Praise for
Hotel on the Corner of Bitter and Sweet
Washington State Book Award Finalist

"A wartime-era Chinese-Japanese variation on *Romeo and Juliet* . . . The period detail [is] so revealing and so well rendered. . . . It's clear on every page how thoroughly Ford, who grew up here, did his research."
—*The Seattle Times*

"A poignant story that transports the reader back in time . . . a satisfying and heart-wrenching tale." —*Deseret Morning News*

"A lovely combination of romantic coincidence, historic detail and realism that is smooth and highly readable . . . Ford does wonderful work in re-creating prewar Seattle." —*The Oregonian*

"Sentimental, heartfelt . . . The exploration of Henry's changing relationship with his family and with Keiko will keep most readers turning pages. . . . A timely debut that not only reminds readers of a shameful episode in American history, but cautions us to examine the present and take heed we don't repeat those injustices." —*Kirkus Reviews*

"Jamie Ford's first novel explores the age-old conflicts between father and son, the beauty and sadness of what happened to Japanese Americans in the Seattle area during World War II, and the depths and longing of deep-heart love. An impressive, bitter, and sweet debut."
—LISA SEE, author of *Snow Flower and the Secret Fan*

"Mesmerizing and evocative, *Hotel on the Corner of Bitter and Sweet* is a tale of conflicted loyalties, devotion, as well as a vibrant portrait of Seattle's Nihonmachi district in its heyday."
—SARA GRUEN, author of *Water for Elephants*

"A tender and satisfying novel set in a time and a place lost forever, *Hotel on the Corner of Bitter and Sweet* gives us a glimpse of the damage that is caused by war—not the sweeping damage of the battlefield but the cold, cruel damage to the hearts and humanity of individual people. Especially relevant in today's world, this is a beautifully written book that will make you think. And, more important, it will make you *feel*."
                                        —GARTH STEIN, author of *The Art of Racing in the Rain*

"Jamie Ford's novel, *Hotel on the Corner of Bitter and Sweet,* is deeply informed by an intimate knowledge of Seattle during World War II, of the tribulations of Asian peoples during the time of Japanese internment, and even of the Seattle jazz scene during that time. His story of an innocent passion across racial barriers—and of the life of a man who forsook the girl he loved—is told with an artistic technique that makes emotion inevitable."   —LOUIS B. JONES, author of *Ordinary Money*

"I loved it! *Hotel on the Corner of Bitter and Sweet* is a beautiful and tender masterpiece, a book everyone will be talking about, and the best book you'll read this year."   —ANNE FRASIER, author of *Garden of Darkness*

"Jamie Ford's novel, *Hotel on the Corner of Bitter and Sweet,* tells a heartwarming story of fathers and sons, first loves, fate, and the resilient human heart. Set in the ethnic neighborhoods of Seattle during World War II and in Japanese American internment camps, this novel brings its era to life with marvelously evocative details."
                                        —JIM TOMLINSON, author of *Things Kept, Things Left Behind*

HOTEL ON
THE CORNER OF
BITTER AND SWEET

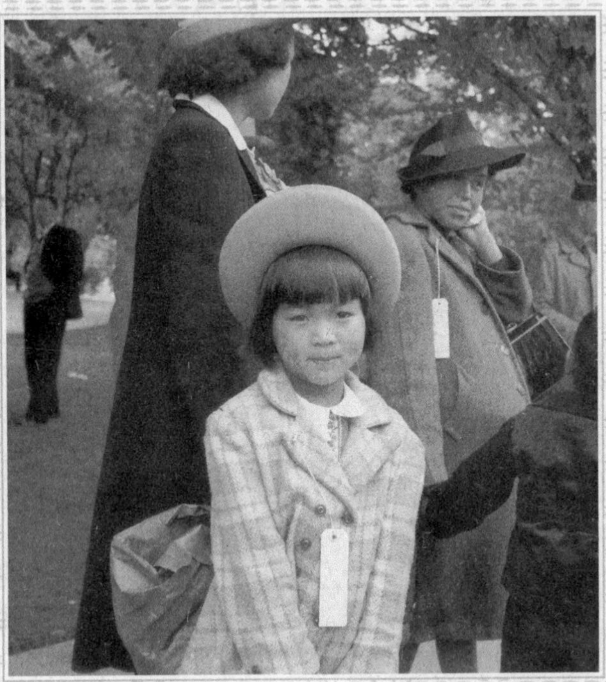

HOTEL ON THE CORNER OF BITTER AND SWEET

A NOVEL

Jamie Ford

BALLANTINE BOOKS TRADE PAPERBACKS • NEW YORK

2009 Ballantine Books Trade Paperback Edition

Copyright © 2009 by James Ford
Reading group guide copyright © 2009 by Random House, Inc.
Excerpt from *Songs of Willow Frost* copyright © 2013 by James Ford

Published in the United States by Ballantine Books,
an imprint of The Random House Publishing Group,
a division of Random House, Inc., New York.

BALLANTINE and colophon are registered trademarks
of Random House, Inc.
RANDOM HOUSE READER'S CIRCLE & Design is a registered trademark
of Random House, Inc.

Originally published in hardcover in the United States by Ballantine Books,
an imprint of The Random House Publishing Group,
a division of Random House, Inc., in 2009.

This book contains an excerpt from the forthcoming book *Songs of Willow Frost* by Jamie Ford.
This excerpt has been set for this edition only and may not reflect the final content of the
forthcoming edition.

Grateful acknowledgment is made to Duke Ellington, courtesy of the
Estates of Mercer K. Ellington and Edward K. Duke Ellington
c/o LICENSEBOX—A MODA Entertainment Company.
Duke Ellington Estate Executor: Paul Ellington.

Frontispiece photo courtesy of the National Archives,
photo no. 210-G-C158.

Library of Congress Cataloging-in-Publication Data
Ford, Jamie.
Hotel on the corner of bitter and sweet: a novel / Jamie Ford.
p.   cm.
ISBN 978-0-345-50534-7
eBook ISBN 978-0-345-51250-5
1. Fathers and sons—Fiction.   2. Japanese Americans—Evacuation and relocation,
1942–1945—Fiction.   3. Widowers—Fiction.   4. Seattle (Wash.)—Fiction.   I. Title.
PS3606.O737H68 2009
813'.6—dc22   2008044398

Printed in the United States of America

www.randomhousereaderscircle.com

26 28 29 27

Book design by Victoria Wong

For Leesha, my happy ending

My poor heart is sentimental
Not made of wood
I got it bad and that ain't good.

—Duke Ellington, 1941

HOTEL ON
THE CORNER OF
BITTER AND SWEET

The Panama Hotel
(1986)

Old Henry Lee stood transfixed by all the commotion at the Panama Hotel. What had started as a crowd of curious onlookers eyeballing a television news crew had now swollen into a polite mob of shoppers, tourists, and a few punk-looking street kids, all wondering what the big deal was. In the middle of the crowd stood Henry, shopping bags hanging at his side. He felt as if he were waking from a long forgotten dream. A dream he'd once had as a little boy.

The old Seattle landmark was a place he'd visited twice in his lifetime. First when he was only twelve years old, way back in 1942—"the war years" he liked to call them. Even then the old bachelor hotel had stood as a gateway between Seattle's Chinatown and Nihonmachi, Japantown. Two outposts of an old-world conflict—where Chinese and Japanese immigrants rarely spoke to one another, while their American-born children often played kick the can in the streets together. The hotel had always been a perfect landmark. A perfect meeting place—where he'd once met the love of his life.

The second time was today. It was 1986, what, forty-plus years later? He'd stopped counting the years as they slipped into memory. After all, he'd spent a lifetime between these bookended visits. A marriage. The birth of an ungrateful son. Cancer, and a burial. He missed his wife, Ethel. She'd been gone six months now. But he didn't miss her as much as you'd think, as bad as that might sound. It was more like quiet relief really. Her health had been bad—no, worse than bad. The cancer in her bones had been downright crippling, to both of us, he thought.

For the last seven years Henry had fed her, bathed her, helped her to the bathroom when she needed to go, and back again when she was all through. He took care of her night and day, 24/7 as they say these days. Marty, his son, thought his mother should have been put in a home, but Henry would have none of it. "Not in my lifetime," Henry said, resisting. Not just because he was Chinese (though that was a part of his resistance). The Confucian ideal of filial piety—respect and reverence for one's parents—was a cultural relic not easily discarded by Henry's generation. He'd been raised to care for loved ones, personally, and to put someone in a *home* was unacceptable. What his son, Marty, never fully understood was that deep down there was an Ethel-shaped hole in Henry's life, and without her, all he felt was the draft of loneliness, cold and sharp, the years slipping away like blood from a wound that never heals.

Now she was gone for good. She needed to be buried, Henry thought, the traditional Chinese way, with food offerings, longevity blankets, and prayer ceremonies lasting several days—despite Marty's fit about cremating her. He was so *modern*. He'd been seeing a counselor and dealing with his mother's death through a support group of some kind. Talking to strangers sounded like talking to no one, which Henry had some firsthand experience in—in real life. It was lonely. Almost as lonely as Lake View Cemetery, where he'd buried Ethel. She now had a gorgeous view of Lake Washington, and was interred with Seattle's other Chinese notables, like Bruce Lee. But in the end, each of them occupied a solitary grave. Alone forever. It didn't matter who your neighbors were. They didn't talk back.

When night fell, and it did, Henry chatted with his wife, asking her how her day was. She never replied, of course. "I'm not crazy or anything," Henry would say to no one, "just open-minded. You never know who's listening." Then he'd busy himself pruning his Chinese palm or evergreen—houseplants whose brown leaves confessed his months of neglect. But now he had time once again. Time to care for something that would grow stronger for a change.

Occasionally, though, he'd wonder about statistics. Not the cancer mortality rates that had caught up with dear Ethel. Instead he thought about himself, and his time measured on some life insurance actuarial table. He was only fifty-six—a young man by his own standards. But he'd read in *Newsweek* about the inevitable decline in the health of a surviving spouse his age. Maybe the clock *was* ticking? He wasn't sure, because as soon as Ethel passed, time began to crawl, clock or no clock.

He'd agreed to an early retirement deal at Boeing Field and now had all the time in the world, and no one to share the hours with. No one with whom to walk down to the Mon Hei bakery for *yuet beng,* carrot mooncakes, on cool autumn evenings.

Instead here he was, alone in a crowd of strangers. A man between lifetimes, standing at the foot of the Panama Hotel once again. Following the cracked steps of white marble that made the hotel look more like an Art Deco halfway house. The establishment, like Henry, seemed caught between worlds. Still, Henry felt nervous and excited, just like he had been as a boy, whenever he walked by. He'd heard a rumor in the marketplace and wandered over from the video store on South Jackson. At first he thought there was some kind of accident because of the growing size of the crowd. But he didn't hear or see anything, no sirens wailing, no flashing lights. Just people drifting toward the hotel, like the tide going out, pulling at their feet, propelling them forward, one step at a time.

As Henry walked over, he saw a news crew arrive and followed them inside. The crowd parted as camera-shy onlookers politely stepped away, clearing a path. Henry followed right behind, shuffling his feet so as not to step on anyone, or in turn be stepped upon, feeling the crowd press back in behind him. At the top of the steps, just inside the lobby, the hotel's new owner announced, "We've found something in the basement."

Found what? A body perhaps? Or a drug lab of some kind? No, there'd be police officers taping off the area if the hotel were a crime scene.

Before the new owner, the hotel had been boarded up since 1950, and in those years, Chinatown had become a ghetto gateway for *tongs*—gangs from Hong Kong and Macau. The city blocks south of King Street had a charming trashiness by day; the litter and slug trails on the sidewalk were generally overlooked as tourists peered up at egg-and-dart architecture from another era. Children on field trips, wrapped in colorful coats and hats, held hands as they followed their noses to the mouthwatering sight of barbecue duck in the windows, hanging red crayons melting in the sun. But at night, drug dealers and bony, middle-aged hookers working for dime bags haunted the streets and alleys. The thought of this icon of his childhood becoming a makeshift crack house made him ache with a melancholy he hadn't felt since he held Ethel's hand and watched her exhale, long and slow, for the last time.

Precious things just seemed to go away, never to be had again.

As he took off his hat and began fanning himself with the threadbare brim, the crowd pushed forward, pressing in from the rear. Flashbulbs went off. Standing on his tippy toes, he peered over the shoulder of the tall news reporter in front of him.

The new hotel owner, a slender Caucasian woman, slightly younger than Henry, walked up the steps holding . . . *an umbrella*? She popped it open, and Henry's heart beat a little faster as he saw it for what it was. A Japanese parasol, made from bamboo, bright red and white—with orange *koi* painted on it, carp that looked like giant goldfish. It shed a film of dust that floated, suspended momentarily in the air as the hotel owner twirled the fragile-looking artifact for the cameras. Two more men brought up a steamer trunk bearing the stickers of foreign ports: Admiral Oriental Lines out of Seattle and Yokohama, Tokyo. On the side of the trunk was the name Shimizu, hand-painted in large white letters. It was opened for the curious crowd. Inside were clothing, photo albums, and an old electric rice cooker.

The new hotel owner explained that in the basement she had discovered the belongings of thirty-seven Japanese families who she presumed had been persecuted and taken away. Their belongings had been hidden and never recovered—a time capsule from *the war years*.

Henry stared in silence as a small parade of wooden packing crates and leathery suitcases were hauled upstairs, the crowd marveling at the once-precious items held within: a white communion dress, tarnished silver candlesticks, a picnic basket—items that had collected dust, untouched, for forty-plus years. Saved for a happier time that never came.

The more Henry thought about the shabby old knickknacks, the forgotten treasures, the more he wondered if his own broken heart might be found in there, hidden among the unclaimed possessions of another time. Boarded up in the basement of a condemned hotel. Lost, but never forgotten.

Marty Lee
(1986)

Henry left the crowd at the Panama Hotel behind and walked to his home up on Beacon Hill. It was not so far back as to have a scenic overlook of Rainier Avenue, but in the more sensible neighborhoods just up the street from Chinatown. A modest three-bedroom home with a basement—still unfinished after all these years. He'd meant to finish it when his son, Marty, went away to college, but Ethel's condition had worsened and what money they'd saved for a rainy day was spent in a downpour of medical bills, a torrent that lasted nearly a decade. Medicaid kicked in near the end, just in time, and would even have covered a nursing home, but Henry stuck to his vow: to care for his wife in sickness and in health. Besides, who'd want to spend their last days in some state-owned facility that looked like a prison where everyone lived on death row?

Before Henry could answer his own question, Marty knocked twice on the front door and walked right in, greeting him with a casual "How you doing, Pops," and immediately headed for the kitchen. "I'll be right out, don't get up, I just gotta get a drink—I hoofed it all the way from Capitol Hill—exercise you know, you should think about a little workout yourself, I think you've put on some weight since Mom died."

Henry looked at his waistline and mashed the mute button on the TV. He'd been watching the news for word on today's discovery at the Panama Hotel, but heard nothing. Must have been a busy news day. In his lap was a stack of old photo albums and a few school annuals, stained and mildew-smelling from the damp Seattle air that cooled the concrete slab of Henry's perpetually unfinished basement.

He and Marty hadn't talked much since the funeral. Marty stayed busy as a chemistry major at Seattle University, which was good, it seemed to keep him out of trouble. But college also seemed to keep him out of Henry's life, which had been acceptable while Ethel was alive, but now it made the hole in Henry's life that much larger—like standing on one side of a canyon, yelling, and always waiting for the echo that never came. When Marty did come by, it seemed like the visits were only to do his laundry, wax his car, or hit his father up for money—which Henry always gave, without ever showing annoyance.

Helping Marty pay for college had been a second battlefront for Henry, if caring for Ethel had been the first. Despite a small grant, Marty still needed student loans to pay for his education, but Henry had opted for an early retirement package from his job at Boeing so he could care for Ethel full-time—on paper, he had a lot of money to his name. He looked downright *affluent*. To the lenders, Marty was from a family with a decent bank account, but the lenders weren't paying the medical bills. By the time his mother passed, there had been just enough to cover a decent burial, an expense Marty felt was unnecessary.

Henry also didn't bother to tell Marty about the second mortgage— the one he'd taken out to get him through college when the student loans ran dry. Why make him worry? Why put that pressure on him? School is hard enough as is. Like any good father, he wanted the best for his son, even if they didn't talk all that much.

Henry kept staring at the photo albums, faded reminders of his own school days, looking for someone he'd never find. I try not to live in the past, he thought, but who knows, sometimes the past lives in me. He took his eyes off the photos to watch Marty amble in with a tall glass of iced green tea. He sat on the couch for a moment, then moved to his mother's cracked faux-leather recliner directly across from Henry, who felt better seeing someone . . . anyone, in Ethel's space.

"Is that the *last* of the iced tea?" Henry asked.

"Yup" was Marty's reply, "and I saved the last glass for you, Pops." He set it on a jade coaster next to Henry. It dawned on Henry how old and cynical he'd allowed himself to become in the months since the funeral. It wasn't Marty. It was him—he needed to get out more. Today had been a good start.

Even so, a mumbled "Thank you" was all Henry could muster.

"Sorry I haven't come by lately—finals were killing me, plus I didn't want to waste all that hard-earned money you and Ma paid to put my butt in college in the first place."

Now Henry felt his face flush with guilt as the noisy old furnace shut off, letting the house cool.

"In fact, I brought you a little token of my appreciation." Marty handed him a small *lai see* envelope, bright red, with shiny gold foil embossed on the front.

Henry took the gift with both hands. "A lucky-money envelope—you paying me back?"

His son smiled and raised his eyebrows. "In a way."

It didn't matter what it was. Henry had been humbled by his son's thoughtfulness. He touched the gold seal. On it was the Cantonese character for prosperity. Inside was a folded slip of paper, Marty's report card. He'd earned a perfect 4.0.

"I'm graduating summa cum laude, that means with highest honor."

There was silence, nothing but the electric hum of the muted television.

"You all right, Pops?"

Henry wiped at the corner of his eye with the back of his callused hand. "Maybe next time, I borrow money from *you*," he replied.

"If you ever want to finish college, I'll be happy to front you the cash, Pops—I'll put you on scholarship."

Scholarship. The word had a special meaning for Henry, not just because he never finished college—though that might have been part of it. In 1949 he'd dropped out of the University of Washington to become an apprentice draftsman. The program offered through Boeing was a great opportunity, but deep down, Henry knew the real reason he dropped out—the painful reason. He had a hard time fitting in. A sense of isolation left over from all those years. Not quite peer pressure. More like peer rejection.

As he looked down at his sixth-grade yearbook, he remembered everything he had hated and loved about school. Strange faces played in his thoughts, over and over, like an old newsreel. The unkind glances of school-yard enemies, a harsh contrast to the smiling innocence of their yearbook pictures. In the column next to the giant class photo was a list of names—those "not pictured." Henry found his name on the list; he was indeed absent from the rows and rows of smiling children. But he'd been there that day. All day.

I Am Chinese
(1942)

Young Henry Lee stopped talking to his parents when he was twelve years old. Not because of some silly childhood tantrum, but because they asked him to. That was how it felt anyway. They asked—no, told—him to stop speaking their native Chinese. It was 1942, and they were desperate for him to learn English. Which only made Henry more confused when his father pinned a button to his school shirt that read, "I am Chinese." The contrast seemed absurd. This makes no sense, he thought. My father's pride has finally got the better of him.

"M-ming bak?" Henry asked in perfect Cantonese. "I don't understand."

His father slapped his face. More of a light tap really, just something to get his attention. "No more. Only speak you American." The words came out in *Chinglish.*

"I don't understand," Henry said in English.

"Hah?" his father asked.

"If I'm not supposed to speak Chinese, why do I need to wear this button?"

"Hah, you say?" His father turned to his mother, who was peeking out from the kitchen. She gave a look of confusion and simply shrugged, going back to her cooking, sweet water chestnut cake from the smell of it. His father turned to Henry again, giving him a backhanded wave, shooing him off to school.

Since Henry couldn't ask in Cantonese and his parents barely understood English, he dropped the matter, grabbed his lunch and book bag, and headed down the stairs and out into the salty, fishy air of Seattle's Chinatown.

The entire city came alive in the morning. Men in fish-stained T-shirts hauled crates of rock cod, and buckets of geoduck clams, half-buried in ice. Henry walked by, listening to the men bark at each other in a Chinese dialect even *he* didn't understand.

He continued west on Jackson Street, past a flower cart and a fortune-teller selling lucky lottery numbers, instead of going east in the direction of the Chinese school, which was only three blocks from the second-floor apartment he shared with his parents. His morning routine, walking upstream, brought him headlong into dozens of other kids his age, all of them going the opposite way.

"Baak gwai! Baak gwai!" they shouted. Though some just pointed and laughed. It meant "white devil"—a term usually reserved for Caucasians, and then only if they really deserved the verbal abuse. A few kids took pity on him, though, those being his former classmates and onetime friends. Kids he'd known since first grade, like Francis Lung and Harold Chew. They just called him Casper, after the Friendly Ghost. At least it wasn't Herman and Katnip.

Maybe that's what this is for, Henry thought, looking at the ridiculous button that read "I am Chinese." Thanks, Dad, why not just put a sign on my back that says "Kick me" while you're at it?

Henry walked faster, finally rounding the corner and heading north. At the halfway point of his walk to school, he always stopped at the arched iron gateway at South King Street, where he gave his lunch to Sheldon, a sax player twice Henry's age who worked the street corner, playing for the tourists' pleasure and pocket change. Despite the booming activity at Boeing Field, prosperity didn't seem to reach locals like Sheldon. He was a polished jazz player, whose poverty had less to do with his musical ability and more to do with his color. Henry had liked him immediately. Not because they both were outcasts, although if he really thought about it, that might have had a ring of truth to it—no, he liked him because of his music. Henry didn't know what jazz was, he knew only that it was something his parents didn't listen to, and that made him like it even more.

"Nice button, young man," said Sheldon, as he was setting out his case for his morning performances. "That's a darn good idea, what with Pearl Harbor and all."

Henry looked down at the button on his shirt; he had already forgotten it. "My father's idea," he mumbled. His father hated the Japanese. Not because they sank the USS *Arizona*—he hated them because they'd been bombing Chongqing, nonstop, for the last four years. Henry's father had never even been there, but he knew that the provisional capital of Chiang Kai-shek had already become the most-bombed city in history.

Sheldon nodded approvingly and tapped the metal tin hanging from Henry's book bag. "What's for lunch today?"

Henry handed over his lunch box. "Same as always." An egg-olive sandwich, carrot straws, and an apple pear. At least his mother was kind enough to pack him an American lunch.

Sheldon smiled, showing a large gold-capped tooth. "Thank you, sir, you have a fine day now."

Ever since Henry's second day at Rainier Elementary, he'd been giving his lunch to Sheldon. It was safer that way. Henry's father had been visibly excited when his son was accepted at the all-white school at the far end of Yesler Way. It was a proud moment for Henry's parents. They wouldn't stop talking about it to friends on the street, in the market, and at the Bing Kung Benevolent Association, where they went to play bingo and mah-jongg on Saturdays. "They take him *scholarshipping,*" was all he ever heard his parents say in English.

But what Henry felt was far from pride. His emotions had gone sprinting past fear to that point of simply struggling for survival. Which was why, after getting beat up by Chaz Preston for his lunch on the first day of school, he'd learned to give it to Sheldon. Plus, he made a tidy profit on the transaction, fishing a nickel from the bottom of Sheldon's case on the way home each day. Henry bought his mother a starfire lily, her favorite flower, once a week with his newfound lunch money—feeling a little guilty for not eating what she lovingly prepared, but always making up for it with the flower.

"How you buy flower?" she'd ask in Chinese.

"Everythingwasonsaletodayspecialoffer." He'd make up some excuse in English, trying to explain it—and the extra change he always seemed to bring home from his errands to the market. Saying it fast, fairly sure she wouldn't catch on. Her look of confusion would coalesce into satisfied acceptance as she'd nod and put the change in her purse. She understood little English, but Henry could see she appreciated his apparent bargaining skills.

If only his problems at school were solved so easily.

For Henry, *scholarshipping* had very little to do with academics and everything to do with work. Luckily, he learned to work fast. He had to. Especially on his assignments right before lunch—since he was always dismissed ten minutes early. Just long enough to find his way to the cafeteria, where he'd don a starched white apron that covered his knees and serve lunch to the other kids.

Over the past few months, he'd learned to shut his mouth and ignore the heckling—especially from bullies like Will Whitworth, Carl Parks, and Chaz Preston.

And Mrs. Beatty, the lunch lady, wasn't much help either. A gassy, hairnet-wearing definition of one of Henry's favorite American words: *broad.* She cooked by hand, literally, measuring everything in her dirty, wrinkled mitts. Her thick forearms were evidence that she'd never used an electric mixer. But, like a kenneled dog that refuses to do its business in the same place it sleeps, she never ate her own handiwork. Instead, she always brought her lunch. As soon as Henry laced up his apron, she'd doff her hairnet and vanish with her lunch pail and a pack of Lucky Strikes.

Scholarshipping in the cafeteria meant Henry never made it out to recess. After the last kid had finished, he'd eat some canned peaches in the storage room, alone, surrounded by towering stockpiles of tomato sauce and fruit cocktail.

Flag Duty
(1942)

Henry wasn't sure which was more frustrating, the nonstop taunting in the school cafeteria or the awkward silence in the little Canton Alley apartment he shared with his parents. Still, when morning came, he tried to make the best of the language barrier at home as he went about his normal routine.

"Jou san." His parents greeted him with "Good morning" in Cantonese.

Henry smiled and replied in his best English, "I'm going to open an umbrella in my pants." His father nodded a stern approval, as if Henry had quoted some profound Western philosophy. *Perfect,* Henry thought, this is what you get when you send your son *scholarshipping.* Stifling a laugh, he ate his breakfast, a small pyramid of sticky rice, flavored with pork, and cloud ear mushrooms. His mother looked on, seemingly knowing what he was up to, even if she didn't understand the words.

When Henry rounded the block that morning, heading to the main steps of Rainier Elementary, he noticed that two familiar faces from his class had been assigned to flag duty. It was an assignment envied by all the sixth-grade boys, and even a few of the girls, who weren't allowed, for reasons unknown to Henry.

Before the first bell, the pair of boys would take the flag from its triangle-shaped rack in the office and head to the pole in front of the school. There they'd carefully unfold it, making sure no part of it touched the ground, since a flag desecrated in such a way was immediately burned. That was the story anyway; neither Henry nor any other kid in recent memory had ever known of such a thing actually occurring. But the threat was legendary. He pictured Vice Principal Silverwood, a blocky, harrumphing old bear of a man, burning the flag in the parking lot while shocked faculty looked on—then sending the bill home with the clumsy boy responsible. His parents surely would be shamed into moving to the suburbs and changing their names so no one would ever find them.

Unfortunately, Chaz Preston and Denny Brown, who were on flag duty, were not likely to move away any time soon, regardless of what they did. Both were from prominent local families. Denny's father was a lawyer or a judge or something, and Chaz's family owned several apartment buildings downtown. Denny was no friend of Henry's, but Chaz was the real menace. Henry always thought Chaz would end up as his family's bill collector. He liked to lean on people. He was so mean the other bullies feared him.

"Hey, *Tojo,* you forgot to salute the flag," Chaz shouted.

Henry kept walking, heading for the steps, pretending he hadn't heard. Why his father thought attending this school was such a great idea, Henry would never know. Out of the corner of his eye, he watched Chaz tie the flag off and amble toward him. Henry walked faster, heading for the safety of the school, but Chaz cut him off.

"Oh, that's right, you Japs don't salute *American* flags, do you?"

Henry wasn't sure which was worse, being picked on for being Chinese, or being accused of being a Jap. Though Tojo, the prime minister of Japan, was known as "the Razor" because of his sharp legalistic mind, Henry only wished he were sharp enough to stay home from school when his classmates were giving speeches about the *Yellow Peril.* His teacher, Mrs. Walker, who rarely spoke to Henry, didn't stop the inappropriate and off-color remarks. And she never once called him to the blackboard to figure a math problem, thinking he didn't understand English—though his improving grades must have clued her in, a little bit at least.

"He won't fight you, he's a yellow coward. Besides, the second bell's gonna ring any minute." Denny sneered at Henry and headed inside.

Chaz didn't move.

Henry looked up at the bully blocking his way but didn't say a thing.

He'd learned to keep his mouth shut. Most of his classmates ignored him, but the few who made a point of pushing him around generally got bored when he wouldn't respond. Then he remembered the button his father had made him wear and pointed it out to Chaz.

" 'I am Chinese,' " Chaz read out loud. "It don't make no difference to me, shrimp, you still don't celebrate Christmas, do you?"

The second bell rang.

"Ho, ho, ho," Henry replied. So much for keeping my mouth shut, he thought. We *do* celebrate Christmas, along with Cheun Jit, the lunar new year. But no, Pearl Harbor Day is not a festive occasion.

"Lucky for you I can't be late or I'll lose flag duty," Chaz said before he faked a lunge at Henry, who didn't flinch. Then Henry watched the bully back up and head into the building. He exhaled, finally, and found his way down the empty hallway to Mrs. Walker's classroom, where she reprimanded him for being tardy—and gave him an hour of detention. Henry accepted his punishment without a word. Not even a look.

Keiko
(1942)

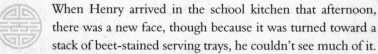 When Henry arrived in the school kitchen that afternoon, there was a new face, though because it was turned toward a stack of beet-stained serving trays, he couldn't see much of it. But it was clearly a girl, probably in his grade, about his height; she was hidden behind long bangs and the black strands of hair that framed her face. She sprayed the trays with hot, steaming water and put them in the dish rack, one by one. As she slowly turned toward Henry, he noticed her slender cheekbones, her perfect skin, smooth and lacking in the freckles that mottled the faces of the other girls at the school. But most of all, he noticed her soft chestnut-brown eyes. For a brief moment Henry swore he smelled something, like jasmine, sweet and mysterious, lost in the greasy odors of the kitchen.

"Henry, this is Keiko—she just transferred to Rainier, but she's from *your* part of town." Mrs. Beatty, the lunch lady, seemed to regard this new girl as another piece of kitchen machinery, tossing her an apron, shoving her next to Henry behind the serving counter. "Heck, I bet you two are related, aren't you?" How many times had he heard that one?

Mrs. Beatty wasted no time and fished out a Zippo lighter, lit a cigarette one-handed, and wandered off with her lunch. "Call me when you're all done," she said.

Like most boys his age, Henry liked girls a lot more than he could bring himself to admit—or actually show to anyone, especially around other boys, who all tried to act cool, as if girls were some strange new species. So, while he did what came naturally, trying his best to show indifference, he was secretly elated to have a friendly face in the kitchen. "I'm Henry Lee. From South King Street."

The peculiar girl whispered, "I'm Keiko."

Henry wondered why he hadn't seen her around the neighborhood before; maybe her family had just come over. "What kind of name is Kay-Ko?"

There was a pause. Then the lunch bell rang. Doors were slamming down the hall.

She took her long black hair in equal handfuls and tied it with a ribbon. "Keiko *Okabe,*" she said, tying on her apron and waiting for a reaction.

Henry was dumbfounded. She was *Japanese.* With her hair pulled back, he could see it clearly. And she looked embarrassed. What was she doing *here*?

The sum total of Henry's Japanese friends happened to be a number that rhymed with *hero.* His father wouldn't allow it. He was a Chinese nationalist and had been quite a firebrand in his day, according to Henry's mother. In his early teens, his father had played host to the famed revolutionary Dr. Sun Yat-sen when he visited Seattle to raise money to help the fledgling Kuomintang army fight the Manchus. First through war bonds, then he'd helped them open up an actual office. Imagine that, an *office* for the Chinese army, right down the street. It was there that Henry's father kept busy raising thousands of dollars to fight the Japanese back home. *His* home, not mine, Henry thought. The attack on Pearl Harbor had been terrible and unexpected, sure, but it paled when compared with the bombings of Shanghai or the sacking of Nanjing— according to his father anyway. Henry, on the other hand, couldn't even find Nanjing on a map.

But he still didn't have a single Japanese friend, even though there were twice as many Japanese as Chinese kids his age, and they lived just a few streets over. Henry caught himself staring at Keiko, whose nervous eyes seemed to recognize his reaction.

"I'm American," she offered in defense.

He didn't know what to say, so he focused on the hordes of hungry kids who were coming. "We'd better get busy."

They took the lids off their steamer trays, recoiling at the smell, looking at each other in disgust. Inside was a brown, spaghetti-like mess. Keiko looked like she wanted to throw up. Henry, who was used to the putrid stench, didn't even flinch. He simply showed her how to dish it up with an old ice-cream scoop as freckled boys in crew cuts, even the younger ones, said, "Look, the Chink brought his girlfriend" and "More chop suey, please!"

At the most they taunted, at the least they sneered and glared suspiciously. Henry kept silent, angry and embarrassed as always, but pretending he didn't understand. A lie he wished he believed—if only in self-defense. Keiko followed suit. For thirty minutes they stood side by side, occasionally looking at each other, smirking as they served up extra-large helpings of Mrs. Beatty's rat-scrabble slop to the boys who teased them the most, or the red-haired girl who pulled at the corners of her eyes and made a hideous bucktoothed face.

"Look, they don't even speak English!" she squealed.

He and Keiko smiled at each other until the last child was served and all the trays and pans were washed and put away. Then they ate their lunch, together, splitting a can of pears in the storage room.

Henry thought the pears tasted especially good that day.

The Walk Home
(1942)

A week after Keiko arrived, Henry had settled into a new routine. They'd have lunch together, then meet by the janitor's
closet after school for the second part of their work duties.
Side by side they'd clean the chalkboards, empty wastebaskets, and
pound erasers behind the school on an old stump. It wasn't bad. Having
Keiko around cut the work he'd previously been doing in half, and he
enjoyed the company—even if she was Japanese. Besides, all the work
after school gave the other kids plenty of time to get on their bikes or
their buses and be on their way long before he stepped out onto the
school yard.

That was how it was supposed to work.

But today as he held the door for Keiko when they left the building,
Chaz was standing at the bottom of the steps. He must have missed his
bus, Henry thought. Or maybe he'd sensed a murmur of happiness since
Keiko had arrived. Just a glance, or a smile between them. Even if he is
here to show me up, Henry thought, that's fine, as long as he doesn't
hurt her.

He and Keiko walked down the steps and past Chaz, Henry on the inside, putting himself between her and the bully. As they descended,
Henry became all too aware that his nemesis was a whole foot taller than
either one of them.

"Where do you think *you're* going?"

Chaz should have been in a higher grade, but he'd been held back—
twice. Henry had long suspected he'd failed on purpose so he could continue to lord over his sixth-grade kingdom. Why give that up to be an
eighth-grade nobody?

"I said, Where do you think you're going—Jap lover?"

Keiko was about to speak when Henry shot her a look, put his arm around her, and kept her walking.

Chaz stepped in front of them. "I know you understand every word I'm saying, I've seen you two talking after class."

"So?" Henry said.

"So." Chaz grabbed him by his collar and jerked him up to his chest, so close Henry could smell his lunch—onions and powdered milk, still ripe on his breath. "How about I make it so you can't talk anymore? How would you like that?"

"Stop it!" Keiko shouted. "Let him go!"

"Leave the kid alone, Charlie," Mrs. Beatty interrupted, walking down the steps, lighting a cigarette. Judging by her nonchalance, Henry figured she was used to Chaz's lapses in behavior.

"My name is Chaz."

"Well, Chaz honey, if you hurt that kid, you're going to be taking his place in the kitchen, you understand me?" She said it in a way that almost sounded like she cared. Almost. The hard look on her face put just enough doubt in Chaz's mind. He let go, shoving Henry to the ground— but not before ripping the button that read "I am Chinese" off Henry's shirt, leaving a small tear. Chaz pinned it on his own collar and gave Henry a bucktoothed smile before finally wandering off, presumably to find other kids to rough up.

Keiko helped Henry up, handing him his books. When he turned to thank Mrs. Beatty, she was well on her way. Not even a good-bye. *Thanks anyway.* Did she care about playground bullying, or was she just protecting her kitchen help? Henry couldn't tell. He dusted off the seat of his pants and wiped the thought from his mind.

After their week in the kitchen together, he hadn't thought he could actually feel any more frustration or embarrassment. What a surprise. But if Keiko thought less of him after their run-in with Chaz, it certainly didn't show. She even touched his hand, offering hers as they walked, but he ignored it. He wasn't really shy around girls. A Japanese girl, though, that was a red flag. Or a white flag with a big red sun on it, as it were. *My father would fall over dead,* he thought. *And in town, some-one would see us.*

"Have you always gone to Rainier?" she asked.

He noticed how cool her voice sounded. Clear and simple. Her English was much better than that of most of the Chinese girls he knew.

He shook his head. "Just since September. My parents want me to get a Western education—university—instead of going back to Canton for my Chinese schooling like all the other kids in my neighborhood."

"Why?"

He didn't know how to say it.

"Because of people like you." As the words came out, he felt bad for venting the day's frustrations. But part of it *was* true, wasn't it? Out of the corner of his eye he watched her undo the ribbon in her hair. Long black strands fell around her face, bangs almost covering her chestnut eyes.

"I'm sorry. It's not your fault. It's because the Japanese army has invaded the northeastern provinces. The fighting is a long way from Canton, but they still won't let me go. Most of the kids on my side of town all go to the Chinese school, then finish back in China. That's what my father always planned for me. Until last fall anyway." Henry didn't know what else to say.

"So you weren't born in China?"

He shook his head again, pointing to First Hill, where Columbus Hospital stood on the outskirts of Chinatown. "I was born right up there."

She smiled. "That's where I was born too. I'm Japanese. But American first."

"Did your parents teach you to say that?" He bit his words as they came out, afraid of hurting her feelings again. After all, his parents told him to say the same thing.

"Yes. They did. My grandfather came over right after the great fire in 'eighty-nine. I'm second generation."

"Is that why they sent you to Rainier?"

They had walked past the black iron arches of Chinatown all the way to Nihonmachi. Henry lived seven blocks over, and had been here only once, when his father had to meet someone for lunch at the Northern Pacific Hotel, at the edge of the Japanese marketplace. Even then, Father had insisted they leave once he found out the place had been built by

Niroku "Frank" Shitamae, a local Japanese businessman. They were gone before their food even arrived.

"No." She stopped and looked around. "This is why they send me."

Everywhere he looked he saw American flags, in every shopwindow and hanging from every door. Yet many more shops had broken windows, and a few were boarded up completely. In front of them an orange public works lift truck blocked three parking spaces. A bearded man in the bucket was taking down the sign for Mikado Street and replacing it with one that read "Dearborn Street."

Henry remembered the button his father had given him and touched the torn fabric over his heart where it had been. He looked at Keiko, and for the first time all day, the first time all week, she looked afraid.

Nihonmachi
(1942)

Saturdays were special to Henry. While other kids tuned in to the radio to listen to *The Adventures of Superman* on the Mutual Broadcasting System, Henry did his chores as fast as he could and ran down to the corner of Jackson and Maynard. Oh, sure, he liked the Man of Steel—what twelve-year-old didn't? But during the war years, the adventures were, well, less than adventurous. Instead of smashing robots from another planet, the son of Krypton spent his days uncovering fifth columnists and Japanese spy rings, which hardly interested Henry.

Although he did wonder about Superman himself. The actor playing the voice of Superman was a mystery in 1942. No one knew who he was. No one. And kids everywhere obsessed over finding his true identity. So as Henry ran down the street, he'd look at the mild-mannered folks who wore suits and glasses, like Clark Kent, wondering if they just might be the voice of Superman. He even looked at Chinese and Japanese men— because you never knew.

He wondered if Keiko listened to Superman on Saturday mornings as well. He thought about wandering over to the Nihonmachi side of town, just to poke around. Maybe he'd run into her. How big could it be?

Then he heard Sheldon playing in the distance and followed the music.

Saturday was the only time of the week he could listen to Sheldon play. Most days when Henry came by after school, Sheldon's instrument case had little more than two or three dollars in change, and by that time, he was usually packing up for the day. But Saturdays were different. With all the impressionable tourists, seamen, and even the crowds of locals who came and strolled down Jackson Street, Saturday was "payday," as Sheldon called it.

That morning, when Henry arrived, there was a crowd, maybe twenty people, swaying and smiling while his friend played some smooth jazz number. Henry squeezed to the front and sat on the sidewalk, enjoying the surprisingly sunny weather. Sheldon saw him and winked, not missing a note.

As he finished, the applause came and went, and the crowd dispersed, leaving behind almost three dollars in pocket change. Sheldon put a small handwritten sign in his case that read "Next Performance in 15 Minutes," and caught his breath. As he inhaled deeply, his wide chest seemed to be testing the limits of his satin vest. A button was already missing from the bottom.

"Good crowd," Henry said.

"Not bad, not bad at all. But, boy, you just look at that, there's a lot of clubs these days—stiff competition." Sheldon pointed with his sax to where rows of signs and sandwich boards marked the nightclubs up and down both sides of Jackson.

Henry had once wandered the whole area, counting thirty-four clubs in all—including the Black & Tan, the Rocking Chair, the Ubangi, the Colony Club, and the Jungle Temple. And those were just the *official* clubs—ones that had glittering neon signs for the world to see. There were countless others tucked away in basements and backroom parlors. His father constantly complained about the racket they made.

On Saturday nights, Henry would look out his window and watch the changing landscape of people walking past. By day, Asian faces were everywhere. But by night, the crowds doubled, mostly white folks in their evening best, heading for an evening of jazz and dancing. On some Saturdays, Henry could hear faint music in the distance, but his mother didn't like him sleeping with the window open, afraid he'd catch his death with a cold or pneumonia.

"How's the tryouts?" Henry asked, knowing Sheldon had been auditioning for a regular job in the evening.

Sheldon handed him a card. It read "Negro Local 493."

"What's this?"

"Can you believe it? I joined the union. The white musicians formed a union to try and get more work, but the black players formed their own, and now we're getting more gigs than we can handle."

Henry didn't quite understand what a union card meant, but Sheldon seemed excited, so he knew it must be good news.

"I even got a cancellation gig at the Black Elks Club—tonight. The regular sax player got thrown in jail for something, so they call the union and the union called *me*. Can you believe that? Me, playing at the Black Elks . . ."

"With Oscar Holden!" Henry finished. He'd never heard the man play, but he'd seen his posters all over town, and Sheldon always talked about him in tones normally reserved for heroes and legends.

"With Oscar Holden." Sheldon nodded, then belted out a few happy bars on his sax. "It's only for tonight, but hey, it's a good gig, with a good man."

"I'm so excited!" Henry grinned. "That's really big news."

"Speaking of big news, who's that little girl I've seen you walking home with, huh? Something I should know about?"

Henry felt blood flushing his cheeks. "She's . . . just a friend from school."

"Uh-huh. Would that be a *girl*friend, perhaps?"

Henry quickly answered in defense. "No, she's a *Japanese* friend. My parents would kill me if they found out." He pointed to the button on his shirt, a new one his father had made him wear after the other one was ripped off by Chaz.

"I am Chinese. I am Lebanese. I am Pekinese. I am the ever-loving bees' knees." Sheldon just shook his head. "Well, the next time you see your Japanese *friend,* you tell her *oai deki te ureshii desu.*"

"Oh I decky tay ooh ree she day sue," Henry mimicked.

"Close enough—it's a compliment in Japanese, it means 'How are you today, beautiful—' "

"I can't say that," Henry interrupted.

"Go on, she'll like it. I use it on all the local geisha girls around here, they always take it the right way, plus she'll appreciate it being in her native tongue. Very sophisticated that way. *Mysterious.*"

Henry tried the phrase out loud a few more times. And a few more times quietly in his head. *Oai deki te ureshii desu.*

"Now why don't you head on over to Japantown and try it out—I'm closing up early today anyway," Sheldon said. "One more performance, then I'm saving my wind for my big spotlight gig with Oscar tonight."

Henry wished he could see and hear Sheldon play with the famed jazz pianist. Wished he could see what the inside of a real jazz club looked like. Sheldon had told him that most of the clubs had dancing, but when Oscar played, people just sat back and listened. He was that good. Henry liked to imagine a dark room, everyone clad in their fine suits and dresses, holding long-stemmed glasses, listening to music drift out of the spotlight onstage, cool fog rolling in off a stretch of cold black water.

"I know you'll do great tonight," Henry said, turning to head south toward Japantown, instead of east toward his family's apartment.

Sheldon flashed him his gold-capped smile. "Thank you, sir, you have a fine day now," he said and went back to his next performance.

Henry practiced the Japanese words, saying them over and over as he kept walking—until the faces on the street turned from black to white to Japanese.

Japantown was bigger than Henry realized—at least four times the size of Chinatown, and the farther he walked through the crowded streets, the more he realized that finding Keiko might be impossible. Sure, he'd walked her partway home from school, but that was just to the fringes of the neighborhood. They'd walk as far as the Hatsunekai Dance School, then he'd say good-bye, watching her head in the direction of the Mount Fuji Hotel. From there he'd cut back over to Jackson and on to South King in the direction of home. Walking down Maynard Avenue was like being dropped into another world. There were Japanese banks, barbers, tailors, even dentists and newspaper publishers. The glowing neon signs still flashed by day, paper lanterns hung outside the stoop of each apartment dwelling, while small children pitched baseball cards of their favorite Japanese teams.

Henry found a seat on a bench and read through a day-old copy of the *Japanese Daily News,* much of which, surprisingly, was printed in English. There was a going-out-of-business sale at the Taishodo Book Store, and a new owner had taken over Nakamura Jewelry. As Henry looked around, there seemed to be a lot of businesses for sale; others were closed in the middle of the day. All of which made sense, as many of the news articles had to do with hard times in Nihonmachi. Apparently business had been bad, even before Pearl Harbor—going all the way back to when the Japanese invaded Manchuria, in 1931. Henry remembered the year only because his father mentioned the war in China so often. According to the news article, the Chong Wa Benevolent Association had called for a boycott of the entire Japanese community. Henry didn't know what the Chong Wa was exactly, some sort of Chinatown committee like the Bing Kung Association, which his family belonged to—but larger and more political, encompassing not only his neighborhood but the entire region and all the tongs—social networks that sometimes resembled gangs. His father was a member.

As Henry looked at the scores of people milling about the streets, shopping and playing, their numbers belied the hard times, boycotts, and the boarded-up, flag-draped storefronts. Poking through the streets, most of the locals ignored him, though some Japanese children pointed and spoke as he walked by, only to be shushed by their parents. There were more than a few black faces speckling the crowd, but no white faces to be seen.

Then Henry stopped in his tracks when he finally saw Keiko's face— or a photo of it anyway—in the window display of the Ochi Photography Studio. There she was, in a dark sepia print of a little girl dressed in her Sunday best, sitting in an oversize leather chair, holding an ornate Japanese umbrella, a bamboo parasol with koi painted on it.

"Konichi-wa," a Japanese man, fairly young by the look of it, greeted him in the doorway. *"Konichi-wa, Ototo-san?"*

Confused by the Japanese greeting, Henry opened his coat and pointed to his button that read "I am Chinese."

The young photographer smiled. "Well, I don't speak Chinese, but how are you today—looking for a photograph? A sitting? Or are you just looking for someone?"

Now it was Henry's turn to be surprised. The young photographer's English seemed near perfect compared with Henry's own grasp of the language.

"This girl, I go to school with her."

"The Okabes? They send their daughter to the Chinese school?"

Henry shook his head, waving his hand. "Keiko Okabe, yes. We both go to Rainier Elementary—the white school across Yesler Way."

A moment of silence vanished in the car engines that roared by. Henry looked on as the photographer regarded the photo of Keiko.

"Then you both must be very special students."

Since when did *special* become such a burden? A curse even. There was nothing special about *scholarshipping* at Rainier. Nothing at all. Then again, he was here looking for someone. Maybe *she* was special.

"Do you know where she lives?"

"No. I'm sorry. But I see them a lot near the Nippon Kan Hall. There's a park, you might look for her there."

"Domo," Henry said. It was the only Japanese word he knew, aside from what Sheldon had taught him earlier.

"You're welcome. Come back, I'll take your picture!" the photographer yelled.

Henry was already down the street.

Henry and Keiko walked through Kobe Park on their way home from school each day, and he knew the hillside park by the numerous rows of cherry trees that lined the streets. Across from the park sat the Nippon Kan Hall, more of a Kabuki theater really, complete with posters for plays he'd never seen, or even heard of—like *O Some Hisamatsu* and *Yuku No Ichiya*—written in kanji and English. Like Chinatown, the whole area around the park apparently woke up on Saturdays. Henry followed the crowds, then the music. In front of the Nippon Kan were street performers, dressed in full traditional costumes, fighting with shimmering swords that flexed and bent as they cut the air. Behind them, musicians played what looked like strange, three-string guitars. Nothing at all like the *yuehu* or *gao wu*, the two-string violins that he was used to hearing when the Peking Opera performed a fighting routine.

With the music and the dancing, Henry forgot all about looking for Keiko, though he occasionally murmured the words Sheldon had taught him—*Oh I decky tay ooh ree she day sue*—mainly out of nervous habit.

"Henry!"

Even through the music he knew the voice was hers. He looked around the crowd, lost for a moment before spotting her sitting on the hillside, the high point of Kobe Park, looking down on the street performers, waving. Henry walked up the hill, his palms sweating. *Oh I decky tay ooh ree she day sue. Oh I decky tay ooh ree she day sue.*

She put down a small notebook and looked up, smiling. "Henry? What are you doing here?"

"Oh-I-decky-tay . . ." The words rolled off his tongue like a Mack truck. He felt a wisp of perspiration on his forehead. *The words?* What was the rest? *"Ooh ree she day . . . sue."*

Keiko's face froze in a smile of surprise, interrupted only by her occasional wide-eyed blinking. "What did you just say?"

Breathe, Henry. Deep breath. One more time.

"Oai deki te ureshii desu!" The words came out perfectly. *I did it!*

Silence.

"Henry, I don't speak Japanese."

"What . . . ?"

"I. Don't. Speak. Japanese." Keiko burst out laughing. "They don't even teach it anymore at the Japanese school. They stopped last fall. My mom and dad speak it, but they wanted me to learn only English. About the only Japanese *I* know is *wakarimasen.*"

Henry sat down beside her, staring at the street performers. "Which means?"

Keiko patted his arm. "It means 'I don't understand'—understand?"

He lay back on the hillside, feeling the cool grass. He could smell the tiny Japanese roses everywhere, dotting the hill with patches of yellow stars.

"Whatever it was, Henry, you said it beautifully. What's it mean?"

"Nothing. It means 'What time is it?' "

Henry glanced at Keiko sheepishly and saw the look of suspicion in her eye. "Did you come all the way over here to ask me what time it was?"

Henry shrugged. "A friend just taught it to me, I thought you'd be impressed, I was wrong—what kind of notebook is that?"

"It's a sketchbook. And I *am* impressed, just that you'd come all the way over here. Your father would be mad if he knew. Or does he?"

Henry shook his head. This was the last place his father would expect to find him. Henry normally hung out at the waterfront on Saturdays, with other boys from the Chinese school, haunting places like Ye Olde Curiosity Shop out on Coleman Dock—looking at the real mummies and genuine shrunken heads, daring one another to touch them. But since he'd begun attending Rainier, they all treated him differently. He hadn't changed, but somehow, in their eyes he was different. He wasn't one of them anymore. Like Keiko, he was *special*.

"It's no big deal. I was just in the neighborhood."

"Really? And which neighbor taught you to speak Japanese?"

"Sheldon, the sax player on South King." Henry's eyes fell to the sketchbook. "Can I see your drawings?"

She handed him her small black sketchbook. Inside were pencil drawings of flowers and plants, and the occasional drawing of a dancer. The last one was a loose sketch of the crowd, the dancers—and a profile of Henry from the host of people below. "It's me! How long did you know I was down there? You just watched me the whole time. Why didn't you say anything?"

Keiko pretended that she didn't understand. "*Wakarimasen.* So sorry, I don't speak English." Joking, she took her sketchbook back. "See you Monday, Henry."

Bud's Jazz Records
(1986)

Henry closed the yearbook in his lap, setting it on the carved cherrywood coffee table, next to the framed photograph of him and Ethel on their thirtieth wedding anniversary. To Henry, her smiling face looked thin, gracefully hiding a certain sadness.

In the photo she was in early remission, but still was missing most of her hair from the radiation treatments. It didn't fall out all at once like you see in the movies. It came apart in uneven clumps, thick in some places, smooth in others. She'd asked Henry to use a set of clippers and shave it all off, which he did, reluctantly. It was the first of many personal moments they would share together. A long sabbatical into her day-to-day care, part of the mechanics of dying. He'd done all he could. But choosing to lovingly care for her was like steering a plane into a mountain as gently as possible. The crash is imminent; it's how you spend your time on the way down that counts.

He thought about moving on but didn't even know where to begin. So he went where he'd always gone to stimulate his senses, even as a little boy—a place where he always found a little comfort. He grabbed his hat and jacket and found himself stalking the dusty aisles of Bud's Jazz Records.

Bud's had been a fixture on South Jackson, near the old Pioneer Square, for as long as Henry could remember. Of course the original Bud Long didn't actually own the place anymore. But the new guy, a grizzled fellow with sagging hangdog cheeks like those of a partially deflated Dizzy Gillespie, filled the part amiably. He tended the record counter, where he readily answered to the name Bud.

"Haven't seen *you* in a while, Henry."

"I've been around," Henry said, flipping through a rack of old 78s, hoping to find something by Oscar Holden—the Holy Grail of Seattle's jazz recordings. The apocryphal story was that Oscar recorded a master-session 78 way back in the thirties, on vinyl, not wax. But of the rumored three hundred printed, none survived. None that anyone knew about anyway. But then again, almost no one knew who Oscar Holden *was*. Seattle greats like Ray Charles and Quincy Jones had moved on to the fame and fortune of Celebrityville. Still, Henry daydreamed that he might find a vinyl copy someday. And now that CDs were starting to outsell records, the used LP bins at Bud's were overflowing with new used records every day.

If one still existed, someone was bound to throw it out, or trade it in, not knowing what that dusty old recording meant to avid collectors like Henry. After all, Oscar *who*?

Bud turned the music down a bit. "You ain't been around *here,* 'cause I'd have seen you if you were around here." Something modern was playing, Overton Berry, Henry guessed, from the deep melancholy of the piano.

Henry thought about his absence. He'd been a regular for most of his adult life, and part of his youth. "My turntable was broken." And it had been, so it wasn't a lie. Besides, how do I tell him my wife died six months ago—no sense in turning Bud's Jazz Records into Bud's *Blues* Records.

"You hear about the Panama Hotel?" the old dealer asked.

Henry nodded, still thumbing through the rack, his nose itchy from the dust that always settled in the basement record shop. "I was standing right there when they started bringing all that stuff up."

"You don't say?" Bud rubbed his bald black pate. "I know what you're always in here looking for. Oh, I gave up looking for Oscar myself. But it sure makes you wonder, doesn't it? I mean they board up that whole building, what, around 1950? And then that new owner buys it, goes inspecting, and finds all that *stuff* sealed up all those years. Newspaper says there ain't much of value in there. No gold bars or nothing. But it makes you wonder . . ."

Henry had wondered nonstop since he'd watched them bring up that first steamer trunk. Since the owner had spun that Japanese parasol.

Henry fished out an LP by the Seattle jazz drummer Webb Coleman and set it on the counter. "I guess this'll do it."

Bud slipped the old record in a used Uwajimaya grocery bag and handed it right back. "This one's on me, Henry—I'm sorry about your wife." Bud's eyes looked like they'd seen plenty of suffering in his *own* time. "Ethel was a fine woman. I know you did right by her."

Henry found a weak smile and thanked him. Some people read the obituaries every day, even in a sprawling place like the Emerald City—but the International District was just a small town. People know everything about everyone. And just as in other small towns, when someone leaves, they never come back.

Dim Sum
(1986)

When the weekend rolled around, Henry headed past the old Nippon Kan Theater, or what was left of it—his feet crunching bits of broken glass and shattered lightbulbs. The colorful marquee that had once lit up the dark streets now was riddled with empty sockets and broken fixtures—the once warm glow, a reflection of how much hope Henry had had as a young boy, sat covered in decades of rust and neglect. Restoration or demolition? Henry didn't know which made more sense. The Nippon Kan had been abandoned decades earlier, like the Panama Hotel. But, like the hotel, it had also been bought in recent years and was in the process of being remodeled. Last he'd heard, the once-beating cultural heart of Japantown would soon be a bus station.

All these years, he'd never been inside, and even though there had been a small reopening party, four decades later, he couldn't bring himself to go. Stopping to soak it in, he watched the construction workers throwing old lavender upholstered chairs out a second-story window into the dumpster below. Must be from the balcony, Henry thought. Not much is left, might be my only time to step past the old ticket window and see that old Kabuki theater the way it was. So tempting. But he was almost late to meet Marty at the Sea Fortune Restaurant for lunch, and Henry hated to be late.

Henry regarded the musty old restaurant as the best in Chinatown. In fact, he'd been coming here for years, going all the way back to his childhood. Although, the first time he came here, it had been a Japanese noodle shop. Since then, it'd been through a merry-go-round of Chinese owners. Smart owners—they always kept the kitchen staff, which kept the food consistent. That was the true key to success in life, Henry thought—consistency.

Marty, on the other hand, wasn't crazy about the dim sum there. "Too traditional," he'd argue, "too bland." He much preferred the newer establishments, like House of Hong or Top Gun Seafood. Personally, Henry didn't favor those trendy restaurants that broke with tradition and served dim sum to the yuppie bar crowd until way after midnight. Nor did he care for nouveau Eurasian cuisine—ingredients like smoked salmon or plantains had no place on a dim sum menu, according to Henry's taste buds anyway.

As father and son settled into the lumpy, cracked cushions of a bright red Naugahyde booth, Henry flipped open the teapot, sniffing its contents, as though he were sampling some vintage wine. It was old. Nothing but brown, tea-stained water with hardly any aroma. He pushed the whole pot, lid up, to the side and flagged down the ancient serving lady pushing a cart of steamed dumplings in their general direction.

Looking over the sampling of shrimp dumplings, egg tarts, and steamed buns called *hum bau,* Henry pointed and nodded, not even asking what Marty wanted—he knew all of Marty's favorites anyway.

"Why do I get the feeling that something new is bothering you?" Marty asked.

"The tea?"

"No, that's just you thinking you're some kind of sommelier of dried leaves in a bag. You've been acting different lately. Something I should know about, Pops?"

Henry unwrapped his cheap wooden chopsticks, rolling them together to rub off any splinters. "My son is graduating, soma coma lode—"

"*Summa cum laude,*" Marty corrected.

"That's what I said. My son is graduating *with highest honor.*" Henry popped a steaming hot shrimp *shui mai* dumpling into his mouth, chewing as he spoke. "What could be wrong?"

"Well, Mom's passed, for starters. And now you're pretty much retired. From your job. From taking care of her. I'm just worried about you. What are you doing to pass the time these days?"

Henry offered a pork *bau* to his son, who took it with his chopsticks and peeled the wax paper off the bottom before taking a large bite. "I just went back down to Bud's. I picked up a little something. I'm getting out," Henry said. To punctuate his statement, he held up the bag from the record store. *See, conclusive evidence that I'm doing just fine.*

Henry watched his son unwrap a lotus leaf and eat the glutinous sticky rice inside. He could tell by the concern in his son's voice that Marty was unconvinced. "I'm heading over to the Panama Hotel. I thought I'd ask if they'd let me look around. They found a lot of old things in the basement. Things from *the war years.*"

Marty finished chewing. "Looking for some long-lost jazz record, perhaps?"

Henry ducked the question, not wanting to lie to his son, who knew he'd been interested in old jazz recordings from a very young age. But that was about all Marty knew of his father's childhood, though he did know that his father had had a hard time of it as a child. Why? He never asked, it somehow seemed sacred, and Henry rarely shared. In return, his son probably thought he was quite boring. A man who had cared for every detail of his wife's last years but had no surprises in him. Mr. Reliable. Without a bone of rebellion or spontaneity. "I'm looking for *something,*" Henry said.

Marty set his chopsticks on the edge of his plate, looking at his father. "Something I should know about? Who knows, Pops, maybe I can help."

Henry took a bite out of an egg custard tart, set it down, and pushed his plate away. "If I find something worth sharing, I'll let you know." *Who knows, I might even surprise you. Wait and see. Wait, and see.*

Marty seemed unconvinced.

"Something bothering *you*? You're the one who looks like he has something on his mind—aside from studying and grades." Henry thought his son was about to say something, then Marty clammed up. Timing seemed to be everything in Henry's family. There had always seemed to be a right time and a wrong time for discussion between Henry and his own father. Maybe his son felt the same.

"He'll deal with it in his own way, and in his own time," Ethel had said, shortly after she learned she had cancer. "He's your son, but he's not a product of *your* childhood, it doesn't have to be the same."

Ethel had taken Henry out on Green Lake, on a boat, beneath a sunny

August sky, to tell him the bad news. "Oh, I'm not leaving anytime soon," she'd said. "But if anything, when I go, I hope my passing brings the two of you together."

She had never stopped mothering her son, and Henry for that matter. Until the treatments began, then everything got turned around. And seemed to stay that way.

Now father and son waited in silence, ignoring the carts of dim sum that rolled by. The awkward moment was interrupted by the crash of plates somewhere in the kitchen, punctuated by men swearing at each other in Chinese and English. There was much to say and ask, but neither Henry nor Marty inched closer to the subject. They just waited for their server, who would soon be bringing more tea and orange slices.

Henry quietly hummed the tune of an old song—he didn't know the words anymore, but he'd never forgotten the melody. And the more he hummed the more he felt like smiling again.

Marty, on the other hand, just sighed, and kept looking for the waitress.

Lake View
(1986)

Henry paid the bill and watched as his son waved good-bye, loading an enormous to-go bag into the front seat of his silver Honda Accord. The extra goodies had been at Henry's insistence. He knew his son did okay with the food on campus, but they didn't have anything that compared with a dozen fresh hum bau—and besides, steamed pork buns could easily be reheated in the microwave in Marty's dorm room.

Content that his son was well on his way, Henry stopped at a flower stand, then stood at the nearest bus stop, where he caught the Number 10 to the far side of Capitol Hill—within walking distance of Lake View Cemetery.

When Ethel died, Henry had sworn he'd visit her grave once a week. But it'd been six months now, and he'd been up to see her only once—on what would have been their thirty-eighth wedding anniversary.

He placed fresh-cut starfire lilies, the kind they grew in their flower garden, on the small granite headstone that was all that reminded the world that Ethel had once lived. He paid his respects, sweeping away the dried leaves and wiping the moss from her grave, where he placed another small bundle of flowers.

Putting his umbrella away, and ignoring the fine Seattle mist, he opened his wallet and took out a small white envelope. On the front was the Chinese character for Lee—Ethel's last name for the last thirty-seven-plus years. Inside had been a piece of hard candy and a quarter. The small envelopes were passed out as he left the Bonney-Watson Funeral Home, where Ethel's memorial service had been held. The candy was so that everyone leaving would taste sweetness—not bitter. The quarter was for buying more candy on the way home—a traditional token of lasting life and enduring happiness.

Henry remembered savoring the candy, a small peppermint. But he didn't feel like stopping at the store on the way home. Marty, ironically, argued that they honor this tradition, but Henry refused.

"Take me home" was all he said when Marty slowed down near the South Gate Grocery.

Henry couldn't bear the thought of spending that quarter. That was all he had left of Ethel. His enduring happiness would have to wait. He'd save it—keeping it with him, always.

He thought about that happiness, reaching into the small envelope he carried with him every day, drawing out the quarter. It was unremarkable—a normal coin anyone would spend on a phone call or a cup of bad coffee. But to Henry it was a promise of something better.

Henry remembered the day of Ethel's service. He'd arrived early, to meet with Clarence Ma, the funeral director assigned to his family. A kindly man in his sixties, prone to talking about his own bodily ailments, Clarence was the patron saint of all things funerary when it came to Chinatown. Each neighborhood had its own advocate. The stately walls of the Bonney-Watson Funeral Home were covered with their framed photos—a United Nations of ethnically diverse funeral directors.

"Henry, you're early—something I can do for you?" Clarence said, looking up from his desk, where he'd been stuffing the coins and candy into envelopes as Henry walked by.

"Just wanted to check the flowers," Henry replied, heading into the chapel where a large portrait of Ethel sat surrounded by flower arrangements of various sizes.

Clarence caught up to him, placing his arm on his shoulder. "Beautiful, isn't it?"

Henry nodded.

"We made sure to place your flowers right next to her picture—she was a lovely woman, Henry. I'm sure she's in a happier place, but hardly one as beautiful." Clarence handed Henry a small white envelope. "In case you don't remember after the service—take it, just in case."

Henry felt the quarter inside. He held the envelope to his nose and could smell the peppermint among the wet, fragrant scents of the floral-filled room. "Thank you" was all he could muster.

Now, standing in the misty rain of Lake View Cemetery, Henry touched the envelope to his nose again. He couldn't smell a thing.

"I'm sorry I haven't been here as often as I should have," he apologized. He held the quarter in his hand, putting the envelope in his pocket. He listened to the sound of the wind blowing through the trees—never really expecting an answer, but always open to the possibility.

"I have some things I need to do. And, well, I just wanted to come by and tell you first. But, you probably know all this." Henry's attention drifted to the marker next to Ethel's—it was his parents'. Then he looked back to where Ethel lay. "You always knew me so well."

Henry brushed the graying hair from his temples, wet from the drizzly rain.

"I'm getting by. But I'm worried about Marty. I've always worried about him. I guess I'd ask that you look out for him—me, I can look out for myself. I'll be okay."

Henry looked around to see if anyone might be watching him having this odd, one-way conversation. He was all alone—he wasn't even sure if Ethel was listening. It was one thing to talk to her at home, where she'd lived. But out here, in the cold ground next to his parents, she was certainly gone. Still, Henry had needed to come out to say good-bye.

He kissed the quarter and placed it on top of Ethel's headstone. This was our promise of happiness, Henry thought. It's all I have left to give. This is so you can be happy without me.

He stood back, hands at his sides, and took three deep bows out of respect.

"I have to go now," Henry said.

Before he left, he drew a lily from Ethel's bundle of flowers and set it on his mother's grave. He even brushed a few leaves from his father's stone before opening his umbrella and walking back down the hill in the direction of Volunteer Park.

He took the long way back, down a winding path that lead to the near-empty parking lot. Lake View Cemetery was a beautiful place, despite the somber graves that stood as cold reminders of so much loss and longing. The final resting place of Chief Seattle's daughter and other notables like Asa Mercer and Henry Yesler, it was a walking tour of Seattle's forgotten history. Not unlike the Nisei War Memorial Monument in the northeast corner. It was a smaller monument, smaller than the headstones of members of the Nordstrom family, dedicated to Japanese American veterans—locals who'd died fighting the Germans. These days it went all but unnoticed, except by Henry, who tipped his hat as he slowly walked by.

Speak Your American
(1942)

 Henry stood in front of the mirror, examining his school clothes. He'd asked his mother to iron them, but they still looked wrinkled. He tried on an old Seattle Indians baseball cap, then thought better of it, combing his hair yet again. Anxiety about Monday mornings was nothing new. In fact, it normally began on Sunday afternoons. Even though he was used to his routine at Rainier Elementary, his stomach would knot up as the hours passed, each minute bringing him closer to his return to the all-white school—the bullies, the heckling, and his lunch duties in the cafeteria with Mrs. Beatty. This Monday morning, though, his ritual of serving the other kids seemed downright exciting. Those forty precious minutes in the kitchen had become time well spent, since he'd get to see Keiko. Silver lining? *Indeed.*

"You one big smile this morning, Henry," his father commented in Chinese, slurping his *jook*—thick rice soup, mixed with diced preserved cabbage. Not a favorite of Henry's, but he ate it politely.

Henry took slices of preserved duck egg out of his own bowl and set them in his mother's before she returned from the kitchen. He liked the salty slices but knew they were her favorite, and she never saved much for herself anyway. On their dark cherrywood table sat a lazy Susan used for serving; he spun it back to its original position just as his mother was returning, her bowl back in front of her.

His father's eyes peeked over his newspaper. The front-page headline read: BRITISH EVACUATE RANGOON. "You liking you school now? Hah?" His father spoke as he turned the page.

Henry, knowing not to speak Cantonese at home, answered with a nod.

"They fix the stairs, hah? The ones you fell down?" Again, Henry nodded, acknowledging his father's Cantonese, and kept eating his thick breakfast soup. He listened to his father during these lopsided, one-way conversations, but he never talked back. In fact, Henry rarely talked at all, except in English to acknowledge his advancing skills. But since his father understood only Cantonese and a little Mandarin, the conversations came as waves, back and forth, tidal shores of separate oceans.

The truth was that Henry had been beaten up by Chaz Preston on that first day of school. But his parents wanted him there so much that not being appreciative would have been a terrible insult. So Henry made up some excuse, *speaking his American*. Of course his parents didn't understand—imploring him *to be more careful next time*. Henry did his best to respect and honor his parents. He walked to school each day, going upstream against a sea of Chinese kids who called him "white devil." He worked in the school kitchen as white devils called him "yellow." But that was okay. I'll do what I have to, Henry thought. But along the way, I think I'm tired of *being careful*.

Finishing his breakfast, he thanked his mother and gathered his books for school. Each had a newly wrapped cover—made from folded jazz-club flyers.

After school that Wednesday, Henry and Keiko did their work duties. Emptied the trash in the classrooms. Pounded erasers. Then they waited for the danger to subside. Chaz and Denny Brown were responsible for retiring the flag each day, which kept them around a little longer than usual. But it'd been thirty minutes since the final bell, and they were nowhere to be seen. Henry gave the all clear to Keiko, who hid in the girls' restroom while Henry scouted the parking lot.

Except for the normal janitorial crew, he and Keiko were typically the last to leave. And today was no different. They walked side by side, down the stairs and past the naked flagpole, dangling their book bags beside them.

Henry noticed Keiko's sketchbook, the one she'd had in the park, in her book bag. "Who taught you how to draw?" he asked. And draw so well, Henry thought, with just a hint of jealousy, secretly admiring her talent.

Keiko shrugged. "My mother, I suppose—mainly. She was an artist when she was about my age. She dreamed of going to New York City and working in a gallery. But she has pain in her hands now and doesn't draw or paint as much, so she gave her art supplies to me. She wants me to go to college at the Cornish Institute on Capitol Hill—that's an art school, you know."

Henry had heard of Cornish, a four-year academy for fine artists, musicians, and dancers. It was a fancy place. A prestigious place. He was impressed. He'd never known a real artist, except for maybe Sheldon, still . . . "They won't take you."

Keiko stopped in her tracks, turning to Henry. "Why not? Because I'm a girl?"

Sometimes Henry's mouth was too big for his face. He didn't know a delicate way around the subject, so he just said what he was thinking. "They won't take you 'cause you're Japanese."

"That's why my mom wants me to apply there. To be the first." Keiko kept walking, leaving Henry a few steps behind. "Speaking of my mother, I asked her what *Oai deki te ureshii desu* means," Keiko said.

Henry walked a step behind, looking around nervously. He noticed Keiko's flowered dress. For someone who appeared so sweet, she sure seemed to know how to needle him. "It was Sheldon's dumb idea," he said.

"It was a nice thing to say." Keiko paused, as if looking at a group of seagulls sweeping by overhead, then looked back at Henry, who caught a glint of mischief in her eyes. "Thank you, *and* Sheldon." She smiled and continued walking.

As they approached Sheldon's usual corner, there was no music, no crowd, and no sign of the sax player anywhere. He normally played across from the Rainier Heat & Power building, its entrance still covered in sandbags from bombing jitters earlier in the year. Tourists walked by as though he'd never existed. Henry and Keiko looked at each other, wondering.

"He was here this morning," Henry said. "He mentioned that his try-out at the Black Elks Club went well. Maybe he got called back?" Maybe he'd landed a regular gig with Oscar Holden, who Sheldon said had regular practice jams on Monday and Wednesday nights. They were free, so a lot of people popped in and played or just enjoyed the music.

Henry stood on the corner, looking up at neon signs marking the jazz clubs that lined both sides of Jackson Street.

"How late do your parents let you play outside?" he asked, looking at the horizon, trying to find the sun hidden somewhere behind the dense, overcast haze of Seattle's waterfront.

"I don't know, I usually take my sketchbook, so until it gets dark, I guess."

Henry looked up at the Black Elks Club, wondering what time Sheldon might be playing. "Mine too. My mother does the dishes and then relaxes, and my father settles in with the newspaper and listens to the news on the radio."

That left Henry with a few hours. Still, evenings could be a dangerous time to be walking the streets. Since so many drivers had painted their headlights blue or covered them with cellophane to comply with blackout restrictions, accidents—either head-on collisions or people simply being run over crossing the street at night—were on the rise. Seattle's thick fog, which slowed down traffic on the streets and made trouble for the ships sailing in and out of Elliott Bay, had become a blanket of comfort, hiding homes and buildings from phantom Japanese bombers or artillery from suspected Japanese submarines. It seemed like there was danger everywhere, from drunken sailors behind the wheel, Japanese saboteurs, and worst of all, his own parents if they caught him.

"I want to go," Keiko insisted. She looked at Henry, then up the street toward the row of jazz clubs. She brushed the hair out of her eyes, looking like she'd already made up her mind about a question he hadn't even asked.

"You don't even know what I'm thinking."

"If you're going to go listen to him play, I'm coming with you."

Henry thought about it. He'd already bent the rules by spending time in Nihonmachi, so why not head up Jackson and see the sights, maybe even hear the songs? It would be okay, as long as they weren't seen, and as long as they made it home before dark. "We're not going anywhere together. My dad will kill me. But if you want to meet me in front of the Black Elks Club at six o'clock, after dinner, I'll be there."

"Don't be late," Keiko replied.

He walked with her through Nihonmachi, the route they always took. Henry had no clue how they'd actually get into the Black Elks Club. *One,* they weren't black. Even if he replaced the button he wore with one that said "I am Negro," it wasn't going to cut it. And *two,* they probably weren't old enough, although he thought he'd seen entire families—young kids in tow—go inside. But that was only on certain nights. Like bingo night at the Bing Kung Benevolent Association. All he knew was that he'd figure it out. They would listen from the street if they had to. It was only a few blocks over, a little farther for Keiko, but not too far. Close to home but a world away—from his parents' world anyway.

"Why do you like jazz so much?" Keiko asked.

"I don't know," Henry said. And he didn't, really. "Maybe because it's so different, but people everywhere still like it, they just accept musicians, no matter what color they are. Plus, my father hates it."

"Why does he hate it?"

"Because it's *too* different, I guess."

As they reached Keiko's apartment building, Henry waved good-bye and turned toward home. Walking away, he watched Keiko's reflection in the side mirror of a parked car. She looked over her shoulder and smiled. Caught peeking, he turned his head and cut through the vacant lot behind Nichibei Publishing and past the Naruto-Yu, a Japanese *sento*—bathhouse. Henry couldn't picture bathing with his parents the way some Japanese families did. He couldn't picture himself doing a lot of things with his parents. He wondered about Keiko's own family—and what they might think of her sneaking out to a jazz club, let alone to meet Henry. He felt his stomach turn a little. His heart raced when he thought about Keiko, but his gut tightened just the same.

In the distance, he heard the faint sound of jazz musicians warming up.

Jamaican Ginger
(1942)

When Keiko arrived outside the Black Elks Club, Henry immediately felt underdressed. Basically, he wore the same clothes he'd had on earlier in the day, the "I am Chinese" button still pinned to his school shirt. Keiko, though, had dressed for the occasion and had on a bright pink dress and shiny brown leather shoes. Her hair, which had been pulled back and bobbed with pins and hot rollers, now hung in swoopy curls to her shoulders. She wrapped herself in a white sweater she said her mother had knitted. Her sketchbook was tucked neatly beneath her arm.

Dumbfounded, Henry said the first thing that came to his mind. "You look beautiful." He said it in English, watching Keiko beam, astonished at how different she looked, only vaguely resembling the silly apron-wearing girl from the school kitchen.

"No Japanese? No *oai deki te ureshii desu*?" she teased.

"I'm speechless."

Keiko returned his smile. "Do we just go in?"

"We can't." Henry shook his head and pointed to a sign that read "No Minors Allowed After 6:00 P.M." "They're serving booze. We're too young. But I've got an idea. Follow me." He pointed to the alley, where he and Keiko looped around, finding the back door. It was framed with thick glass blocks, but music emanated from the screen door, which was slightly ajar.

"Are we sneaking in?" Keiko asked, concerned.

Henry shook his head. "They're bound to see us and toss us." Instead he scrounged up a pair of wooden milk crates, and they both sat down, listening to the music, ignoring the pungent smells of beer and mold in the alley. I can't believe I'm *here,* Henry thought. The sun was still out, and the music was brisk and lively.

After the first fifteen-minute set, the screen door creaked open and an old black man stepped out to light a cigarette. Startled, Henry and Keiko jumped up to run; they were sure they would be shooed away for loitering.

"What are you kids doing hanging out back here, trying to scare the bejeezus out of this old man?" He patted his chest above his heart, then sat down where Henry had been sitting. The rumpled old man wore long trousers, held up by gray suspenders, over a wrinkled button-down shirt, the sleeves rolled up. To Henry, he looked like an unmade bed.

"Sorry," Keiko offered, flattening out the wrinkles in her dress. "We were just listening to the music—we were just about to leave—"

Henry interrupted. "Is Sheldon playing with the band tonight?"

"Sheldon who? We got a lot of new faces in there tonight, son."

"He plays the saxophone."

The old man wiped his sweaty hands on his pants and lit his smoke. Hacking and coughing, he puffed away as if it were a competition and he was the losing team working toward a comeback. Henry listened as the old man caught his breath between draws. "He's in there, doing a fine job—you a fan of his or something?"

"I'm just a friend—and I wanted to come down and hear Oscar Holden. I'm a fan of Oscar's."

"Me too," Keiko added, getting swept up in the moment, crowding close to Henry.

The old man stubbed his cigarette out on the worn heel of his shoe, then tossed the butt in the nearest garbage can. "You a fan of Oscar's, huh?" He pointed at Henry's button. "Oscar got an all-Chinese fan club these days?"

Henry covered the button with his coat. "This is just . . . my father's . . ."

"It's okay, kid, some days I wish I was Chinese too." The old man laughed a gravelly smoker's laugh that trailed into a cough, wheezing and spitting on the ground. "Well, if you're friends of *Sheldon the Sax Man* and fans of *Oscar the Piano Man,* I figure Oscar probably wouldn't mind having a couple little kids from the fan club in his house tonight. Now you won't tell no one about this, will you?"

Henry looked at Keiko, unsure if the old man was kidding or not. She just kept smiling; her eager grin was larger than his. Both shook their heads no. "We won't tell a soul," Keiko promised.

"Great. I need you two fan club kids to do me a little favor if you want admittance to the club tonight."

Henry deflated a bit as he watched the old man take some slips of paper out of his shirt pocket, handing one to each of them. He compared his note with Keiko's. They were almost identical. Some sort of scribbled writing and a signature—from a doctor.

"Now you take these to the pharmacy on Weller—you tell 'em it's on our account, you bring it back, and you get in."

"I don't think I understand," Henry said. "This is medicine . . ."

"It's a prescription for Jamaican Ginger—a secret ingredient around here. This is how the world works, son. With the war, everything's being rationed—sugar, gasoline, tires—*booze.* Plus, they don't let us have a liquor license in the colored clubs, so we do what *they* did a few years back, during the Prohibition. We make it and shake it, baby." The old black man pointed to a neon sign of a martini tumbler that hung above the doorway. "For medicinal purposes, you all know—go on now."

Henry looked at Keiko, not sure what to do or what to believe. It didn't seem like that big a request. He must have gone to the drugstore a hundred times for his mother. Besides, Henry loved to snack on dried ginger. Maybe this was something like that.

"We'll be right back." Keiko tugged at Henry's coat, leading him back out the alley and around to Jackson Street. Weller was one block over.

"Does this make us bootleggers?" Henry asked, when he saw the rows of bottles through the drugstore window. He was both nervous and excited at the prospect. He'd listened to *This Is Your FBI* on the radio as G-men busted up smuggling rings coming down from Canada. You rooted for the good guys, but when you played cops and robbers outside the next day, you always wanted to be the bad guy.

"I don't think so. It's not illegal anymore—besides, we're just running errands. Like he said, they sell it, but they can't buy from the white places, so they make it."

Henry gave up any concern about wrongdoing and headed into the Owl Drug Store, which conveniently stayed open until eight. Bootleggers don't go to pharmacies, he told himself. You can't go to jail for picking up an order, can you?

If the skinny old druggist thought it was odd for two little Asian kids each to be picking up a bottle that was 80 percent alcohol, he didn't say a word. Truth be told, by the way he squinted at the prescriptions and labels with an enormous handheld magnifying glass, he probably didn't even see much of anything. But the clerk, a young black man, just winked and flashed them a knowing smile as he slipped their bottles into separate bags. "No charge," he said.

On their way out, Henry and Keiko didn't even pause to moon over the jars of penny candy. Instead they looked at each other in mock nonchalance, each feeling a little bit older, striding across the street with ten-ounce bottles of liquor swinging at their sides. Small victors in a grown-up scavenger hunt.

"What do they do with this stuff, drink it?" Henry asked, looking at his bottle.

"My papa told me how people used to use it to make bathtub gin."

Henry pictured the sailors who were known to stagger down the street and cause fights late at night. Stumbling around like their legs belonged to someone else. "Jake-legged," people called it—from bad gin. Sailors and soldiers from Paine Army Air Field were banned from certain uptown clubs for fighting, so they wandered into the jazz alleys of South Jackson, or even into Chinatown on occasion, looking for a bar that would serve them. Henry couldn't believe people still drank this stuff. But when he saw the crowds that gathered outside the Black Elks Club, he knew they were here for the same thing he was. They were here to partake of something lush, intoxicating, and almost forbidden—they were here for the music. And tonight, at the front of the building, where latecomers lined up to get in, some were even being turned away. A huge crowd for a weeknight. Oscar sure packed them in.

In the alley, behind the club, Henry could hear musicians tuning up for their next set. He thought he heard Sheldon, tweaking his saxophone.

On the back step, a younger man dressed in a white apron and black bow tie was waiting for them. He opened the screen door and rushed them through a makeshift service kitchen, where they put their bottles of Jamaican Ginger in a tub of ice with other odd-shaped bottles of mysterious properties.

Out in the main room, near a worn wooden dance floor, their escort pointed at some chairs beside the kitchen door, next to where a busboy was folding a pile of cloth napkins into perfect little white triangles. "You sit over there and stay out of trouble, and I'll go see if Oscar is ready," he told them. Henry and Keiko gazed in awe through the dark, smoky lounge, speckled with tall glasses on burgundy tablecloths and jewelry that sparkled on the patrons huddled around the small candlelit tables.

The chatter dimmed as an old man found his way to the bar, where he poured himself a tall glass of ice water, wiping the sweat from his brow. It was the old man from behind the club, the one who'd been smoking in the alley. Henry's jaw dropped as the old man headed onstage, flexed his wrists, and popped his knuckles before sitting down at the upright piano in front of a large jazz ensemble. Sheldon was perched behind a bandbox with the rest of the horn section.

The old man shucked his suspenders from his shoulders, giving his upper body room to roam, and slid his fingers across the keyboard as the rest of the band fell into rhythm. To Henry, the crowd appeared to be holding their breath. The old man at the piano spoke as he started playing an intro. "This is for my two new friends—it's called 'Alley Cats.' It's a little different, but I think you gonna like it."

Henry had listened to Woody Herman and Count Basie once or twice on the radio, but to hear a twelve-piece orchestra *live* was unlike anything he'd ever experienced. Most of the music he heard vicariously spilling out of the clubs up and down South Jackson was of the small-ensemble variety, with simple, broken beats. A few musicians playing freestyle. This was a speeding freight train by comparison. The double bass and drums drove the tune while magically cutting away all at once to allow Oscar to take the spotlight with his featured piano solos.

Henry turned to Keiko, who had opened up her sketchbook and was doing her best to pencil in the scene. "It's swing jazz," she said. "This is what my parents listen to. My mom says they don't play it like this at the white clubs; it's too crazy for some people."

When Keiko mentioned her parents, Henry began noticing the makeup of the crowd. Nearly all were black, some sitting and swaying while others strutted on the floor, dancing spontaneously to the frenetic pace of the band. Standing out in the crowd were several Japanese couples, drinking and soaking in the music, like flowers turned toward the sun. Henry looked for Chinese faces. There were none.

Keiko pointed to one of the small tables where three Japanese couples sat, sipping their drinks and laughing. "That's Mr. Toyama. He was my English composition teacher at the Japanese school for one quarter. That must be his wife. I think the other two are teachers as well."

Henry watched the Japanese couples and thought about his own parents. His mother busy with her housework or community service at the Bing Kung Benevolent Association, where she'd trade in her gasoline coupons for ration stamps—red stamps for meat, lard, and oil, and blue stamps for beans, rice, and canned goods. His father with his ear tuned to the radio, listening for the latest news about the war in Russia. The war in the Pacific. The war in China. Spending his day leading fund-raising drives to support the Kuomintang—the nationalist army fighting the Japanese in the northern provinces of China. He was even ready to fight the war here, having volunteered as a block warden for the Chinatown area. He was one of the few civilians issued a gas mask as a precaution against the impending Japanese invasion.

The war affected everyone. Even here at the Black Elks Club, the blackout curtains were drawn, making the mood feel secretive to Henry. Like a place hidden from the troubles of the world. Maybe that was why they all came here. To escape—running away with a martini made from Jamaican Ginger, chasing it with Oscar Holden's rendition of "I Got It Bad and That Ain't Good."

Henry could have stayed all night. Keiko too, probably. But when he peeked behind the heavy curtain, the sun was setting over Puget Sound and the Olympic Mountains in the distance. He looked out the window as teenagers, older than he and Keiko, ran up and down the sidewalk shouting, "Put out your lights! Put out your lights!"

Inside, Oscar took another break.

"It's almost dark, time to go," Henry said.

Keiko looked at Henry like he'd woken her from a wonderful dream.

They waved at Sheldon, who finally saw them and waved back, looking happy and surprised to see them. He met them by the kitchen door.

"Henry! And this must be . . ." Sheldon looked at him with eyes wide. Henry saw the expression; he looked more impressed than surprised.

"This is Keiko. She's my friend from school. She's on scholarship too."

Keiko shook Sheldon's hand. "Nice to meet you. It was Henry's idea, we hung out back and then—"

"And then Oscar put you to work, that's how it happened, isn't it? He's like that, always looking out for his club. Looking out for his band. What'd you think?"

"The best. He should put out a record," Keiko gushed.

"Now, now, we gotta walk before we can run—bills to pay, you know. Okay, we're about to light it up again for the eight o'clock session, so you two better run along now. It's almost dark, and I don't know about you, miss, but I *know* Henry can't be out that late. Little man ain't got no brother, so *I'm* his big brother, gotta look out for him. In fact, we look alike, don't we?" Sheldon put his face next to Henry's. "That's the only reason he wears that button, so they don't confuse the two of us."

Keiko smiled and laughed; she touched Sheldon's cheek with the palm of her hand, her eyes lighting up as they met Henry's.

"How long are you playing here?" Henry asked.

"Just through the weekend, then Oscar said *we'd talk.*"

"Knock 'em dead," Henry said as he and Keiko headed through the swinging kitchen door.

Sheldon smiled and held up his sax. "Thank you, sir, you have a fine day now."

Henry and Keiko threaded their way through the kitchen, between a large butcher block on wheels and racks of dishes, glasses, and silverware. A few of the kitchen staff looked puzzled as the two of them smiled and walked on by, heading for the back landing in the alley.

The evening had been incredible. Henry wished he could tell his parents about it. Maybe he would, at breakfast tomorrow, in English.

The door leading to the alley had been closed and locked. It was almost blackout time. When Henry opened the heavy wooden sway, lurching in the doorway were two white faces in plain black suits that blotted out what little light remained in the dusky twilight. Henry stopped breathing, frozen, as he heard for the first time the cold metal tumble of a revolver being cocked. Each man gripped a fistful of gunmetal. Short, piercing barrels pointed directly at his smallish twelve-year-old frame as he broke his paralysis to step in front of Keiko, shielding her the best he could. On their suit coats hung badges. They were federal agents. Music inside the Black Elks Club clattered to a halt. The only sounds Henry heard were his own racing heartbeat and men everywhere shouting, *"FBI."*

Henry knew it. They were being busted up for bootlegging. For hauling bottles of Jamaican Ginger to some speakeasy where they'd get fingered for making bathtub gin. But as shocked as he was, stunned was more like it, Keiko looked terrified.

Henry felt the heavy hands of the two FBI men as they escorted them both back through the kitchen, ignoring workers in the pantry, who Henry saw were busy pouring bottles of whiskey and gin down the drain. The agents ignored them. *It doesn't make sense,* Henry thought.

In the ballroom the agents ordered them to sit in the very same chairs they had been occupying previously. From there Henry counted at least a half dozen other agents, some with shotguns, pointing them into the crowd, shouting at some, pushing others out of the way.

Henry and Keiko both looked for Sheldon, who'd been lost in the jumbled shuffle of agents and members of the jazz orchestra, who were quietly and carefully putting their instruments away, protecting the valuables with which they earned a living.

Patrons grabbed their coats and hats if they were nearby; others left them behind, heading for the exits.

Henry and Keiko looked on as Oscar Holden himself stood at the edge of the stage, microphone in hand, imploring everyone to stay calm. He lost his cool when an FBI agent tried to shout him down at gunpoint. Oscar kept on hollering, "They just listening to music. Why you taking them away?" The old man in his white, sweat-stained shirt hoisted his suspenders, casting a long shadow across the dance floor from the halcyon lights behind him, like God yelling down from the mountain. In his shadow lay the Japanese patrons, both men and women—facedown on the dance floor, guns pointed to their heads.

Henry looked at Keiko, who was frozen—staring at a Japanese man sprawled on the floor. "Mr. Toyama?" Henry whispered.

Keiko nodded, slowly.

Oscar kept shouting until Sheldon broke through the crowd and peeled him away from the FBI agent who stood just below. Sax still in hand, he did his best to try to calm the bandleader, and the agent who had just chambered a shell in his shotgun.

The club seemed hollow without music, replaced by the barking of federal agents and the occasional clicking of handcuffs. The dimly lit dance hall still sparkled now and then as the candles on empty tables flickered light on half-empty martini glasses.

The six Japanese patrons were handcuffed and taken to the door, the women sniffling, the men asking *"Why?"* in English. Henry heard *"I'm an American"* being shouted as the last one was arrested and taken outside.

"What the heck are we supposed to do with these two?" the agent next to them shouted to a portly man in a dark brown suit. He looked older than the rest.

"What . . . do we have here?" The brown-suited man holstered his pistol and removed his hat, rubbing his balding forehead. "A little young for spies, I'd say."

Henry slowly opened his coat, showing his button. "I am Chinese."

"Jeezus, Ray, you collared a couple of Chinks by mistake. They were probably just working the kitchen. Nice job. Good thing you didn't have to rough 'em up, they might have got the best of you."

"You leave them kids alone, they work for me!" Oscar slipped past Sheldon and barged through the remaining crowd, heading for the agents nearest Henry. "I didn't leave the South to come all the way up here and see people treated like that!"

Everyone darted out of his way. All but two younger agents, who holstered their guns, freeing both hands to restrain the larger man; a third agent wrestled his way in with a set of handcuffs. Oscar shook his arms free and pitched his shoulder into one of the agents, almost knocking him over a table—sending martini glasses to the ground, where they shattered with soft pinging sounds, dotting the floor with broken glass that crunched under their feet.

Sheldon did his best to keep things from getting even more out of hand. He managed to wedge himself between the agents and Oscar— saving Oscar from the agents or the agents from the angry black man, Henry wasn't sure which. Sheldon backed his bandleader up once again as the agents shouted warnings but let them go. They'd already collared the Japanese they came for. There seemed to be little interest in busting up a gin joint, or its proprietor.

"Why are you taking those people?" Henry heard Keiko ask softly amid the fracas. The door that Mr. Toyama had been taken out of slammed shut, cutting off the remaining light from the outside world.

The brown-suited man put his hat back on, as if his job was finished and he was ready to go, "Collaborators, kid. Secretary of the Navy says there were Jap scouts working in Hawaii—all of them locals. That ain't happening around here. Too many ships over in Bremerton, and parked right out there." He thumbed in the direction of Puget Sound.

Henry stared at Keiko, wishing she could read his thoughts, hoping she would read his eyes. *Please don't say it. Don't tell him that man, Mr. Toyama, was your schoolteacher.*

"What's going to happen to them?" Keiko asked, the sound of concern in her small voice.

"They can get the death penalty if they're found guilty of treason, but they'll probably just spend a few years in a nice safe jail cell."

"But he's not a spy, he was—"

"It's almost dark, we have to go," Henry said, cutting her and the agent off, tugging at Keiko's elbow. "We can't be late, remember?"

Her face was wrinkled with confusion and flushed with anger. "But—"

"We have to go. Now." Henry urged her to the nearest exit. "Please . . ."

A bulky agent stood aside to let them out the front door. Henry looked back and saw Sheldon guarding Oscar near the front of the stage, keeping him quiet. Sheldon looked back and waved, urging them to get home.

Past rows of dark police cars, Henry and Keiko stood on the stoop of an apartment building across the street. They watched as uniformed officers dispersed the crowd. A white reporter from *The Seattle Times* took notes and pictures, the flashbulbs from his camera sporadically lighting up the front of the Black Elks Club. He'd take out a handkerchief to change the hot bulb, dropping the old bulb on the ground, stepping on it, grinding it into the pavement. The reporter shouted questions at the nearest officer, whose only reply was "No comment."

"I can't watch this anymore," Keiko said, stalking away.

"I'm sorry I brought you here," Henry offered as they walked to the edge of South Main, where they would split up for their separate walks home. "I'm sorry our big night was ruined."

Keiko halted and looked at Henry. She looked down at his button, the one his father made him wear. "You *are* Chinese, aren't you, Henry?"

He nodded, not knowing how to answer.

"That's fine. Be who you are," she said, turning away, a look of disappointment in her eyes. "But *I'm* an American."

I Am Japanese
(1986)

Henry woke to the sound of a police cruiser, its siren wailing in the distance. He'd dozed off a bit, daydreaming, on the long bus ride from Lake View Cemetery all the way back down to the International District—the I.D., as Marty called it. Henry covered his mouth in a yawn and looked out the window. To him the area northeast of the Kingdome was simply Chinatown. That's what he'd called it growing up, and he wasn't likely to change now—despite the influx of Vietnamese karaoke clubs, Korean video stores, and the occasional sushi bar, frequented by a mainly Caucasian lunch crowd.

Marty didn't know much about Henry's childhood. Henry talked about his youth only in reflection, as he told stories about his own parents—Marty's grandmother, mainly. Or occasionally the grandfather Marty never knew. The lack of meaningful communication between father and son was based on a lifetime of isolation. Henry had been an only child, without siblings around to talk to, to share things with constantly. And Marty was the same. Whatever stumbling methods of communication Henry had used with his own father seemed to have been passed down to Marty. Over the years, they'd both used Ethel to bridge that gap, but now Henry would have to ford the divide himself. He just wasn't sure what to tell his son and when. For one growing up Chinese, decorum and timing were everything. After all, Henry hadn't spoken to his own parents, not much anyway, for three years—during the war.

But now, deep down, Henry wanted to tell his son everything. How seemingly unfair life was in retrospect, and how remarkable it was that they'd all just accepted what they had and made the best of it. He wanted to tell his son about Keiko—and about the Panama Hotel. But Ethel had only been gone six months. Sure, she'd been gone seven years and six months, but Marty probably wouldn't understand. It was too soon to tell him. And besides, what was there to tell now? Henry didn't know exactly.

Thinking of that painted bamboo parasol, Henry did his best to reconcile his feelings—the loss of Ethel, and the possibility of something to be found in the basement of that broken-down hotel. He'd lamented what else might be down there, right under his nose all these years, and wondered how much he could allow himself to hope for, how much his heart could take. But he couldn't wait any longer. A few days had passed, the news had come and gone. It was time to find out.

So Henry found himself stepping off the bus three stops early and wandering over to the Panama Hotel, a place between worlds when he was a child, a place between times now that he was a grown man. A place he had avoided for years, but now he couldn't keep himself away.

Inside, there were dusty workers in hard hats everywhere Henry looked. The water-stained ceiling tiles were being replaced. The floor was being sanded down to its original finish. The walls in the upstairs hallway were being sandblasted. The noise from the compressor alone made Henry cover his ears as he watched dust and grit settle at the top of the staircase.

Aside from the occasional transient who broke in a back window, or the flocks of pigeons that made their roost in the rooms of the upper floor, no one had occupied the hotel since 1949. Even when Henry was a boy, it had been sparse and half-empty. Especially during and after the war, from around 1942 all the way to V-J Day. Since then it had been abandoned.

"Is Mr. Pettison here?" Henry yelled the question over the screaming sounds of power saws and sandblasters to the construction worker closest to him. The man looked up and pried back his ear protection.

"Who?"

"I'm looking for Palmer Pettison."

The worker pointed to an old coatroom that appeared to have been transformed into a temporary office while the building was undergoing its rehab. From the various blueprints and construction documents pinned to a corkboard just outside the room, it looked like the hotel was on its way back to its former glory.

Henry took his hat off and stuck his head in. "Hello, I'm looking for Mr. Pettison."

"I'm *Ms.* Pettison—Palmyra Pettison. I'm the owner, if that's who you're looking for. Who am I talking to?"

Henry nervously introduced himself, talking faster than he normally would. His heart was racing just being in the old hotel—the place frightened and excited him. It was a forbidden place, according to his father's rules, a place deeply mysterious and beautiful. Even with all the neglect and water damage, the hotel was still stunning inside.

"I'm interested in the personal belongings that were found in the basement—the stored belongings."

"Really? It was an amazing discovery. I bought the building five years ago, but it took me five whole years to get the financing and approvals for the renovation. Before we started doing some of the interior demolition, I wandered down to the basement to inspect the furnace—and there it all was. Steamer trunks and suitcases, row after row, piled to the ceiling in some places. Are you looking to buy something?"

"No, I'm . . ."

"Are you from some museum?"

"No . . ."

"Then what can I do for you, Mr. Lee?"

Henry rubbed his forehead, a little flustered. He wasn't used to dealing with fast-talking business folk. "I don't know how to say this—I'm just looking for *something,* I don't really know what it is, but I'll know it when I see it."

Ms. Pettison closed the ledger at her desk. The look on her face somehow told Henry that she understood. "Then you must be a relative?"

Henry was surprised that after forty-some-odd years, people still on occasion thought he was Japanese. He thought about the button his father had made him wear each and every day—all those months at school, even during the summer. How he was taught by his parents to be ultra-Chinese, that his family's well-being depended on that ethnic distinction. How he had hated being called a Jap at school. But life is nothing if not ironic.

"Yes! I'm Japanese." Henry bobbed his head. "Of course I am. And I'd really like to look around if I could." If that's what it takes to get in the basement, I'll be Japanese. *I'll be a blue-blooded half-Martian Canadian immigrant if that's what it takes,* he thought.

"Just write your family's name on the list," she said and handed Henry a clipboard. "You can go on down and take a look. I'd just ask that you don't remove anything, not right now. We're still holding out hope of tracking down more of the relatives of the families that left their belongings here."

Henry was surprised. There were only three other names on the sheet. The big discovery had made the local news, but few people had come forward to lay claim to what had been left behind.

"No one's come to retrieve their belongings?"

"That was a long time ago. A lot can happen in forty-plus years. People move on." Henry watched her choose her words. There was a reverent tone that belied her hard-driving business nature. "Sometimes people *pass on* as well. In all likelihood, many of the owners are deceased."

"What about their relatives? Someone must have heard, wouldn't they have called . . ."

"I thought that too at first, but I think a lot of people just don't want to go back. Sometimes that's the best thing to do—to live in the present."

Henry understood. Honestly, he did. He knew what it was like to leave something behind. To move on and live the future and not relive the past.

But his sweet Ethel was gone now, and with it his responsibility to her.

Henry thanked Ms. Pettison and wrote a single name on the sheet: "Okabe."

The Basement
(1986)

Henry headed down a paint-chipped stairwell, through a thick wooden door that opened on creaking hinges. The door spilled into a large expanse of subbasement beneath the old hotel itself. The only illumination came from a handful of utility bulbs, hung like Christmas tree lights along the ceiling by large staples; a long tail of bright orange extension cord led the way.

Stepping inside, Henry drew several deep breaths, feeling a chest-pressing wave of claustrophobia. The underground storeroom was packed. He could hardly comprehend the quantity of personal items stored here. A narrow path, shoulder-wide, wound through a forest of crates, suitcases, and steamer trunks stacked as high as the ceiling, many rows deep. Some yellow. Some blue. Large and small. A thin veneer of dust coated everything. The belongings had been here untouched for decades.

On first impression, the room looked like a secondhand store. There was an old Luxus bicycle, the kind Henry wished he'd had as a child. There were large metal buckets, filled with rolls of paper and what appeared to be art prints. A 1941 Sears, Roebuck order form jutted out from a box beside an old issue of *Physical Culture* magazine. A finely carved marble chess set was piled up in a wooden rice bowl.

Aside from the parasol that was brought up the first day, nothing looked even remotely familiar, but then he couldn't be sure if the bamboo umbrella had been Keiko's or not. He'd seen it only in an old black-and-white photograph of her as a child, what, forty years ago? Yet, as much as he tried to dismiss it as sheer coincidence, his heart told him otherwise. It was hers. Her family's possessions were here. Some of the things most precious to her were here. And he would find them. What was left of them, anyway.

Henry eased down a small suitcase, popped the rusty clasps, and opened it, feeling like an intruder in someone's home. In the leather case was a shaving kit, an ancient bottle of Farnesiana cologne, and a rat's nest of old silk neckties. The name on the inside of the suitcase read "F. Arakawa." Whoever *he* was.

The next suitcase, a large leather number with a clear Lucite handle, practically fell apart as Henry opened it. The fabric was damp and moldy from decades of humidity. Upon closer inspection, Henry saw it for what it was. The beaded pearls. Silk-covered buttons. Lifting it out of the suitcase, he could see the gauzy white fabric was someone's wedding dress. Inside were a matching pair of white pumps and a lace garter. In a small hatbox, tucked beneath the dress, was a dried wedding bouquet, brittle and delicate. There were no photos or other identification in the suitcase.

Next Henry hauled down an old Wenatchee Valley apple crate overflowing with baby things. Bronzed shoes on a plaque, with the name Yuki engraved on the base. Tucked beside the crate were a tiny pair of red galoshes. Mixed in were a few things of more than personal value—silver rattles, a silver tea set, the American kind, plus a rolled up set of gold-plated flatware. Beneath the forks and spoons was a photo album. Henry sat on a leather stool and opened the dusty binder in his lap. There were photos of a Japanese family he didn't recognize—parents, small children, many taken in and around South Seattle, even photos of them swimming at Alki Beach. Everyone in the photos looked so serious. As Henry leafed through the album, he saw that there were blank spaces. Sometimes entire pages were empty. More than half the photos were gone. They'd been removed, leaving behind white squares where the hidden page had been preserved from yellowing in the wet Seattle air.

Henry hesitated, then pressed his nose to the page, inhaling. He thought he had imagined the smell at first, then he inhaled again. He was right the first time—the pages smelled like smoke.

Executive Orders
(1942)

Henry woke the next morning to the delightful smell of *siu beng,* baked sesame buns—a breakfast favorite of his father's and a real treat since sugar coupons were in short supply. At the table his father sat dressed in his finest suit, actually, his only suit. He'd had the dark gray number custom-made by a tailor who'd just moved here from Hong Kong.

Henry sat and listened to his father read from the daily newspaper, citing each new arrest of Japanese locals. All of them now bound for federal prison. Henry didn't understand. They were taking schoolteachers and businessmen. Doctors and fishmongers. The arrests seemed random, and the charges were vague. His father sounded satisfied—small battles won in a larger conflict.

Henry blew on his honey-brown sesame bun, right from the oven, cooling it as best he could. He watched his father, who seemed engrossed in an article, wondering about Keiko and the arrests at the Black Elks Club. His father turned to show the story to Henry—all Henry could tell was that it was written in Chinese, a message from the Bing Kung Benevolent Association; their *chop,* a stamp of their name, was evident at the bottom.

"This is *important news* for us, Henry," his father explained in Cantonese.

Henry finally took a bite and nodded, listening and chewing.

"Do you know what an executive order is?"

Henry had a vague idea, but, forbidden to answer in his father's native tongue, he simply shook his head no. But you're going to tell me, aren't you?

"It's a very important declaration. Like when Sun Yat-sen proclaimed January first, 1912, as the first day of the first year of the Republic of China."

Henry had heard his father speak of the Republic of China on many occasions, even though his father hadn't set foot on Chinese soil since he was a young man. It had been years, back when he was Henry's age and he'd been sent to finish his Chinese schooling in Canton.

Father also spoke in reverent, worshipful tones of the late Dr. Sun Yat-sen, a revolutionary who brought about *a government of the people*. Henry fancied the name: Dr. Sun. It sounded like someone Superman would do battle with.

His father had devoted most of his life to nationalist causes, all aimed at furthering the Three People's Principles proclaimed by the late Chinese president. So naturally, as Henry slowly grasped the point of his father's enthusiasm in these small local conflicts with Japanese Americans, it was mixed with a fair amount of confusion and contradiction. Father believed in a government *of the people* but was wary of who those people were.

"President Roosevelt just signed *Executive Order 9102*—which creates the War Relocation Authority. This is in addition to *Executive Order 9066*—which gives the United States power to designate new military areas."

Like a new base or army fort, Henry thought, looking at the clock to make sure he wouldn't be late to school.

"Henry, the *entire West Coast* has been designated as a military area." Henry listened, not understanding what this meant. "Half of Washington, half of Oregon, and most of California are now under military supervision."

"Why?" Henry asked, in English.

His father must have understood the word, or maybe he just felt like Henry should know. "It says: 'I hereby authorize and direct the Secretary of War, and the Military Commanders,' "—Henry's father paused, doing his best to read it correctly in Cantonese—" 'to prescribe military areas in such places and of such extent as he or the appropriate Military Commander may determine, from which any or all persons may be excluded, and with respect to which, the right of any person to enter, remain in, or leave shall be subject to whatever restrictions the Secretary of War may impose in his discretion.' "

Henry gulped down the last bite of his sesame bun; the executive order might have been in German for all he cared. The war was everywhere. He'd grown up with it. The presidential memorandum didn't seem out of the ordinary.

"They can exclude anyone. They can exclude us. Or German immigrants." His father looked at Henry, setting the letter down. *"Or the Japanese."*

That last part worried Henry—about Keiko, and her family. He looked out the window, barely noticing his mother. She'd come in with a pair of kitchen shears and cut the stem off the starfire lily he'd bought for her days ago, placing it back in its vase on their tiny kitchen table.

"They can't take them *all* away. What would happen to the strawberry farms on Vashon Island and the sawmill on Bainbridge? What about the fishermen?" she said. Henry listened to their conversation in Cantonese as if it were coming from a distant radio station.

"Hah? Plenty of Chinese workers—plenty of colored workers. They so short on labor even Boeing hiring Chinese now. Todd Shipyards is hiring and paying the same wage as Caucasian," his father said, smiling.

Henry grabbed his book bag and headed for the door, wondering what might happen to Keiko if her father was arrested. He didn't even know what her father did to earn a living, but it didn't really matter now.

"Henry, you forgetting your lunch?" his mother said.

He told her he wasn't hungry, in English. She looked at Henry's father, puzzled. She didn't understand. Neither of them did.

Henry walked past the corner on South Jackson; it was quiet and empty without Sheldon there to send him off. Henry was happy that his friend had found a job up the street, but having Sheldon around was like an insurance policy. No bully who followed Henry home made it past Sheldon's corner and his protective eye.

In class that day, Mrs. Walker told everyone that their classmate Will

Whitworth would be gone for the rest of the week. His father had been killed while serving onboard the USS *Marblehead*. Japanese dive-bombers struck his convoy near Borneo in the Makassar Strait. Henry didn't know where that was, but it sounded like someplace warm, tropical, and far away—he wished he was there as he felt the eyes of his classmates drill into him, tiny, piercing darts of accusation.

Henry had had only one run-in with Will, and it was earlier in the year. Will seemed to fancy himself a war hero, doing his part to fight the yellow menace on the home front, even if it was only on the playground after school. Despite the black eye Will had given him, Henry genuinely felt sorry for him when he heard this news. How could he not? Fathers weren't perfect, but even a bad one seemed better than no father at all—at least in Henry's case.

When lunchtime mercifully approached, Henry was excused. He ran, then walked, then ran again, down the hall and into the cafeteria kitchen.

Keiko wasn't there.

Instead, Denny Brown, one of Chaz's friends, stood there wearing a white apron, ladle in hand. He sneered at Henry like a rat caught in a trap. "What are you looking at?"

Mrs. Beatty stomped around the kitchen—patting herself, trying to find where she'd left her matches. "Henry, this is Denny. He'll be subbing for Kay-Ko. He got caught stealing from the school store. So Vice Principal Silverwood wants me to put him to work." Henry watched, mortified. Keiko was gone. His kitchen haven was now occupied by one of his tormentors. Mrs. Beatty called off her search for a pack of matches and lit her cigarette on the stove's pilot light, then grumbled something about *staying out of trouble* as she wandered off to eat her lunch.

At first, Henry had to listen to Denny grumble about being caught, getting kicked off flag duty and cornered into working in the kitchen— forced to do the work of a Japanese girl. But when the lunch bell rang and hungry kids rolled in, Denny's attitude changed as they smiled and chatted him up. They all wanted him to serve them, holding back their trays, leering suspiciously at Henry as they passed.

To *them,* Henry thought, we're at war and *I'm the enemy.*

He didn't wait for Mrs. Beatty to get back. He set his scoop down, removed his apron, and walked away. He didn't even return to his class-room. He left his books, and his homework, passing down the hall and out the front door.

In the distance—in the direction of Nihonmachi, he noticed small plumes of smoke disappearing in the gray afternoon sky.

Fires
(1942)

Running toward the smoke, Henry avoided Chinatown altogether. Not because he was afraid of being seen by his parents during school hours, though that *was* part of it, but because of the truant officers. It was almost impossible to skip school where Henry was from. Truant officers patrolled the streets and parks, even small noodle factories and canneries, looking for migrant children whose parents often sent them to work full-time rather than to school. The families probably needed the extra money, but locals like Henry's father believed that educated children meant less crime. Maybe they were right. The International District was normally quite peaceful, aside from occasional gang violence by rival tongs, or by enlisted men who wandered in, then staggered out, drunk and ripe for trouble. Plus, any police officer seeing an Asian kid on the street during school hours would usually pick him up as well. He'd be sent home, where the poor kid's punishment by his parents would probably make him regret not being thrown in jail.

So Henry cautiously edged his way along Yesler Way, on the Nihonmachi side, all the way to Kobe Park, which was now deserted. Walking through the corridors of Japantown, he saw few people out. Like a Sunday morning in downtown Seattle, when all the shops and businesses were closed, and those that were open had few patrons.

What am I doing here? he asked himself, looking up from the barren streets to the cold sky, plumes of black smoke snaking skyward from places unseen. I'll never find her. Still, he kept busy wandering from building to building. Avoiding the strange looks on the faces of the few men and women who passed him.

In the heart of Japantown, Henry found the Ochi Photography Studio once again. He couldn't miss the young proprietor, who stood outside on a milk crate looking through a large camera mounted on a wooden tripod. He was shooting in an alley that ran in the same direction as Maynard Avenue, where Henry saw the source of the fires. They weren't Japanese homes or businesses, as he'd feared. They were large burning barrels and garbage cans set ablaze in the alley, fire and smoke pluming up and over the apartment buildings on either side.

"Why are you taking a picture of garbage fires?" Henry asked, not sure if the photographer even recognized him.

The man looked through Henry. Then his eyes blinked as he seemed to remember him. It must have been the button Henry wore. The photographer turned back to his camera, his hands shaking. "They're not burning garbage."

Henry stood at the T where the alley met the street, next to the photographer on his milk crate with his camera and his flashbulbs. Looking down the alley, he could see people coming and going from the apartment buildings, throwing things into the burning barrels. A woman yelled out of a third-story window to a man below and threw down a plum-colored kimono that looped and swirled, settling like falling snow on the dirty, slug-trailed pavement of the alley. The man below scooped it up, regarded it for a moment, hesitated, then threw it on the fire. The silky fabric lit, and burning pieces floated out of the heat like butterflies whose wings caught flame, fluttering on the draft, flickering out and raining down as black, ashy dust.

An old woman brushed by Henry with an armload of papers, throwing them into the fire, where they made a whooshing sound. Henry felt the rush of heat on his cheeks and stepped back. Even from a distance, he could see they were scrolls—artwork, written and drawn by hand. Large Japanese characters disappearing into the heart of the fire.

"Why are they doing this?" Henry asked, not fully understanding what he was seeing with his own eyes.

"They arrested more people last night. Japanese, all over the city. All over Puget Sound. All over the state, maybe," the photographer told him. "People are getting rid of anything that might connect them to the war

with Japan. Letters from Nippon. Clothing. It all must go. Too dangerous to keep. Even old photos. People are burning photos of their parents,
of their families."

Henry watched an old man wearily place a neatly folded Japanese flag
into the nearest burning barrel, saluting it as it burned.

The photographer snapped the shutter on his camera, capturing the
scene.

"I burned all *my* old photos last night." He turned to Henry, the tripod shaking as he held it. With his other hand he wiped his mouth with
a handkerchief. "I burned my own wedding photos."

Henry's eyes stung as they filled with smoke and soot. He heard a
woman yelling something in Japanese, somewhere in the distance. It
sounded more like crying.

"We had a traditional wedding right here in Nihonmachi. Then we
took our photos at the Washington Park Arboretum in front of the mag-
nolias and rockroses. We wore kimonos—Shinto dressing that had been
in my family for three generations." The photographer looked haunted
by the scene in front of him. Haunted by the destruction of touchable,
tangible reminders of life.

"I burned it all."

Henry had seen all he could take. Turning, he ran home, still tasting
the smoke.

Old News
(1986)

Henry searched through the dusty basement of the Panama Hotel, sneezing and coughing, for nearly three hours. In that time he'd found countless photo albums of babies and faded black-and-white snapshots of families celebrating Christmas and New Year's. Boxes and boxes of fine dishware and utensils, and enough clothing to fill a small department store. The items were so random. It was easy to forget that people once cared enough for these things to hide them, hoping to retrieve them another day—presumably after the war had ended.

But serving as somber reminders were the names—like Inada, Watanabe, Suguro, and Hori. Most of the boxes and trunks had hanging name tags of some sort. Others had names painted directly on the sides or tops of the suitcases themselves. Quiet reminders of the lives displaced so long ago.

Henry stretched his aching back and spied a rickety aluminum lawn chair that he imagined had seen better days at barbecues and backyard picnics. It creaked as he unfolded it, in chorus with his knees, which popped when he sat down, his body tired from being hunched over boxes and crates.

Resting from his labors, he fished out a newspaper from a nearby bundle. It was an old copy of the *Hokubei Jiji—The North American Times,* a local newspaper still in circulation. It was dated March 12, 1942.

Henry scanned the old-style news articles, printed in English in neat vertical rows. Headlines about local rationing and the war in Europe and the Pacific. Straining to read the fine print in the dimly lit basement, he noticed an editorial on the cover. The headline read: FINAL ISSUE. "We re-

gret that this will be our final issue until further notice, but wish to acknowledge our deepest loyalty and support of the United States of
America, its allies and the causes of freedom . . ." It was the last newspaper printed in Nihonmachi before the internment, before they took
them all away, Henry thought. There were other articles, one on relocation opportunities farther inland—in places like Montana and North
Dakota. And a police report about a man posing as a federal agent, then
accosting two Japanese women in their apartment.

"You finding anything?" Ms. Pettison came down, flashlight in hand,
startling Henry, who'd grown accustomed to the lonely silence of the
basement.

He set the paper down and stood up, brushing himself off a bit, wiping his hands on his pants, leaving two palm-size streaks of dust. "Well, I
haven't exactly found what I'm looking for. There's just so much of . . .
everything."

"Don't worry, we need to close up for the day, but you're more than
welcome to come back next week. The dust needs to settle so we can
clean up, and we're sealing the brick tomorrow, but after that all clears,
feel free to come back and keep looking."

Henry thanked her, disappointed that he hadn't found anything belonging to Keiko or her family. But he didn't give up hope. For years he'd
walked past the hotel. Decades even—never suspecting anything of value
remained. He'd assumed that everything from the war years had been re-
claimed long ago, accepted that fact and tried to move on. Tried to live
his life. But looking at the mountains of boxes he'd yet to search, he
felt Keiko's presence. Something of her remained. Inside. He strained
to hear her voice in memory. Lost among his thoughts. It's in there. *I
know it.*

He thought of Ethel too. What would she think? Would she approve
of him snooping around down here, digging into the past? The more he
thought about it, the more he realized what he'd known all along. Ethel
would always approve of things that might make Henry happy. Even
now. Especially now.

"I'll be back this time next week, if that's all right?" Henry asked.

Ms. Pettison nodded and led the way back upstairs.

Henry squinted, allowing his senses to adjust to the daylight and the cold, gray Seattle sky that filled the paned windows of the Panama Hotel lobby. Everything, it seemed—the city, the sky—was brighter and more vivid than before. So modern, compared with the time capsule downstairs. As he left the hotel, Henry looked west to where the sun was setting, burnt sienna flooding the horizon. It reminded him that time was short, but that beautiful endings could still be found at the end of cold, dreary days.

Marty's Girl
(1986)

The next day Henry spent the afternoon in Chinatown, at the barber, the bakery—any excuse to walk by the Panama Hotel. He peered in the open windows, each time seeing nothing but construction workers and clouds of dust everywhere. When he finally found his way back home, Marty was waiting for him on his doorstep. He had a key, but by all appearances he'd locked himself out. Sprawled across the cement steps, Marty tapped his foot, his arms folded across his chest, looking nervous and expectant.

Henry had sensed that something was bothering Marty at lunch the day before, but had allowed himself to be distracted by the thought of finding something—anything—of Keiko's in the basement of the Panama Hotel. Now he was here. *He's here to have it out with me.* To tell me I was wrong in how I cared for his mother, Henry thought.

Ethel's last year had been a rough time. When she'd been lucid enough to engage the both of them, he and Marty had seemed to get along famously. But once her health declined, and the word *hospice* came up, the real disagreements had begun.

"Pops, you can't keep Mom here—this place smells like old people," Marty argued.

Henry rubbed his eyes, weary of the discussion. "We *are* old people."

"Have you even been to the new Peace Hospice? It's like a resort! Don't you want Mom to spend her last days in a *nice place*?" As Marty said it, he rolled his eyes to the ceiling, which was a dingy yellow color from Ethel's years of smoking cigarettes. "This place is a dump! I don't want my mom to be stuck here when she could be at a state-of-the-art facility."

"This *is* her home," Henry shot back, standing up from his easy chair. "She wants to be here. She doesn't want to die in someplace unfamiliar—no matter how nice it is."

"*You* want her to be here. You can't live without her—without controlling everything!" Marty was practically in tears. "They'll take care of her medicine, Pops, they have nurses . . ."

Henry was angry, but he didn't want to make the situation worse by getting into another pointless shouting match, especially with Ethel sleeping in the next room.

The home hospice service had brought in everything to make her last few months more comfortable—a hospital bed and enough morphine, atropine, and Ativan to keep her relaxed and free from pain. They called each day, and a home health worker popped by as needed, but never as often as Henry had hoped.

"Henry . . ." Both he and Marty froze at the sound of Ethel's weak voice. Neither had heard her speak in at least a week.

Henry went to their bedroom. *Their bedroom.* He still called it that, even though he'd been sleeping on the couch for the last six months, or occasionally in a recliner next to Ethel's bed. But only on the nights when she grew restless or scared.

"I'm here. Shussh-shhhhh. I'm here . . . ," he said, sitting on the edge of the bed, holding his wife's frail hand, leaning in close to try to hold her attention.

"Henry . . ."

He looked at Ethel, who was staring wide-eyed out their bedroom window. "It's okay—I'm here." As he said it, he straightened out her nightgown and pulled her covers back up around her arms.

"Take me home, Henry," Ethel pleaded, gripping his hand. "I'm so sick of this place, take me home . . ."

Henry looked up at his son, who was standing in the doorway, speechless.

After that day, the arguing had ceased. But so had their conversations.

"Pops, I think we need to talk."

Marty's voice woke Henry from his melancholy. He walked up the steps, partway, until he stood looking at his son, eye to eye. "Shouldn't we go inside and sit down and talk about what's on your mind?" he asked.

"I'd rather talk out here."

Henry noticed his son staring at his clothes, covered with dust from watching the renovation at the hotel. "Are you okay? What'd you hit, a line drive and slide into third base?"

"You have your long story, I have mine." Henry sat down next to his son, watching the long, dark shadow of Beacon Hill fall behind the trees, stretching the width of the avenue. The streetlamps above them flickered and hummed to life.

"Pops, we haven't talked about much of anything since Mom died, you know?"

Henry nodded stoically, bracing himself for an onslaught of criticism.

"I've busted my tail on my grades, I've tried to be the son you want me to be."

Henry listened, feeling remorseful. Maybe I spent too much time taking care of Ethel—*maybe I left him out,* he thought. If I did, it wasn't intentional. "You don't need to apologize for anything. I'm immensely proud of you," he said.

"I know you are, Pops. I see it—I know you are. Which is why I've been dodging talking to you about this. One, because there was so much going on with Mom, and two, well, because I just didn't know how you'd react."

Henry furrowed his brow; now he *was* worried. His mind checked off all the things his son could possibly tell him under these circumstances: *He's on drugs. He's been kicked out of school. He's wrecked his car, joined a gang, committed a crime, going to jail, he's gay . . .*

"Dad, I'm engaged."

"To a girl?"

Henry asked the question in all seriousness. Marty laughed. "Of course to a girl."

"And you're scared to tell me this?" Henry searched his son for some meaning in his face, his eyes, in his body language. "She's pregnant." Henry said it as more of a statement than a question. The way you'd say "We surrender" or "We lost in overtime."

"Dad! No. Nothing like that."

"Then why are we talking out here . . ."

"Because she's inside, Pops. I want you to meet her."

Henry lit up. Sure, he was hiding a pang of hurt that this mystery girl had been kept a secret, but his son was busy, he was sure Marty had a reason.

"It's just that, well, I know how crazy your own folks were. I mean, they weren't just Chinese, they were super-Chinese, if you know what I mean. They were like ice cubes in America's melting pot, you know—they had one way of seeing things." Marty struggled for the words. "And you know, you married Mom and did the whole traditional wedding thing. And you sent me to Chinese school, like your own old man did—and you always talk about me finding a nice Chinese girl to settle down with, like Mom."

There was a pause, a moment of silence. Henry watched his son, waiting for him to continue. Nothing stirred but the shadows cast on the steps as the fir trees swayed in the slight breeze.

"I'm not like Yay Yay—not like your grandfather," Henry said, as he realized where this was going, stunned to be categorized in the same breath as his own father. He loved his father, deep down, what son doesn't? He'd only wanted the best for him. But after all Henry had gone through, all he'd seen and done, had he changed that little? Was he so much like his own father? He heard a click as the door opened behind them. A young woman poked her head out, then stepped out smiling. She had long blond hair, and cool blue eyes—the kind Henry called Irish eyes.

"You must be Marty's father! I can't believe you've been out here this whole time. Marty, why didn't you say something?" Henry smiled and watched her look in surprise at his son, who looked nervous, as if caught doing something wrong.

Henry offered his hand to his future daughter-in-law.

She shone like a light. "I'm Samantha, I've been dying to meet you." She stepped past his hand and threw her arms around him. Henry patted her, trying to breathe, then gave in and hugged her back. Looking over her shoulder—smiling—Henry gave Marty a thumbs-up.

Ume
(1986)

 In the backyard, Henry put on garden gloves and pruned dead limbs off an old plum tree—dotted with small green fruit used in Chinese wine.

The tree was as old as his son.

Marty and his fiancée sat on the back steps and watched while sipping iced green tea with ginger. Henry had tried making iced tea with Darjeeling or pekoe, but they always tasted too bitter, no matter how much sugar or honey he added.

"Marty told me this was some sort of a surprise, I hope I didn't completely ruin it—it's just that he's told me everything about you, and I've been dying to meet you."

"Oh, not much to tell, really," Henry said politely.

"Well, for starters, he told me that's your favorite tree," Samantha said, doing her best to fill the awkward silence between father and son, "and that you planted it when Marty was born."

Henry continued pruning, clipping off a twig with delicate white blossoms. "It's an *ume* tree," he said, slowly pronouncing it "ooh-may." "Its flowers bloom even during the harshest weather—even in coldest winter."

"Here we go . . . ," Marty whispered to Samantha, just loud enough for his father to hear. *"Viva la revolución . . ."* he joked.

"Hey, what's that supposed to mean?" Henry asked, pausing from his labors.

"No offense, Pops, it's just that—"

Samantha interrupted. "Marty told me that tree has a special meaning for you. That it's a symbol of some kind."

"It is," Henry said, touching a small, five-petaled plum blossom. "Ume flowers are used as decoration during Chinese New Year. It's also the symbol of the ancient city of Nanjing and now the national flower of all of China."

Marty stood up partway and offered a mock salute.

"What's that for?" Samantha asked.

"Tell her, Pops."

Henry kept pruning, attempting to ignore his son's jest. "The flower was also my own father's favorite." He struggled against his pruning shears before finally clipping off a large dead branch. "It's a symbol of perseverance in the face of adversity—a revolutionist symbol."

"Your father was a revolutionary?" Samantha asked.

"Hah!" Henry caught himself laughing at the thought. "No, no—he was a nationalist. Always scared of the communist. But he still believed in one China. The ume tree was special to him that way, understand?"

Samantha smiled and nodded, sipping her tea. "Marty said that tree came from a branch of your father's tree—that you planted it here when he died."

Henry looked at his son, then shook his head and clipped another branch. "His mother tell him this."

Henry felt bad for mentioning Ethel. For bringing up such sadness on what was an otherwise happy day.

"I'm very sorry," Samantha said. "I wish I could have met her."

Henry just smiled solemnly and nodded, while Marty put his arm around his fiancée and kissed her on the temple.

Samantha changed the subject. "Marty tells me you were an incredible engineer, they even let you retire early."

Henry could see Samantha out of the corner of his eye as he tended to the tree; it was like she was checking off an imaginary list. "You're a great cook, you like to garden, and you're the best fisherman he's ever known. He told me about all the times you took him out on Lake Washington for sockeye."

"That so . . . ," Henry said, looking at his son, wondering why he never said these things to *him*. Then he thought about the communications gaps, more like chasms really, between him and his own father and knew the answer.

Samantha sipped her iced tea, stirring the ice cubes with her finger. "He says you love jazz music."

Henry looked at her, intrigued. *Now we're talking.*

"And not just any jazz. The roots of West Coast jazz and swing, like Floyd Standifer and Buddy Catlett—and that you're a big Dave Holden fan, and a really big fan of his father, Oscar Holden, as well."

Henry pruned a small branch and tossed it in a white bucket. "I like her," he said to Marty, loud enough for her to hear it. "You did good."

"I'm glad you approve, Pops. You know, you surprise me."

Henry did his best to communicate without words. To give his son that smile, that knowing look of approval. He was certain Marty picked up every phrase of their wordless communication. After a lifetime of nods, frowns, and stoic smiles, they were both fluent in emotional short-hand. Smiling at each other as Samantha showed off her impressive knowledge of Seattle's rich prewar music history. The more Henry listened, the more he thought about going back to the Panama Hotel next week. About sifting through the basement. All those crates. All those trunks, and boxes, and suitcases. And about how much easier it would be if he had help.

But more than that, Henry hated being compared with his own father. In Marty's eyes, the plum hadn't fallen far from the tree; if anything, it was clinging stubbornly to the branches. That's what I've taught by my example, Henry thought, realizing that having Marty help him in the basement might ease more than the physical burden.

Henry took off his garden gloves, setting them on the porch. "The ume tree *was* my father's favorite, but the sapling I planted—it didn't come from him. It came from a tree in Kobe Park . . ."

"But wasn't that part of old Japantown?" Marty asked.

Henry nodded.

The night Marty was born Henry had cut an incision in the small branch of a plum tree—one of many that grew in the park—placing a toothpick in the cut and wrapping it with a small strip of fabric. He came back weeks later and took the rest of the branch—new roots had grown. He planted it in the backyard. And tended to it, always.

Henry had thought about grafting a cherry tree. But the blossoms were too beautiful—the memories too painful. But now, Ethel was gone.

Henry's father was long since gone. Even Japantown was gone. All that remained were days filled with long, endless hours, and the plum tree he had tended to in his backyard. Grafted the night his son was born, from a Chinese tree in a Japanese garden, all those years ago.

That tree had grown wild during the years Ethel fell ill. Henry had had less time to tend to the massive branches that had grown to fill the small confines of their backyard. But once Ethel had passed, Henry had started taking care of the tree once again, and it had begun to bear fruit.

"What are you two doing next Thursday?" Henry asked.

He watched them look at each other and shrug. His son's face still bore a wrinkle of confusion. "No plans," Samantha said.

"Meet me at the tearoom of the Panama Hotel."

Home Fires
(1942)

Henry burst through his front door, fifteen minutes earlier than the time he normally came home from school. He didn't care, and his parents didn't seem to mind. He needed to talk to someone. Needed to tell his parents what was going on. They'd know what to do, wouldn't they? Shouldn't they? Henry needed to do something. But what? What could he do? He was only twelve.

"Mom, I need to tell you something!" he yelled, trying to catch his breath.

"Henry, we were hoping you'd be home soon! We have guests for tea." He heard his mother in the kitchen, speaking in Cantonese.

She came out, speaking broken English, shushing him, urging him to their modest living room. "Come, you come."

Henry found himself indulging in a terrible fantasy. Keiko had run away; she was here, safe. Maybe her entire family had fled, just before the FBI broke down their door, leaving them to find an empty house—the window open, curtains blowing in the wind. He'd never met them but could picture them clearly, running down the alley, leaving the FBI agents flat-footed and confused.

He walked around to the sitting area and felt his stomach drop, as if hitting the floor, rolling under the couch, lost somewhere.

"You must be Henry. We've been waiting for you." An older Caucasian man in a fine tan suit sat across from Henry's father. Sitting next to the man was Chaz.

"Sit. Sit." Henry's father motioned, speaking Chinglish.

"Henry, I'm Charles Preston. I'm a building developer. I think you know Junior here—we call him Chaz, in our house anyway. You can call him whatever you want." Henry had a few choice names. In two languages even. He waved at Chaz, who smiled so sweetly Henry noticed his dimples for the first time.

Still, he didn't understand what was going on—in his own home no less. "What . . ." What are *you* doing here? He thought it, but the words were stuck somewhere in his throat as he realized why his father had worn his suit—the one he always wore to important meetings—that morning.

"Your father and I were trying to discuss a business matter, and he indicated you'd be a perfect translator. He says you're learning English over at Rainier Elementary."

"Hi, Henry." Chaz winked, then turned to his father. "Henry's one of the smartest kids in class. He can translate anything. *Japanese too,* I bet." Those last words came out like mumbled ice cubes as Chaz once again beamed at Henry. Henry could tell Chaz didn't like being there any more than he did, but he was content playing cat and mouse with Henry while innocently seated at Mr. Preston's elbow.

"Henry, Mr. Preston owns several apartment buildings around here. He's interested in developing some property on Maynard Avenue, in Japantown," Henry's father explained in Cantonese. "Since I'm a Chong Wa board member, he needs my support, and the support of the Chinese community in the International District. He needs our support for the approval of the city council." He said it in a way—his tone, his eyes, his mannerisms—that made Henry realize this was a very big deal. Very serious, but also very enthusiastic. His father didn't get excited about too many things. Victories in China over the invading Japanese army, which were few, and Henry's *scholarshipping* at Rainier were the only things he'd ever talked about with such electric enthusiasm. Until now anyway.

Henry sat on the footstool between them, feeling small and insignificant. Caught between a rock and another rock, two towering pieces of adult-shaped granite.

"What do I need to do?" he asked in English, then in Cantonese.

"Just translate what each of us is saying, the best you can," Mr. Preston said. Henry's father nodded, trying to follow the English words Chaz's father spoke slowly.

Henry rubbed grit and soot from the corners of his eyes, wondering about Keiko and her family. He thought about those three Japanese couples lying facedown on the dirty floor of the Black Elks Club in their evening finery. Being hauled out and jailed somewhere. He stared back at Mr. Preston, a man trying to buy land out from under families who were now burning their most precious possessions to keep from being called traitors or spies.

For the first time Henry realized where he was, standing on one side of an unseen line between himself and his father, and everything else he'd known. He couldn't recall when he'd crossed it and couldn't see an easy way back.

He looked at Mr. Preston and Chaz, then at his father, and nodded. Go ahead, I'll translate. I'll do my *best,* he thought.

"Henry, can you tell your father that I'm trying to buy the vacant lot behind the Nichibei publishing company? If we can force the Japanese newspaper out of business, will he approve us to buy that land as well?"

Henry listened intently. Then he turned to his father, speaking in Cantonese. "He wants to buy the land behind the Japanese newspaper and the building too."

His father evidently knew this area well, answering, "That property is owned by the Shitame family, but the head of the family was arrested weeks ago. Make an offer to the bank, and they will sell it out from under them." The words came out slowly, presumably so Henry wouldn't miss a thing in translation.

Henry was shocked at what he was hearing. He looked around for his mother. She was nowhere to be seen—probably downstairs doing laundry, or making tea for the guests. He hesitated for a moment, then looked at Mr. Preston and in all seriousness said, "My father won't approve of the sale. It was once a Japanese cemetery and it's very bad luck to build there. That's why the lot is empty." Henry pictured a dive-bomber, augering toward its target, loaded with ordnance.

Mr. Preston laughed. "He's kidding, right? Ask him if he's joking."

Henry could hardly believe that for the first time in months he was actually talking to his father—and telling him lies. *But necessary ones,* Henry thought. He looked over at Chaz, who just stared at the ceiling, seemingly out of boredom.

Henry's father was hanging on his every Cantonese word. "Mr. Preston says he wants to turn the building into a jazz club. That kind of music is very popular, and there's a lot of money to be made." Henry pictured his imaginary bomber releasing its payload, the bombs raining down . . . *screeeeeeeeeeeee* . . .

His father looked more offended than confused. Bull's-eye. The bombs exploded on impact. The International District needed many things, his father argued, but more nightclubs and more drunken sailors were evidently not very high on Henry's father's agenda for progressive community development, even if they displaced some of the Japanese in Nihonmachi.

The conversation went significantly downhill from there.

Mr. Preston grew angry, accusing Henry's father of indulging in Japanese superstition. Henry's father accused Mr. Preston of indulging too often in the spirits that he intended to sell at his proposed jazz club.

After more mixed translation on Henry's part, they ended their bilingual discussion, agreeing to disagree, each warily eyeing the other.

But they still argued, bypassing Henry altogether, hardly understanding a word each other was saying. Chaz stared at Henry, not even blinking. He opened his coat and showed Henry the button he'd stolen from him. Neither parent noticed, but Henry saw. Chaz flashed him a bucktoothed grin, then closed his coat again and smiled angelically as his father said, "We're done talking about this. I can see coming here was the wrong thing to do. You people will never be able to handle real business anyway."

Henry's mother walked in with a fresh pot of her best chrysanthemum tea, just in time to see Chaz and Mr. Preston stand up and storm out, looking like gamblers who'd lost their last sawbuck on a round of pitch and toss.

Henry took a cup of tea and graciously thanked his mother—in English. She didn't understand the words, of course, but seemed to appreciate the tone.

After finishing his tea, Henry excused himself to his room. It was early, but he felt weary. He lay down, closing his eyes, and thought about Mr. Preston, the adult version of Chaz, greedily carving up Japantown, and his own father, so eager to help with these important *business* matters. Henry half-expected to feel happy about disrupting their plans, but all he felt was exhausted relief, and guilt. He'd never disobeyed his father so blatantly. But he had to. He had seen the fires in Nihonmachi and people burning their prized possessions—ashen remainders of who they had been, who they still were. Boarded-up storefronts with American flags in the windows. He didn't know much about business, but he knew times were tough and getting worse. He needed to find Keiko, needed to see her. As darkness fell, he pictured her in some family photograph, a portrait on fire, curling, burning, and turning to ash.

Hello, Hello
(1942)

When Henry finally opened his eyes again, he saw nothing but darkness. *What time is it? What day? How long have I been asleep?* His thoughts raced as he rubbed his eyes and blinked, doing his best to wake up. A sliver of moonlight peeked between the blackout curtains on his bedroom window.

Something had woken him. What was it? A sound? Then he heard it again, a ringing in the kitchen.

He stretched, reorienting once again to time and place, then rolled his feet to the cold wooden floor, sitting up. His eyes adjusting to the darkness, Henry could make out the silhouette of a serving tray in his room. His mother had thoughtfully left him dinner. She'd even put the vase with her starfire lily on the tray for simple decoration.

There it was again—the unmistakable sound of their telephone ringing. Henry still wasn't quite used to its loud, jarring bell. Fewer than half of the homes in Seattle had telephones, and even fewer had them in Chinatown. His father had insisted on having one installed when the United States had declared war on the Axis powers. He was a block warden, and his responsibilities included staying in touch, with whom exactly Henry didn't know.

The phone rang again, clanging like a windup alarm clock.

Henry started to yawn but froze partway as he thought about Chaz. *He now knows where I live.* He could be outside waiting for me right now. Waiting for me to come wandering out unawares, taking out the trash or bringing in the laundry. Then he'd pounce, getting even, without teachers and playground monitors to get in the way.

He peered through the heavy, musty curtains, but the street, two stories below, looked cold and empty, damp from a recent rainstorm.

In the kitchen, he could hear his mother answering, *"Wei, wei?"* Hello, hello.

Henry opened his door, padding down the hallway toward the bathroom. His mother was mumbling something on the phone about not speaking English. She waved at Henry, pointing to the phone. The call was for him. Sort of.

"Hello?" he asked. Henry was used to handling all the wrong numbers. They were usually in English, or calls from census takers polling the Asian community. Strange women, asking Henry how old he was and if he was the man of the house.

"Henry, I need your help." It was Keiko. She sounded calm but direct.

He hesitated, not having expected Keiko's soft voice. He started speaking in whispered tones, then remembered his parents didn't speak English anyway. "Are you okay? You weren't at school. Is your family okay?"

"Can you meet me at the park, the park we met at last time?"

She was being vague. Deliberately vague. Henry could talk freely, but obviously she couldn't. He thought about the operators who often listened in and understood. "When? Now? Tonight?"

"Can you meet me in an hour?"

An hour? Henry's mind raced. It's already after dark. What'll I tell my parents? Finally he agreed. "One hour, I'll try my best." I'll find a way.

"Thank you, good-bye." She paused for a moment. Just as Henry thought she might say something, she hung up.

A sharp, chirpy female voice cut in on the line. "The other party has disconnected, would you like for me to assist you in another call?"

Henry hung up immediately, as if he'd been caught stealing.

His mother was standing there when he turned around. She had a look Henry couldn't distinguish between curiosity and concern. "What? You have a *girlfriend,* maybe?" she asked.

Henry shrugged and spoke in English. "I don't know?" And truth be told, he didn't. If his mother thought it was odd that the little girl calling her son didn't speak Chinese, she didn't say anything. Maybe she thought all parents were forcing their children to *speak their American.* Who knew? Maybe they all were.

Henry thought about how he'd get to Kobe Park, after hours, after blackout. He was glad he'd slept earlier. It was shaping up to be a very long night.

Henry waited most of the hour in his room. It had been almost nine o'clock when Keiko called. His parents had settled into bed around nine-thirty, not because they were particularly tired but because going to bed early was the prudent thing to do. Saving electricity for the war effort was like a sacrament to Henry's father.

After briefly listening and hearing no sign of his parents, Henry opened his window and crept down the fire escape. The ladder reached only halfway to the ground but near enough to a closed dumpster for re-cycled tires. Henry removed his shoes and leapt for the dumpster, which made a muffled clanging as his stocking feet landed on the heavy metal lid. Getting up again would be a bit of a scramble but doable, he thought, putting his shoes back on.

As he walked along the damp sidewalks, his breath came out in a swirling mist, adding to the fog rolling in off the water. He tried to stay in the shadows, despite the fear that crept into his mind and curdled his stomach. Henry had never been out this late by himself. Though with the crowds of people that bustled up and down the avenues, he hardly felt alone.

All the way down South King, the street was awash in the stain of neon signs that defied the blackout restrictions. Signs for bars and night-clubs reflected greens and reds in each puddle he jumped over. The oc-casional car would drive by, bathing the street in its dim blue headlights, illuminating the men and women, Chinese and Caucasian, enjoying the nightlife—despite the rationing.

Crossing Seventh Avenue and entering Nihonmachi was like step-ping onto the dark side of the moon. No lights. No cars moving. Every-thing locked down. Even the Manila Restaurant had boards across its windows to protect them from vandals, despite being owned by

Filipinos—not Japanese. The streets were empty all the way along May-nard Avenue. From the Janagi Grocery to the Nippon Kan Hall, Henry saw no one, except for Keiko.

At Kobe Park, across from the Kabuki theater, he waved as he found her sitting on the hill, like last time, surrounded by a grove of cherry trees whose blossoms were beginning to bud. After walking up the steep hill of the terraced park, Henry caught his breath and sat on a rock beside her. She looked pale in the moonlight, shivering in the cold Seattle air.

"My parents made me stay home from school, they were afraid some-thing might happen, that our family would be separated," she said. Henry watched as she brushed her long hair out of her face. He was sur-prised at how peaceful she looked, how calm. "The police and FBI came and took our radios, cameras, and a few people from our building, but then they left. We haven't seen them since."

"I'm sorry." It was all he could think of—what else could he say?

"They came and arrested scores of people back in December, right after Pearl Harbor, but it's been quiet for months now. Too quiet, I guess. Papa said the navy has given up worrying about an invasion and now they're more concerned about sabotage, you know—people blowing up bridges and power plants and stuff like that. So they swept through and arrested more Japanese."

Henry thought about the word *sabotage*. He'd sabotaged Mr. Preston's plans to buy up part of Japantown. Didn't feel bad about it either. But weren't these people taken away American? Japanese by descent, but American born? After all, Keiko's father had been born here.

"There's even a curfew now."

"Curfew?"

Keiko nodded slowly, contemplating its effects as she looked around the barren streets. "No Japanese are allowed outside of our neighbor-hoods from eight o'clock at night to six in the morning. We're prisoners at night."

Henry shook his head, struggling to believe what she was saying but knowing it must be true. From the arrests at the Black Elks Club to the victorious smile on his father's face, he knew it was really happening. He felt bad for Keiko and her family, for the wrongs done to everyone in Nihonmachi. Yet he was so selfishly grateful to be with her—feeling guilty at his own happiness.

"I cut class today and went looking for you," he said. "I was worried . . ."

She looked at him, a small smile turning into a crooked grin. He felt nervous, stumbling over his words.

"I was worried about school," Henry said. "It's important that we don't fall behind, especially since the teachers don't pay attention to us very much anyway . . ."

There was silence for a moment, then they both heard the swing-shift horn—blaring all the way from Boeing Field. Thousands of workers would be going home. Thousands more would be starting their day at ten o'clock at night, making airplanes to fight in the war.

"It's nice of you to care so much about my schooling, Henry."

He could see the disappointment in her eyes. The same look she'd had when they departed last night, after the arrests at the Black Elks Club. "I wasn't just worried about school," he admitted. "It's more than that. I was worried about—"

"It's okay, Henry. I don't mean to get you in trouble. Either at school or at home with your father."

"I'm not worried about my troubles . . ."

She looked at him and took a deep breath. "Good, 'cause I need a favor, Henry. A big favor." Keiko got up, and Henry followed her down the hill a bit, behind a bench where a red Radio Flyer wagon was partially hidden. In the back were stacks of photo albums and a box of prints. "These belong to my family. My mother told me to take them to the alley and burn them. She couldn't bring herself to do it. Her father was in the Japanese navy. She wanted me to burn all her old photos from Japan." Keiko looked at Henry with sad eyes. "I can't do it, Henry. I was hoping you might hide them for us. Just for a while. Can you do that for me?"

Henry remembered the horrible scene in Japantown that afternoon, the photographer from the Ochi Studio—visibly shaken but determined.

"I can hide them in my room. Do you have more?"

"This is the important stuff. My mom's keepsakes—family memories. The stuff we have from my baby years is okay for us to keep, I think, and some families in our neighborhood are trying to find someplace else to store things. Bigger things. We'll probably put other stuff there if we have to."

"I'll keep this safe, I promise."

Keiko hugged Henry for a brief moment. He found himself hugging her back. His hand touched her hair. She was warmer than Henry had imagined.

"I need to get back before they know I'm gone," Keiko said. "I guess I'll see you in school tomorrow?"

Henry nodded, taking the handle of the little red wagon, heading for home, down the darkened, empty streets of Japantown. Pulling behind him a lifetime of memories. Memories that he'd hide, and a secret he would keep, somewhere back home.

Downhill
(1942)

Henry knew just where he'd hide the photo albums when he got to his Canton Alley apartment—in that shallow empty space between his lower dresser drawers and the floor below. Just enough room to stash all of Keiko's precious family photos, if he spread them out properly.

He'd go up the fire escape and come back down with a pillowcase. It'd probably take two trips to bring everything up, but it shouldn't be any real trouble. My father snores, Henry thought, and my mother compensates by being a heavy sleeper; as long as I don't cause a racket, I should be able to pull it off without a hitch.

Doing his best to stay in the shadows and zigzagging through darkened alleyways, Henry crept back toward Chinatown. A young boy out at night by himself might not normally draw that much attention, but with the blackout restrictions and the new curfew imposed on the Japanese, he would surely be stopped by any police officer patrolling the street.

Through the darkness Henry pulled the little red wagon, cargo and all, down Maynard Avenue—backtracking the way he'd come earlier. The streets in Japantown were barren. It felt empty but safe. The wagon's back wheels squeaked and whined once in a while, piercing the quiet, peaceful evening. Only a few more blocks, then he'd be able to head north and down the hill into the heart of Chinatown and the direction of home.

Still worrying about Keiko, Henry rolled past the Rodo-Sha publisher and the Yada Ladies Tailor, with its Western-size, American-looking mannequins in the display window. Then he passed Eureka Dentistry, with its giant modeled tooth hanging outside, looking pale, almost transparent in the moonlight. If he could somehow block out the American flags and slogans that hung in every window—or were plastered on every boarded-up storefront—he could almost mistake this part of town for Chinatown, only bigger. More developed.

As Henry left the quiet sanctuary of Japantown and warily headed north on South King, in the direction of home, he saw someone—a boy. He could barely make out his shadow in the moonlight, backlit by the streetlamps that buzzed and hummed, surrounded by moths bouncing off the glass. As Henry rolled closer, he could see the boy wiping down the poster of an American flag that had been posted over the window of the Janagi Grocery. The door had a plank of plywood covering the glass near the doorknob, but the large windows were intact. Probably newly installed, Henry thought. Covered with flags, serving as protectors.

To Henry, it looked like the boy was painting, moving a brush over the surface of the paper. He's out at night, Henry thought, still doing his best to declare his citizenship. Trying to protect his family's property. Henry relaxed for a moment, comforted that other kids his age were out at this hour.

The young boy heard the squeaking of the wagon and froze. He turned away from his handiwork, stepping clear of the shadow to where Henry could see him and, likewise, he could see Henry.

It was Denny Brown.

In his hand was a paintbrush, dripping red paint all over the sidewalk, tear-shaped splotches trailing behind him.

"What are *you* doing here?" he said. Henry could see a flicker of fear in Denny's eyes. He was scared, *caught*. Then Henry saw his startled, wide-eyed look change to anger when Denny's eyes narrowed with anticipation. Henry was all alone; there was no one else. And Denny seemed to know it, drawing closer—all while Henry looked on stunned, holding the handle of Keiko's little red wagon.

"What are you doing?" Henry asked, knowing the answer but needing to hear it from Denny himself. It was a vain attempt at understanding. He understood who, where, and what. But for the young life of him, he couldn't fathom *why*. Was it fear? Hatred? Or just youthful boredom that drove Denny here, to Japantown, where families hid and locked their doors, hiding their precious possessions, fearing arrest. While Denny stood on the corner, painting "Go Home Japs!" over American flags posted on store windows.

"I told you he was a Jap on the inside!"

Henry knew the voice. Turning around, he saw Chaz. Crowbar in one hand, and a wadded-up poster of an American flag in his other. *A different kind of flag duty,* Henry thought. The wooden door behind Chaz had long gashes where he'd scraped the poster off. Behind Chaz stood Carl Parks, another bully from school. The three converged on Henry.

Looking around, Henry saw no one else. Not a soul. Not even a light was visible from the nearby apartments.

Chaz smiled. "Taking your wagon out for a walk, Henry? Whatcha got in there? You delivering some Jap newspapers? Or is that stuff a Japanese spy would be delivering?"

Henry looked down at Keiko's things. The photo albums. The wedding album. Things he'd promised to protect. He could barely stand up to one, let alone the three of them. Without thinking, Henry slammed the handle of the Radio Flyer back into the wagon and took off running, pushing the wagon from behind. He leaned his whole body into it as he ran, legs pumping the wagon up the crest of the hill and down the steep slope—down South King.

"Get him! Don't let that Jap lover get away!" Chaz shouted.

"We're coming after you, Henry!" he heard Denny shouting, his feet pounding the pavement. Henry didn't look back.

As the wagon sped faster down the steep hill, Henry thought he'd fall face-first into the sidewalk while it sped away. Instead he jumped, like playing leapfrog on a moving playground. He flung his feet wide, knees out, as the seat of his pants landed in the back of the wagon, right on top of Keiko's photo albums—legs splayed out, one on each side, the rubber of his shoes suspended over the ground as he flew along.

Henry gripped the handle, steering as best he could. The wagon, cargo and all, careened down South King, rumbling on the cracked pavement. Henry could hear the shouts of the boys closing in behind him, giving chase. He briefly felt a hand on the back of his shirt, grasping at his collar. Henry leaned forward over the wagon handle, shifting his weight. Looking back for a moment, he saw his pursuers fall behind as he flew down the hill faster than a sled in wintertime. The squeaky wheels were now just a shimmering hum, as the revolutions of the wagon's axles made a spinning noise like a top.

"Make way! Watch out! Move!" Henry yelled as bar patrons wandering the streets skipped out of the way. He nearly clipped a man in overalls, but the racket was so loud, and the scene before him so hysteric that most people jumped out of the way with plenty of time to spare. One woman dove into the open window of a parked car. Henry leaned back, slipping just beneath her wriggling stocking feet.

He heard a clatter and a cry, and looked back to see Chaz and Carl skidding to a halt as Denny tumbled to the pavement face-first. They'd given up their pursuit, far back, up the hill.

Henry turned around just in time to graze a parking meter. Jerking back on the handle, he lost what little control he had, ricocheting into the rear wheel of a car slowly rolling through the intersection of South King and Seventh Avenue. A police car. He'd slammed into the wheel and rear fender, a black slope of metal against the white chassis of the car.

His shoes left black skid marks on the sidewalk as he slammed them down, trying to stop—wobbling and bouncing until his knees felt like two defective springs. Flying forward, Henry flipped over the handle, his side hitting, then bouncing off the whitewall of the tire. The wagon tipped, spilling its contents alongside and underneath the car in a fan of loose photos and torn pages.

Lying there in pain, Henry heard the brakes of the police car release and the engine idle into park. The pavement was cold and hard. His bruised body ached. His legs throbbed and his feet felt hot and swollen.

People on the street regained their senses, some yelling, others cheering in what Henry figured must have been drunken celebration. The bullies from school had disappeared. Henry rolled to his hands and knees and slowly began scooping up the photos by the armload, dumping them back into the wagon.

He looked over and saw the star-shaped emblem on the car door. Out stepped a uniformed patrol officer. "Judas Priest! You're gonna get yourself killed pulling a stunt like that—at night no less. If you had a little more horsepower in that thing I might have run you over." To Henry he sounded more concerned than angry over the child-shaped projectile that had just torpedoed his cruiser.

But I was dead if I stayed behind, Henry thought, while trying to discreetly shuffle the last of the pictures and photo albums back into the wagon. He looked at the car. As far as he could tell in the dimly lit night, there was no damage. He'd blocked most of the impact with his own body as he flipped over the front end of the wagon. He was sporting a second skin of bruises and a knot on his head, but he'd be okay.

"I'm sorry, I was just trying to get home . . ."

The officer picked up a photo that had slid partway under his patrol car. He examined it with his flashlight, then showed it to Henry—a dog-eared photo of a Japanese officer, posing beneath a white flag with a red sun, a sword at his side. "And where is *home* exactly? You know I could take you to jail for being out after curfew?"

Henry patted his shirt, finding the button, holding it out for the officer to see. "I'm Chinese—a friend at school asked me . . ." He couldn't think of what to say; the truth would have to do. "A friend asked me to hold them. A Japanese American family."

Spies and traitors came in all shapes and sizes, Henry prayed, but not as sixth graders out too late with a wagonload of photographs.

The officer pawed through the mess of photos and flipped through the albums. No secret scouting shots of airplane hangars. No detailed photos of shipyards. Just wedding photos. Holiday photos, though many were in traditional Japanese dress.

Henry squinted, blinded by the light the officer directed at his button, then straight at Henry. He couldn't see the officer, just a black shape with a silver badge. "Where do you live?"

Henry pointed in the direction of Chinatown. "South King." He was more worried about his father's reaction to a police officer bringing him home with a wagonload of Japanese photos than he was about going to jail. Jail would be a cakewalk by comparison.

The officer looked more annoyed than offended. It was a busy night, surely he had better things to do than run in a twelve-year-old Chinese boy for reckless driving—of a Radio Flyer. "Go home, kid, and take this stuff with you. And don't let me catch you out after dark again! Got it?"

Nodding vigorously, Henry shuffled off with the wagon in tow, his heart still pounding. He was only one block from home. He didn't look back.

Within fifteen minutes, Henry was in his room, sliding the bottom drawers of his dresser back in place. The Okabes' photo albums were safely hidden. He'd put the photos back in place as best he could. He could sort them out later. Keiko's wagon found a home beneath the stairs in the alley behind Henry's apartment building.

He climbed into bed and kicked off the covers. Rubbing his head, he could feel the goose egg that had appeared. Hot and still sweaty from the running and scrambling, Henry left his bedroom window up, feeling the cool air come off the water. He could smell the rain that would be coming soon and hear the horns and bells of the ferries along the waterfront signaling their last run for the night. And in the distance he could hear swing jazz being played somewhere, maybe even the Black Elks Club.

Tea
(1986)

Henry looked up from his paper, smiling as he saw Marty and his fiancée, Samantha, waving in the window. They entered the tiny storefront café that sat at the base of the Panama Hotel, their entrance ringing with a string a Buddhist bells that jangled from the front door.

"Since when did you start hanging out in Japanese teahouses?" Marty asked, holding out a black wicker chair for Samantha.

Henry folded his paper nonchalantly. "I'm a regular."

"Since when?" Marty asked, more than surprised.

"Since last week."

"You must be turning over a whole new *tea leaf* then. This is all news to me." Marty turned to Samantha. "Pops would never ever come here. In fact, he hated coming over to this side of town, pretty much from here to Kobe Park—outside that new theater, the Nippo Con—"

"The Nippon Kan Theater," Henry corrected.

"Right, that place. I used to accuse Pops of being a Nippo-phobe—someone that was afraid of all things Japanese." As he said it, Marty waved his hands in mock fright.

"Why?" Samantha asked, in a way that made it seem she thought Marty was joking or teasing.

The waitress brought a fresh pot of tea, and Marty refilled his father's cup and poured a cup for Samantha. Henry in turn filled Marty's. It was a tradition Henry cherished—never filling your own cup, always filling that of someone else, who would return the favor.

"Pop's pop, my grandfather, was a crazy traditionalist. He was like a Chinese Farrakhan. But he was famous around here. He raised money to fight the Japanese back home. You know, during the whole war in the Pacific, he was helping the war efforts in northern China. It was a big deal back then, huh, Pops?"

"That. Is. An understatement," Henry said, slurping his tea, holding the small cup with both hands.

"Growing up, Pops was never allowed in Japantown. It was verboten. If he came home smelling of wasabi, he'd be kicked out of the house or some craziness like that."

Samantha looked intrigued. "Is that why you never came here, or to Japantown—because of your father?"

Henry nodded. "It was a different time back then. Around 1882, the Chinese Exclusion Act was passed by Congress—no more Chinese were allowed to immigrate. This was when competition for jobs was fierce. Chinese laborers like my father were used to working harder for less, so much so that when the local fisheries added canning machines, those machines were called 'iron Chinks.' But still, the local businesses needed cheap labor, so they went around the exclusion act—they allowed Japanese workers to come over. Not just workers but picture brides too. Japantown flourished, while Chinatown remained stagnant. My father resented that—and when Japan invaded China—"

"But what about afterwards?" she asked. "After you were grown up—after he passed away? Did you feel like all bets were off and you could run wild if you wanted to? Man, I would. Being told I can't have something would just drive me crazy, even if I didn't know what to do with it in the first place."

Henry looked at his son—who was waiting for an answer to a question even he had never asked.

"When I was a little boy, most of the International District *was* Japantown, or Nihonmachi as they called it then. So it was a big place that my father forbade me to enter. It had a"—Henry searched for the word—"a *mystique* about it. And over the years, much of it changed. At the time it was illegal to sell property to nonwhites, except in certain areas. There were even districts for Italian immigrants, Jewish people, black people— that's just the way it was. So after the Japanese were taken away, all these other people moved in. It was like wanting to go into a certain bar to have a drink, but by the time you turn twenty-one, the bar has turned into a flower shop. It just wasn't the same."

"So you didn't want to go?" Marty asked. "After all those years of being told not to. When you finally had your chance, you still didn't want to wander over, just to see?"

Henry poured more tea for Samantha, furrowing his brow. "Oh, I didn't say that."

"But you said it changed—"

"It did. But I still *wanted* to go."

"Then why didn't you? Why now?" Samantha asked.

Henry finally pushed his teacup away, drumming his fingers on the glass tabletop. He let out a heavy sigh, one that seemed to reveal a part of him like a curtain drawing back from a darkened stage that was slowly coming to life. "The reason I never went to Nihonmachi . . . is because it was too *painful* to do so." Henry felt his eyes gloss with wetness, but not quite tears.

There was a moment of silence. Another customer left the tearoom; the door chimes rang again, breaking the pregnant pause between them.

"I don't get it. Why would it be painful if you never went there in the first place, if your father forbade it?" Samantha asked, before Marty could.

Henry looked at the two of them. So young. So handsome together. But so much they didn't know.

"Yes, my father forbade it." He sighed, staring longingly at the framed photos of Nihonmachi that hung on the walls. "He was vehemently against all things Japanese. Even before Pearl Harbor, the war in China had been going on for almost ten years. For his son to be frequenting *that other* part of town—Japantown—would have been bad form. Shameful to him . . . But, oh, how I went—I went anyway. *Despite him.* I went deep into the heart of Nihonmachi. Right here, where we sit now, this was all Japantown. I went and saw many things. In many ways, the best and worst times of my life were spent on this very street."

Henry could see the confusion in his son's eyes, more like shock really. Marty had grown up, all these years, assuming Henry was like his grandfather. A zealous man, passionate about the old ways and the Old

Country. Someone who harbored enmity toward his neighbors, especially the Japanese ones. Clinging to leftover feelings from *the war years*. It never dawned on his son that Henry's steeped passion for tradition, his stodgy old-world habits, could be for any other reason.

"Is this why you invited us here for tea?" Marty asked. The impatience in his voice seemed to soften. "To tell us about Japantown?"

Henry nodded yes, then said, *"No,"* correcting himself. "Actually, I'm glad Samantha asked, because it certainly makes the rest of this easier to explain."

"The rest of what?" Marty asked. Henry recognized the look in his son's eyes. It reminded him of the halting, half-spoken conversations he'd had with his own father all those years ago.

"I could use your help—in the basement." Henry stood up and took out his wallet. He put a ten-dollar bill on the table to cover the tea, then walked up the steps connecting the tearoom to the hotel lobby, which was still under renovation. "Are you coming?"

"Coming where?" Marty asked. Samantha took his arm and pulled him along, his confusion mirrored by her excitement and anticipation.

"I'll explain when we get there," Henry said with a subdued smile.

Together, they went through the frosted Art Deco doors into the glowing lobby of the Panama Hotel. It smelled of dust and mold but felt new as Henry touched the brick where it had just been sandblasted and sealed, stripping away decades of chipped paint and dust. Swept and cleaned, and swept again. It was just as Henry remembered from when he was a boy, peering through the ornate window. The hotel was the same all over again, as if nothing had changed. Maybe he hadn't changed that much either.

Henry, Marty, and Samantha stopped in at the makeshift office of the Panama Hotel and waved a hello to Ms. Pettison, who was on the phone—negotiating with a builder or a contractor. She had plans spread across her desk and was discussing details of the renovation. Something about not wanting to change. About wanting to restore the hotel to the way it was. Apparently buildings like this were either torn down or turned into high-priced condominiums.

From the few conversations Henry had had with Ms. Pettison, he knew she was having nothing of it. She wanted to restore the Panama Hotel to its former glory. Retaining as much of the original architecture as possible. The marble *sento* baths. The simple rooms. Much the same way she had restored the teahouse.

Henry signed in, whispering, "We'll be in the basement. I brought help this time . . . ," pointing to his son and soon-to-be daughter-in-law.

She nodded and waved them on as she kept talking on the phone.

Heading down the old stairwell, Marty was getting impatient again. "Um, where exactly are we going, Pops?"

Henry kept telling him, "Wait and see, wait and see."

Through the heavy, rust-hinged door, Henry led them into the basement storage room. He flipped the light switch and the makeshift string of utility lights crackled to life.

"What is this place?" Samantha asked, running her hands along the dusty stacks of suitcases and old boxes.

"This is a museum, I think. It just doesn't know it yet. Right now it's sort of a time capsule from before you were born," Henry said. "During the war, the Japanese community was evacuated, for their own safety, *supposedly*. They were given only a few days' notice and were forced inland to internment camps. A senator at the time—I think he was from Idaho—called them 'concentration camps.' They weren't that bad, but it changed the lives of many. People had to leave everything behind, they could take only two suitcases each and one small seabag, like a duffel bag." Henry approximated the size with his hands. "So they stored their valuable belongings in places like this hotel, the basements of churches, or with friends. What was left in their homes was long gone by the time they returned—looters took everything. But most didn't return anyway."

"And you saw all this, didn't you—when you were a boy?" Marty asked.

"I lived it," Henry said. "My father was *for* the evacuation. He was excited about 'E-day,' as many called it. I didn't understand it completely, but I was caught in the middle of everything. I saw it all happen."

"So that's why you never came back to Japantown—just too many bad memories?" Marty asked.

"Something like that," Henry said. "In a way, there was nothing for me to come back to. It was all gone."

"But I don't get it, why is this stuff still here?" Samantha asked.

"This hotel was boarded up with the rest of Japantown. The owner himself was taken away. People lost everything. Japanese banks closed. Most people didn't come back. I think the hotel changed owners a few times, but it stayed boarded up all these years—decades in fact. Ms. Pettison bought it and found all of this still here. Unclaimed. She's trying to find the owners. My guess is that there are things here belonging to thirty to forty families. She waits for contact, someone to come forward and claim, but very few have."

"There's no one left alive?"

"Forty years is a long time," Henry explained. "People have moved on. Or passed on, I'm afraid."

They looked at the stacks of luggage in silence. Samantha touched the thick cloak of dust on a cracked leather steamer trunk.

"Pops, this is fascinating, but why are you showing us this?" Marty still looked a little confused eyeing the rows of boxes piled to the ceiling. "Is this what you really brought us here for?"

For Henry, it was as if he had stumbled into some unseen room in the house he had grown up in, revealing a part of his past Marty never knew existed. "Well, I asked you to come here because I could use your help looking for something."

Henry looked at Marty, seeing the dim ceiling lights flicker in his son's eyes.

"Let me guess, an old forgotten Oscar Holden record? One that supposedly doesn't exist anymore. You think you're going to find one here, in all this stuff from, what—forty-five years ago?"

"Maybe."

"I didn't know Oscar Holden made an album," Samantha said.

"That's been Pops's Holy Grail—rumor is they printed a handful back in the forties, but none survive today," Marty explained. "Some people don't even believe it ever actually existed, because when Oscar died, he was so old even *he* didn't remember recording it. Just some of his bandmates, and of course Pops here—"

"I bought it. I *know* it existed," Henry interrupted. "But my parents' old Victrola wouldn't play it."

"So where is it now, the one you bought?" Samantha asked, prying the lid off an old hatbox, wrinkling her nose at the musty smell.

"Oh, I gave it away. Long time ago. I never even listened to it."

"That's so sad," she said.

Henry just shrugged.

"So you think one might be in here? Among all these boxes? One might have survived all these years?"

"That's what I'm here to find out," Henry said.

"And if so, who did it belong to?" Marty interrupted, wondering. "Someone you knew, Pops? Someone your old man didn't want you hanging out with on the wrong side of town?"

"Maybe," Henry offered. "Find it and I'll tell you."

Marty looked at his father, and the mountains of boxes, crates, trunks, and suitcases. Samantha squeezed Marty's hand for a moment, smiling. "Then I guess we'd better get started," she said.

Records

(1942)

When Henry told Keiko about his wild ride down South King the night before, she burst out laughing. She searched the lunch line and giggled almost as hard when she saw Denny Brown appear. He wore a defeated scowl, like an angry, whipped mutt. His cheeks and nose were scabbed over from where his face had skidded along the pavement after his fall.

Denny disappeared into the herd of hungry kids. They stampeded by, making their normal abnormal faces as Henry and Keiko dished up a gray mess that Mrs. Beatty soberly called Spam à la king. The bubbling sauce had a subtle green tint to it, almost metallic in its sheen, glossy like a fish's eyeball.

All week long, they scraped out the empty steamer trays and dumped the leftovers in the garbage. Mrs. Beatty didn't believe in saving leftovers. Ordinarily, she had Henry and Keiko place the food scraps in separate buckets, to be retrieved by local pig farmers, who used the dregs as slop each night. This time, though, the leftovers went in the regular garbage cans. Even pigs have standards.

By Monday, lunch was back to the same routine. In the storage room, Henry and Keiko sat on a pair of upturned milk crates, splitting a can of peaches and talking about what had happened at the Black Elks Club the night that Keiko's English teachers had been arrested and how the curfews were affecting everyone. The papers didn't say much. What they did say about the arrests got lost in the big headline of the week—that General MacArthur had miraculously escaped the Philippines, proclaiming: "I came out of Bataan and I shall return." Buried beneath that news was a small column about the arrest of suspected *enemy agents*.

Maybe that was what Henry's father had been talking about. The conflict that had seemed so far away suddenly felt closer than ever.

Especially with bullies like Chaz, Carl Parks, and Denny Brown still out there waging war on the playground. Even though no one ever wanted to be the Japs or the Jerrys, they usually made some little kid play the enemy, hounding him mercilessly. If they ever got tired of it, Henry never saw it. But here, in this dusty storage closet, there was shelter, and company.

Keiko smiled at Henry. "I have a surprise for you," she said.

He looked at her expectantly, offering the last peach, which she speared with a fork and ate in two big bites. They shared drinks of the sweet, syrupy juice that was left.

"It's a surprise, but I'm not going to show it to you until after school."

It wasn't his birthday, and Christmas had been months ago; still, a surprise was a surprise. "Is this because I'm storing all your photographs? If so, no need, I'm happy to—"

Keiko cut him off. "No, this is for taking me to the Black Elks Club with you."

"And almost getting us thrown in jail," Henry muttered sheepishly.

He watched her purse her lips and consider that comment, then dismiss his concern, beaming at Henry. "It was worth it."

Together they enjoyed a moment of silence that was interrupted by a knock on the half-open door. Scientific proof that time sometimes passes all too quickly.

"Shoofly, shoo." That was Mrs. Beatty's way of telling them to get a move on. Time to get back to their classes. After lunch she usually thundered back into the kitchen, working her teeth with a fresh toothpick, sometimes holding a copy of *Life* magazine—rolled up like a billy club or a fish bat. She used it to swat flies, which she left lying there, their flattened guts smeared on the metal kitchen counters.

Henry held the door for Keiko, who let her hair down and headed back to her classroom. Henry followed, looking back as Mrs. Beatty settled in with her magazine. It was last week's issue. The cover read "Bathing Suits in Fashion."

. . .

After school they pounded erasers, wiped desks, and mopped the bath-rooms. Henry kept asking about Keiko's surprise. She coyly deferred. "Later. I'll show you on the way home."

Instead of walking south toward Nihonmachi, Keiko led him north, to the heart of downtown Seattle. Every time Henry asked where they were going, she'd just point to the massive Rhodes Department Store on Second Avenue. Henry had been there a few times with his parents—only on those special occasions when they needed something important, or something that couldn't be found in Chinatown.

Rhodes was a local favorite. Being in the massive six-story building was like taking a life-size stroll through the Sears catalog, but with a cer-tain charm and real-world grandeur. Especially with its massive pipe organ, which was played during lunchtime and dinner, special concerts for hungry shoppers—at least it had been until a few months ago, when the organ had been dismantled and moved to the new Civic Ice Arena over on Mercer.

Henry followed Keiko to the audio section, a corner on the second floor with cabinet radios and phonographs. There was an aisle with long cedar racks of disk records—which to Henry felt lighter and more frag-ile than shellac records. Shellac supplies had been limited, apparently—another conscript of the war effort—so vinyl was now being used for the latest hit music, like "String of Pearls" by Glenn Miller and Artie Shaw's "Stardust." Henry loved music. But his parents had only an old Victrola. I doubt it'd even play any of these newer records, Henry thought.

Keiko stopped in front of one of the rows of records. "Close your eyes," she said, taking Henry's hands and moving them to his face.

Henry looked around first, then complied. He felt a little awkward but covered his eyes anyway, standing in the middle of the record aisle. He heard Keiko shuffling in the racks and couldn't resist peeking through his fingers, watching her from behind for a moment as she flipped through rows of records. He squeezed his eyes shut as she turned around, holding something.

"Open them!"

Before his eyes was a shiny vinyl record in a white paper sleeve. The simple, pressed label read: "Oscar Holden & the Midnight Blue, The Alley Cat Strut."

Henry was speechless. His jaw hung open, but no sound came out.

"Can you believe it?" She gushed with pride. "This is our song, the one he played for us!"

Holding it in his hands, he couldn't believe it. He'd never known an actual recording artist—never met one in person. The only famous person he'd ever seen was Leonard Coatsworth, the last man on the Tacoma Narrows Bridge before it bucked and bent and crashed into the water. Coatsworth had been on the newsreels, walking down the middle of the twisting bridge. Henry saw him ride by in the Seafair Parade and thought he was just an ordinary-looking fool. Not a performer like Oscar Holden.

Sure, Oscar had been famous on South Jackson, but this was *real* fame. Fame you could buy and hold in your hand. As he tilted the perfect record, he looked at the grooves and tried to hear the music again, the swinging sound of the horn section, Sheldon on saxophone. "I can't believe it." Henry spoke in awe.

"It just came out. I saved up to buy it. For you."

"For us," Henry corrected. "Besides, I can't even play it, we don't even have a record player."

"Then come to my house. My parents want to meet you anyway."

The thought of her parents wanting to meet him left him feeling flattered and shocked. Like an amateur fighter being given a shot at a prizefight. Excitement, custom-fit with doubt and anxiety. Fear too. His parents probably would have nothing to do with Keiko. Were her parents that different? What could they possibly think of him?

Henry and Keiko took the record to the checkout counter. A middle-aged woman with long blond hair pulled back under a clerk's hat kept busy counting change at the register, sorting it into a larger tray.

Keiko reached up and set the record on the counter, then opened a small purse and pulled out two dollars—the price of a new record.

The blond clerk kept counting.

Patiently, Henry and Keiko waited for the clerk to finish counting what was in her till. She made detailed notations of the amounts, writing on a sheet of paper.

While he and Keiko waited, another woman came up behind them, holding a small windup wall clock. Henry watched in confusion as the clerk took the clock, over his and Keiko's heads, and rang it up. The clerk took the money and handed the change back, and the clock, in a large green Rhodes shopping bag.

"Is this counter open?" Keiko asked.

The clerk just looked around for another customer.

"Excuse me, ma'am, I'd like to buy this record, please."

Henry was becoming more annoyed than the clerk looked—her hip cocked, her jaw set. She leaned down and whispered to them, "Then why don't you go back to your own neighborhood and buy it?"

Henry had been given dirty looks before but he'd never experienced something like this. He'd heard about things like this in the South. Places like Arkansas or Alabama, but not Seattle. Not the Pacific Northwest.

The clerk stood there, her fist dug into her hip. "We don't serve people like you—besides, my husband is off fighting . . ."

"I'll buy it," Henry said, putting his "I am Chinese" button on the counter next to Keiko's two dollars. "I said, I'll buy it, please."

Keiko looked ready to cry or storm out. Her fists rested on the counter, two white-knuckled balls of frustration.

Henry stared at the clerk, who looked confused, then annoyed. She relented, snatching the two dollars and flicking his button to one side. She handed the record to him, without a bag or a receipt. Henry insisted on both, afraid she'd yell for store security and report that they had stolen the record. She scratched a price on a yellow receipt and stamped it "paid"—shoving it at Henry. He took it, thanking her anyway.

He put his button in his pocket along with the slip of paper. "C'mon, let's go," he said to Keiko.

On the long walk home, Keiko stared blankly ahead. The joy of her surprise had popped like a helium balloon, loud and sharp, leaving nothing to hold but a limp string. Still, Henry held the record and tried his best to calm her down. "Thank you, this is a wonderful surprise. This is the best present I've ever been given."

"I don't feel very giving, or grateful. Just angry," Keiko said. "I was born here. I don't even speak Japanese. Still, all these people, everywhere I go . . . they hate me."

Henry found a smile and waved the record in front of her, handing it to her. Seeing it made her forget. "Thank you," she said.

She looked at the record as they walked. "I guess I'm used to the teasing at school. After all, my dad says they're just dumb kids that would pick on weak boys and little girls no matter what part of town they're from. That being Japanese or Chinese just makes the heckling that much easier—we're easy targets. But this far from home, in a grown-up part of town . . ."

"You'd think grown-ups would act different," Henry finished her sentence, knowing from his own experience that sometimes grown-ups could be worse. Much worse.

At least we have the record, Henry thought. A reminder of a place where people didn't seem to care what you looked like, where you were born, or where your family was from. When the music played, it didn't seem to make one lick of difference if your last name was Abernathy or Anjou, Kung or Kobayashi. After all, they had the music to prove it.

On the way home, Henry and Keiko debated who should keep the record.

"It's a gift from me to you. You should keep it, even if you can't play it. Someday you'll be able to," she insisted.

Henry thought Keiko should have it since she had a record player that could play the new vinyl disks.

"Besides," he argued, "my mother is always around, and I'm not sure if she'd approve—because my father doesn't like modern music."

In the end, Keiko relented and accepted it. Because her parents liked jazz, but also because she realized how late they were going to be if they didn't hurry home.

They walked as fast as they could along the scenic waterfront, their feet crunching on the occasional fragment of clamshell that littered the sidewalk. Hovering seabirds had dropped the shells whole, cracking them on the pavement so they could swoop down and feast on the squishy, meaty contents. To Henry the splattered shellfish just looked gross. He was wary of the messy sidewalk, almost to the point of distraction. So much so that he almost didn't notice a thin line of soldiers near the ferry terminal.

He and Keiko were forced to stop on the north side of the terminal, along with dozens of cars and a handful of people milling about the sidewalk. Most looked more curious than annoyed. A few looked happy. Henry didn't understand the commotion.

"Must be a parade, I think. I hope so," Henry said. "*I love parades.* The Seafair Parade was even better than the Chinese New Year's one on Main Street."

"What day is it?" Keiko asked, handing Henry the record, breaking out the sketchbook she kept in her book bag.

She sat on the curb and began drawing the scene in pencil. There was a row of soldiers in uniform, bayoneted rifles slung across their shoulders. All looked crisp, civil, and polite. Efficient even, Henry thought. The ferry *Keholoken* sat moored in the background, moving almost imperceptibly with the ebb and flow of the dark green waters of the frigid Puget Sound.

Henry thought about it. "It's March thirtieth—no holiday I know of."

"Why are they here? That's the Bainbridge Island ferry, isn't it?" Keiko tapped her pencil on her cheek in confusion.

Henry agreed. Looking down at Keiko's drawing, he was more impressed than ever. She was good. Better than good, she had real talent.

Then they heard a whistle.

"It must be starting," Henry said. Looking around, he saw there were more people lining the streets, frozen, as if waiting for a broken red light to change.

Another whistle and a long line of people began walking off the ferry. Henry could hear the rhythmic *plink-plank* of leather shoes on the metal ramp. In a neat row they ambled across the street and south—where to, Henry couldn't fathom. As best he could figure, they were heading in the direction of Chinatown, or maybe Nihonmachi.

The line went on forever. There were mothers with small children in tow. Old people, with faltering steps, pitching forward in the same general direction. Teenagers ran ahead, then walked when they saw the soldiers everywhere. All were carrying suitcases, wearing hats and raincoats.

That was when Henry realized what Keiko already knew. By the occasional chatter, he realized they were all Japanese. Bainbridge Island must have been declared a military zone, Henry thought. They're evacuating everyone. Hundreds. Each group was shadowed by a soldier who counted heads like a mother hen.

Looking around, Henry could see that most of the crowd watching was almost as surprised as he was. Almost. Yet quite a few just looked annoyed, as if they were late and were caught behind a long, never-ending train. Others looked pleased. Some clapped. He looked at Keiko, whose drawing was half-finished; her hand held the pencil above the page, the lead broken, her arm like a statue.

"C'mon, let's go around. We should go home, now," he said. He took the sketchbook and pencil from her hands and put them away, helping her to her feet. He turned her away from the scene, putting his arm around her shoulder, trying his best to gently guide her home. "We don't want to be here."

They crossed the street, passing in front of idling cars waiting for the parade of Japanese citizens to end. We can't be here. *We need to get home.* Henry realized they were the only Asian people on the street who didn't have suitcases in hand, and he didn't want to get swept up in the comings and goings of the soldiers.

"Where are they going?" Keiko asked in a hushed whisper. "Where are they taking them?"

Henry shook his head. "I don't know." But he did know. They were heading in the direction of the train station. The soldiers were taking them away. He didn't know where, but they were being sent packing. Maybe it was because Bainbridge was too close to the naval shipyard in Bremerton, or maybe because it was an island and it was easier to round them all up there than in a place like Seattle, where the confusion, the sheer numbers would make a similar feat impossible. It can't happen here, Henry thought. There's too many of them. *Too many of us.*

Henry and Keiko fought the crowd all the way back to Seventh Avenue, the neutral zone between Nihonmachi and Chinatown. News had spread in advance of their arrival. People of every color littered the streets. Throngs were talking and facing in the direction of the train station. There were no soldiers to be seen in this part of town. No trouble.

Henry found Sheldon, standing in a crowd of onlookers, his sax case hanging at his side. "What are you doing here?" Henry said, tugging on his sleeve.

Sheldon looked down, startled for a moment, then smiled his cap-toothed grin at Henry. "I was just breaking down for the day—Oscar's club has been temporarily shut down after the raid, so until they open up, and soon I hope, I'm back on the street trying to make a living. And this ain't helping business any."

Henry held out the Rhodes bag with the record. Sheldon smiled and winked at him. "I've got a copy myself."

Sheldon put his arm on Henry's shoulder as they watched the scene. Neither felt like talking about music. "They evacuated the whole island. Said it was for their safety. Can you believe that nonsense?" Sheldon said.

Keiko brushed the hair from her eyes, holding on to Henry's arm. "Where are they taking them?" she asked.

Henry was scared for Keiko; he didn't want to know the answer. He leaned his head until his temple rested next to hers, wrapping his coat around her.

"I don't know, miss," Sheldon said. "I don't know. California, I reckon. I heard they build some kind of prisoner of war camp down there near Nevada. They pass some order saying they can round up all the Japanese, Germans, and Italians—but do you see any Germans in that crowd? You see them rounding up Joe DiMaggio?"

Henry looked around. What few Japanese people there were in the crowds were all heading home, some of them running. "You'd better go, your parents are probably worried sick right now." He handed her the record.

Sheldon agreed, looking at Henry. "You better get home too, young man. Your family's going to be just as worried. Button or no button."

Keiko hugged Henry, lingering a long time. Looking up, Henry could see the fear in her eyes. Not just for herself—for her entire family. He felt it too. They said a wordless good-bye before splitting up, each running in a different direction of home.

Parents
(1942)

Within a week, the evacuation of Bainbridge Island was already old news—within a month it was almost forgotten, on the surface, anyway—everyone was doing their best to go about business as usual. Even Henry felt the restless calm as he and Keiko made plans for lunch on Saturday. She had surprised him by calling his home. Henry's father had answered the phone. As soon as she spoke in English, he handed the receiver to Henry. His father didn't ask who it was, just asked if it was a girl—knowing full well the answer.

I guess he just wanted to hear it from my lips, thought Henry. "Yes, it's a girl" was all he offered. The words came out in meaningless English, but he nodded and explained, "She's my friend." His father looked confused, yet seemingly resigned to the fact that his son was practically in his teens. Back in China, *the Old Country,* marriages happened as early as thirteen or fourteen. Sometimes they were arranged at birth, but only for the very poor or the very rich.

His father would probably be more concerned if he knew the purpose of the call—to meet Keiko's family. No, Henry realized, *concerned* was too gentle a word, his father would be livid.

Henry, on the other hand, was less worried until he realized that lunch might qualify as a date—a thought that made his stomach churn and his palms sweat. He reassured himself that it was nothing fancy, just lunch with the Okabes.

At school, things seemed abnormally normal—so restrained and peaceful that he and Keiko didn't know what to think. The other children, and even the teachers, seemed unaware of the Japanese exodus from Bainbridge Island. The day had come and gone in relative quiet.

Almost like it never happened. Lost in the news of the war—that the U.S. and Filipino troops were losing at Bataan and that a Japanese submarine had shelled an oil refinery somewhere in California.

Henry's father had become more adamant than ever that Henry wear his button. "On the outside—wear it on the outside, where everyone can see it!" his father demanded in Cantonese as Henry was heading out the door.

Henry unzipped his coat and left it open so the button was plainly visible, slumping his shoulders, awaiting his father's stern approval. He had never seen his father so serious before. His parents even went one step further, each wearing an identical button. Some sort of collective effort, Henry reasoned. He understood his parents' concern for his own well-being, but there was no way that they'd be mistaken for Japanese—because they rarely left Chinatown. And if they did, there were simply too many people to round up in Seattle. Thousands.

Henry and Keiko's plan was to meet in front of the Panama Hotel. It had been built thirty years earlier by Sabro Ozasa—some architect that Henry's father had mentioned once or twice. Japanese, but of some renown, according to Henry's father anyway, who rarely acknowledged anything in the Japanese community in a positive light. This being the rare exception.

The hotel was the most impressive building in Nihonmachi, or the entire district for that matter. Standing as a sentinel between two distinct communities, it provided a comfortable home for people fresh off the boats, rooming by the week, or the month, or as long as it took to find a job, to save a little money, and to become an American. Henry wondered how many immigrants had rested their weary heads at the Panama Hotel, dreaming of a new life that began the day they stepped off the steamship from Canton or Okinawa, counting the days until they could send for their families. Days that usually turned to years.

Now the hotel stood as a run-down shell of its former glory. Immigrants, fishermen, and cannery workers who weren't allowed to bring their families with them from the Old Country used it as a permanent bachelor hotel.

Henry had always wanted to go down to the lower level. To see the two marble bathhouses, the *sento,* Keiko called them. They were supposedly the largest and most luxurious on the West Coast. But he was too scared.

Almost as scared as he was to tell his parents he was meeting Keiko. He'd hinted to his mother—in English no less—that he had a Japanese friend, and she had immediately shot him her stink-eye, a look of shock so profound he immediately dropped the subject. Most Chinese parents were indifferent to the Japanese, or the Filipinos who were arriving daily, fleeing the war or seeking better fortunes in America. Some Chinese harbored ill feelings, but most simply kept to themselves. His parents were different—they checked his shirt for an "I am Chinese" button every time he walked out the door. Father's nationalistic pride, his banner of protection, just kept swelling.

When he walked Keiko home, a polite wave or an occasional "Hello" to her parents was about as far as Henry got. He had been certain his father would somehow find out, so he kept his visits to a minimum. Keiko, on the other hand, gushed to her parents. About her friend Henry, his musical interests, and about wanting to meet for lunch today.

"Henry!" There she was, sitting on the front step waving. An early spring was showing signs of new life, and cherry blossoms were beginning to bloom—the streets, lined in pink and white flowers, finally smelled of something other than seaweed, salty fish, and low tide.

"I can be Chinese too," she teased him, pointing at Henry's button. *"Hou noi mou gin."* It meant "How are you today, beautiful?"—in Cantonese.

"Where did you learn that?"

Keiko smiled. "I looked it up at the library."

"Oai deki te ureshii desu," Henry returned.

For an awkward moment, they just looked at each other, beaming, not knowing what to say, or in which language to say it. Then Keiko broke the silence. "My family is shopping in the market, we'll meet them for lunch."

They raced through the Japanese market to meet her parents. He let her win, a courteous gesture his father would have expected of him. And of course, Henry didn't know where he was going anyway. He followed her to the lobby of a Japanese noodle shop—recently renamed the American Garden.

"Henry, so nice to see you again." Mr. Okabe wore gray flannel pants and a hat that made him look like Cary Grant. Like Keiko, he spoke beautiful English.

The manager sat them at a round table near the window. Keiko sat across from Henry, while her mother found a booster seat for Keiko's little brother. Henry guessed he must have been all of three or four. He was playing with his black lacquered chopsticks, his mother scolding him gently, telling him it was bad luck.

"Thanks for walking Keiko home every day, Henry. We appreciate your being such a conscientious friend."

Henry wasn't exactly sure what *conscientious* meant, but as Mr. Okabe said it, he poured him a cup of green tea, so he took it as a compliment. Henry took the cup of tea with both hands, a sign of respect his mother had taught him, and offered to fill Mr. Okabe's cup, but Keiko's father had already begun pouring his own, using the marble lazy Susan to work his way around the table.

"Thank you for inviting me." Henry wished he'd paid more attention in English class. Until he was twelve, he had been forbidden to speak English in his own home. His father had wanted him to grow up Chinese, the way he had done. Now everything was upside down. Yet the cadence of his words seemed to have more in common with that of the fishermen who came over from China than with the English Keiko and her family spoke so fluently.

"That's an interesting button you have on, Henry," Keiko's mother observed in a sweet, grandmotherly way. "Where did you get it?"

Reaching up, Henry covered it with his hand. He'd meant to take it off on the way over but had forgotten it in the race to the restaurant. "My father gave it to me; he said I'm supposed to wear it at all times—it's embarrassing."

"No, your father is right. He's a very wise man," Mr. Okabe said.

You wouldn't think that if you met him.

"You shouldn't be ashamed of who you are, never more than right now."

Henry looked at Keiko, wondering what she thought about this conversation. She just smiled and kicked him under the table, obviously feeling more at home here than in the school cafeteria.

"It's easy to be who you are here, but it's harder at school," said Henry. "At Rainier, I mean." *What am I saying? It's hard being who I am in my own house,* with my own family, he thought.

Mr. Okabe sipped his tea, reminding Henry to sip his own. It was lighter, with a flavor more subtle and transparent than the black oolong teas his own father favored.

"I knew going to a Caucasian school was going to present certain challenges for Keiko," Mr. Okabe said. "But we tell her, Be who you are, no matter what. I warned her that they may never like her, some might even hate her, but eventually, they will respect her—as an American."

Henry liked where the conversation was going, but he felt a little guilty too, wondering about his own family. Why hadn't anyone ever explained it that way? Instead he got a button and was forced to *speak his American.*

"There's a free outdoor jazz concert on Jackson Street tonight— Oscar Holden will be playing," Keiko's mother said. "Why don't you invite your family to join us?"

Henry looked at Keiko, who was smiling and raising her eyebrows. He couldn't believe what he was hearing. He'd seen Oscar Holden only that one time with Keiko. He'd heard him a few times before that, but only by pressing his ear to the back-alley door of the Black Elks Club, where the legendary jazz pianist happened to be practicing. The offer was tempting. Especially since he'd seen so little of Sheldon now that he was subbing for Oscar's usual sax man—"a once in a lifetime gig," Sheldon had called it. Indeed.

But, unlike Keiko's parents, Henry's didn't care for *colored* music. In fact, they didn't seem to listen to music at all anymore. Classical or modern. Black or white. The only thing they listened to on the radio these days was the news.

It was a kind offer from the Okabes, but one he'd have to decline. Henry could picture the scene like a ten-cent horror matinee at the Atlas Theater—complete with Chinese subtitles. A dark tragedy springing to life as he explained that not only did he have a Japanese friend but her whole family wanted to take his to a jazz concert.

Before he could fake a polite answer to Mrs. Okabe, a half-empty bottle of *shoyu* began skipping around the table. Henry grabbed it and felt the ground tremble.

Through the rattling window, he could see a large deuce-and-a-half army truck belching black diesel fumes as it rumbled into the square. Its metal frame creaking and piercing the lumbering thunder of its massive engine. Even before its gas brakes squealed, people on the street began scattering in all directions. Only the very old or the very young stayed to observe the truckload of soldiers who sat stoically in the back of the massive rig.

More trucks kept coming, one after another, unloading American soldiers and military police with rifles who began canvassing the neighborhood, nailing small posters to doors, storefronts, and telephone poles. Merchants and customers alike poured out to see the commotion. Henry and the Okabes stepped onto the sidewalk as soldiers walked past, handing out copies of the flyer—"Public Proclamation 1," which was written in English and Japanese.

Henry looked at the paper in Keiko's hand. The bold type screamed: INSTRUCTIONS TO ALL PERSONS OF JAPANESE ANCESTRY. It was all about Japanese families being forced to evacuate, for their own safety. They had only a few days and could bring next to nothing—only what they could carry. At the bottom, it was signed by the president of the United States and the secretary of war. The rest of the flyer was a mystery to Henry, but not to Keiko's family. Her mother immediately began crying. Her father looked upset but remained calm. Keiko touched her heart with her finger and pointed to Henry. He touched his and felt the button his family wore. "I am Chinese."

Better Them Than Us
(1942)

Henry burst into the little apartment he shared with his parents. His father sat in his easy chair calmly reading *Hsi Hua Pao,* the *Seattle Chinese Post.* His mother was in the kitchen, slicing vegetables from the sound of it—a knife rhythmically tapping a cutting board.

Henry handed a copy of the proclamation to his father, trying to breathe. He rubbed his side where it ached from running ten city blocks. Father glanced at it—Henry could tell by the look in his eyes that he was waiting for an explanation, in *American,* of why Henry was so upset. No, not this. Not now. *Just speak to me* was all Henry could think. He said the same in Chinese.

Father shook his head sternly, cutting Henry off as he tried to explain.

"No! You can't ignore me. Not anymore," Henry argued in English before slipping back into Chinese. "They're taking everyone away. All the Japanese. The army is taking everyone away!"

His father handed the proclamation back. "Better them than us."

His mother appeared from the kitchen, speaking Chinese, looking for an explanation. "Henry, why does this matter? We're at war. And we're our own community. We take care of each other. You know this as well as anyone."

Henry didn't know what to say—or in which language to say it. He looked at both of his parents, and the words fell out. "It matters to me," he said in Chinese. Then he switched back to English. "It matters because *she's* Japanese."

He stormed to his bedroom, slamming the door. The images of his parents' dumbfounded expressions lingering in his troubled mind. Through the door, he could hear them begin to argue.

Henry opened his window and climbed out onto the fire escape, leaning against the stiff metal railing, dejected. He could hear the army trucks thundering in the distance. Beyond the alley, in the streets of Chinatown, people simply went about their business; some were looking, talking, or pointing in the direction of Nihonmachi, but for the most part, everyone was calm.

Henry watched as a car packed to the windows with boxes rolled up to the back door of the Kau Kau restaurant. To his surprise a young Japanese couple hopped out as people from the restaurant poured into the alley, hauling boxes of what Henry could only presume were personal effects into the restaurant. The things left unboxed were what gave it away. A floor lamp. A long rug, rolled and tied to the roof of the rusty green sedan. It all went inside, all but four suitcases, which the couple shouldered as best they could. There were hugs all around between this Japanese couple and their Chinese friends.

The Japanese couple walked off, out the alley and down the street, looking as though they were being dragged toward the train station. Henry looked up and down the alley one last time, thinking about Keiko and her family. About how they'd left the American Garden restaurant to try to make their own arrangements.

Henry went back inside and sprawled on his bed as his mother came in. He pawed through a stack of comic books, then saw the cover of *Marvel Mystery Comics Number 30,* the last issue he'd bought. The cover featured the Human Torch battling a Japanese submarine. The war is everywhere, Henry thought, shoving the comics under his bed as his mother set a plate of butter-almond cookies on his nightstand.

"Do you need to talk, Henry? If so, then please talk to me." She spoke in Cantonese, her eyes not masking her concern for him.

He looked at the open window. The blackout curtains hung stiff and heavy, barely moving in the breeze. He couldn't understand the chatter of the people on the street below. It drifted in and out like his longing to understand what was going on around him.

"Why won't he talk to me?" Henry asked his mother in Cantonese, still looking out the window.

"Who talk? Your father?"

After a long pause, Henry looked at her and nodded.

"He talks to you every day. What do you mean, why won't he talk?"

"He talks, but he doesn't listen to me."

Henry sat there as she patted him on the arm, on his belly, searching for the words to make her son understand.

"I don't know how to tell you so it makes sense. You were born here. *You're American.* Where your father comes from, it was nothing but war. War with Japan. They invaded northern China, killing many, many people. Not soldiers but women and children, the old and the sick. Your father, he grew up this way. He saw this happen to his *own family.*" She pulled a knit handkerchief out from her sleeve and dabbed her eyes, even though she wasn't crying. Maybe she couldn't cry anymore, Henry thought. It was just habit now.

"Your father came here, as an orphan, but he never forgot who he was, where he came from. Never forgot about his *home.*"

"*This* is his home now," Henry protested.

His mother got up and looked out the window before closing it. "This is where he *lives,* but it will never be his home. Look at what is happening to Japantown. Your father is afraid that might happen to us someday. That's why—as much as he loves his China—he wants this to be your home. For *you* to be accepted here."

"There are other families . . ."

"I know. There are some families. Chinese families. American families. Families that right now, even as we are speaking, are hiding Japanese. Taking their belongings. *Very dangerous.* You, me, all of us risk going to jail if we help them. I know you have a friend. The one who calls on the telephone. The girl from the Rainier school? *She is Japanese?*"

Henry didn't see her as Japanese anymore. "She's just my friend," he said in English. *And I miss her.*

"Hah?" his mother said, not understanding.

Henry switched back to Cantonese, thinking of what to say, how much to say. He looked his mother in the eye. "She's my best friend."

His mother looked at the ceiling, letting out a heavy sigh. The kind of sigh you give when you just accept that something bad has happened. When a relative dies, and you say, "At least he lived a long life." Or when your house burns to the ground and you think, "At least we have our health." It was a sigh of resigned disappointment. A consolation prize, of coming in second and having nothing to show for it. Of coming up empty, having wasted your time, because in the end, what you do, and who you are, doesn't matter one lousy bit. Nothing does.

For the rest of the weekend Henry's father wouldn't speak of what was going on in Japantown. Henry tried arguing, but his father cut him off every time he attempted to speak to him in Chinese. His mother had softened a bit, if only to ease his unhappiness. She had argued with Henry's father, a rare occurrence, about Keiko—about Henry's *friend*—but now it was time to move on, and she too found little value in Henry discussing it further. Being told in Cantonese that he'd understand it all when he was older only infuriated him. And all Henry could do was grumble about it in English, to no one.

He even tried calling Keiko before his parents woke up Sunday morning, but there was no answer. The operator thought the phone had been disconnected. School on Monday did nothing to lessen his anxiety. Keiko was absent there as well. Everyone in Nihonmachi had become occupied with packing—or selling what they couldn't carry.

So on Tuesday morning, instead of walking to school, Henry ran toward Union Station, which had become the central assembly area for the residents of Nihonmachi. Running down South Jackson, he saw lines of Pullman cars stretched out on the tracks leading toward the train depot. Greyhound buses too, creaking and groaning, filled to capacity with soldiers, who looked out of place stepping off with rifles slung over their shoulders.

They're taking them away, Henry thought. They're taking all of them away. There must be five thousand Japanese. How can they take them all? Where will they go?

A few blocks from the station itself, crowds filled the street. There was a mix of crying toddlers, shuffling suitcases, and soldiers checking the paperwork of local citizens—most of whom were dressed in their Sunday best, the one or two suitcases they were allowed packed to the point of bursting. Each person wore a plain white tag, the kind you'd see on a piece of furniture, dangling from a coat button.

Public Proclamation 1 instructed all Japanese citizens, foreign-born and even second-generation Americans, like Keiko, to gather at the train station by nine in the morning. They would be leaving in waves, by neighborhood, until they were all removed. Henry had no idea where they'd be going. The Japanese from Bainbridge Island had been sent to Manzanar—someplace in California, near the Nevada border. But one camp couldn't possibly handle the crowd that had been herded to the train station.

Scanning the area for Keiko, Henry tried to ignore the mobs of angry whites who stood behind barricades, shouting at the families walking by. The entire span of the sky bridge leading to the ferry terminal was packed as well, no one moving, everyone lingering over the railing, staring down at the cordoned-off military zone. It seemed that eyes were everywhere. Men and women alike perched in open office windows high above the street, whistling.

Henry hadn't spoken to Keiko since they left the restaurant. He'd called again from a pay phone on the way over, but the phone just rang and rang until an operator cut in asking if there was a problem. He hung up. If he was to find them, this was the place. But had they left already? He had to find her. He hated the thought of going back to school without her and was surprised at how much he missed her already.

There were a few Chinese people, mainly rail workers, here and there. No one Henry recognized. He picked them out of the crowd by the buttons they wore, identical to his. Once the army and military police had arrived, the small print shop that was making them had run out. *This is what gold feels like,* Henry thought, touching the button he wore. *Small and precious.*

Standing on a red, white, and blue mailbox, he frantically scanned the crowd, which crept slowly in the direction of the train station. Henry watched another large army truck rumble mercilessly through and stop, but instead of soldiers, the canvas-covered flatbed was filled with elderly Japanese. Some appeared to be almost crippled by the way they walked. Soldiers helped them down, putting some in wheelchairs, their hair unkempt and messy. A Japanese doctor was in tow. Henry realized what was happening. They had cleared the hospital. The sick and infirm were being evacuated as well. Many looked bewildered, obviously not knowing what was happening to them, or why.

Henry watched a white man holding hands with a Japanese woman. He couldn't help but wonder what must be happening to those families where a Caucasian had taken a Japanese bride. Mixed marriages were illegal. Then again, maybe they'd be spared the hardship of internment after all. But he thought otherwise when he saw the suitcase in the woman's hand and the baby stroller.

Watching the crowd mill by, he heard the nine o'clock whistle go off miles away at Boeing Field. He'd been searching the crowd for— what?—forty minutes now. Henry knew time was slipping away, and he was beginning to panic. "Keiko!" he shouted from atop the mailbox. He felt people's stares on him as they passed by. They must think I'm mad. Maybe I am. Maybe it's okay to be mad. "Keiko! Keiko Okabe!" he shouted until a soldier looked at him as though he were disturbing the peaceful reverie of the morning. Then he saw something. A familiar sight.

Yes, there it is! Mr. Okabe's Cary Grant hat looked regal even as he crossed the street carrying his only remaining belongings. Henry recognized his dignified posture, but his charming demeanor had been replaced with a detached stare. He walked slowly, holding his wife's hand. She in turn was holding Keiko's. Keiko's little brother walked in front, playing with a wooden airplane, spinning the propeller, unaware that today was unlike any other day.

Henry waved his arms and shouted. It didn't matter, they didn't notice. They might not have noticed if it were raining or the buildings around them were on fire. Like most of the Japanese families heading toward the train station, they had their heads down, eyes ahead, or stayed busy keeping track of one another.

One person did notice Henry, though.

It was Chaz. Even from where Henry stood, he recognized the bully's ruddy, pimpled face. Chaz stood behind the barricade laughing, waving at Henry, smiling before going back to screaming at the children and crying mothers walking by.

Henry spied the button Chaz wore and dropped down off the mailbox, pressing through the crowd, zeroing in on Chaz's flattop haircut, following the sound of his cackling laugh. *He's going to kill me,* Henry thought. He's bigger, faster. But I don't care anymore. Henry's spine had fused with anger.

Chaz sneered as Henry slipped beneath the barricade directly in front of him. "Knew I'd find you here, Henry ol' buddy. How's your daddy doing?"

"What are you doing here?" Henry asked.

"Just enjoying the sights like everyone else. Thought I'd take a stroll down here and see who's not leaving. But it looks like everybody is going bye-bye. Guess I'm going to be busy looking after their things while they're gone." Chaz stuck out his lower lip, pretending to pout.

Henry had heard about the looting that had begun the night before in some neighborhoods. Families hadn't even left, and people strolled right in and took lamps, furniture, anything that wasn't nailed down. If it was, they had claw hammers to fix that too.

"Since the army closed off Nip-ville, there's not much to see. Just thought I'd come down here and say *sayonara.* You were just a bonus find." As he said it, Chaz grabbed a handful of Henry's collar.

Henry struggled against his grip. Chaz was a whole foot taller, looming over him. Henry scanned the crowd for a friendly face, but no one noticed. No one cared. *Who am I in all this? What do I matter?*

Then his eyes found the button on Chaz's shirt. The one he had stolen from Henry. A trophy, pinned to his jacket like a merit badge of cruelty. More gold.

Henry curled his fists so tightly his fingernails cut tiny half crescents into the tender flesh of his palms. He punched Chaz as hard as he could, feeling the impact all the way into his shoulder. He was aiming for his nose but caught cheekbone instead. Before Henry could land another blow, the ground slammed into his back. His head hit the concrete, and all he saw were meaty fists raining down.

Defending himself the best he could, Henry reached up to grab Chaz and felt a sharp pain in his hand. Despite the blows to the side of Henry's head, a piercing in his hand was the only pain he felt. The only pain that mattered.

As Henry rolled away from the punches, covering up, Chaz seemed to float up and off of him. The crowd had parted. No one appeared to care that a white kid was beating the snot out of a little Chinese boy. No one but Sheldon—who'd seen him and pulled the larger boy off him.

Chaz shrugged the black man away. "Get your dirty hands off of me!" He brushed the dust off his shirt, looking embarrassed and humiliated— a tomcat dunked in an icy bath. He eyed the crowd around him for a friendly face, but the few spectators who noticed rolled their eyes at the noisy troll that he'd become. "I forgot you were friends with this rice nigger," Chaz grunted, almost in tears. Skulking away, he added, "See you tomorrow, Henry. Next time you'll get worse."

"You all right, kid?" Sheldon asked.

Henry rolled to his side and sat up, wiping a small spot of blood from his nose with his sleeve. His eye felt puffy and would surely be purple to-morrow. He licked his teeth with his tongue, taking inventory. Nothing broken. Nothing missing.

He opened his hand and looked down at the button, the pin sticking in partway. Henry smiled and said in his best English, "Never felt better."

Henry sprinted through the crowd, unnoticed in the chaos—searching for Keiko's family, worried that his scuffle with Chaz may have blown his one chance to see her. He knew the direction they were headed, but in-side the station, there would be any number of trains to board. He thought of the people from the Kau Kau restaurant. The ones who were caring for the belongings of that Japanese couple. He'd heard his mother mention others. Chinese families who took people in, hiding them— there had to be a chance.

With each step, he plotted how he would convince his parents. Would they take Keiko in? Their first thought was to protect themselves, then others in their own community. He'd have to make them understand, somehow. How could they not? Father was closed-minded, but knowing soldiers were herding thousands of people to an unknown destination, an unknown fate—this would change everything. How could they sit back and do nothing when this many people were being taken away— when they could be next?

Henry ran past a mountain of luggage. Trunks, bags, and suitcases stacked almost as high as the roofs of the silvery buses that rolled by. Families were arguing about how much or how little they were allowed to bring. The excess found its way to the top of the ever-growing heap. Next to the mound was a truckload of confiscated radios. Giant Philco consoles and small Zenith portables with bent wave-magnet antennas were piled up in the back like discarded shoes. Across the street sat Union Station, a courtly looking mass of red brick, its thick iron awning held aloft by massive stretches of black chain anchored to the building. Above it sat an enormous clock face. Nine-fifteen. Time was slipping away.

From the steep marble steps of the station, Henry looked out over the swirling sea of people, clusters of families and loved ones trying desperately to stay together. The occasional lost child cried alone as soldiers marched by. The rest were packed like cattle; group by group they were being checked onto four large passenger trains—bound for where? Crystal City, Texas? Winnemucca, Nevada? So many rumors. The last one had them bound for an old Indian reservation.

Henry spotted the hat again. One of many, to be sure, but the walk, the gait, it looked like her father. Sprinting down the stairs to the ground floor, he half-expected a soldier to stop him, but too much was going on. Get them onboard. Make them leave. Now. That was all that mattered to those in uniform.

Henry shuffled around the grown-ups, some standing, others sitting on their luggage looking frightened and confused. A priest said a rosary with a young Japanese woman. Other couples took photos of each other, smiling as best they could, before exchanging hugs and polite handshakes.

There he was.

"Mr. Okabe!" Bruised and out of breath, Henry felt the side of his head start to hurt.

The defeated old gentleman who turned around had a wide mustache. Henry's disappointment was punctuated by the ringing of a porter's bell. For the first time all morning, Henry stopped searching the crowds and crumpled to his knees, staring at the dirty, tiled floor. *She's gone, isn't she?*

"Henry?"

He turned, and there they were. Keiko and her family. Her little brother making airplane noises with his lips. They smiled, each wearing an identical hangtag that read "Family #10281." They seemed delighted to see a face that wasn't going to the unknown place they were.

Henry scrambled to his feet. "I thought you'd left." He looked at Keiko, her family, not wanting them to go.

"I brought this. Wear it, and they'll let you walk out of here," he said and put the button he'd retrieved from Chaz into Keiko's hand, pleading to Mr. Okabe, "She can stay with us, or my aunt. I'll find a place where she can stay. I'll get more. I'll go back and get more for all of you. You can have mine. Take it and I'll go back and get more."

Henry's heart raced as he fumbled, trying to take his own button off.

Mr. Okabe looked at his wife, then touched Henry's shoulder. Henry saw the flicker of a chance in their eyes. Just a chance. Then he watched it slip away. They would go. Like the rest. They would go.

"You just gave me hope, Henry." Mr. Okabe shook Henry's small hand and looked him in the eye. "And sometimes hope is enough to get you through anything."

Henry let out a deep breath, his shoulders drooping as he gave up trying to remove his button.

"Your cheek?" Keiko's mother asked.

"It's nothing," Henry said, remembering the scrapes and bruises from his scuffle.

Mr. Okabe touched the hangtag dangling from his coat. "No matter what happens to us, Henry, we're still Americans. And we need to be together—wherever they take us. But I'm proud of you. And I know your parents must be too."

Henry choked on the thought and looked at Keiko, who had slipped her hand into his. It felt softer and warmer than he'd ever imagined. She touched Henry's shirt, where his button was, the space above his heart. She smiled, with a sparkle in her eye. "Thank you. Can I keep this anyway?" she asked, holding up the button he had given her.

Henry nodded. "Where are they taking you?"

Keiko's father looked at the train that was nearly full. "We only know they're taking us to a temporary relocation center—called Camp Harmony. It's at the Puyallup Fairgrounds, about two hours to the south. From there . . . we don't know, we haven't been told. But the war can't last forever."

Henry wasn't so sure. It was all he'd known growing up.

Keiko wrapped her arms around him and whispered in his ear, "I won't forget you." She pinned the button reading "I am Chinese" to the inside cover of her diary, holding it close.

"I'll be here."

Henry watched them board the train, herded in with dozens of other families. Soldiers with white gloves, batons in hand, blew whistles and pointed as the doors closed. Henry lingered at the edge of the boarding area, waving good-bye as they pulled away from the station, disappearing from sight. He wiped warm tears from his cheeks, his sadness diluted by the sea of families waiting for the next train. Hundreds of families. Thousands.

He avoided eye contact with the soldiers as he walked away, thinking about what he'd say to his parents, and which language to say it in. Maybe if he *spoke his American,* he wouldn't have to say anything at all.

Empty Streets
(1942)

Henry walked upstream against the current of Japanese families that continued flowing toward Union Station. Almost everyone was on foot, some pushing handcarts or wheelbarrows weighed down with luggage. A few cars and trucks crept by with suitcases and bags tied to the hoods, the grilles, the roofs—any flat surface became ample cargo space as families loaded up their relatives and their belongings and drove off toward the army's relocation center—Camp Harmony, Mr. Okabe had called it.

Henry looked out at the endless ribbon of people. He didn't know where else to go. He just wanted to walk *away,* wherever that was.

School was out of the question for the day. The thought of being tardy and facing the ridicule of his classmates was almost as horrible as the thought of enduring their happiness—their joy and satisfaction at knowing that Keiko's family, and her whole neighborhood, were being taken away. All smiles. Victorious in their home-front battle with a hated enemy. Even if that enemy spoke the same language and had said the Pledge of Allegiance alongside them since kindergarten.

Of course, deep down, Henry didn't know if schools were open at the moment. The commotion downtown seemed to have created a holiday atmosphere—a monstrous, carnival-like celebration. A record player somewhere blared "Stars and Stripes Forever"—a harsh contrast to the Japanese melancholy and quiet sadness.

As Henry slipped away from the train station, the possibility of being caught by truant officers looking for schoolchildren cutting class seemed very small. There was too much going on, too many people crowding the streets. Businesses closed as office workers downtown stopped everything to watch the commotion. Those leaving. Those watching. And the soldiers on the streets all seemed to be consumed with the task at hand—herding groups of people with tags hanging from their coats. They barked commands for people to stay lined up, blew the occasional whistle to catch the attention of those who spoke little or no English.

Henry wandered away, finding himself drawn down Maynard Avenue to the edge of Nihonmachi. There he found Sheldon sitting on a bus bench, sipping black coffee from a thermos cup, his sax case tucked between his feet. He looked up at Henry, shaking his head as the remaining residents of Nihonmachi drifted away.

"I'm sorry, Henry," Sheldon said, as he blew on his coffee to cool it down.

"Not your fault," Henry offered, sitting next to his friend.

"Sorry all the same. There was nothing you could've done. Nothing anyone could've done. They'll be okay. The war will be over soon, they'll be coming back, you wait."

Henry couldn't even bring himself to nod in agreement. "What if they send them back to Japan? Keiko doesn't even speak Japanese. What'll happen to her then? She's more of an enemy there than she is here."

Sheldon offered his coffee to Henry, who shook his head no. "I don't know about all that, Henry. I can't say. All I know is, all wars end. This'll end. Then everything will be made right." Sheldon put the cap back on his thermos. "You want me to walk you to school?"

Henry stared at nothing.

"Going home?"

"I'll go home later," Henry said, shaking his head.

Sheldon looked up the street, as if waiting for a bus that was late and might never arrive. "Then come with me."

Henry didn't even ask. He followed Sheldon down the center of Maynard Avenue, walking along the dotted white line into the heart of Japantown, a street littered with copies of Public Proclamation 1 and small paper American flags that stuck to the wet pavement. The streets were barren of people, the sidewalks too. Henry looked up and down the avenue—no cars or trucks anywhere. No bicycles. No paperboys. No fruit sellers or fish buyers. No flower carts or noodle stands. The streets were vacant, empty—the way he felt inside. There was no one left.

The army had removed the barricades from the streets, except those flowing in the direction of the train station. All the buildings were boarded up. The windows were covered with plywood slabs, as if the residents had been waiting for a typhoon that had never arrived. Banners that read "I am an American" still hung over the Sakoda Barber Shop and the Oriental Trading Company. Along with signs that read "Out of Business."

The streets were so quiet Henry could hear the squawking seagulls flying overhead. He could hear the porters' whistling from the train station, several blocks to the south. He could even hear his shoes squishing on the damp Seattle pavement, quickly drowned out by the rattle of an army jeep as it turned onto Maynard. He and Sheldon hopped to the sidewalk, looking at the soldiers as they drove by, staring back. For a moment Henry thought he might be rounded up, like the rest of Seattle's Japanese citizens. He looked down and touched the button on his coat. It wouldn't be so bad, would it? He might be sent to the same camp as Keiko and her family. His mother would miss him, though, maybe even his father. The jeep drove past. The soldiers didn't stop. Maybe they knew he was Chinese. Maybe they had more important things to do than round up a lost little kid and a black out-of-work sax player from South Jackson.

He and Sheldon walked all the way to the steps of the Nippon Kan Theater, across from Kobe Park and in the shadow of the Japanese-owned Astor Hotel, which stood silent like an empty coffin. The prettiest part of Japantown, even vacant as it was, looked beautiful in the afternoon. Cherry blossoms covered the sidewalks, and the streets smelled alive.

"What are we doing here?" Henry asked, as he watched Sheldon open his case and take out his saxophone.

Sheldon slipped his reed into the mouthpiece. "We're living."

Henry looked around the deserted streets, remembering the people, the actors, the dancers, the old men gossiping and playing cards. Children running and playing. Keiko sitting on the hillside drawing in her sketchbook. Laughing at Henry. Teasing him. The memories warmed him, just a little. Maybe there was life to be lived.

His ears perked up as Sheldon drew a deep breath, then began a slow wailing on his sax. A sad, melancholy affair, the kind Henry had never heard him play on the street or in the clubs. It was heartbreaking, but only for a moment. Then he slipped into something festive—something up-tempo, with a soul and a heartbeat. He played for no one, but at the same time Henry realized he was playing for everyone.

Henry waved good-bye, Sheldon still playing in the distance. Half-way home, he entered Chinatown. He was far from the soldiers at the train station, so he removed his button and put it in his pocket, not wanting to think about it.

Then he stopped and bought his mother another starfire lily.

Sketchbook
(1986)

 In the dimly lit basement of the Panama Hotel, Samantha drew a deep breath and blew the dust off the cover of a small book. "Look at this!" she said.

She and Marty hadn't been as much help as Henry had hoped. They were caught up in the detail of each item they found, trying to interpret some meaning—to place historical value, or at least appreciate why such an item would be stored here, whether it be an important-looking document or a simple bundle of dried flowers.

Henry had explained that much of what many families had treasured was sold for pennies on the dollar in the hastened days before the army arrived to take everyone away. Storage space was hard to come by, and no one was sure of the safety of anything left behind. After all, no one knew when they might be coming back. Still, a lot of what Henry, Marty, and Samantha found was obviously of high personal value—photo albums, birth and wedding certificates, carbon copies of immigration and naturalization papers. Even neatly framed diplomas from the University of Washington, including a handful of doctorates.

Henry had paused the first day to look at some of the photo albums, but the sheer volume of belongings kept him focused on what he was really looking for. If he didn't breeze past all else, he'd be here for weeks.

"This is incredible! Look at these books," Marty said from across the dusty basement. "Pops, come look at these things."

Henry and his makeshift crew had been mining the luggage for old disk records for two hours. In that time Henry had been called over to ooh and aah over piles of costume jewelry, a Japanese sword that had miraculously avoided confiscation, and a case of old brass surgical instruments. He was growing weary of the novelty of the hour.

"Is it a record?" he mumbled.

"Sort of, it's a record of *something*—it's a sketchbook. A whole box of sketchbooks in fact. Come check 'em out."

Henry dropped the bamboo steamer he had been taking out of an old shipping trunk and shuffled over boxes and suitcases as quickly as he could.

"Let me see, let me see . . ."

"Easy now, there's plenty to share," Marty said.

Henry held the tiny sketchbook in his hand—the dusty black cover was old and brittle. Inside were sketches of Chinatown and Japantown. Of the piers jutting out to Elliott Bay. And of cannery workers, ferryboats, and flowers in the marketplace.

The sketches looked rough and imperfect, occasionally dotted with little notations of time or place. No name was written in them, none that he could find anyway.

Marty and Samantha sat on suitcases beneath the spotlight of a single hanging bulb, paging through the sketchbooks. Henry couldn't sit. He couldn't stand still either.

"Where did you find these? Which pile?"

Marty pointed, and Henry began digging through a crate of old maps, half-painted canvases, and jars of ancient art supplies.

"Pops?"

Henry turned around and saw a bewildered look in his son's eyes. He looked to the page in front of him, then up at his father and back again. Samantha just looked confused.

"Dad?" Marty stared at his father in the dim light. *"Is this you?"*

Marty held out an open, dog-eared page. It was a pencil drawing of a young boy sitting on the steps of a building. Looking somewhat sad and alone.

Henry felt like he was looking at a ghost. He stood staring at the image.

Marty turned the page. There were two more drawings, less detailed but obviously of the same boy. The last one was a close-up of a young, handsome face. Beneath it was the word "Henry."

"It's you, isn't it? I recognize it from pictures and photos of you as a kid growing up."

Henry swallowed hard and caught his breath, no longer aware of the dust from the basement tickling his nose or making him want to scratch his eyes. He didn't feel the dryness anymore. He touched the lines on the page, feeling the pencil marks, the texture of the graphite smoothed out to define shadow and light. He took the small sketchbook from his son and turned the page. Pressed in it were cherry blossoms, old and dried, brown and brittle. Pieces of something that had once been so completely alive.

The years had been unkind.

Henry closed the sketchbook and looked at his son, nodding.

"I found something!" Samantha had gone back to work in the boxes where the sketchbooks had been found. "It's a record!" She pulled out a dingy white record sleeve; its size was odd by contemporary standards. It was an old 78. Samantha handed it to him. It was twice as heavy as today's records; still, he felt it give. He didn't even have to take the old record out to know it was broken in half. Henry opened the sleeve and saw the two halves bend, held together by the record label. A few splintered pieces settled in the bottom of the sleeve. He carefully slipped out the record, which otherwise looked shiny and brand-new. No scratches on the surface, and the thick grooves were free from dust. He rested it, slightly bent, in his palm. As it reflected in the light, he could make out fingerprints at the edges of the vinyl. Small fingerprints. Henry placed his fingers over them, sizing them up; then his hand drifted across the label, which read "Oscar Holden & the Midnight Blue, The Alley Cat Strut."

Henry breathed a sigh of quiet relief and sat down on an old milk crate. Like so many things Henry had wanted in life—like his father, his marriage, his life—it had arrived a little damaged. Imperfect. But he didn't care, this was all he'd wanted. Something to hope for, and he'd found it. It didn't matter what condition it was in.

Uwajimaya
(1986)

Henry and Marty leaned against the hood of his son's Honda in the parking lot of the Uwajimaya grocery store. Samantha had gone inside to pick up a few things—she insisted on making dinner for all of them, a Chinese dinner. Why, or what she might be trying to prove, Henry couldn't ascertain, and honestly, he didn't care. She could have made huevos rancheros or coq au vin and he'd have been fine with it. He had been so anxious about what might be found in the basement of the Panama Hotel that he'd skipped lunch completely. Now it was nearing dinnertime and he was excited, emotionally exhausted . . . and famished.

"I'm sorry you found your Holy Grail and it was all damaged like that." Marty tried his best to console his father, who was actually in terrific spirits, despite his son's perceptions of the day.

"I found it, that was all that mattered. I don't care what condition—"

"Yeah, but you can't play it," Marty interrupted. "And in that condition it's not worth anything, the collectible value is nil."

Henry thought about it for a moment, casually looking at his watch as they waited for Samantha to return. "Worth is determined only by the market, and the market will never determine that—because I would *never* sell it, even if it were in mint condition. This is something I've wanted to find off and on for years. Decades. Now I have it. I'd rather have found something broken than have it lost to me forever."

Marty screwed a smile on his face. "Sort of like, 'Better to have loved and lost than never to have loved—' "

" 'At all,' " Henry finished. "Something like that. Not quite as much of a Hallmark moment as how you put it, but you're in the same zip code."

He and Marty had searched through the rest of the trunks and boxes near where they had found the sketchbooks and the old record, but none were clearly marked. He did find several loose name tags, including one that read "Okabe," but it had settled atop a pile of magazines. A mouse or rat had probably confiscated the twine from the hangtags long ago. Most of the nearby cases contained art supplies. Most likely Keiko's or her mother's. When he had more time, Henry planned to go back and see what else he could find. But for now, he had found exactly what he wanted.

"So are you going to explain that box in the backseat then?" Marty asked, pointing to the small wooden crate of sketchbooks in the back of his Honda Accord.

Ms. Pettison had let Henry take the collection of Keiko's sketchbooks and drawings, temporarily, after he showed her the illustrations with his name inside. She asked only that he bring them back later to be cataloged with the rest of the belongings and allow a historian to photograph them. Oscar Holden's old vinyl 78 managed to find its way into the box as well, somewhat unnoticed. But the old jazz record was broken and not worth anything anyway, right? Henry felt guilty nonetheless, though Marty convinced him that some rules were worth bending.

Henry leaned on the hood of the car, making sure it wouldn't dent or buckle, then got comfortable. "Those books belonged to my best friend—when I was just a boy during *the war years*."

"A Japanese friend, I take it?" Marty asked, but his question was more of a declarative.

Henry raised his eyebrows and nodded, noticing the knowing look on his son's face. Marty's eyes glimmered with a hint of sadness and regret. Henry was unsure why that was.

"Yay Yay must have flipped his lid when he found out," Marty said.

Henry always marveled at how his son stood with his feet planted firmly in two worlds. One, traditional Chinese; the other, contemporary American. Modern even. Running a computer bulletin board for the chemistry program at Seattle University but still calling his grandfather by the traditional Chinese honorific Yay Yay (and Yin Yin for his grandmother). Then again, his grandmother had always sent Marty letters in college addressed to "Master Martin Lee"; the formalities seemed to work both ways.

"Oh, your grandfather was busy at the time, fighting the war on two fronts, in America and back in China." *But yes, you don't know the half of it.*

"What was he like—your friend? How did you meet?"

"She."

"Who?"

"He was a *she.* Her name was Keiko. We met as the only two Asian children sent to an all-white prep school—this was during the height of the war, you know. Each of our parents wanting us to grow up *American,* and as quickly as possible."

Henry smiled, on the inside anyway, as his son popped up off the hood, turned around, tried to speak—then turned around again. "Let me get this straight. Your best *friend* was a Japanese girl while you were living under Yay Yay's one-man Cultural Revolution at home? I mean—" Henry watched his son grasping for the words, stunned, gape-mouthed at his father's revelation. "Was she like . . . a girlfriend? I mean, this is not the most comforting discussion to have with one's own father, but I have to know. I mean, weren't you practically in an arranged marriage? That's how you made it sound whenever you mentioned how you and mom met."

Henry looked up and down South King. There were people of every walk of life strolling the boulevard—all kinds of races. Chinese and Japanese, but also Vietnamese, Laotian, Korean, and of course, plenty of Caucasian. As well as a mix of *hapa,* as they say in the Pacific Islands, meaning "half." People who were a little bit of everything. "We were very young," he said. "Dating was not like it is today."

"So she was . . . someone·*special* . . ."

Henry didn't answer. So much time had passed, and he didn't know how to explain it in a way his son would understand. Especially now that he had met Samantha. In Henry's day, it was common to meet a girl's parents before you started dating her, rather than the other way around. And dating was more like courting, and courting leads to . . .

"Did Mom know about all this?"

Henry felt the Ethel-shaped hole in his heart grow a little emptier, a little colder. He missed her terribly. "A little. But when I married your mother, I never looked back."

"Pops, you've been full of surprises lately. I mean, big, perception-altering surprises. I'm stunned. I mean, this whole time—us looking for the record. Was it really about the record, or were you looking for memories of Keiko, of your long-lost *friend*?"

Henry felt a little awkward as his son said the word *friend* in a way that insinuated more. But she *was* more than a friend, wasn't she?

"It started with the record, the one I always wanted to find again," Henry said, not sure if that was entirely true. "I wanted it for someone. Sort of a dying wish for a long-lost brother. I vaguely remembered her stuff had been put there, but I'd just assumed it had been recovered or claimed decades earlier. I never dreamed it would *still* be there, right under my nose. I walked by that hotel off and on for years and years, never knowing. Then they start bringing up all that stuff—that bamboo parasol. All those things left behind. I had no idea what I'd find. But I'm grateful for the sketchbooks. The memories."

"Wait a minute," Marty stopped him. "One, you're an only child, and two, you just said you'd never sell that record, no matter what shape it was in."

"I didn't say I wouldn't *give* it away—especially to an old friend—"

"I'm ba-ack." Samantha appeared, heavy plastic shopping bags dangling from each arm. Henry took a few, and Marty took the others. "You're in for a treat this evening. I'm making my special black-bean crab." She reached in and pulled out a wrapped bundle that looked from the size of it like fresh Dungeness crab. "I'm also making *choy sum* with spiced oyster sauce."

Two of Henry's favorites. He was famished—now he was famished *and* impressed.

"I even got a little green-tea ice cream for dessert."

Marty's face was frozen in a polite grimace. Henry smiled and was grateful for such a kind and thoughtful future daughter-in-law, even if she didn't know the ice cream was Japanese. It didn't matter. He'd learned long ago: perfection isn't what families are all about.

Camp Harmony
(1942)

Henry pretended he was sick the next day, even refusing to eat. But he knew he could fool his mother only so long, if he was fooling her at all. He probably wasn't; she was just kind enough to go along with his manufactured symptoms. As well as the excuse he'd employed to explain away his black eye and bruised cheek, courtesy of Chaz. Henry had told her they were from "bumping" into someone in the crowded streets. He hadn't elaborated further. The ruse was effective only if his mother was a willing accomplice, and he didn't want to push his luck.

So on Thursday, Henry did what he'd been dreading all week. He started preparing to go back to school, back to Mrs. Walker's sixth-grade class. Alone.

At the breakfast table, Henry's mother didn't ask if he was feeling better. She knew. His father ate a bowl of jook and read the newspaper, fretting over a string of Japanese victories at Bataan, Burma, and the Solomon Islands.

Henry stared at him but didn't say a word. Even if he'd been allowed to speak to his father in Cantonese, he wouldn't have said a thing. He wanted to blame him for Keiko's family being taken away. To blame him for doing nothing. But in the end, he didn't know what to blame him for. For not caring? How could he blame his own father, when no one else seemed to care either?

His father must have felt his stare. He set his newspaper down and looked at Henry, who stared back, not blinking.

"I have something for you." His father reached in his shirt pocket and drew out a button. This one read "I'm an American," in red, white, and blue block lettering. He handed it to Henry, who glared and refused to take it. His father calmly set the new button on the table.

"Your father wants you to wear this. Better now that the Japanese are being evacuated from Seattle," his mother said, dishing up a bowl of the sticky, plain-tasting rice soup, placing it hot and steaming in front of Henry.

There was that word again. *Evacuated.* Even when his mother said it in Cantonese, it didn't make sense. Evacuated from what? Keiko had been taken from him.

Henry snatched the button in his fist and grabbed his book bag, storming out the door. He left the steaming bowl of soup untouched. He didn't even say good-bye.

On the way to school, the other kids heading to the Chinese school didn't tease him as they walked by. The look on his face must have carried a warning. Or maybe they too were shocked into silence by the empty, boarded-up buildings of Nihonmachi a few blocks over.

A few blocks from home, Henry found the nearest trash can and threw his new button on the heap of overflowing garbage—broken bottles that couldn't be recycled for the war effort and hand-painted signs that forty-eight hours earlier were held up by cheering crowds in favor of the evacuation.

At school that day, Mrs. Walker was absent, so they had a substitute, Mr. Deacons. The other kids seemed too preoccupied with how much they could get away with as the new teacher stumbled through the day's assignments and left Henry alone in the back of the classroom. He felt as if he might disappear. And maybe he had. No one called on him. No one said a word, and he was grateful.

The cafeteria, though, was an entirely different affair. Mrs. Beatty seemed genuinely annoyed that Keiko was gone. Henry wasn't sure if her disappointment was because of the unjust circumstances of his friend's sudden departure or simply because the lunch lady had to help out more with the kitchen cleanup. She cursed under her breath as she brought out the last pan of the day's lunch meat, calling it "chicken katsu-retsu." Henry wasn't sure what that meant, but it looked like Japanese food. American Japanese food anyway. Breaded chicken cutlets in a brown gravy. Lunch actually looked good. Smelled good too. "Let 'em try that, see what they have to say about it" was all she grumbled before she wandered off with her cigarettes.

If Henry's fellow grade-schoolers knew that the main course at lunch was Japanese food, they didn't notice and didn't seem to mind. But the irony hit Henry like a hammer. He smiled, realizing there was more to Mrs. Beatty than met the eye.

The other kids, though, they weren't full of such surprises.

"Look, they forgot one!" A group of fourth graders taunted as he dished their lunches. "Someone call the army; one got away!"

Henry didn't have his button. Not the old one. Or the new one. Neither would have mattered. How many more days? he thought. Sheldon said the war wouldn't go on forever. How many more days of this do I have to put up with?

Like a prayer being answered by a cruel and vengeful god, Chaz appeared, sliding his tray in front of Henry. "They take your girlfriend away, Henry? Maybe now you'll learn not to frater . . . fraten . . . *not to hang out with the enemy*. Dirty, backstabbing Jap—she probably was poisoning our food."

Henry scooped up a heaping spoonful of chicken and gravy, cocking his arm, eyeing Chaz's bony, apelike forehead. That was when he felt thick, sausage fingers wrap around his forearm, holding him back. He looked up, and Mrs. Beatty was standing behind him. She took the serving spoon from his hand and eyeballed Chaz. "Beat it. There's not enough food left," she said.

"What do you mean? There's plenty—"

"Kitchen's closed to you today. Scram!"

Henry looked up and saw what he could only describe as Mrs. Beatty's war face. A hard look, like the one you'd see in those Movietone newsreels of soldiers in training, that stony expression of someone whose occupation is killing and maiming.

Chaz looked like a puppy that had been caught making a mess and had just had his nose rubbed in it—slinking off with an empty tray, shoving a little kid out of the way.

"I never liked him anyways," Mrs. Beatty said as Henry went back to serving the last few kids in line, who looked delighted to see the school bully taken down a peg. "You want to make some money Saturday?" the stout lunch lady asked.

"Who? Me?" Henry asked.

"Yeah, you. You got other work you got to do on Saturday?"

Henry shook his head no, partly confused and scared of the tanklike woman who had just left tread marks on the seat of Chaz's dungarees.

"I've been asked to help set up a mess hall—as a civilian contractor for the army—and I could use someone that works hard and knows how I like things done." She looked at Henry, who wasn't sure what he was hearing. "You got a problem with that?"

"No," he said. And he didn't. She cooked, Henry set up and served, he broke down and cleaned. It was hard work, but he was used to it. And as hard as she made him work here in the school kitchen, she had never said a mean word to Henry. Of course, she'd never said a kind word either.

"Good. Meet me here at nine o'clock Saturday morning. And don't be late. I can pay you ten cents an hour."

Money was money, Henry thought, still stunned from seeing Chaz walk away with his tail between his legs. "Where are we going to work?"

"Camp Harmony—it's at the Puyallup Fairgrounds near Tacoma. I've got a feeling you've heard of it." She stared at Henry, her face as stonelike as ever.

Henry knew exactly where it was. He'd gone home and found it on a map. I'll be there, Saturday morning, nine o'clock sharp, wouldn't miss it for the world, he wanted to say, but "Thank you" were the only words Henry could muster.

If Mrs. Beatty knew how much this meant to him, she didn't let it show. "There they are . . ." She grabbed a book of matches and headed out back again with her lunch. "Call me when you're all done in here."

When Saturday came, Henry had one goal. One mission. Find Keiko. After that, who knew? He'd figure that out later.

Henry wasn't quite sure what to make of Mrs. Beatty's offer, but he didn't dare to question it either. She was an intimidating mountain of a woman—and a person of few words. Still, he was grateful. He told his parents she was paying him to help out in the kitchen on Saturdays. His story wasn't quite the truth, but it wasn't a lie either. He would be helping her in the kitchen—at Camp Harmony, about forty miles to the south.

Henry was sitting on the stoop outside the kitchen when Mrs. Beatty drove up in a red Plymouth pickup truck. It looked like the old rambler had been recently washed, but its enormous whitewall tires were splattered with mud from the wet streets.

Mrs. Beatty threw a cigarette butt into the nearest puddle, watching it fizzle. "Get in," she snapped as she rolled the window up, the entire truck rocking with the motion of her meaty arm.

Good morning to you too, Henry thought as he walked around the front of the truck, hoping she meant the passenger seat and not the back. When he peered into the bed of the pickup, all he could make out were boxlike shapes hidden beneath a canvas tarp and tied down with a heavy rope. Henry popped onto the seat. His parents didn't own a car, although they had finally saved up enough to buy one. With gasoline rationing, buying one now didn't make any sense, according to Henry's father anyway. Instead, they took the transit coach, or the bus. On rare occasions they would catch a ride with his auntie King, but that was usually if they were going to a family affair—a wedding, a funeral, or the golden birthday or anniversary of some old relative. Being in a car always felt so modern and exciting. It didn't even matter where they were going, or how long it took to get there—it always made his heart race, like today. Or was that just the thought of seeing Keiko?

"I'm not paying you for travel time."

Henry wasn't sure if that was a statement or a question. "That's fine," he answered. I'm happy just to go. *I'd do it for free, in fact.*

"The army doesn't pay me for miles, just tops off my gas tank each way."

Henry nodded as if this all somehow made sense. Mrs. Beatty was somehow employed in the mess hall, a part-time assignment as far as Henry could tell.

"Were you in the army?" Henry asked.

"Merchant Marines. Daddy was, anyway, even before it was officially called that by the Maritime Commission. He was head cook on the SS *City of Flint*—I'd help out whenever he was in port. Procurement lists, menu planning, prep and storage. I even spent two months onboard during a run to Hawaii. He used to call me his 'little shadow.' "

Henry couldn't imagine Mrs. Beatty as a little *anything*.

"I got so good at it, he'd call me to help out whenever his old ship was in port—put me to work for a few days here and there. His best friend, the ship's steward—he's practically my uncle, you'd like him—he's Chinese too. That's the way it is on those ships, all the cooks are either colored or Chinese, I suppose."

That caught Henry's attention. "Do you see them much?"

Mrs. Beatty chewed on her lip for a moment, staring ahead. "He used to send me postcards from Australia. New Guinea. Places like that. I don't get them anymore." There was a tremor of sadness in her voice. "Daddy's old ship was captured by the Germans two and a half years ago. Got a photo of him from the Red Cross in some POW camp, a few letters at first, but haven't heard from him in over a year."

I'm so sorry, Henry thought but didn't say. Mrs. Beatty had a way of having one-sided conversations, and he was used to being on the quiet end.

She cleared her throat, puffing out her cheeks. Then she tossed a half-smoked cigarette out the window and lit another. "Anyway, someone down here knew I was handy at cooking for a whole herd, and could portion-control for feeding kids too, so they gave me a call and I couldn't find it in me to say no." She looked at Henry like it somehow was his fault. "So, here we are."

And there they were. In Mrs. Beatty's pickup, bouncing down the highway, past dusty miles of tilled farmland south of Tacoma. Henry wondered about Mrs. Beatty and her missing father as he stared at fields of cows and draft horses, larger and more muscular than he had ever seen. These were real working farms, not the victory gardens in front yards and corner lots of homes in Seattle.

Henry had no idea what to expect. Would it be like where Mrs. Beatty's father was being held? It couldn't be that bad. He'd heard Camp Harmony was a temporary place, just until the army could figure out how and where to build more permanent camps farther inland. *Perma-*

nent. He didn't like the sound of that word. Still, they kept calling it a "camp"—which sounded nice in a way that even Henry knew was probably false. But, the beautiful scenery and countryside managed to get his hopes up. He'd never been to a summer camp but had seen a picture once in *Boys' Life* magazine—of cabins by a beautiful glass lake at sunset. Of campfires and fishing. People smiling, carefree, and having fun.

Nothing at all like the quaint town of Puyallup, a small farming community surrounded by lush acres of daffodils. Greenhouses dotted vast yellow fields and snowcapped Mount Rainier dominated the horizon. As they cruised down the main boulevard, past rows of Craftsman homes toward Pioneer Park, signs in many shopwindows read "Go Home Japs!" The signs were grim reminders that Camp Harmony was no summer camp. And no one would be going home any time soon.

Henry rolled down the window and was hit by the pungent smell of fresh horse manure, or was it from cows? Was there really a whiff of difference? The ripe stench could have been goat or chicken for all he could tell. Either way, it sure smelled a long way from the crisp, salty air of Seattle.

Near the heart of Puyallup they peeled into a wide expanse of gravel parking. Henry looked in awe at the long stables and outbuildings surrounding the Washington State Fairgrounds. By the giant grain silos, he could tell this was definitely farm country. He'd never been to the fair, and the whole place was larger than he'd ever imagined. The fairground area was probably as large as, if not larger than, Chinatown itself.

There was a big wooden stadium in need of a fresh coat of paint and what appeared to be a rodeo or livestock pavilion of some kind. Behind that was an open expanse with hundreds of chicken coops in neat little rows. The whole area was surrounded by a barbed-wire fence.

Then he saw people walking in and out of those tiny buildings. With dark hair and olive skin. And he noticed the towers near the fence line. Even from a distance he could see the soldiers and their machine guns. Their dormant searchlights were aiming at the barren ground below. Henry didn't even need to see the sign above the barbed-wire guard gate. This was Camp Harmony.

. . .

Henry had never been to jail. The one time he'd gone to City Hall with his father to pick up a meeting permit, the serious nature of the place had spooked him. The marble facade, the cold granite tiles on the floor. Everything had a weight to it that was inspiring and intimidating at the same time.

Henry felt that way again as they drove inside a holding pen between two large metal gates. Both were covered with new barbed wire and a row of springy coil with jutting points that looked as sharp as kitchen knives. Henry sat stiff—terrified was more like it. He didn't move as the army MP came to the window to check Mrs. Beatty's papers. Henry didn't even move to make sure his "I am Chinese" button was clearly visible. This is a place where someone like me goes in but doesn't come out, he thought. Just another Japanese prisoner of war, even if I'm Chinese.

"Who's the kid?" the soldier asked. Henry looked at the man in uniform, who didn't look like a man at all—more of a boy really, with a fresh, pimply complexion. He didn't look thrilled to be stuck in a place like this either.

"He's a kitchen helper." If Mrs. Beatty was worried about Henry getting into Camp Harmony, her concern didn't show. "I brought him to be a runner, help switch out serving trays, stuff like that."

"You got papers?"

This is where they take me, Henry thought, looking at the barbed wire, wondering which chicken coop he'd be assigned to.

He watched as the barrel-chested lunch lady pulled out a small file of papers from beneath the driver's seat. "This is his school registration, showing him as a kitchen worker. And this is his shot record." She looked at Henry. "Everyone here had to have a typhoid shot first, but I checked and you're clear." Henry didn't understand completely, but he was suddenly grateful for being sent to that stupid school in the first place. Grateful to have been stuck *scholarshipping* in the kitchen all these months. Without having to work the kitchen, he'd never have made it this far—this close to Keiko.

The soldier and Mrs. Beatty argued for a moment, but the stronger man—or in this case, woman—won out, because the young soldier just waved her through to the next holding area, where other trucks were unloading.

Mrs. Beatty backed into a loading spot and set the parking brake. Henry stepped out into ankle-deep mud, which made hollow, sucking sounds as he stuck and unstuck each foot until he reached the row of two-by-four boards that had been set down as a makeshift walkway. Shaking the mud off as best he could and wiping his feet on the boards as he went, he followed Mrs. Beatty into the nearest building, his wet socks and shoes squishing with each step.

On the way, Henry could smell something cooking. Not something necessarily pleasant but *something*.

"Wait here," Mrs. Beatty said, entering the cookhouse. Moments later she reemerged with a uniformed clerk trailing behind as she untied the tarp to reveal boxes of shoyu, rice vinegar, and other Japanese cooking staples.

The two of them carried the supplies in, helped by Henry and a few young men in white aprons and caps—soldiers assigned to cooking duty. They set up in a mess hall that was maybe forty feet long, with rows and rows of tables and brown, dented folding chairs. The planks of the wooden floor were a tapestry of grease stains mottled by muddy boot prints. Henry was surprised at how comfortable he felt. The camp was intimidating, but the kitchen, the kitchen was home. He knew his way around.

He peeked under the lids of rows of steamer trays, twice as many as back at school. Evidently lunch had already been prepared. Henry stared at the wet piles, some brown, some gray—canned sausages, boiled potatoes, and dry stale bread—the greasy smell alone made him long for the food back at Rainier Elementary. At least the condiments that Mrs. Beatty had brought would help in some small way.

Henry watched as she and another young soldier went over papers and order forms of some kind. He'd been assigned to serve, along with another aproned soldier, who looked at Henry and did a double take. Was it Henry's age or his ethnicity that caused the young man in uniform to pause? It didn't matter; the soldier just shrugged and started serving. He was used to following orders, Henry supposed.

As the first of the Japanese prisoners were let in single file, their hair and clothing was dotted with rain. A few chatted eagerly with one another, although some scowled, and most frowned when they saw what Henry was putting on their plate. He felt like apologizing. As the chow line inched forward, Henry could see young children outside, playing in the mud as their parents waited.

"*Konichiwa . . . ,*" a young boy said as he slid his tray along the metal countertop in front of Henry's serving trays.

Henry just pointed to his button. Again and again. Each time, the person saying *hello* looked brightly hopeful, then disappointed, and later confused. Maybe that's a good thing. Maybe they'll talk about me. And maybe Keiko will know where to find me, Henry thought.

He was sure he'd see Keiko in line. As each young girl entered, his hopes rose and fell, his heart inflating and deflating like a balloon—but she never appeared.

"Do you know the Okabes? Keiko Okabe?" Henry asked occasionally. Mostly, he was met with looks of confusion, or mistrust; after all, the Chinese were Allies, fighting against Japan. But one older man smiled and nodded, chatting excitedly about something. What that something was, Henry couldn't tell, since the man spoke only Japanese. The old man might have known exactly where Keiko was, but he couldn't explain it in a way that helped at all.

So Henry kept serving, for two hours, from 11:30 to 1:30. Near the end of his shift he fidgeted, shifting his weight back and forth on the apple crate he was standing on to reach over the serving pans. In that time he never saw any sign of the Okabes. Not a glimmer.

He watched the crowds come in, some looking hopeful, but the food did away with their optimism as the reality of their environment must have been settling in. Even so, no one complained about the food, to him anyway, or to the young man serving next to him. Henry wondered how this white soldier must have felt, now that *he* was the minority in the lunchroom—but then again, he could leave when his shift was over. And he had a rifle with a long blade on the end.

"Let's go, we need to set up dinner in the next area." Mrs. Beatty appeared as he was breaking down the last of the serving dishes and collecting loose trays.

Henry was used to following orders in the kitchen. They drove to another section of Camp Harmony, which had fewer stock buildings and more shade trees and picnic areas that sat vacant. Mrs. Beatty's map showed an overview of the entire camp, which had been divided up into quarters—each with its own mess hall. There was still a chance to find Keiko, or three chances, as it were.

At the next mess hall, lunch had finished. Mrs. Beatty had him wash and wipe down trays while she coordinated with the kitchen manager on needed supplies and menu planning. "Just hang out if you get done early," she said. "Don't go wandering off unless you want to stay here for the rest of the war." Henry suspected that she wasn't joking and nodded politely, finishing his work.

By all accounts, the mess hall was off-limits to the Japanese when it wasn't mealtime. Most were restricted to their chicken shacks, although he did see people occasionally slogging through the mud to and from the latrine.

When he was done, Henry sat on the back step and watched smoke billowing from the stovepipes fitted into the roofs of the makeshift homes—the collective smoky mist filled the wet, gray sky above the camp. The smell of burning wood lingered in the air.

She's here. Somewhere. Among how many people? A thousand? Five thousand? Henry didn't know. He wanted to shout her name, or run door to door, but the guards in the towers didn't look like they took their jobs lightly. They stood watch, for the protection of the internees—so he'd been told. But if that were so, why were their guns pointed inside the camp?

It didn't matter. Henry felt better knowing he'd made it this far. There was still a chance he'd find her. Among the sad, shocked faces, maybe he'd find her smile again. But it was getting dark. Maybe it was too late.

Visiting Hours
(1942)

After seven restless days had passed, Henry repeated the process—starting with the same hopes. He met Mrs. Beatty on the back step of the school, and together they drove south to Puyallup and through the barbed-wire gates of Camp Harmony—this time into the third and fourth areas, which were even bigger. The last one included the livestock pavilions that had been converted into housing, one family to each stall, or so he'd been told.

Back at home, his parents were so proud of him. "You keep saving, you be able to pay your own way back to China," his father praised him in Cantonese. His mother simply nodded and smiled every time she saw him deposit the money he earned in a jelly jar on his nightstand. Henry didn't know what else to do with so much spending money in a time when sugar and shoe leather were being rationed. To spend it on penny candy and more comic books just seemed wasteful, especially at Camp Harmony, where there was so little of everything.

"More of the same today," Mrs. Beatty grunted, as she began unloading the Japanese sundries from the back of the truck. During the week Henry realized where they were coming from. She was ordering extra supplies from the school, then bringing them down to the camps, discreetly passing them out to the prisoners and their families. She was trading them for cigarettes that had been provisioned to each household. Whether she sold them or smoked them all herself, Henry never knew.

What Henry did know was that the fourth area held the most evacuees. This quadrant of the fairgrounds was the largest, with an enormous trophy barn that had been converted into a mess hall.

"Your parents okay with you working a few extra days when school lets out for vacation?" Mrs. Beatty asked, picking what was left of her breakfast from her teeth with a matchbook cover from the Ubangi Club.

"Yes, ma'am." Henry nodded eagerly. That was the one benefit of not being able to communicate with his parents. They would assume he had summer school, or extra work at Rainier Elementary—paying work. They asked all sorts of wild questions. Was he taking extra classes? Was he tutoring other kids? *Imagine, their son, a tutor of white kids!* Henry just smiled and nodded and let them assume what they wanted.

Another language barrier Henry ran into was within Camp Harmony. Just seeing a Chinese kid standing on an apple crate behind the serving counter was strange enough. But the more he questioned those who came through his chow line about the Okabes, the more frustrated he became. Few cared, and those who did never seemed to understand. Still, like a lost ship occasionally sending out an SOS, Henry kept peppering those he served with questions.

"Okabes? Does anyone know the Okabes?" To Henry it was a unique name, but really, there could be hundreds of people at the camp with that name. It might be like the name Smith or Lee.

"Why are you looking for the Okabes?" A voice came from somewhere in the crowded line. A man stepped up, tray in hand, sheepishly peering ahead. He was wearing a buttoned-up shirt that had once been white but now was the same color as the overcast sky. His trousers were wrinkled and muddy about the ankles. His messy hair was countered only by his close-cropped beard and mustache—the black yielding to a sprinkling of gray that made him look collegiate and dignified, despite his condition.

As Henry dished up the man's lunch, a stew of corn and boiled eggs, he recognized him. It was Keiko's father.

"Henry?" the older man said.

Henry nodded. "Would you like some stew?" Henry couldn't believe that was all he could think of to say. He felt ashamed for Mr. Okabe's circumstances, like walking into someone's home and seeing him in a state of undress. "How are you? How is your family—how is Keiko?"

Mr. Okabe ran his fingers through his hair, straightening it. He rubbed his beard, then broke into an enormous smile. "Henry! What are you doing here?" It was as if a layer of suffering that had hardened around him these past two weeks cracked and fell to dust. He reached across the serving counter and held Henry's arms, eyes sparkling with life. "I can't believe . . . I mean . . . how did you get here?"

Henry looked at the line forming behind Mr. Okabe. "Mrs. Beatty, the cafeteria lady at school, asked me to work with her for a while. In her own way, I think she's trying to help. I've been working my way through all the areas—trying to find you and Keiko. How is she, how have you all been?"

"Fine. Fine." Mr. Okabe smiled, seeming to forget all about the meager lunch Henry loaded on his plate, with extra bread. "This is the first vacation I've had in years. I just wish it were someplace sunny."

Henry knew that Mr. Okabe might get his wish. He'd heard the army was building permanent camps in Texas and Arizona. Hot, miserable places.

Mr. Okabe stepped out of the way to let the others inch forward in the chow line. Henry kept serving as they talked. "Where is Keiko, is she eating?"

"She's back with her mom and little brother, she's okay. Half of us in this area fell ill from food poisoning of some kind yesterday, including most of our family. But Keiko and I are doing fine now. She stayed back to help out, and I was going to give her my portion." Mr. Okabe warily looked at his food before regarding Henry again. "She misses you."

Now it was Henry's turn to light up. He didn't do backflips or cartwheels, but never in his entire life had he felt this good about anything.

"Do you know where the visitors' station is?" Mr. Okabe asked. The words rang like a pitch-perfect note on a beautifully tuned instrument. *Visitors?* He'd never even considered the possibility.

"There's a visiting area? Where?" The next man in line had to clear his throat, politely, to get Henry to keep serving.

"Out this door and left, toward the main gate on the west side of Area Four. It's a fenced-off area just inside the gate. You can probably get to the visitors' side if you go out the back of the building. When are you done here?"

Henry looked at the old army-surplus clock that hung on the wall above the front door. "In one hour . . ."

"I'll ask Keiko to meet you there." Mr. Okabe headed for the door. "I need to get back. Thank you, Henry."

"For what?"

"I'm just thanking you, in case I don't see you for a while."

Henry exhaled as he watched Mr. Okabe leave, waving as he slipped out the door holding his tray of food. The other people in line now viewed Henry as some sort of celebrity, or perhaps a confidant, smiling and saying hello in Japanese and English.

After lunch had been served and all the trays rounded up, cleaned, and put away, Henry found Mrs. Beatty, who was in a meeting with a young mess officer. As she had the previous week, she was planning out menus and arguing over whether to cook potatoes (which there were in abundance) or rice, which Mrs. Beatty insisted they order, even though it wasn't on their list. Henry figured they would be there awhile, and Mrs. Beatty's backhanded wave, dismissing him to the rear step of the mess hall, all but confirmed it.

Henry traced the dirt road to the nearest gate and followed the path between the two barbed-wire fences. This no-man's-land was actually a modestly trafficked walkway leading a few hundred yards to a latticed area designated for visitation with the prisoners (as they called themselves) or evacuees (as the army made a habit of calling them).

The path led to a seating area along the interior fence line, where a small procession of visitors came and went, chatting and sometimes crying as they held hands through the barbed wire separating the prisoners from those on the outside. A pair of soldiers in uniform sat at a makeshift desk on the prisoners' side, their rifles leaning against a fence post. They looked as bored as could be, playing cards, stopping occasionally to inspect letters that were being handed out or whatever care packages were being delivered.

Because he'd been working inside the camp, Henry could have walked right up to the soldiers at the desk from the mess hall, but the fear of straying too far and being mistaken for a resident of Camp Harmony was very real. That was why Mrs. Beatty had him hang out behind the mess hall, either on the steps where the kitchen workers knew who he was or in her truck when they were preparing to leave. Even with his special access, it seemed safer to go about visiting the camp's residents the proper way, if only to keep Mrs. Beatty happy so she'd continue bringing him with her.

Henry stood at the fence, tapping the wire with a stick, unsure if it was electrified—he was certain it wasn't, but was wary nonetheless. To his surprise, the soldiers didn't even seem to notice him there. Then again, they were busy arguing with a pair of women from a local Baptist church who were trying to deliver a Japanese Bible to an elderly internee, a woman who looked ancient to Henry.

"Nothing printed in Japanese is allowed!" one of the soldiers argued.

The women showed him their crosses and tried to hand the young soldiers pamphlets of some kind. They refused.

"If I can't read it in *God's* plain English, it ain't coming into the camp," Henry overheard one of the soldiers say. The women said something to the Japanese lady in her native tongue. Then they touched hands and waved their good-byes. The Bible left the camp the way it came, and the old woman retreated empty-handed. The soldiers went back to their card game.

Henry watched and waited until he saw a beautiful slip of a girl walk up the muddy path in a faded yellow dress, red galoshes covered in mud, and a brown raincoat. She stood on the other side of the fence, her smiling face, pale from food poisoning, framed by cold metal and sharp wire. A captured butterfly. Henry smiled and exhaled slowly.

"I had a dream about you last week," Keiko said, looking relieved but happy, and even a little confused. "I keep thinking, this must still be a dream."

Henry looked along the fence, then back at Keiko, touching the metal points between them. "This *is* real. I'd rather have the dream too."

"It was a nice dream. Oscar Holden was playing. And we were dancing—"

"I don't know how to dance," Henry protested.

"You knew how to dance in *my* dream. We were dancing in some club, with all kinds of people, and the music—it was the song he played for us.

The song from the record we bought. But it was slower somehow . . . we were slower."

"That's a nice dream." Henry felt it as much as she did.

"I think about that dream. I think about it so much I dream it during the day, while I'm walking around the dirty camp, walking back and forth to the infirmary to help the old people and the sick with my mom. I dream it all the time. Not just at night."

Henry rested his hands on the barbed-wire fence. "Maybe I'll dream it too."

"You don't have to, Henry. In here, I think my dream is big enough for the both of us."

Henry looked up at the nearby guard tower, with its menacing machine guns and sandbags to protect them. Protect them from what? "I'm sorry you're here," he said. "I didn't know what else to do after you left. So I just came here trying to find you. I still don't know what to do."

"There is something you can do—" Keiko touched the fence too, her hands on top of Henry's. "Can you bring us a few things? I don't have any paper or envelopes—no stamps either, but if you bring me some, I'll write to you. And could you bring us some fabric—any kind, just a few yards. We don't have any curtains, and the searchlights shine through our windows and keep us up at night."

"Anything, I'll do it—"

"And I have a special request."

Henry traced his thumbs over the backs of her soft hands, looking into her chestnut brown eyes through the jagged coils of fence.

"It's my birthday next week. Could you bring all that stuff back by then? We're going to have a record concert outside that day, right after dinner. Our neighbor traded with the soldiers for a record player, but they only have a scratchy Grand Ole Opry recording—something like that, and it's terrible. The soldiers are going to let us have a record concert, outdoors, if the weather clears up. They might even play the music for us through the loudspeakers. And I'd really like to have a visit on my birthday. We can sit right here and listen."

"What day is your birthday?" he asked. Henry knew she was a few months older than he was but had completely forgotten her birthday in the confusion of recent events.

"It's actually a week from tomorrow, but we're trying to have our first camp social, something to make this more of a camp, and less of a prison. Next Saturday is the day they've proposed for the record concert, so we'll just celebrate it then."

"Do you have the record we bought?" Henry asked.

Keiko shook her head, biting her lip.

"Where is it?" Henry asked, remembering the empty streets of Nihonmachi, the rows of boarded-up buildings.

"It's probably in the basement of the Panama Hotel. There's a lot of stuff there. It's where Dad put some of the things we couldn't fit in our suitcases, things we didn't want to sell either—personal things. But it was being boarded up as we left. I'm sure it's shuttered now. You'll never get in, and if you do, I don't know if you could ever find it. There's so much."

Henry thought about the old hotel. The last he recalled the ground floor had been boarded up completely. The windows on the upper floors—the ones left uncovered—had all been broken by rocks thrown by kids below in the days since the evacuation. "That's okay. I'll get what I can and bring it back next Saturday."

"Same time?"

"Later. Next week we're back here in Area Four, helping with dinner, but I can meet you here afterward, around six. I'll probably see you at dinner if you come through my line."

"I'll be here. Where am I going to go?" She looked around, eyeing the long stretch of barbed wire, then glanced down, seemingly noticing how muddy she was. Then she reached in her pocket. "I have something for you."

Henry reluctantly let go of her other hand as she pulled out a small bundle of dandelions, tied with a ribbon. "These grow between the floorboards of our house. Not really a floor, just wooden planks spread out on the dirt. My mom thought it was horrible to have all these weeds growing at our feet, but I like them. They're the only flowers that grow here. I picked them for you." She handed them to Henry through a gap beneath the wire.

"I'm sorry," Henry said; he suddenly felt foolish having come empty-handed. "I didn't bring you anything."

"That's okay. It's enough that you came. I knew you would. Maybe it was my dream. Maybe I was just wishing it. But I knew you'd find me." Keiko looked at Henry, then took a deep breath. "Does your family know you're here?" she asked.

"They don't know," Henry confessed, ashamed of his mother's ambivalence and his father's joyfulness. "I'm sorry I didn't tell them. I couldn't . . . they'd never let me come. I *hate* my father, he's—"

"That's okay, Henry, it doesn't matter."

"I—"

"It's okay. I wouldn't want my son coming to a prison camp either."

Henry turned his hands upward, feeling Keiko rest hers in his as they both felt the sharp metal of the wire sway between them, unyielding. Looking down, he noticed there was dried mud beneath her fingernails. She saw it too, curling her fingers in, then looking up to meet Henry's eyes.

The moment, for what it was, ended abruptly as Henry heard honking in the distance. It was Mrs. Beatty in her truck, waving him back. Evidently she suspected where she might find him.

"I have to go. I'll be back next week, okay?" Henry said.

Keiko nodded, swallowing her tears but finding a smile. "I'll be here."

Home Again
(1942)

Henry woke up Sunday morning feeling like a new man, even if he was only twelve—going on thirteen, actually. He'd found Keiko. He'd seen her face-to-face. And somehow, just knowing where she was became a comfort, even if that place was a mud-soaked prison camp.

Now all he had to do was find a few items to bring back to Camp Harmony by next Saturday. But what about the Oscar Holden record? That'd be a nice birthday gift, he thought. If he could find it.

In the kitchen Henry found his father, still in his robe, poring over a map of China from a *National Geographic* magazine he used to keep track of the war. His father had pasted it to a corkboard with small sewing pins stuck here and there to indicate major battles—blue for victories and red for defeats. There were several new blue pins. Still, Father was shaking his head.

"Good morning," Henry said.

"Jou san," Henry's father replied, tapping a spot on the map with his worn fingernail. He kept muttering a phrase in Cantonese that Henry didn't understand, *"Sanguang Zhengce,"* over and over again.

"What does that mean?" Henry asked. It sounded like "three lights."

He and his father had settled into a pattern of noncommunication months ago. Henry knew when his father was lamenting something; all he had to do was ask a question. Even if it were in English, if the tone sounded *like* a question, Henry would get an explanation of some kind.

"It means 'three tiny lights'—it's a joke," Father said in Cantonese. "The Japanese call it 'three fires.' They call it 'Kill All. Burn All. Loot All.'"

They closed the Burma Road, but since the bombings at Pearl Harbor, we're finally getting supplies, from the Americans."

Aren't *you* an American? Henry thought. Aren't we Americans? Aren't they getting supplies from *us*?

Henry's father kept talking, whether to himself or his son, Henry couldn't be sure. "Not just supplies. Planes. The Flying Tigers are helping Chiang Kai-shek and the nationalist army defeat the Japanese Imperial invaders—but they're destroying everything now. The Japanese are killing civilians, torturing thousands, burning cities."

Henry saw the conflict in his father's eyes, in how he stared at the map, happy and sad. Victorious and defeated.

"There's good news for us, though. Hong Kong is secure. The Japanese have been contained in the north for months. Next school year, you can go to Canton."

He said it like it was a birthday, Christmas, and Chinese New Year's all rolled into one. Like this would be welcome news. His father had spent most of his school years in China, finishing his education. An expected rite of passage. Sending their children to stay with relatives to attend Chinese school was what most families—traditional Chinese families like Henry's—did.

"What about my scholarship to Rainier? What about just going to the Chinese school on King Street, like the other kids? What if I don't want to go?" Henry said the words, knowing his father would understand only a few: *scholarship, Rainier, King Street.*

"Hah?" his father asked. "No, no, no—back to *Canton.*"

The thought of going to China was terrifying. It was a foreign country to Henry. One without jazz music or comic books—or Keiko. He envisioned staying at his uncle's house, which was probably more of a shack, and being teased by the locals for not being Chinese enough. The opposite of here, where he wasn't American enough. He didn't know which was worse. It made Keiko's situation, while bleak, seem so much more appealing. Henry caught himself feeling a twinge of jealousy. At least she was with her family. For now anyway. At least they understood. At least they wouldn't send *her* away.

Before Henry could press his bilingual argument, his mother appeared from the kitchen and handed him a shopping list and a few dollars. She often sent him to the market when there was only a little buying to be done, especially since Henry seemed to have a knack for negotiating bargains. He took the note and a steamed pork bau for breakfast on the way and headed down the stairs and out into the cold morning air, relieved to get away for a while.

Walking down South King toward Seventh Avenue and the Chinese marketplace, Henry thought of what to get Keiko for her birthday—aside from paper for writing, fabric for curtains, and the Oscar Holden record, which he was bound and determined to find. The first two items would be easy. He could pick up stationery and fabric at Woolworth's on Third Avenue any time during the week. And he knew where the record was. But what would she want for a birthday present? What could he buy that would make a difference in the camp? He'd saved all his money from working with Mrs. Beatty. What could he buy? Maybe a new sketchbook or a set of watercolors? Yes, the more he thought about it, art supplies would be perfect.

How he'd actually *get* the record, though, that question remained unanswered as he walked past the marketplace and into Nihonmachi. Two blocks over on South Main, he stood before the boarded-up facade of the Panama Hotel. There was no way in—it would take a crowbar and more muscle than rested on Henry's small shoulders. And once he made his way in, where would it be?

He had the money—why not buy a new one? That made more sense than trying to break his way into the old hotel. But that too seemed fruitless as he walked from Nihonmachi toward downtown and the Rhodes Department Store. He had doubts about whether they'd sell it to him, especially after all the trouble he and Keiko had gone through the first time. Those doubts were magnified when he walked past the Admiral Theater. The marquee featured a new movie called *Little Tokyo, U.S.A.,* which piqued his curiosity yet made Henry wary and nervous.

The publicity photos were of big Hollywood stars—Harold Huber and June Duprez, made up to look Japanese. They were playing spies and conspirators who'd helped plot the bombing of Pearl Harbor. Judging from all the torn ticket stubs and cigarette butts that dotted the damp sidewalk, the movie was a hit.

Rhodes was out of the question. Henry wasn't trusted in these parts of town. And the Black Elks Club was still closed down—no hope of going to the source, Oscar Holden himself, to buy a new record. Henry kicked a can on the sidewalk, his stomach knotted in frustration.

Maybe Sheldon?

Henry zigzagged back in the direction of South Jackson, where Sheldon sometimes played on Sunday afternoons; usually when there was a new ship in town, bringing restless sailors and their dates to the neighborhood.

His walk back took him past the Panama Hotel again. The massive marble entrance that he was never allowed to enter was now boarded up. Henry looked at the shopping list his mother had given him. He probably had another thirty minutes before his parents would worry about him being late.

Thinking there must be a back way in, Henry slipped down the alley, behind the vacant and boarded-up Togo Employment Agency. The alley itself was piled with boxes and heaps of garbage, stacks of clothing and old shoes. Belongings that no one wanted, thrown out, but still here since the garbage service to this area had evidently been suspended. Behind the hotel, Henry looked for a freight entrance or a fire escape he could shimmy up to one of the many broken windows on the second floor.

Instead he found Chaz, Will Whitworth, and a small gathering of other boys trying to gain entrance too. They were looking and pointing at the second-story windows. Some threw rocks, while others pawed through the boxes left behind. One boy Henry didn't recognize had found a box of dishes and began throwing them against a brick wall, shattering them, pieces of fine porcelain china raining down.

Before Henry could yell, or run, or hide, they saw him. One, then all of them.

"It's a Jap!" one of the boys yelled. "Get him!"

"No, it's a Chink," Will said, stopping the boy for a moment as they all stalked in Henry's direction.

Chaz took control of the situation. "Henry!" Smiling, he seemed more happy than surprised. "Where's your girlfriend, Henry? She's not home if you're looking for her—and your nigger friend ain't around today, is he?" he taunted. "Better get used to me. My dad's going to buy all these buildings, so we might end up neighbors."

Henry's knees felt wobbly, but his jaw was clenched tighter than his fists. On a pile of garbage lay an old broom handle, almost as tall as Henry. He picked it up with both hands and gripped it like a baseball bat. He swung it once, then twice for good measure. It felt light and sturdy. Sturdy enough to hit a curveball the size of Chaz's head.

All of the boys stopped, except for Chaz, who inched closer to Henry, staying just out of range of his makeshift club.

"Go home, Chaz." The anger in his voice surprised Henry. He felt the blood drain away from his fists where they clenched the broom handle until his knuckles turned pale.

Chaz spoke softly, a mock gentleness to his voice. "This *is* my home, this is the United States of *America*—not the United States of Tokyo. And my dad is probably going to end up owning this whole neighborhood anyway. What are you going to do, take us all on? You think you can beat us all up?"

Henry knew he didn't stand a chance against all seven of them. "You might get to me eventually, but I know one of you'll be going home with a limp." Henry swung the club, smacking it on the dirty, gritty pavement between him and the larger boy. He vividly remembered the bruised cheek and black eye he'd received outside the train station, courtesy of Chaz.

The boys in the back hesitated. Retreating, they dropped the items they'd pilfered from the alley, then turned and fled around the corner. Henry swung fiercely at Chaz, who backed up too, looking pale and even a little scared. The spiked hair of his crew cut seemed to wilt. Without a word, Chaz spit on the ground between them and then walked away.

Henry held on to the broom handle, resting it on the pavement, his whole body shaking and his heart pounding. His legs felt limp. *I did it. I beat them. I stood up to them. I won.*

Henry turned around and walked face-first into a soldier, actually two soldiers—with army MP bands on their arms. Their rifles were slung across their shoulders, and each had a long black baton dangling from a short leather strap attached to his wrist. One of the soldiers looked down, poking Henry's chest with his baton, tapping his button.

Henry dropped the broom handle, which made a wooden, clattering sound on the pavement.

"No more looting, kid. I don't care who you are—beat it."

Henry backed up, then walked away as fast as his wobbly legs would carry him. Out on South Main, he hustled in the direction of Jackson, Sheldon's neighborhood. He saw the lights of a police car reflected in the wet pavement and the puddles he tried to avoid. Looking back, he saw Chaz and his friends sitting on the sidewalk being questioned by a police officer who had a notepad out and was busy writing something. It looked like the officer wasn't buying whatever excuse Chaz was stringing along. There had been too much vandalism and looting. And now he'd been caught in the act.

Dinner
(1986)

Much to Henry's surprise, Samantha was an incredible cook. Henry had a special affinity for anyone with talent in the kitchen, since he himself did most of the cooking in his own home. Even before Ethel fell ill, he had liked to cook. But after the cancer hit, all of the cooking—and the cleaning, the washing—everything fell to Henry. He didn't mind. She was in such pain, always sick, always suffering from the cancer or the radiation treatments that were designed to kill parts of her insides. Both ravaged her small, frail body. The least Henry could do was cook her favorite panfried noodles or make her fresh mango custard with mint. Even though near the end, as wonderful as it sounded, she'd had little appetite. It was all Henry could do to get her to drink fluids. And at the very end, she really just wanted to go, needed to go.

He thought of that, and fought off a wave of melancholy as his son offered a toast, raising his teacup of *heung jou,* a fermented wine that tasted more like grain alcohol.

"To a successful find, in the basement time capsule of the Panama Hotel."

Henry raised his glass but followed up with only a sip as Marty and Samantha downed their cups, wincing and grimacing at the strong, eye-watering taste.

"Geez, that burns," Marty groaned.

Smiling, Henry filled his son's cup again with the clear, innocent-looking liquid that could just as easily be used to strip the grease from used car parts.

"To Oscar Holden, and long-lost recordings," Samantha toasted.

"No. No. No. I'm done. I know my limit," Marty said, lowering her arm, grounding it once again to the round table in the corner of the small dining room that also functioned as Henry's living room. It was a quiet, reflective place, alive with potted plants, like the jade plant that Henry had nurtured since Marty was born. The walls were covered with family photos, colorful and bright against the once-white surface that now looked tarnished and yellow, darkened in the corners like coffee-stained teeth.

Henry looked at his son and the young woman he was obviously enchanted with. Holding their cups. Feeling the burn. How different they were. And how little it mattered. Their differences were unnoticeable. So alike, and so happy. Hard to tell where one person ended and the other began. Marty was happy. Successful, good grades, *and* happy. What more could any father want for his son?

And as Henry looked at the vast pile of crab shells and the empty platter of choy sum, he realized Samantha's cooking rivaled that of Ethel's in her heyday—even his own cooking. Marty had chosen well.

"Okay, who's ready for dessert?"

"I'm so full," Marty groaned, pushing his plate away.

"There's always room," Henry taunted as Samantha stepped into the kitchen and returned, bringing out a small platter.

"What's this?" Henry asked, stunned. He'd expected green-tea ice cream.

"I made this especially for my future father-in-law—the ice cream's for me. But this"—she set a plate of delicately spun white candies in front of Henry—"this is something for a special occasion. It's dragon's beard candy."

The last time Henry had had dragon's beard candy was long before Ethel got sick. As he bit into the thread-thin strands of sugar, wrapped around a filling of grated coconut and sesame seeds, he watched Marty smile, nodding in approval—as if to say, "See, Pops, I knew you'd like her."

It was delicious. "This takes years to learn to make, how did you . . ."

"I've been practicing," Samantha explained. "Sometimes you have to just go for it. Try for what's hardest to accomplish. Like you and your childhood sweetheart."

Henry choked a little on his dessert, tasting the sweet filling and clearing his throat. "I see my son's been sharing stories."

"He couldn't help it. And besides, haven't you ever wondered what happened to her? No disrespect to your wife, but this girl, whoever she may be, might still be out there somewhere. Aren't you curious where she is, where she might be?"

Henry looked at his cup of wine, then finished it in one slow pour. Biting back the sting and watery sensation it brought to his eyes, he felt his sinuses clearing as it burned. Setting the cup down, he looked at Samantha and Marty. Weighing their expressions, equal parts hope and wishful thinking.

"I have thought about her." Henry searched for the words, unsure of Marty's reaction. Knowing how much his son loved Ethel, not wanting to trample her memory. "I have thought about her." All the time. Right now, in fact. It would be wrong to tell you that, *wouldn't it*? "But that was a long time ago. People grow up. They marry, start families. Life goes on."

Henry had thought about Keiko off and on through the years—from a longing, to a quiet, somber acceptance, to sincerely wishing her the best, that she might be happy. That was when he realized that he did love her. More than what he'd felt all those years ago. He loved her enough to let her go—to not go dredging up the past. And besides, he had Ethel, who had been a loving wife. And of course, he had loved her as well. And when she fell ill, he would have changed places with her if he could. To see her get up and walk again, he'd gladly have lain down in that hospice bed. But in the end, he was the one who had to keep living.

When he saw those things coming up from the basement of the Panama Hotel, he had allowed himself to wonder and to wish. For an Oscar Holden record no one believed existed. And for evidence of a girl who'd once loved Henry for who he was, even though he was from the other side of the neighborhood.

Marty watched his father, deep in thought. "You know, Pops, you have her stuff, her sketchbooks anyway. I mean, even if she's married and all, I think she'd still appreciate getting those back. And if you were the one to give them to her, what a nice coincidence that might be."

"I have no idea where she is," Henry protested as his son filled his cup with more wine. "She might not even be alive. Forty years is a long time. And almost no one has claimed anything from the Panama. Almost no one. People didn't look back, and there was nothing to return to, so they moved on."

It was true. Henry knew it. And from the look on his face, Marty knew it too. But still, no one had thought the record still existed, and it was found. Who knew what else he might find if he looked hard enough?

Steps
(1986)

After dinner, Henry insisted on doing the dishes. Samantha had done a marvelous job. When Henry walked in, he half-expected to find take-out boxes from the Junbo Seafood Restaurant hidden beneath the sink or at least oyster-sauce-stained recipe books strewn about. Instead, the kitchen was neat and tidy—she'd washed the pans as she cooked, the way Henry did. He dried and put away what few dishes remained and put some serving platters in the sink to soak.

When he poked his head out to thank her, it was too late. She'd already kicked off her shoes and was asleep on the couch, snoring gently. Henry looked at the half-empty bottle of plum wine and smiled before covering her up with a green afghan Ethel had knitted. Ethel had always been crafty, but knitting had become a necessary pastime. It gave her something to do with her hands while she sat there during chemotherapy. Henry had been amazed that she could knit so well with an IV in her arm, but she didn't seem to mind.

Henry felt a draft and noticed the front door was open. He could see his son's silhouette behind the screen door. Moths flitted in the porch light, pinging against the bulb, helplessly drawn to something they could never have.

"Why don't you stay the night?" Henry asked, as he opened the screen door. He sat down next to Marty, waiting for an answer. "She's asleep, and it's too late to be out driving."

"Says who?" Marty snapped back.

Henry frowned a little. He knew his son hated it when he appeared to be bossing him around, even if the offer was genial. These were the times when he and Marty seemed to argue for the sake of arguing. And no one ever won.

"I'm just saying that it's late . . ."

"Sorry, Pops," Marty said, checking his reaction. "I think I'm just tired. This year has been a rough one." He palmed an unlit cigarette. Ethel had finally succumbed to the cancer when it spread to her lungs. Henry had quit smoking years ago, but Marty still struggled—having quit when his mother became ill but sneaking smokes now and then. Henry knew how guilty his son felt about smoking while his mom was dying of lung cancer.

Marty tossed the cigarette into the street. "I can't help thinking about Mom and how much things have changed the last few years."

Henry nodded, looking out across the sidewalk. He could see into the front window of his neighbors' house. Their TV was on, and they were watching a Hispanic variety show of some kind. *The neighborhood keeps changing*, Henry thought as he looked down the block past the Korean bakery and a dry cleaner run by a nice Armenian family.

"Can I ask you something, Pops?"

Henry nodded again.

"Did you keep Mom at home to spite me?"

Henry watched a low-ride pickup truck boom down the alleyway. "What do you think?" he asked, knowing the answer but surprised that his son would ask such a direct question.

Marty stood up and walked to the cigarette he'd tossed into the street. Henry thought he might pick up the dirty cigarette and light it. Instead Marty stepped on it, grinding it to pieces. "I used to think that. It didn't make sense to me, you know? I mean, this isn't exactly a plush neighborhood—we could have put her someplace with a view, with a rec room." Marty shook his head. "I think I get it now. It doesn't matter how *nice* home is—it just matters that it *feels* like home."

Henry listened to the booming truck in the distance.

"Did Yay Yay know about Keiko?" Marty asked. "Did Mom know?"

Henry stretched and sat back. "Your grandfather knew, because I told him." He looked at his son, trying to gauge his reaction. "He stopped talking to me after that . . ."

Henry had told his son little about his childhood, and stories of Marty's grandfather were seldom shared. Marty rarely asked. Most of what he knew he'd gleaned from his mother.

"But what about Mom?"

Henry let out a big sigh and rubbed his cheeks where he'd forgotten to shave in the commotion of the last few days. The stubble reminded him of all those months, years caring for Ethel. How days would pass without his ever leaving the house, how he'd shave for no real reason, just out of habit. Then he'd occasionally let himself go—living with someone who didn't notice, who couldn't notice.

"I'm not sure what your mom knew. We didn't talk about it."

"You didn't talk about old flames?" Marty asked.

"What old flames?" Henry laughed, a little. "I was the first boy she'd ever dated. It was different back then—not like now."

"But you had one, evidently." Marty held out a sketchbook that had been sitting on the steps next to his jacket.

Henry took it, flipping through the pages, touching the impressions where Keiko's pencil had danced across the paper. Feeling the texture of the drawings, he wondered why she had left her sketchbooks. Why she'd left everything behind. Why he had too.

All these years, Henry had loved Ethel. He had been a loyal and dedicated husband, but he would walk blocks out of his way to avoid the Panama Hotel and the memory of Keiko. Had he known her belongings were still there . . .

Henry handed the sketchbook back to his son.

"You don't want it?" Marty asked.

Henry shrugged his shoulders. "I have the record. That's enough." *A broken record,* he thought. Two halves that will never play again.

Sheldon's Record
(1942)

When Monday came, Henry was still beaming from finding Keiko and seeing Chaz hounded by the police. There was a bounce in his step as he left school and ran, walked, then ran some more, weaving around the smiling fishmongers of South King all the way over to South Jackson. People on the streets seemed happy. President Roosevelt had announced that Lieutenant Colonel James Doolittle had led a squadron of B-25s on a bombing raid of Tokyo. It seemed that morale had been boosted everywhere. When asked where the planes had launched from, the president had joked, telling reporters they'd come from *Shangri-La*—which happened to be the name of a jazz club Henry wandered by on his way to find Sheldon.

Locating him this late in the afternoon was an easy task. Henry just followed his ears, homing in on the bluesy notes coming from Sheldon's instrument, a tune Henry recognized—called "Writin' Paper Blues." It was one Sheldon had played in the club with Oscar. Most appropriate considering Henry still had to round up stationery for Keiko, among other things.

Plunked down on an apartment step near where Sheldon was performing, Henry spotted a small mountain of change in the open sax case. That, and a vinyl record, a 78, propped up on a little wooden display. It was the same kind Henry's mother used in the kitchen to display what few pieces of fine china they could afford. A small, hand-painted sign read "As featured on Oscar Holden's new disk record."

To Henry, the crowd looked about the same, but to his pleasant surprise, they clapped with much more vigor as Sheldon played his heart out. They clapped harder as he ended on a sweet, stinging note that echoed in the clatter and din of nickels, dimes, and quarters pinging into the sax case. The mound of coins was more money than Henry had ever seen, in pocket change anyway.

Sheldon tipped his hat to the last of the crowd as they dispersed. "Henry, where you been, young sir? I haven't seen you running the streets on a weekend for two, three weeks now."

It was true. Henry had been so busy at Camp Harmony, and hiding that fact from his parents, that he hadn't seen Sheldon since E-day. He felt a little guilty about his absences. "I've picked up a weekend job—at Camp Harmony, it's that place—"

"I know. I know all about *that* place—been in the paper now for weeks. But how—tell me, how on God's green earth did this bit of intrigue come about . . . this job?"

It was a long story. And Henry didn't even know the ending. "Can I tell you later? I'm running errands and I'm running late—*and I need a favor.*"

Sheldon was fanning himself with his hat. "Money? Take what you need," he said, pointing to the case filled with silvery coins. Henry tried to guess how much was in there, twenty dollars at least, in half-dollars alone. But that wasn't the flat, round object Henry needed.

"I need your record."

There was a moment of stunned silence. In the distance Henry heard drums from a rehearsal upstairs at one of the other clubs.

"That's funny, that sounded a lot like 'I need your record,' " Sheldon said. "It sounded a lot like 'I need your *last* record.' The only record I own—of my *own* playing. The only record that was left at the music store since Oscar sold them out like hotcakes just last week."

Henry looked at his friend, biting his lip.

"Is that what I heard?" Sheldon asked, seemingly joking, but Henry wasn't entirely sure.

"It's for Keiko. For her birthday . . ."

"Owwww." Sheldon looked like he'd been stabbed. His eyes closed and his mouth screwed up in a grimace of pain. "You got me. You got me right here." He patted his heart and cracked a toothy smile at Henry.

"Does this mean I can have it? I can replace it. Keiko and I bought one together, but she wasn't allowed to bring it to the camp and now it's stored somewhere, I can't get to it—it's probably lost now."

Sheldon put his hat back on and adjusted the reed on his sax. "You can have it. Only because it's for a *higher* power."

Henry didn't pick up on Sheldon's gibe, otherwise he would have blushed horribly and denied that *love* was driving him in any way imaginable.

"Thank you. I'll pay you back someday," he said.

"You go play that thing. You go play that thing in that camp down there. You go. I kinda like the sound of that," Sheldon said. "It'd be the first time I ever played in a *white* establishment—even if it's for a bunch of Japanese folks, bit of a captive audience."

Henry smiled and looked at Sheldon, who was obviously waiting for a reaction to this pun. Henry tucked the record under his coat and ran, yelling back, "Thank you, sir, and you have a fine day." Sheldon shook his head and smiled before warming up for another afternoon performance.

Henry stopped by Woolworth's on the way home from school the next day. The old five-and-dime was unusually crowded—packed in fact. Henry counted twelve different booths, each selling war bond stamps. The Elks lodge had a booth. So did the Venture Club. Each group had a giant craft-paper thermometer showing how much they'd sold, each competing to outsell the others. One even had a life-size cutout of Bing Crosby wearing an army uniform. "Make every payday bond day!" a man yelled as he passed out slices of pie and cups of coffee.

Henry waded through the crowd, past the bright red vinyl booths and spinning stools of the soda counter, heading for the back of the store. There he gathered writing paper, art supplies, fabric, and a sketchbook whose blank pages looked so promising, a future unwritten. He quickly paid a young woman who simply smiled when she saw his button, then ran the rest of the way home, arriving maybe ten minutes late. Nothing really. Not even enough time to give his mother pause. He stashed Keiko's things with the record in an old washtub beneath the stairs in the back alley, then bounded up the steps, two at a time, light on his feet.

Things were looking up as word had already spread that Chaz and his friends had been picked up by the Seattle police for at least part of the damage they'd caused in Nihonmachi. Whether they'd actually received any punishment, no one could say. The Japanese citizens, even though they were Americans, were now considered enemy aliens—did anyone care what happened to their homes? Still, Chaz's father would probably find out soon enough that his golden boy had a heart of coal, and that was punishment enough, Henry reasoned, feeling more relief than joy.

Then there was Sheldon, who was finally enjoying the monetary fruits of his musical labors. He'd always drawn a crowd, but now it was a *paying* crowd, not just lookie-loos tossing in pennies.

And along with the birthday gift, the last copy of Oscar Holden's 78 record would soon be on its way to Keiko. The song was something they could share, even if a barbed-wire fence kept them apart and a machine-gun tower kept watch from above.

Despite the bitterness of all he'd seen, and the sadness of the forced exodus to Camp Harmony, things were manageable, and the war couldn't last forever. Eventually Keiko would come home, wouldn't she?

Henry whistled as he opened the door to his little apartment and saw his parents. That was when his pursed lips fell silent and Henry lost his breath. Both of them sat at their tiny kitchen table. Spread across the table were Keiko's family albums. The ones he'd so carefully hidden beneath his dresser drawers. Hundreds of photos of Japanese families, some in traditional dress, others in military uniforms. Piles and piles of black-and-white images. Few of the people in them were smiling. But none looked as dour as his parents—their faces cemented in expressions of shock, shame, and betrayal.

His mother muttered something in disgust, her voice cracking with emotion as she banged her way to the kitchen, shaking her head.

Henry's eyes met his father's furious gaze. His father picked up a photo album, tore the spine in two, and threw it to the floor—yelling something in Cantonese. He seemed more angry at the photos themselves than at Henry. But his turn was coming. Henry knew it.

Well, at least we're probably going to have a real conversation, Henry thought. And, Father, *it's about time.*

Henry set his shopping items on the table by the front door, took off his coat, and sat down in the chair opposite his father, looking down at the scattered photos of Keiko and her family—her Japanese family. Her parents' wedding photos in kimonos. Images of picture brides. Photos of an old man, probably her grandfather, in the dress uniform of the Imperial Japanese Navy. Some Japanese families had burned these things. Other families hid their treasured memories of who they were and where they came from. Some even buried their photo albums. *Buried treasure,* Henry thought.

It had been almost eight months since his father had insisted he only speak English. That was about to change.

"What do you have to say? Speak up!" his father was snapping in Cantonese.

Before Henry could answer, his father lashed out.

"I send you to school. I negotiate your way—into a *special* school. I do this for *you.* A top white school. And what happens? Instead of studying, you're making eyes with this Japanese girl. Japanese! She's a daughter of the butchers of my people. *Your* people. Their blood is on her! She stinks of that blood!"

"She's American," Henry protested, speaking softly in Cantonese. The words felt strange. Foreign. Like stepping onto a frozen lake, unsure if it would hold your weight or send you crashing through to the icy depths.

"Look! Look with your own eyes." Henry's father held up a page from an album, practically shoving it in Henry's face. "This is not American!" He pointed at the image of a stately man in traditional Japanese dress. "If the FBI find this here—in our home, our Chinese American home—they can arrest us. Take everything. They can throw us in jail and fine us five thousand dollars for helping the enemy."

"She's not the enemy," Henry said, speaking a little louder, his heart racing and his hands beginning to shake, trembling with frustration—with anger he never allowed himself to feel. "You don't even know her. You've never met her." He clenched his jaw and gritted his teeth.

"I don't need to—she's Japanese!"

"She was born in the same hospital I was born in, the same year I was born. She's an *American*!" Henry shouted back, so loudly it frightened even himself. He'd never spoken that way to any grown-up, let alone his own father, whom he was taught to revere and respect.

His mother had walked out of the kitchen for a moment to remove a flower vase from the table. He saw her, a look of shock and disappointment on her face that Henry would ever be so disobedient. The look quickly faded to a quiet acceptance, but with it, so much guilt settled on Henry's small shoulders. He rested his head in his hands, ashamed for speaking so loudly in front of his mother. She turned away, as if he hadn't said a thing. As if he weren't there. She swept back into the kitchen before Henry could say another word.

When Henry turned back, his father was already at the open window with an armload of Keiko's photos. He looked back at Henry, on his face a blank expression that was probably a mask of his disappointment. Then he dropped the photos, the albums, and boxes. They scattered to the ground, covering the the alley with white squares, lost faces staring back at no one.

Henry bent down to pick up the torn album. His father snatched it from his hands and tossed it too. Henry heard the pieces hitting the pavement outside, wet slapping sounds.

"She was born here. Her family was born here. *You* weren't even born here," Henry whispered to his father, who looked away, oblivious to his son's words.

He'd be thirteen in a few months; maybe this was what it meant to stop being a boy and start being something else, Henry thought as he put his coat back on and headed for the door. He couldn't leave the photos outside.

He turned to his father. "I'm leaving to get her photos. I told her I'd keep them for her—just until she gets back. And I'm going to keep my promise."

His father pointed at the door. "If you walk out that door—if you walk out that door *now,* you are no longer part of this family. You are no longer Chinese. You are not part of us anymore. Not a part of me."

Henry didn't even hesitate. He touched the doorknob, feeling the brass cold and hard in his hand. He looked back, speaking his best Cantonese. "I am what you made me, Father." He opened the heavy door. "I . . . am an American."

Camp Anyway
(1942)

Henry had managed to save most of Keiko's photos. He'd wiped the mud and garbage off on his coat sleeve and stored them in the old washbasin beneath the stairs until he could give them to Sheldon for safekeeping. But from that moment on, he began to feel like a ghost in the little brick apartment he shared with his parents. They didn't speak to him; in fact, they barely acknowledged his presence. They'd speak to each other as if he weren't there, and when they looked his way, they'd each pretend to look right through him. He hoped they were pretending anyway.

At first he'd talked to them regardless, in English—just table conversation—then later, pleading in Chinese. It didn't matter. Their great wall of silence was impervious to his best attempts to subvert it. So he too said nothing. And since his parents' conversations often had to do with Henry's *schooling,* Henry's *grades,* Henry's *future,* in Henry's *absence,* they said very little. The only sounds heard in their tiny home came from the rustling of the daily newspaper or the squelch and static of the wireless radio—playing news bulletins on the war and the latest local updates on rationing and drills of the Civil Air Defense. On the radio, nothing was ever mentioned of the Japanese who had been led out of Nihonmachi—it was as if they'd never existed.

After a few days, his mother did acknowledge his existence, in her own way. She did his laundry and packed him a lunch. But she did it with little ceremony, presumably so as not to go against the wishes of Henry's father, who had followed up on his threat to disown him figuratively, if not literally.

"Thank you," Henry said, as his mother set out a plate and rice bowl for him. But as she reached for another set of chopsticks—

"Are you expecting a guest for dinner?" Henry's father interrupted in Chinese, setting down his newspaper. "Answer me," he demanded.

She looked apologetically at her husband, then quietly removed the dish, avoiding eye contact with her son.

Henry, not to be discouraged completely, brought his own plate and served himself from then on. Eating in all but silence, the only sounds those of chopsticks occasionally tinging the side of his half-empty rice bowl.

The deafening silence continued at Rainier Elementary, even though Henry had thought about following his old friends to the Chinese school, or even up the hill to Bailey Gatzert Elementary, which was a mixed-race school that some of the older kids went to. But then again, he knew he'd have to register somehow, and without his parents' coopera- tion, it seemed impossible. Maybe when the school year was over, he'd convince his mother to switch him. No, his father was too proud of his son's *scholarshipping*. She would never go along with it.

So Henry accepted the fact that he would finish out the next two weeks of the sixth grade right where he was. And he had to, didn't he? Mrs. Beatty was still taking him to Camp Harmony on the weekends, and if he didn't work in the grade-school kitchen all week, his weekend furloughs to see Keiko might be in jeopardy.

By the time Saturday rolled around, Henry longed to talk to someone—anyone. He had tried to catch Sheldon during the week, but there was never any time before school. After school, Sheldon was al- ways performing at the Black Elks Club, which had just reopened.

When Mrs. Beatty rolled up, she seemed as good a conversationalist as Henry could hope for. She smoked while she drove, flicking her ashes out the window and blowing the smoke out the side of her mouth. It al- ways caught the draft and billowed back in, settling on the two of them. Henry rolled his window down a few inches, trying to draw the smoke away from the presents that sat on his lap.

In addition to a bag of sundries from Woolworth's, he had two boxes, each wrapped in lavender paper with white ribbon that he'd snuck from his mother's sewing box. One box contained a sketchbook, pencils, brushes, and a tin of watercolors. The other was the Oscar Holden record; the one Sheldon gave him. Henry had delicately wrapped it in tissue to keep it safe.

"Little early for Christmas," Mrs. Beatty commented, flicking her butt out the window of the speeding truck.

"It's Keiko's birthday tomorrow."

"That so?"

Henry nodded, waving the last of the smoke away.

"Mighty thoughtful of you," Mrs. Beatty said. Just as Henry was about to speak, she interrupted. "You know they're not going to let you take those in looking like that? I mean, that could be a gun, a couple of hand grenades, who knows—all wrapped up with a pretty bow, special delivery."

"But I thought I'd just have her open them at the fence . . ."

"Don't matter, dearie, all gifts are opened by the sentry on duty. Rules are rules."

Henry shook the larger box on his lap, the one with the record, thinking that he might as well take the ribbon off and just get it over with.

"Don't worry, I'll take care of it," Mrs. Beatty said. And she did.

On the outskirts of Puyallup, Mrs. Beatty pulled over into the parking lot of a Shell Oil gas station. She pulled off to the side, near the back, avoiding the pumps and the service attendant, who watched them quizzically.

"Grab those boxes and come with me," she barked, putting the truck in park before stepping out and walking to the rear of the still running vehicle.

Henry followed, holding the presents as she climbed up into the back of the truck. Grunting as she bucked a fifty-pound sack, she pulled it toward Henry, then untied the knot, jerking it open. Inside, Henry could see it was filled with Calrose rice.

"Gimme that."

Henry handed her the presents and watched her stuff each one in a bag, then bury them with handfuls of rice before sealing the bags again. He looked at all the bags, wondering what else must be in there. He'd seen her trading tools with soldiers and occasionally camp residents.

Things like files, small saws, and other woodworking tools. For an escape? Henry wondered. No, he'd seen old men working outside their shacks, building chairs, building shelves. That was probably where their tools came from. Mrs. Beatty's corner stand on the black market.

"Hey, what're you doing with that Jap over there?" The gas station attendant had walked around the building and must have been curious about this old woman and this little Asian kid.

"He ain't no Jap. He's a Chinaman—and the Chinese are our allies, so shove off, mister!" Mrs. Beatty hefted the last bag, the one with the record in it, and set it upright against the back of the cab with a heavy thud.

The attendant backed off immediately, taking a few steps back to the service station, offering a feeble wave. "Just trying to be helpful. That's my job, you know."

Ignoring him, Henry and Mrs. Beatty climbed into the truck—and rolled on. "Not a word, you understand," she said.

Henry nodded. And kept his mouth shut the rest of the drive, all the way to Camp Harmony and right through the main gates.

In Area 4, Henry went about his normal routine of dishing up lunch. Gradually Mrs. Beatty had won over the local kitchen steward, who now ordered mealtime staples appreciated by the Japanese residents—namely rice, but also miso soup with tofu, which Henry thought smelled delicious.

"Henry!"

He looked up and saw Mrs. Okabe standing in line. She wore dusty trousers and a sweater-vest with a large O sewn on one side.

"Are you responsible for putting an end to that awful potted meat? It suddenly changed to a steady flow of rice and fish—your doing?" she asked, smiling at him.

"I can't take credit for it, but I'm happy to be serving something I'd actually eat too." Henry dished her up a plateful of rice and pork *katsu*. "I have a couple of birthday presents for Keiko. Would you give them to her for me?" Henry set his ladle down for a moment and turned to pick up the presents, which sat at his feet.

"Why don't you tell her yourself?" Mrs. Okabe pointed to the back of the line. Keiko peeked her head through the crowd, smiling and waving.

"Thank you, I will. Is there anything you need? Anything your family needs? I can sometimes bring stuff into the camp, stuff that's not normally allowed."

"That's very sweet of you, Henry, but I think we'll be just fine for the moment. At first some of the men wanted tools, but some of that's coming in now. Just a hammer would have been a priceless treasure only a few weeks ago. Now there's so much hammering and sawing going on each day, it's a wonder why they go through the trouble . . ."

"What trouble?" Henry asked, not understanding.

"They're just going to move us anyway—this is only temporary. Can't sleep in a horse stall for the duration of the war, can I? I hope not anyway. One month is bad enough. In a few months they're sending us to permanent camps that are being built farther inland. We don't even know where we'll go. Either Texas or Idaho—probably Idaho, that's what we're hoping for anyway, since it's closer to home, or what used to be home. They might even split off some of the men—those with job skills needed elsewhere. They're making us build our own prisons, can you believe that?"

Henry shook his head in disbelief.

"How's the old neighborhood?"

Henry didn't know what to say. How could he begin to tell her that Nihonmachi was like a ghost town? Everything boarded up—a disaster of broken windows and doors, as well as other vandalism.

"It's fine" was all he could muster.

Mrs. Okabe seemed to sense his hesitation. Her eyes glossed over with sadness for a moment, and she wiped the corner of one eye as if there were a mote of dust bothering her. "Thank you for coming here, Henry. Keiko's missed you so much . . ."

Henry watched her smile bravely, then take her tray and disappear into the crowd.

"*Oai deki te ureshii desu!*" Keiko stood across the serving pans, smiling, almost glowing. "You came back!"

"I told you I would—and you look beautiful too. How are you?"

Henry looked at her and found himself feeling light-headed and slightly out of breath.

"It's so funny. They throw us in here because we're Japanese, but I'm *nisei*—second generation. I don't even *speak* Japanese. At school they teased me for being a foreigner. In here, some of the other kids, the *issei*—the first generation—they tease me because I can't speak the language, because I'm not Japanese enough."

"I'm sorry."

"Don't be, it's not your fault, Henry. You've done so much since I've been here. I was afraid you might forget about me."

Henry thought about his parents. About how they hadn't spoken a word to him in nearly a week. His father was stubborn, and traditional. He hadn't just threatened to disown him—he'd gone through with it. All because Henry couldn't stop thinking about Keiko. His mother knew, somehow she knew. Maybe it was the loss of appetite; mothers notice those things. That distracted longing. Feelings can only be hidden so long from those who really pay attention. Still, his mother obeyed his father, and Henry was alone now. *All because of you,* he thought. I wish I could think of something else—someone else—but I can't. Is this what *love* feels like? "How could I ever forget you?" he asked.

An old man behind Keiko began tapping his tray on the steel railing of the counter and clearing his throat.

"I better go," Keiko said, sliding her tray down as Henry filled it.

"I have those things you asked for—and a birthday present for you."

"Really?" Keiko smiled with delight.

"I'll meet you at the visitors' fence an hour after dinner, okay?"

Keiko beamed a smile back before disappearing into the crowded mess hall. Henry went back to work, serving meal after meal until everyone had been fed. Then he carried the serving pans to the dish pit, where he hosed them down with icy cold water, thinking of how Keiko would be leaving again—going to someplace unknown.

Keiko walked past a different set of guards this time and met Henry at the visitors' area of the fence, just like they'd planned. There were three or four other clusters of visitors along the fence line, with five or ten feet between them, creating intimate spots to converse through the barbed-wire fencing separating the internees from the outside world.

It was getting late, and a chilling wind had rolled in thick storm clouds, replacing the normally bleak, overcast sky. Rain was coming.

"They just canceled our record party—bad weather."

Henry looked at the darkening sky, disappointed more for Keiko than for himself. "Don't worry," he said, "there will be another time. You can count on it."

"I hope you're not disappointed." Keiko sighed. "You came all this way. I really did want to sit here along the fence and listen with you."

"I . . . didn't come for the music," Henry said.

He rubbed his eyes, trying to forget the news that she and her family would soon be leaving again. Everything felt so serious—and final. He interrupted the moment with a smile of his own. "This is for you. Happy birthday."

Henry handed Keiko the first of the two presents he'd brought, slipping it carefully between the rows of barbed wire to keep from snagging the wrapping paper. Keiko took it graciously and carefully untied the ribbon, folding it into a neat bundle. "I'm saving this. Ribbon like this, in camp, is like a present in itself." Henry watched as she did the same with the lavender wrapping paper before opening the package, the size of a small shoe box.

"Oh, Henry . . ."

She took out the sketchbook, the tin of watercolors, and the set of horsehair brushes. Then a set of drawing pencils, each of a different softness of lead.

"Do you like it?"

"Henry, I absolutely adore it. This is so wonderful . . ."

"You're an artist. Seemed like it would be a shame to be here, away from what you're so good at," Henry said. "Did you look inside the sketchbook?"

Keiko set the small box down on a dry patch of dirt; the mud from the previous week had hardened, creating a desert of textured soil. She opened the small black, hand-bound sketchbook and read the price tag. "A dollar twenty-five."

"Ooops, here . . ." Henry reached in and peeled off the price tag from the stationer where he'd bought it. "You weren't supposed to see that. Look on the next page."

Keiko turned the page and read the inscription aloud. "To Keiko, the sweetest, most beautiful American girl I've ever known. Love, your friend, Henry."

He watched her eyes moisten as she read it again.

"Henry, that's so sweet, I don't know what to say."

He had felt awkward writing the word *love* in the sketchbook. He must have stared at that blank page worrying about what to write for twenty minutes, before he finally just wrote it in ink. No turning back then. "Just say thank you and that'll be fine."

She looked at him between the wires. The wind picked up and blew her hair away from her face. Thunder could be heard rumbling somewhere over the foothills, but neither looked away. "I don't think 'thank you' is enough. You've come a long way to bring me this. And I know your family . . . your father . . ."

Henry looked down and exhaled softly.

"He knows, doesn't he?" Keiko asked.

Henry nodded.

"But we're just friends."

Henry looked her in the eye. "We're more than friends. We're the same people. But he doesn't see it—he only sees you as a daughter of the enemy—he's disowned me. My parents stopped speaking to me this week. But my mother still sort of acts like I'm around." The words came out so casually, even Henry was surprised at how normal it felt. But communication in his home had been far from ordinary for almost a year; this was just a new, final wrinkle.

Keiko looked at Henry, shocked, with sadness in her eyes. "I'm sorry. I never meant for any of this to happen. I feel terrible. How could a father treat his son—"

"It's all right. He and I never talked that much to begin with. It's not your fault. I wanted to be with you. When you first came to the school, I was shocked and a little surprised. But going to school without you, it just hasn't been the same. I . . . miss you."

"I'm so glad you're here," Keiko said as she touched the pointed metal of the fence. "I miss you too."

"I brought you something else." Henry offered her the other package through the barbed wire. "It's just a little surprise, might not be too handy now, with the poor weather and all."

Keiko unwrapped the second package as carefully as she had the first. "How did you find this?" she whispered in awe, holding up the Oscar Holden record in its faded paper sleeve.

"I couldn't get into the Panama Hotel, and they were sold out in town, but Sheldon gave me his. I guess it's from both of us. Too bad you can't play it tonight, with the concert canceled and all."

"We still have the record player in our building. I'll play it anyway, just for you. Actually, just for us."

That made Henry smile. Parents, what parents?

"You couldn't possibly know how happy I am to have this. This is almost like having you here with me—not that I'd want to subject you to a place like this. But we've had no music. I'll be playing this every day."

Thunderclaps struck overhead, turning what had become a drizzle into a cloudburst, first in a few, spare droplets, then widening into a thick, drenching downpour. Henry gave Keiko the last bag, the one from Woolworth's, with stationery, stamps, and fabric for blackout curtains.

"You'd better go," he insisted.

"I don't want to leave you. We just got here."

"You'll get sick in this weather, living in a place like this. You need to go. I'll be back next week. I'll find you."

"Visiting hours are over!" a soldier barked, wrapping himself in a green raincoat as he gathered up his files. "Everyone away from the fence!" The rain was rippling the ground, the sound drowning out their voices.

To Henry, it seemed to go from six o'clock to nine o'clock as the dark clouds dimmed the skyline, hiding the sun altogether. A dull gray glow illuminated the surface of the ground as it transformed back into the muddy, soggy field it had been earlier that week.

Keiko reached through the fence and held Henry's hands. "Don't forget about me, Henry. I won't forget about you. And if your parents don't want to speak to you, I'll speak to them, and tell them you're wonderful for doing this."

"I'll be here, every week."

She let go and fastened the top button on her coat. "Next week?"

Henry nodded.

"I'll write to you then," Keiko said, waving good-bye as the last of the visitors filed away from the fence line and back toward the main gate. Henry was the last to leave, standing there soaking wet, watching Keiko as she made it all the way back to a small outbuilding near the livestock pavilion that had become her new home. He could almost see his breath, it was growing so cold, yet inside he felt warm.

As it grew darker, Henry noticed the searchlights in the machine-gun towers torched to life. The tower guards shone them up and down the fence line, illuminating Henry and the other visitors as they puddle-jumped their way back past the main gate. Henry turned down the hill toward Mrs. Beatty's truck. In the dark, he could see her massive outline strapping down empty fruit crates in the back, her face illuminated by the cherry red embers of her lit cigarette, dangling from her mouth.

Through the slosh of the rain, Henry heard music from the camp. The song grew louder and louder, straining the limits of the speakers it came from. It was the record. Their record. Oscar Holden's "Alley Cat Strut." Henry could almost pick out Sheldon's part. It shouted at the night. Louder than the storm. So loud a guard near the gate started hollering, *"Turn off that music."* The searchlights swept down on the buildings in Area 4, beaming down a menacing eye, searching for the source.

Moving
(1942)

 Henry finally received the news he'd been dreading all summer. He'd known it was only a matter of time. Keiko would be moving farther inland.

Camp Harmony was always intended to be temporary, just until permanent camps could be built—away from the coastlines, which were seen as a vulnerable target for bombing or invasion. In these coastal communities, every Japanese citizen was a potential spy—able to keep track of the comings and goings of warships and ocean-based supply lines. So the farther inland the Japanese could be sent, the better. The safer we'll all be—that was what Henry's father had told him, at least back in the days when he actually spoke to him. It didn't matter. The words still rang in his ears, even in the awkward silence of their little Canton Alley apartment.

Keiko had taken to writing him once a week. Sometimes she'd include a wish list of items that he and Mrs. Beatty could smuggle into the camps. Small things, like a newspaper, or big things, like forgotten records and copies of birth certificates. Other times it was practical things, like tooth powder and soap. There was a shortage of everything inside the camps.

Henry wasn't sure if he'd even get Keiko's letters at first. He was certain his father would tear up any letter or note coming from Camp Harmony. But somehow Henry's mother, sorting the mail first, found the letter each week and slipped it underneath his pillow. She never said a word, but Henry knew it was her doing. She did her best to be an obedient wife, to honor her husband's wishes, but to look out for her son as well. Henry wanted to thank her. But even in private, expressing his gratitude would have been bad form—just acknowledging that she was bending the rules set by Henry's father would be taken as an admission of guilt, so he too said nothing. But he was indeed grateful.

Keiko's current letter said that her father had left already. He had volunteered to go to Camp Minidoka in Idaho, near the Oregon border. He'd offered to be part of a work detail—to help build the camp, the mess halls, the living quarters, even a school.

Keiko had mentioned that her father used to be a lawyer but now was working alongside doctors, dentists, and other professional men—all were now day laborers, toiling in the hot summer sun for pennies a day. Evidently their efforts were worth it. The men who volunteered all wanted to stay as close to their original homes as possible. Plus, they were promised that their families could join them as soon as the camp was ready. Other families had been split up, some to Texas and others to Nevada. At least the Okabes would be together.

Henry knew he didn't have much time. This Saturday would probably be his last visit to Camp Harmony. His last chance to see Keiko for a very long while.

Henry had been inside Area 4 almost a dozen times now, in the kitchen, in the mess hall, or up at the visitors' fence, talking to Keiko, and occasionally her parents, through the barbed wire, lost among the half dozen other groups of visitors who usually populated the fence during the day. But he'd never been into the camp itself, the large common area, the parade grounds that once were the heartbeat of the state fair. Now it was a dusty (occasionally muddy) field, beaten down by the thousands of footsteps of restless internees.

Today would be different. Henry had become used to the strangeness of the place. The guard dogs that patrolled the main gate. The machine-gun towers. Even the sight of men everywhere with bayoneted rifles slung across their backs. It all seemed so normal now. But today, during the normal routine of his Saturday in the mess hall, Henry planned to visit Keiko. Not at the fence. He was going into the camp. He was going to find her.

So when most of the prisoners had been served their dinner, when the crowd began to thin, Henry excused himself to go to the latrine. The other kitchen helper could handle the small crowds that trickled in late. He hadn't seen Keiko come through yet. She tended to come late; that way she'd be able to spend time talking to Henry without holding up the line.

Henry returned to the kitchen and left through the back door, right past Mrs. Beatty, who was out smoking a cigarette and talking to one of the supply sergeants. If she noticed him, she didn't say a thing, but then again, she rarely did anyway.

Instead of heading for the latrine, Henry looped back around the building and blended into a crowd of Japanese prisoners heading to the large trophy barn that had become a makeshift home for what he guessed were three hundred people. He stuffed his "I am Chinese" button into his pocket.

If I'm caught, Henry thought, they'll probably never let me come here again. Mrs. Beatty will be furious. But if Keiko is leaving, I won't be coming back anyway, so what does it matter? Either way, this is my last weekend at Camp Harmony—Keiko's too.

If the men and women thought it was odd that a Chinese boy was following them back to their quarters, they didn't say a word. They just spoke to each other in English and Japanese both, talking about the impending move—the conversation that seemed to echo in every area of the camp. It would be this coming week, Henry was certain of it now.

Nearing the large building where most of the families in Area 4 lived, Henry was amazed at how normal life had become here. Grandfatherly old men sat in homemade chairs smoking pipes while small children played hopscotch and four square. Clusters of women tended to long lines of laundry and even weeded small gardens that had been planted in the barren soil.

Henry slipped through the main entrance of the building—a huge, sliding barn door that had been left open to allow cool air to seep into the sweltering interior. Inside were rows and rows of stalls, most covered with makeshift privacy curtains hung by pieces of rope. Henry realized that the lucky ones had windows, bringing fresh air inside. The unlucky ones, well, they made do the best they could. Henry could hear a flute playing somewhere, among the noise of the crowds, which was surprisingly subdued the farther in he walked. Each stall accommodated one family, but they had evidently been cleaned by the new residents and didn't smell like horses or cows. Not in the slightest, much to Henry's surprise.

Walking down the hallways between the rows of makeshift homes, Henry had no idea how he would find Keiko or her family. Some families had put up signs, or banners—in Japanese, English, and sometimes both. But many more stalls were left bare. Then he saw a sign above a curtain and knew this was where Keiko lived. The banner was written in English and read "Welcome to the Panama Hotel."

Henry knocked on a wooden beam making up one corner of the stall. He knocked again. *"Konichi wa."*

"Donatà deu ka?" came from behind the curtain. Henry recognized the phrase as "Who is it?" The voice was Keiko's. When had she learned to speak Japanese? Then again, when had Henry started saying *"Konichi wa"*?

"Is there a vacancy at the hotel?" he asked.

There was a pause.

"Maybe, but you might not like it, the sento bath in the basement is awfully crowded these days."

She knew.

"I'm just passing through, wouldn't mind staying for a while if you have room."

"Let me check with my manager. Nope, sorry, we're all full. Maybe if you try the pig barn two buildings over. I hear they have some very nice rooms."

Henry wandered off, taking noisy, exaggerated steps. "Okay, thanks for the tip, have a nice day . . ."

Keiko pulled back the curtain. "For the boy who chased me down in the train station with soldiers running around, you sure give up easy!"

Henry spun on his heel and walked back to where Keiko stood, then looked around the building, taking it all in. "Where's your family?"

"Mom took my little brother to see the doctor about an earache he's been having, and you know about my dad—he left a week ago. He's finishing the roofing at the camp in Idaho. Our next stop. I've always wanted to travel, I guess this is my chance." Henry watched Keiko's face turn serious. "You've crossed some sort of line coming all the way down here, haven't you, Henry?"

He just looked at her. She wore a yellow summer dress and sandals. Her hair was pulled back with a white ribbon from the present he had given her on her birthday. Strands of black hair fell at the sides of her face, which had tanned quite a bit since she'd been at Camp Harmony.

He shrugged. "I'm breaking a lot of rules to be down here right now, but it's okay . . ."

"Of course you know I'm leaving then, don't you?" Keiko asked. "You got my letter. You know we're *all* leaving."

Henry nodded, feeling sad but not wanting to show it, afraid that it might make Keiko feel even worse.

"They're taking us to Minidoka next week. Buses have already taken some families from the other areas. I wish you could come with us."

"Me too," Henry confessed. "I would if I could. Don't tell me you haven't thought about it."

"About you coming with us, or me leaving with you?"

"Either, I guess."

"There's no place for me to go, Henry. Nihonmachi doesn't exist anymore. And I need to be here with my family. And you need to be with yours. I understand. We're not that different, you know."

"I don't have much to go home to. But I can't go with you either, though I've thought about trying to blend in—how easy it would be to just get swept up in it all, to tag along. But I'm Chinese, not Japanese. They'd find out. Everyone would find out. I can't hide who I am. My parents would find out too, and they'd know where I'd gone. We'd all get in a lot more trouble than we'd know what to do with."

"So what brings you all the way down here? Or is Mrs. Beatty with you?" Keiko asked, looking up and down the rows of stalls.

How do I say this? Henry thought. What can I say that will make any difference, to anyone? "I just had to come see you, face-to-face. To tell you how sorry I am for the way I acted that first day at school."

"I don't understand . . ."

"I was afraid of you. Honestly. Afraid of what my father might say or do. My father had said so many things—I just didn't know what to think.

I didn't have any Japanese friends, let alone any . . ." Henry couldn't bring himself to say the word *girlfriends,* but he trailed off in a way that he was certain Keiko knew what he meant.

Keiko smiled and looked up at him, her brown eyes unblinking.

"It's just that, this is probably our last time together—for a very long time. I mean, we don't know when you're ever coming back, or if you'll even be let back. I mean, there are senators that want to send you all back to Japan, win or lose."

"It's true." Keiko nodded. "I'll still write—if you want me to? Does your father know about the letters?"

Henry shook his head no. He reached out and took her hands in his, feeling her soft skin, looking at her slender fingers, slightly dirty from working in the camp.

"I'm sorry I've caused so much trouble in your family," Keiko said. "I'll stop writing if that will make it better for you at home."

Henry exhaled deeply. "I'll turn thirteen soon. The same age my father was when he left home and began working full-time back in the Old Country. I'm old enough to make my own decisions."

Keiko leaned in closer. "And what decision is that, Henry?"

He searched for the words. Nothing he ever learned in English class at Rainier Elementary could describe what was going on inside him. He'd seen movies where the hero takes the girl, where the music comes to a crescendo. He wanted so badly to wrap his arms around her and hold her and somehow keep her from going. But he also lived in a home where the most dramatic display of emotion was usually a nod and occasionally a smile. He'd just assumed all families were that way—all people too. Until he met Keiko and her family.

"I . . . it's just that . . . ," Henry stammered.

What am I doing? I need to let her go, so she can be with her family—with her own community. *I need to let her move on.*

"I'm going to miss you," he said, letting go of her hands and putting his own in his pockets, looking at his feet.

Keiko looked crushed. "More than you know, Henry."

For the next hour, Henry stayed there, listening to Keiko talk about the little details. Like what kinds of toys her father was making for her little brother. Or how difficult it was to sleep with the noisy old lady who snored and broke wind through the night, even though she herself never woke up. The time passed quickly. Never once did they mention missing each other or how they felt again. They were together, alone even, but they might as well have been standing up at the visitors' fence—Henry on one side, Keiko on the other—separated by razor wire.

Stranger
(1942)

The ride home was more quiet than usual. Henry stared out the passenger window, watching the sun set one last time. Watching the farmland give way to the landscape of Boeing Field, its enormous buildings draped in camouflage netting—a feeble attempt to keep entire factories hidden from enemy bombers. Henry didn't say a word, and Mrs. Beatty, perhaps out of sympathy, didn't either. She just left him to his thoughts. All of which were about Keiko.

With the last of the prisoners taken to camps farther inland, Camp Harmony would revert back to being the site of the Washington State Fair just in time for the fall harvest season. Henry wondered if anyone going to the fair this year would feel different walking through the trophy barn, admiring prized heads of cattle. He wondered if anyone would even remember that, two months earlier, entire families had been sleeping there. Hundreds of them.

But what now? Keiko would be on her way to Minidoka, Idaho, in a few days. A smaller work camp somewhere in the mountains near the Oregon border, he presumed. It was closer than Crystal City, Texas, but still seemed like a world away.

Their good-bye had been a formal one. After he'd decided to let her go (for her own good, he reminded himself), he'd kept a polite distance, not wanting to make it any harder on either of them. She was his best friend. More than a friend, really. Much more. The thought of her leaving was killing him, but the thought of telling her how he really felt and *then* watching her go, that was more than his small heart could manage.

Instead, he said good-bye with a wave and a smile. Not even a hug. She looked away, wiping her eyes with the backs of her hands. He'd done the best thing, right? His father had said once that the hardest choices in life aren't between what's right and what's wrong but between what's right and what's best. The best thing was to let her go. And Henry had done just that.

But his mind had filled with doubts.

To his surprise, no one had even noticed he was gone. Or if they had, they hadn't cared enough to say anything. The truth was, the residents of Camp Harmony would be leaving, and the camp workers, the soldiers, all just wanted to go back to their lives. They had done their duty and were ready to wash their hands of the whole ugly matter once and for all.

Mrs. Beatty was thoughtful enough to drop Henry off in Chinatown, a block from the apartment he shared with his family. She had never done that before.

"I guess that's that," she said. "Stay out of trouble this summer—and don't go changing schools on me now. I still expect to see you in the kitchen this fall, got it?" Mrs. Beatty let the engine idle as she stubbed out a cigarette in a beanbag ashtray she kept on the dashboard for when the truck's ashtray got too full.

"I'll be careful. I hope you hear some news about your father. I'm sure he's doing okay," Henry said, thinking about Mrs. Beatty's father and the crew of the SS *City of Flint*—merchant marines imprisoned somewhere in Germany, like Keiko and her family.

Mrs. Beatty smiled slightly, nodding. "Thank you, Henry. Mighty thoughtful of you. I'm sure he'll get by. You will too." She struggled to put the truck in gear, then regarded Henry once more. "And so will Keiko."

He watched her drive off, bumping along the potholed streets, her arm waving out the window. Then she rounded the corner and was gone. The streets were peaceful. Henry listened for Sheldon playing over on Jackson but heard only the rumble of trucks, the squeal of brakes, and a dog barking in the distance.

He walked up the steps and down the hall to his apartment, the steamy smell of rice in the air. When he reached his home, the door was partially open and light spilled out. A shadow moved, the silhouette of an older man, but not that of his father.

Henry stepped inside. His mother was sitting at the kitchen table, sniffling into a handkerchief, her eyes red and her nose puffy from crying. Henry recognized the man immediately by the stethoscope that hung around his neck. Dr. Luke, one of the few Chinese doctors who had a practice on South King—and still made house calls. He'd once come by when Henry had "fallen off the swing" at school (a beating actually, courtesy of Chaz Preston) and had a concussion. Henry had thrown up and passed out, and his mother had immediately called the local doctor. But Henry had been fine, and his mother, despite the tears, looked reasonably well. This time, she looked scared, her body shaking. That's when Henry knew.

"Henry—your mother was just talking about you. You look like you've grown since my last visit." Dr. Luke was being polite, speaking in Chinese, but nervous too. What *isn't* he telling me? Henry thought.

Henry's mother left her chair and fell to her knees, hugging him so hard it hurt.

"What's the matter? Where's Father?" Henry asked, guessing the answer.

She propped herself up, wiping the tears from her eyes, and spoke in a positive tone that somehow didn't fit the news she was about to share. "Henry, your father's had a stroke. Do you know what that is?"

He shook his head no. Though he had some vague recollection of Old Man Wee in the fish market, who always talked funny and used only his right arm to weigh the day's catch.

"Henry, it's a very bad stroke," Dr. Luke said, putting his hands on Henry's small shoulders. "Your father is tough, and stubborn. I think he's going to pull through, but he's going to need rest—for at least a month. And he can barely talk. He might gain some of that back, but for right now, it's going to be difficult for all of us. Especially him."

The only words Henry heard were "he can barely talk." Father had barely said anything when he could, and in the last two months hadn't said a single word to Henry. Not even a good night. Not a hello, or a good-bye.

"Is he going to die?" was all Henry could think of to ask, his voice cracking.

Dr. Luke shook his head, but Henry saw through to the truth. He looked at his mother, and she looked terrified, not saying a thing. What could she say?

"Why did this happen? . . . How?" Henry asked his mother as well as Dr. Luke.

"These things just happen, Henry," Dr. Luke answered. "Your father gets worked up about so many things, and he's not a young man inside. He lived such a hard life back in China. It ages a body. And now so much worry, with the war . . ."

A wave of guilt crashed over Henry. He was sinking beneath it. His mother took his hand. "Not your fault. Don't think this. Not your fault—his fault, understand?"

Henry nodded to make his mother feel better, but he was torn inside. He had so little in common with his father. He had never understood him. But still, he was the only father he had, the only one he would ever have.

"Can I see him?" Henry asked.

Henry watched his mother's eyes meet Dr. Luke's; the doctor paused, then nodded. At the door of his parents' room, Henry could smell Buddhist incense burning, along with some kind of cleaning solution. His mother turned on a small lamp in the corner. As Henry's eyes adjusted, he beheld his father, looking small and frail. He lay like a prisoner of his bed—the covers pulled up tight around his chest, which seemed to move in a jerky, uneven rhythm. His skin was pale, and one side of his face looked bloated, like it had been in a fight while the other side watched and did nothing. His arm lay at his side, palm up; a long tube connected at his wrist led to a bottle of clear fluid that hung from the bedpost.

"Go on, Henry; he can hear you," Dr. Luke said, prodding him forward.

Henry walked to the side of the bed, afraid that touching his father would injure him or push him closer to his ancestors.

"It's okay, Henry, I think he'd want to know you're here." His mother gently caressed his nervous shoulder, taking his hand and putting it in his father's frail, limp fingers. "Say something, let him know you're here."

Say something? What can I possibly say now? And in what language? Henry took the "I am Chinese" button off his shirt and set it on the nightstand near what he assumed to be his father's medicine. There were assorted brown glass bottles, some with labels in English while others, herbal concoctions, were labeled in Chinese.

Henry watched his father open his eyes, blinking twice. Henry couldn't tell what lurked behind that stricken, expressionless face. Still, he knew what he had to say. *"Deui mh jyuh."* It meant, "I am unable to face," a formal apology when you're admitting guilt or fault. Henry felt his mother's hand on his face for a moment, a caress of comfort.

His father looked up at him, his mind straining to force his disobedient body into activity. Each movement of his mouth took incredible effort. Just breathing in and out enough to generate sound appeared nearly impossible. Still, his fingers gripped Henry's so slightly it was almost imperceptible. And a single phrase slipped out. *"Saang jan."*

It meant "stranger." As in "You are a stranger to me."

Thirteen
(1942)

One month later Henry grew up, or so it felt. He turned thirteen, the age that many laborers had left China two generations earlier in search of Chinshan—the Gold Mountain, seeking their fortunes in America. It was the same age his father had been when he took a job as a laborer, the age Henry's father considered a boy to be a man. Or a girl to be a woman, for that matter, since arranged marriages often happened as early as thirteen—the age a girl's education typically ended—and only for those who could afford such arrangements.

Henry's birthday came and went with little fanfare. His mother made *gau,* a favorite dessert cake of glutinous sticky rice she normally reserved for special holidays like the lunar new year. His extended family of aunties and cousins came over for a dinner of black bean chicken and choy sum with oyster sauce—also favorites of Henry's. His rich auntie King gave him a lai see envelope, filled with ten crisp one-dollar bills, more money than he'd ever received at one time. She gave Henry's mother one too; his mother gushed her appreciation but didn't open it. That was when Henry realized that Auntie King and her husband, Herb, were probably helping support Henry's family now that his father was bedridden.

Henry's father was confined to his bed or a wheelchair that his mother pushed around the apartment, positioning him next to the radio, or the window so he could get some fresh air once in a while. He said nothing to Henry but would whisper words to Henry's mother, who doted on him as best she could.

Occasionally, Henry would catch his father watching him, but when he'd make eye contact, his father would look away. He wanted to say something, feeling guilty for having disobeyed, for having caused his father's weakened condition. But in a way, he was his father's son, and he could be equally stubborn.

Keiko had been gone more than a month. She'd left on August 11 with the last of the prisoners of Camp Harmony, bound for Minidoka. And she'd never once written. Of course, no one could be sure what that *really* meant. Maybe there wasn't mail service up there. Or maybe Henry had been too clear with his good-bye and she was moving on without him. Forgetting him once and for all. Either way, he missed her so much it hurt.

Especially at school, when the fall semester started. Henry had two more years before he'd go to Garfield High, which he'd heard was far more integrated, and where most of the Chinese and black kids ended up going. A mixed-race class would be such a change from Rainier, where he was, once again, the only nonwhite student. He still worked in the kitchen at lunchtime with Mrs. Beatty, who never spoke of Keiko.

Henry rarely saw Chaz anymore. Since getting caught vandalizing homes in Nihonmachi, he had been kicked out of Rainier. Rumor had it he was now bullying kids at Bailey Gatzert, where all the blue-collar kids went. Occasionally Henry would see him shadowing his father around town, but that was it. He'd grin at Henry, but Henry wasn't afraid of him anymore. Chaz looked the way he'd look for the rest of his life, Henry thought, bitter and defeated. Henry, on the other hand still felt like he hadn't learned his best trick yet.

Still, Henry's work duties after school felt empty, and his walk home was a lonely affair. All he could do was think of Keiko, how happy he'd felt when she was around. And how numb and sad he'd felt watching her wipe the tears from her eyes when he'd said good-bye. He didn't regret watching her go as much as he regretted not telling her how much he cared. How much she meant. His father was a horrible communicator. After all the time he'd rebelled against his father's wishes and his father's ways, Henry hated the fact that he wasn't that different from him at all— not where it mattered, anyway.

Henry walked back to the black iron arches of Chinatown, alone again, following the unmistakable sound of Sheldon's sax and the roar of applause that always seemed to accompany his performances these days.

Sheldon was playing in small clubs around South Jackson, but Oscar Holden was on a police watch list now, for speaking out against the treatment of the residents of Nihonmachi, and had a hard time getting gigs. The price you pay for speaking your mind—you lose the ability to have your singing voice heard. A tragedy, Henry thought. No, more than a tragedy, it was a crime, having that ability stolen from him. His record had sold out and became sort of a collectors' item, for a while anyway.

"Hear anything from up yonder?" Sheldon saw Henry and pointed with his chin, eastward, in the direction of Idaho. In the direction of Minidoka.

Henry shook his head no, trying not to look as down as he felt.

"I've been to Idaho once, it's not that bad. I had a cousin that would run liquor across the border into Post Falls years ago, during Prohibition. It's pretty, all those mountains and such."

Henry slouched on the curb. Sheldon handed him his empty lunch pail.

"Oh, it's been a long time since I was what anyone might have called a 'young man,' but boy," he said, "I can see it in your eyes. I know you trying to put on your brave face—that face that even your mama might not see through. But me, Henry, I've seen enough hard luck in my lifetime. I know what you got, and you got it *bad.*"

Henry stole a peek at Sheldon. "What? That obvious?"

"We all felt it, boy. Watching everyone get rounded up like that. That's enough heartbreak to last a lifetime for some people. Down here, in the *so-called International District*—you, me, the Filipinos, them Koreans coming over, even some of the Jews and Italians, we all felt it. But you, it hurt you in a different way, watching *her* go."

"I let her go."

"Henry, she was *going* whether you let her go or not. It's not your fault."

"No—*I let her go.* I didn't even really say good-bye as much as I sent her away."

There was a moment of silence as Sheldon fingered the keys on his sax. "Then you get yourself to some pen and paper and you write to her—"

Henry interrupted. "I don't even know her address. I let her go, and she hasn't even written to me."

Sheldon pursed his lips and let out a big sigh, closing his sax case and sitting on the cold cement curb next to Henry. "You know where Minidoka is, right?"

"I can find it on a map . . ."

"Then let's go see her—they must have visiting hours up there just like down in Puyallup. Let's you and me jump in the *belly of the big dog* and go see her."

"Big dog . . ."

"Greyhound, boy! I have to spell it all out for you? We catch a bus, I ain't got nothing but time right now anyway. We leave on a Friday, come back on a Sunday, you don't hardly miss no school or nothing."

"I can't do that . . ."

"Why, you're thirteen now, ain't you? You're a man in your daddy's eyes. You can make a man's decision and do what you gotta do. That's what I'd do."

"I can't just leave my mother, and what about my father?"

"What about him?"

"I can't just leave him. If he found out I'd gone all the way to Idaho to see a Japanese girl, his heart would give out completely . . ."

"Henry." Sheldon looked at him more seriously than he'd ever done before. "Your daddy having himself a heart fit, that ain't your fault either. He's been fighting the war in his head, in his heart, ever since he was your age back in China. You can't take credit for stuff that goes back to before you were even born. You understand me?"

Henry stood up and brushed the dirt off the seat of his pants. "I gotta go. I'll see you around." He smiled, as much as he could, and walked off in the direction of home.

Sheldon didn't argue.

He's right, Henry thought. I *am* old enough to make my own decisions. But Idaho, that's too far, too dangerous. What business do I have running off like that, to a place I've never been? If something happened to me, who would take care of my mother? With my father bedridden, I'm the man now. I might even have to quit school and go to work to help pay bills. And besides, running off wasn't responsible. The more he thought about it, the more he realized that money wasn't an issue. The money from working at Camp Harmony was more than enough to pay his way, and the windfall from Auntie King would cover everything else.

No, I can't do it. It just isn't practical right now.

When Henry got home, his father was in bed, sound asleep. Since the stroke, he didn't even snore as loudly as he used to. Seemed like everything he did was a pale shadow of his former self. Except his spotlight of condemnation, which always seemed to shine on Henry. No matter where Henry was, he felt it.

His mother came up the stairs behind him with a basket of laundry taken from the clothesline shared by others in the alley. "You have a birthday card," she said in Cantonese. She took it out of her apron pocket and handed it to him. It was a bright yellow envelope, slightly bent and dirty. Henry recognized the stamp.

He knew who it was from just by the handwriting—it was from Minidoka. From Keiko. She hadn't forgotten him.

He looked at his mother, a little bewildered but not apologizing.

"It's okay" was all she said as she walked away with the basket of clean laundry.

Henry didn't even go to his room to open it. He carefully peeled it open right there and read the letter inside. At the top of the page was a small pen-and-ink drawing of a birthday cake, colored with watercolor. It read "Happy Birthday, Henry! I didn't want you to go, but I knew I was going anyway, so what could you do? I don't want to trouble your family or make things worse between you and your dad. I just wanted to let you know I was thinking about you. And miss you more than you'll know."

The rest was about camp life. How they had a school there, and how her father was doing. His law degree wasn't much good to him when it came time to pick sugar beets every day.

And the letter closed with, "I won't write you again, I don't want to bother you. Maybe your father is right. Keiko."

Henry's fingers shook when he read the last line again and again. He looked at his mother, who was now in the kitchen and had been watching him from the corner of her eye. She held her hand to her lips, looking concerned.

Henry half-smiled at her and found his way to his room, where he counted out the money he'd saved all summer and the lucky money from Auntie King. He then found an old suitcase at the top of his closet and filled it with enough clothes and clean underwear to last a few days.

Walking out of his room, he felt like an entirely different person from the one who had walked in. His mother looked at him, blanketed in confusion.

Suitcase in hand, he headed for the door. "I'm going to the bus station, I'll be back in a few days. Don't wait up for me."

"I knew you'd do the right thing," Sheldon said, smiling from the aisle passenger seat of the Greyhound bus bound for Walla Walla. "I knew you had it in you—saw it in your eyes."

Henry just looked out the window as the city streets of Seattle gave way to green hills up and toward the pass between western and eastern Washington. He'd found Sheldon, and his suitcase in hand was all the prompting his friend had needed. "Let me get my hat" was Sheldon's only response, and the two of them gathered their things and headed for the bus depot, where they bought two round-trip tickets to Jerome, Idaho, the closest town to Camp Minidoka. The tickets cost twelve dollars each—Henry offered to pay for Sheldon's out of the money he'd saved up from working that summer, but Sheldon declined.

"Thanks for coming with me. You didn't have to pay, I had enough—"

" 'Sokay, Henry, I never get out of the city enough anyway."

Henry was grateful. Deep down, he'd wanted to save enough money. At least enough for *three* return tickets. He was going to ask Keiko to leave with him. He would give her his button and try to sneak her out during a visit. Anything was worth trying at this point. She could stay at his auntie King's house on Beacon Hill, or so he thought. Unlike his father, Auntie King had no qualms about her Japanese neighbors. She had said so herself, one time, much to Henry's surprise—somehow, she was more forgiving, more accepting. It was a long shot, but it was his last, best hope in the current situation.

"You know where this place is?" Sheldon asked.

"I know how it was in Puyallup, at Camp Harmony. If we get close enough, we're gonna have a hard time not knowing where it is."

"How can you be so certain—"

Henry cut him off. "There's supposed to be nine thousand people imprisoned there. That's like a small city. It's not going to be a problem finding the camp. The problem will be finding Keiko among all those people."

Sheldon whistled, to the dismay of an elderly woman in a fur hat, who turned around and scowled at him.

Henry didn't mind sitting in the back of the bus. But for some reason Sheldon seemed to resent it. Grousing once in a while about how *this was the Northwest and not the Deep South* and the bus driver had had no business jerking his thumb toward the back of the bus when he and Henry boarded. Still, they went. Going this far, to someplace unknown, was potential trouble enough. The good thing about sitting in the last row was not having anyone behind them to stare or ask questions. Henry pretty much disappeared into the rear corner of the bus, looking out the window, and those glaring back didn't even make eye contact with Sheldon.

"What happens if we get there and no one rents us a place to lay our heads for the night?" Henry asked.

"We'll manage. Not the first time I slept out-of-doors, you know."

But despite Sheldon's optimistic attitude, Henry had a very real concern. Right before all the Japanese were evacuated from Bainbridge Island, Keiko's uncle and his family had tried to resettle somewhere farther inland—where the Japanese were scrutinized less. Some Japanese families were encouraged to leave voluntarily. Some even thought doing so would prevent incarceration. The problem was that no one would sell gasoline to those families fleeing the city, or rent them a room. Even places that were virtually vacant turned them away or put up their closed signs as the Japanese families got out of their cars. Keiko's uncle had made it as far as Wenatchee, Washington, before being forced to turn back because no one would sell him any gas. He turned back and was rounded up like the rest.

Henry thought about sleeping outside and was grateful he had brought extra clothing. September brought rain and cold weather, at least in Seattle. Who knew what it would be like in Idaho this time of year?

. . .

Six hours later they made it to Walla Walla, a small farming community known for its apple orchards. Henry and Sheldon had forty-five minutes for lunch, then they'd board again for Twin Falls—then on to Jerome, Idaho, which, they assumed, would lead to Camp Minidoka.

As soon as he stepped out on the sidewalk, Henry immediately felt self-conscious. Like the eyes of the world were on him, and Sheldon too. There wasn't a person of color anywhere in sight. Not even an Indian, which Henry had expected to find in a town named after an Indian tribe. Instead, they were greeted with buttoned-up white folk, all of whom seemed to take notice. Despite that, no one appeared unfriendly. They simply regarded him and Sheldon and went about their business. Still, Henry fidgeted with his "I am Chinese" button, and Sheldon said, "Let's go find something to eat. Just don't make eye contact, you hear?"

Henry knew that Sheldon wasn't originally from Seattle; he'd grown up in Tacoma but was born in Alabama. His parents had left the South when he was five or six, and evidently he'd seen enough to never want to return. He still called grown men and little boys "sir" and tipped his hat and said "ma'am," but aside from that, he wanted no part of the South. And judging by Sheldon's hurried reaction to the people on the streets of Walla Walla, this might as well have been Birmingham.

"Where we gonna go?"

Sheldon looked at the windows of stores and restaurants. "I don't know—maybe this isn't as bad as I'd thought."

"What do you mean, bad?"

"I mean, look and you see for yourself. Ain't no one even really concerned with us. And I don't see any 'whites only' signs in the windows."

They walked down the street past people who seemed to notice them, but instead of pulling their children to the far side of the road, they just waved. Which was all the more bewildering.

He and Sheldon finally stopped at the grand entrance of what must have been the tallest building in town, the Marcus Whitman Hotel. Inside, a coffee shop could be plainly seen. "What do you think?" Henry asked.

"This is as good as any. Let's go around back and order something to go."

"Out back?" Henry asked.

"Ain't no need to be taking chances, Henry, we've come this far—"

"Can I help you two with something?" An older gentleman must have crossed the street behind them. His question made Sheldon bolt upright, and Henry stepped behind him. "You two aren't from around here are you?"

Henry swallowed hard.

"No sir, we're just passing through. In fact, we're heading back to our bus right now . . ."

"Well, since you've come all the way down, might as well go on in and grab a cup of something warm." Henry watched the man crane his neck and look down the street to the bus depot. "Looks like you've got time. Welcome to Walla Walla, and I hope you come back and see us again." He handed Henry and Sheldon a small pamphlet and tipped his hat. "God bless."

Henry watched him walk away, confused. What place is this, he wondered. Does he think I'm Japanese? He looked at his button, then up at Sheldon, who was skimming the brochure and scratching his head—a surprised yet relieved look on his face. The small pamphlet was from an Adventist church, a group Henry had known was lending charitable aid to imprisoned Japanese families. Volunteering as teachers and nurses. As it turned out, there was a large congregation, even a private church college, here.

As he and Sheldon grabbed a quick meal of coffee and toast, they looked around and made eye contact with the folks around them. Not everyone was afraid. Some even smiled back.

Finding the camp was easy—in a way that made Henry feel more than a little saddened. As he and Sheldon stepped off the bus in Jerome, Henry couldn't help but notice an enormous sign that read "Minidoka Wartime Relocation Center—18 miles." There were dozens of people loading into trucks and cars, all bound for what had become the seventh largest city in Idaho.

Sheldon adjusted his hat. "Relocation Center—they make it sound like it's the Chamber of Commerce helping people find a new home or something."

"It's *their* new home now" was all Henry could muster.

A woman with a nurse's cape rolled down the window of a blue sedan. "You two must be going to the camp. Need a ride?" she asked.

Henry and Sheldon looked at each other. Was it that obvious? It seemed that everyone in the bus depot had business up north. They both nodded vigorously.

"That truck behind me is taking visitors, if that's what you're planning."

Henry pointed to a large flatbed hay truck, with makeshift benches and rickety boarded siding. "That truck?"

"That's the one. Better hurry if you're planning on going, they won't wait much longer."

Sheldon tipped his hat and grabbed his suitcase, nudging Henry. "Thank you, ma'am—we're much obliged."

They walked to the back of the truck and climbed up, sitting next to a pair of nuns and a priest who spoke to one another in what appeared to be Latin, occasionally mixing in some conversational Japanese.

"Looks like this might be easier than you thought," Sheldon said, sliding his suitcase between his feet. "Bigger than you thought too."

Henry nodded, looking around. He was the only Asian person in sight, let alone in the truck. But he was Chinese; China was an ally of the United States—and he was a U.S. citizen to boot. That had to count for something, right?

Looking at the horizon, Henry could see the camp from five miles away. A massive rock chimney rose above the dry, dusty fields, which eventually revealed the layout of a small city. Everything appeared to be still under construction. Even from a distance Henry could make out the skeletal frames of enormous rows of buildings.

Sheldon saw it too. "That must be one thousand acres, easy," he said. Henry didn't know how much that was, but it was huge.

"Can you believe that?" Sheldon asked. "It's like a city rising up out of the Snake River. Everything's so dry and barren this far north, now they just dump everyone here."

Henry stared at the arid landscape. There were no trees or grass or flowers anywhere, and barely any shrubs. Just a living, breathing landscape of tar-paper barracks spotting the dry desert terrain. And people. Thousands of people—most of them seemed to be working on the buildings, or in the fields picking corn, potatoes, or sugar beets. Even small children and elderly people could be seen hunched over in the dusty furrows. Everyone was very much alive and in motion.

The truck lumbered over a patchwork of potholes, brakes squealing as it rattled to a halt. As passengers unloaded, camp workers were pointed in one direction and visitors in another. Henry and Sheldon followed the small herd of people who crowded into a stone visitors' room. With the wind blowing, Henry could taste the dust in the air, and feel the grit on his skin. The land was dry and parched, but there was an indescribable smell. Sweetgrass, and the smell of rain coming. Being from Seattle, Henry knew that smell all too well. A storm was blowing in.

Inside, they were instructed on what could and could not be brought to and from the camp. Things like cigarettes and alcohol were allowed in small quantities, but fairly benign things like nail files were forbidden. "I guess a huge pair of wire cutters is out of the question," Henry whispered to Sheldon, who just nodded and tipped his head.

If the sight of a Chinese boy was unusual, it was hardly noticed in the hectic comings and goings of Camp Minidoka. Even Henry, who at first was certain he'd be swept up at bayonet point and taken into the heart of the camp, was surprised at how hardly anyone noticed him. How could they? There were thousands of prisoners to process. And more buses of prisoners were arriving by the hour. The camp was still breathing and lurching to life, finding its rhythm—a growing community behind barbed-wire fences.

"Hope you took a bath before we left," Sheldon said, looking out the window. " 'Cause those are sewer lines they're digging in out there."

Henry sniffed at his sleeve, smelling sweaty and musty, like the bus ride.

Sheldon wiped his brow with a handkerchief. "It'll be months before they get hot water or flushing toilets."

Henry looked at the Japanese workers laboring in the sun. The sight made him thankful for being indoors as he and Sheldon waited in line. It was thirty minutes before they were allowed to register as visitors. Finally a file clerk checked camp records to see if the Okabe family had arrived.

"They're Quakers," Sheldon commented to Henry, nodding in the direction of the office staff.

"Like the oatmeal guy?"

"Something like that. They objected to the war and all that. Now they volunteer in the camps, teaching, filling in as nurses and stuff—least that's what I hear. Most of the white folks here is Quakers. Though this *is* Idaho, so some of 'em are Adventists probably. Same thing, I guess."

Henry peeked at the white woman behind the desk. She looked like Betty Crocker—average, plain, and pleasant.

The woman looked up from her papers, smiling. "Okabes? They're here, along with a dozen other families with that name, but I think I found who you're after."

Sheldon patted Henry on the shoulder.

"Just head on over to that visitors' room." She pointed. "And they'll help you get oriented. The camp is organized like a city, with streets and blocks. Ordinarily, visits are arranged by letter or by outgoing phone calls, which can occasionally be made from the main office. Otherwise a runner will be sent into that area of the camp and a notice will get posted outside the barracks assigned to that family."

Henry tried to follow along, blinking his eyes and rubbing his forehead.

"It normally takes at least a day," she said, "since most of the children are in temporary schoolrooms and the adults do work inside the camp."

"What kind of work?" Henry wondered, remembering all the activity outside.

"Just labor. Either harvesting sugar beets or doing construction. Plenty of office work for the women too." She sighed as she said it, returning to the pile of papers in front of her.

Henry filled out a slip for Keiko, who he'd been told was assigned to Block 17—not too far from this side of Camp Minidoka. He wanted to surprise her, so he just put down "visitor" and left the name blank. A runner, an older Japanese man who ironically walked with a limp, took the paper and wandered off.

"This could take a while," Henry said.

Sheldon nodded and watched the crowds of visitors shuffle in and out.

Sitting on a hard bench between an older man with several boxes of hymnals and a young couple with baskets of pears, Henry looked at Sheldon, watching him crack his knuckles, wishing he'd brought along his saxophone. "Thanks for coming with me," he said.

Sheldon patted Henry's knee. "Needed to be done. That's all. Your old man know you're all the way out here?"

Henry solemnly shook his head no. "I told my mother I was leaving for a few days. She must know. I don't think she knows I'm *here*, but she knows enough. I'm not saying she likes it, but she let me go and didn't ask—that was the best she could do, I suppose, her way of helping. She'll be worried and all, but she'll be okay. I'll be okay. I just had to come. I may never see Keiko again, and I didn't want what I said or didn't say at Camp Harmony to be the last thing she ever heard from me."

Sheldon stared off at the people coming and going. "There's hope for you yet, Henry. You wait and see. Might take a while, but there's always hoping."

That *while* lasted for six hours, as he and Sheldon waited and waited—sometimes inside, other times pacing outside the stone visitors' center. Thunderheads had rolled in, darkening the sky, even though there were still several hours before sunset.

Finally, Henry patted his suitcase, looking at a sign that said visiting hours ended at 5:30. "It's almost time to go back. We left our message. She must not have seen it yet." But we'll come back tomorrow. She'll find it soon enough, he thought.

Outside, thick and heavy raindrops dotted the parched ground. As it hit the tin roofs of the makeshift buildings and half-finished barracks, the rain created a slow warbling, drumming sound. People everywhere headed for shelter. Henry thought about the tar-paper roofs and unfinished buildings. He hoped they were vacant and the camp's residents occupied the rows sheltered by completed roofs.

"There's a bus for visitors over here." Sheldon pointed, balancing his suitcase on his head with one hand to keep the rain off as it turned into a downpour. Thunder rumbled far away, but no lightning could be seen. It wasn't that dark yet.

Henry tried to imagine what Keiko must have been doing right then. Heading home from school with the other Japanese kids. What a strange mix that must be—some spoke nothing but English, others spoke only Japanese. He thought about Keiko and her family settling into their one-room quarters, huddled around a pipe stove trying to stay warm, rain dripping into buckets through holes in the roof. He thought about her playing their Oscar Holden record. *Does she think about me? Does she think about me as much as I've thought about her. Could she?* No, Henry thought about her so much he could see her on the streets of Seattle, even hear her voice. Simple and small. Sparkling, with perfect English, like now, speaking his name through the rolling thunder of the rainstorm. As if she was there. As if she'd never left. He was always amazed at how he liked hearing her call his name.

Henry. From the day they met in the kitchen. *Henry.* To that horrible day when he watched helplessly as she and her family boarded the train for Camp Harmony. *Henry.* And finally, when she said *good-bye* in a sheltered, guarded way he'd never seen, as he said farewell and let her go, not wanting to complicate things any more than they already were, wanting to be a *good son.*

That voice had haunted him all these weeks.

"Henry?"

She was there. Standing in the rain, outside the stone visitors' center, which was closing for the day, behind the locked gate and rows of barbed wire. Wearing that yellow dress and a gray sweater hanging wet from her small shoulders. Then she was skipping over mud puddles, running to the fence that stood between them. "Henry!" The note from the messenger was wet and crumpled in her hand.

Looking through watery eyes, wiping the rain from his face with his sleeve, Henry caught her arms through the fence as they leaned in, his hands slipping down to feel hers—incredibly warm, despite the cold rain. Pressing his forehead to hers between the gap in the rows of barbed wire, Henry was so close he could almost feel her eyelashes when she blinked; their proximity kept their faces somewhat dry as the rain fell along their cheeks and soaked their collars.

"What are you doing here?" She blinked away the drops of rain that sprinkled her eyes, running down from a wet strand of hair.

"I . . . I turned thirteen." Henry didn't know what else to say.

Keiko didn't say a word; she just reached through the wire and wrapped her arms around his waist.

"I left. I came to see you. I'm old enough to make my own decisions, so I took a bus with Sheldon. I needed to tell you something."

Henry looked down, and Keiko's brown eyes seemed to reflect something unseen in the gray September sky. Something glowed from inside.

"I'm sorry . . ."

"For what?"

"For not saying good-bye."

"You did say good-bye . . ."

"Not the way I should have. I was so worried about my family. Worried about everything. I was confused. I didn't know what I wanted. I didn't know what good-bye really was."

"So you came all this way, all those miles, just to tell me good-bye?" Keiko asked.

"No," Henry said, feeling fuzzy inside. The rain splashing him was cold, but he didn't feel it. His jacket caught and tore on the barbed wire as his hands gently framed her waist, his fingers feeling the soaked sweater. He was leaning in, his forehead pressed against the cold metal wire; if there was something sharp there, he didn't feel it. All he felt was Keiko's cheek, wet from the rain, as she leaned in too.

"I came to do that," Henry said. It was his first kiss.

Sheldon Thomas
(1986)

Henry stepped out of the rain and into the winding corridors of the Hearthstone Inn, a nursing home over in West Seattle, not too far from the Fauntleroy Ferry Terminal, which connected Seattle with Vashon Island. Henry had been coming more often now that Ethel had passed and he had a surplus of time on his hands.

The Hearthstone Inn was one of the nicer nursing homes in West Seattle, nice to Henry anyway—not that he was an expert on nursing homes. He was more of an expert on the ones he didn't like. Those cold, gray places—like those state institutions that he'd fought so hard to keep Ethel out of. Those small-windowed, cinder-block buildings where people gathered to die, alone. The Hearthstone, by contrast, was more like a rustic hunting lodge or a resort than a rest home.

The entrance featured a chandelier made from deer antlers. A nice touch, Henry thought as he found his way to the one wing he was somewhat familiar with. He didn't bother stopping at the nurses' station. Instead, he went directly to Room 42, knocking lightly just below the nameplate that read "Sheldon Thomas."

There was no answer, but Henry peeked in anyway. Sheldon slept half-upright in his elevated hospital bed. His once-robust cheeks, which had ballooned when he played his sax, now simply draped the bones of his face. An IV ran to his wrist, where it was taped along the weathered, crumpled-paper-bag skin of his forearm. A clear plastic tube went around his ears and hung just below his nose, whistling oxygen into his lungs.

A young nurse, someone new whom he didn't recognize, came up to Henry and patted him on the arm. "Are you a friend or a family member?" She whispered the question in his ear, trying not to disturb Sheldon.

The question hung there like a beautiful chord, ringing in the air. Henry was Chinese, Sheldon obviously wasn't. They looked nothing alike. Nothing at all. "I'm distant family," Henry said.

The answer seemed sufficient. "We were just about to wake him up to give him some meds," the nurse said. "So now's a good time to go on in for a visit. He'll probably be waking up soon anyway. If you need anything, I'll be right outside."

Henry closed the door halfway. A Lava lamp with a bright purple bow on top was the only light on in the room, aside from the red lights on the various monitors hooked up to his old friend. The curtains were open, and light from the cloudy early afternoon twilight warmed up the room.

A gold 45 record hung on the wall in a dusty frame, a single Sheldon's band had recorded in the late fifties. Alongside were photos of Sheldon and his family—children and grandchildren. Drawings in crayon and marker dotted the bathroom door and the wall just beneath where the television hung from the ceiling. A bedside table was covered with small piles of photos and sheet music.

Henry sat in the well-worn chair next to the bed and looked at a recent birthday card. Sheldon had turned seventy-four last week.

One of the many monitors began beeping, then went quiet again.

Henry watched as Sheldon's mouth opened first in a silent yawn, then his eyes, blinking and adjusting to the light. He looked at Henry and smiled an old gold-toothed grin. "Well, well . . . How long have you been hanging out?" he asked, stretching and rubbing his balding pate, flattening out the white hair he had left.

"Just got here."

"Is it Sunday already?" Sheldon asked, waking up, shifting in his hospital bed.

In the months since Ethel had died, Henry had made a habit of coming over on Sunday afternoons to watch the Seahawks game with Sheldon. A nurse would help Sheldon into a wheelchair, and they'd go down to the big rec room. The one with the giant rear-projection TV. But in recent weeks, Sheldon hadn't had the energy. Now they just watched the game in the quiet of his room. Occasionally Henry would sneak in a bag of buffalo wings, clam chowder from Ivar's, or another of Sheldon's favorite foods that the nurses wouldn't normally allow. But not today.

It wasn't Seahawk Sunday, and he had brought something different to share with Sheldon. "I came early this week," Henry said. Loud enough so Sheldon could hear without his hearing aids in.

"What, you think I ain't gonna make it to Sunday?" Sheldon laughed.

Henry just smiled at his old friend. "I found something I thought you would like to have. Something I've been looking for—something you've been looking for—for years."

Sheldon's wide, bloodshot eyes looked at Henry; youthful wonder filled out his sagging face. It was a look Henry hadn't seen in a long time.

"You got a surprise for me, Henry?"

Henry nodded, smiling. He knew that the old Oscar Holden record meant as much to Sheldon as it did to himself. Maybe for different reasons, but it meant the world to each of them. Oscar Holden had given Sheldon his big break back in 1942. He'd played with Holden for a year after the war ended and the club reopened. Then Sheldon had formed his own band when Oscar passed away years later. The street cred Oscar gave him landed him a lot of long-term gigs and even earned him a modest recording contract with a local label.

"Well, I ain't getting any younger, and Christmas is coming," Sheldon said.

"Now I found it, but there's one problem—it's going to need a little restoration before you can play it."

"That don't matter none." As Sheldon spoke, a shaky finger tapped his forehead. "I still play that song in my head every night. I've heard it. I was there, remember?"

Henry reached into his bag and pulled out the old 78 record, still in its original sleeve. He held it out to show Sheldon, reading him the words on the record label as his friend pawed the side table for his reading glasses. "Oscar Holden and . . ."

"The Midnight Blue." Sheldon finished Henry's sentence.

Henry handed the record to his old friend, who draped it across his chest. His eyes closed as if he were listening to the music play somewhere, sometime, long ago.

Waiting
(1942)

Henry woke up on a dingy, straw-filled mattress on the floor, hearing the rain leak through the roof and plip-plop into a half-full laundry basin in the middle of what was the Okabes' living room. To his right was a curtained area where Keiko and her little brother slept on one side, and her parents on the other.

He could hear Keiko's mother snoring softly, along with the pinging of the rain on the tin roof—a relaxing, melodic sound that made Henry feel like he was still dreaming. Maybe it was a dream. Maybe he was really at home in his own bed, with his window overlooking Canton Alley, the window cracked open despite the wishes of his mother. Henry closed his eyes and inhaled, smelling the rain but not the fishy, salty air of Seattle. He was here. He had made it all the way to Minidoka. He'd made it even farther, all the way to Keiko's *house*.

She didn't want him to leave, and he didn't want to go. So he'd met Keiko on the other side of the visitors' building. Everything was designed to keep people from escaping, not to keep people from sneaking in. And much to Henry's surprise, he didn't even have to try very hard. He'd just told a surprised yet approving Sheldon that he would meet him the next day, grabbed a stack of schoolbooks being carried by a group of Quaker schoolteachers, and followed them in past the guards. For once in his life, there was a benefit to Caucasian people thinking that he was one of *them*—that he was Japanese.

Henry rolled over, rubbing his eyes, and froze midyawn. Keiko was lying in her bed, facing him, her chin propped up on her arms and her pillow, staring at him. Her hair was messy, hanging down and sticking out at odd angles, yet somehow it just worked. She smiled, and Henry came alive. He couldn't believe he was here. Even more than that, he couldn't believe that her parents were okay with him being here. His would have thrown him out probably. But she'd said it would be okay, and somehow it was. Her parents had looked flattered and strangely honored to have a guest in their makeshift home, surrounded by barbed wire, searchlights, and machine-gun towers.

When Keiko had walked in, Henry could barely bring himself to step through the door. Her parents were bewildered and flattered that Henry had come all this way, but somehow, they didn't seem *too* surprised. He gathered that Keiko hadn't forgotten about him. In fact, it may have been quite the opposite.

Henry turned around so he was closer to Keiko, wrapping the hand-sewn quilt around him as he lay down facing her. She was a few feet away, brushing the hair from her eyes.

"I dreamed you came to see me last night," Keiko whispered. "I dreamed you came all this way because you missed me. And when I woke up, I was so sure it was a dream, and then I looked over and there you were."

"I can't believe I'm here. I can't believe your parents—"

"Henry, this isn't about us. I mean it is, but they don't define you by the button you wear. They define you by what you do, by what your actions say about you. And coming here, despite your parents, says a lot to them—and me. And they're Americans first. They don't see you as the enemy. They see you as a person."

The words were a strange comfort. Was this acceptance? Was that what this was? The sense of belonging was foreign to him, something alien and awkward, like writing with your left hand or putting your pants on inside out. Henry looked at her parents sleeping. They seemed more restful here, in this cold, wet place, than his own parents in their warm, cozy home.

"I'll have to leave today. Sheldon and I have a bus to catch tonight."

"I know. I knew you couldn't stay forever. Besides, one of the other families might turn us in. You're a secret we wouldn't be able to keep for-ever."

"Can you keep a secret?" Henry asked.

Keiko sat up. That must have got her attention, Henry thought as she fluffed the pillow in her lap, pulling her blanket around her shoulders. She held up two fingers. "Scout's honor, Kemosabe."

"I came here thinking I'd be sneaking you out, not you sneaking me in."

"And how were you going to do that?"

"I don't know. I guess I thought I'd give you my button, like at the train station—"

"You are the sweetest, Henry. And I wish I could, I really do. But you're going to be in enough trouble when you get home. If you came home with me, you'd really get it. We'd both be thrown in jail."

"Do *you* want to know a secret?"

Henry liked this game, nodding.

"I would go. So don't ask, because I would go back with you. I'd try anyway."

Henry was flattered. Touched even. The meaning sank in.

"Then I guess I'll just wait for you."

"And I'll write," Keiko said.

"This can't last forever, right?"

They both turned toward the window, looking out at the nearby buildings through the rain-streaked glass. Keiko lost her smile.

"I don't care how long. I'll wait for you," Henry said.

Keiko's mother stopped snoring and stirred, waking up. She looked at Henry, confused for a moment, then smiled brightly. "Good morning, Henry. How's it feel to be a prisoner for a day?"

Henry looked at Keiko. "Best day of my life."

Keiko found her smile all over again.

Breakfast with Keiko's family was rice and *tamago*—eggs, hard-boiled. It wasn't fancy, but it was filling, and Henry enjoyed it immensely. The Okabes seemed happy to be settled into someplace more permanent than the ramshackle horse stalls of the Puyallup Fairgrounds. Keiko's mother made a pot of tea while her father read a newspaper printed inside the camp. Aside from the simple confines and their modest clothing, they seemed like any other American family.

"Is it nice not having to go to the mess hall all the time?" Henry tried his best to make polite table conversation in English.

"On rainy days, it's always nice," Keiko's mother said, smiling between bites.

"I still can't believe I'm here. Thank you."

"There are almost four thousand of us here now, Henry, and you're our first guest, we're delighted," Mr. Okabe said. "There's supposed to be another six thousand coming in the next month, can you believe that?"

Ten thousand? It was a number that still seemed unimaginable to Henry. "With that many people, what's to keep you from just taking over the camp?"

Mr. Okabe poured his wife another cup of tea. "Ah, that's a very profound question, Henry. And it's one I've thought about. There are probably two hundred guards and army personnel—and there are so many of us. Even if you counted just the men, we'd have a whole regiment in here. You know what keeps us from doing just that?"

Henry shook his head. He had no idea.

"Loyalty. We're *still* loyal to the United States of America. Why? Because we too are Americans. We don't agree, but we will show our loyalty by our obedience. Do you understand, Henry?"

All Henry could do was sigh and nod. He knew that concept all too well. Painfully well. Obedience as a sign of loyalty, as an expression of honor, even as an act of love, was a well-worn theme in his household. Especially between him and his father. But that wasn't the case now, was it? *Did I cause my father's stroke? Was it brought on by my disobedience?* As much as Henry reasoned otherwise, he had a hard time convincing himself the answer was no. His guilt remained.

"But even that's not enough for them," Keiko's mother added.

"It's true, in a way," Mr. Okabe said, sipping his tea. "There is a rumor that the War Relocation Authority plans to have each male seventeen and over sign an oath of loyalty to the United States."

"Why?" Henry asked, confused. "How can they put you here and then expect you to swear an oath of loyalty to them?"

Keiko broke in. "Because they want us to go to war for them. They want to draft men to fight the Germans."

That made about as much sense to Henry as his father sending him to an all-white school wearing an "I am Chinese" button.

"And we would go, gladly. I would go," Mr. Okabe said. "Many of us offered to join the army right after the bombings at Pearl Harbor. Most were refused, many were attacked outright."

"But why would you do that, why would you want to?" Henry asked.

Mr. Okabe laughed. "Look around you, Henry. It's not like we're living on Park Avenue. And anything I could do to help ease the suffering, and even more, the scrutiny and dishonor done to my family, I would do that. Many of us would do that. But what's more, for some, the only way we can prove we are American is to bleed for America's cause—despite what's being done to us. In fact, it's even more important, in the face of what's been done."

Henry began to understand and appreciate the sentiment within that complex web of injustice and contradiction. "When are they going to let you fight?" he asked.

Mr. Okabe didn't know, but he suspected it wouldn't be long after the completion of the camp. Once their labor here was done, they could be used elsewhere.

"Enough about all that fighting, Henry," Keiko's mother interrupted. "We need to figure out how we're going to get you out of here today."

"She's right," said Mr. Okabe. "We're honored that you would come all this way to court Keiko, but it is a very dangerous place. We're so used to it that the soldiers seem normal to us. But there was a shooting a week before we arrived here."

Henry blanched a little, feeling the color drain from his face. He wasn't sure what made him more nervous: that his being here was considered part of a formal courtship, which he supposed it was, or that someone had been shot.

"Um, I suppose I haven't asked permission . . . ," Henry said.

"To leave?" said Keiko's mother.

"No. Permission to court your daughter." Henry reminded himself again that he was now the same age his father had been when he was betrothed to his mother. "May I?"

Henry felt awkward and strange. Not because he still felt so young but because he'd grown up with the Chinese tradition of a go-between—someone who would act as a mediator between families. Traditional courtship involved an exchange of gifts from family to family, tokens of betrothal. None of that was possible now.

Mr. Okabe gave him a proud look, the kind Henry always wished his father had given him. "Henry, you have been incredibly honorable in your intentions toward my daughter, and you are a constant help to us as a family. You have my full permission—as if being here sleeping on our floor wasn't permission enough."

Henry perked up, disbelieving what he had asked and what he'd heard in reply. He grimaced a bit as he worried about his father, then saw Keiko smiling at him from across the table. She reached over and poured Henry a fresh cup of tea, offering it to him.

"Thank you. For everything." Henry sipped his tea still stunned. The Okabes were so casual and relaxed, so American. Even in the way they mentioned the terrible things that happened to them at Camp Minidoka.

"What was that about a shooting?" Henry asked.

"Oh that . . ." The way Mr. Okabe said it made it sound all the more strange. It was obviously something bad, but he was so used to living with the pain. Living here must do that to a person, Henry thought.

"A man, I think his name was Okamoto, was shot for stopping a construction truck from going the wrong way. One of the soldiers escorting the convoy shot him. Killed him right there," Mr. Okabe said, swallowing hard.

"What happened to him?" Henry asked. "The soldier, not the man who was shot."

"Nothing. They fined him for unauthorized use of government property, and that was it."

Henry felt the silence settle heavily on all of them.

"What use? What property?" he asked after a moment.

Mr. Okabe choked up as he looked to his wife and drew a deep breath.

"The bullet, Henry." Keiko's mother finished the story. "He was fined for the unauthorized use of the bullet that killed Mr. Okamoto."

Farewell
(1942)

Since it was Saturday, Keiko had no school, and since Henry was a very special visitor, her parents let her skip her chores for the day—just this once. So while her mother did the laundry and the mending, and her father helped new families settle in on their block, Henry sat on the steps outside their building and talked to Keiko for the better part of the afternoon. If there had been a more quiet, more romantic part of the camp, they would have found it. But there wasn't a park, or even a tree taller than a shrub for that matter. So they sat on cement blocks, side by side, their feet touching.

"When are you leaving?" Keiko asked.

"I'm going to leave with the volunteers when the five-thirty whistle blows. I'll just cluster in with them at the gate, wear my button, and hope to get through. That's where Sheldon will be meeting me, so at least I'll have someone to vouch for me."

"And what if you get caught?"

"That wouldn't be so bad, would it? I'd get to stay here with you."

Keiko smiled and rested her head on Henry's shoulder. "I'm going to miss you."

"Me too," Henry said. "But I'll be waiting for you when this is all over."

"What if it's years?"

"I'll still wait. Besides, I need time to get a good job and save money." Henry could hardly believe what he was saying. A year ago, he'd been working in the kitchen of Rainier Elementary. Now he was talking about taking care of someone. It sounded so grown-up and somewhat frightening. He hadn't even dated Keiko, really, not when they were both on the outside of the fences. But a courtship could take a year, or several years. Even in his family, where his parents often argued over the tradition of using a matchmaker for Henry, nothing was decided. Would they even let him date American girls? It didn't matter now that his father was so frail. Despite Henry's guilt, he would have to make his own decisions from now on. He'd follow the intent of his own heart.

"How long will you wait for me, Henry?"

"As long as it takes, I don't care what my father says."

"What if I'm an old woman?" Keiko said, laughing. "What if I'm in here until I'm old and my hair is gray—"

"Then I'll bring you a cane."

"You'd wait for me?"

Henry smiled, nodded, and took Keiko's hand. He didn't even look, their two hands just seemed to fall together. They spent the better part of the day beneath that cloudy sky. Henry looked up expecting rain, but the wind, which kept them a little chilly, blew the clouds south of the camp. There would be no more rain.

As the hours passed, they talked about music, Oscar Holden, and what life would be like when Keiko's family came back to Seattle. Henry couldn't bear to tell her that Nihonmachi was disappearing. Building by building and block by block, it was being transformed, bought out and renovated. He wondered how much, if anything, would be left by the time they got out. The Panama Hotel, like the rest of Japantown, was boarded up now, slumbering like a patient in a coma—you never knew if they would sit up, or just drift off and never wake up again.

As the evening shift changed for the many volunteers who worked inside Camp Minidoka, Henry said good-bye to Keiko's family once again. Her little brother even seemed to regard Henry with a sense of longing. *I guess even he knows I have a connection to the outside, a freedom he's not allowed,* Henry thought.

Holding Keiko's hand, he walked with her as close to the volunteer gate as possible without being seen. They stood behind an outbuilding and waited for a crew of workers and missionaries to pass by, then Henry would disappear into the crowd and head to the gate. He hoped Sheldon would be waiting on the other side.

"I don't know when I'll see you again. It took all I had to come see you this time," he told Keiko.

"Don't come. Just wait, and write. I'll be here—you don't have to worry about me. I'm safe here, and it won't be forever."

Henry hugged her close and felt her small arms around his shoulders. Leaning in, he felt the warmth of her cheek in the cool autumn air. Their foreheads touched as he looked down into her eyes, rolling clouds moving slowly in the reflections. His head turned to the left as hers did the same, and a simple kiss found a home between their lips. When he opened his eyes, hers were beaming back at him. He hugged her one more time, then let her go—walking backward, waving, trying not to smile too broadly, but he couldn't help it.

I love her. Henry paused at the thought. He didn't even know what that was, or what it meant, but he felt it, burning in his chest—feeling fuzzy inside. Nothing else seemed to matter. Not the somber crowd of camp workers drifting to the barbed-wire gate. Not the machine guns in the towers above.

Henry began to wave, then lowered his hand slowly as the words "I love you" rolled off his tongue. She was too far away to hear it, or maybe he didn't make a sound, but she knew, and her mouth echoed the same statement as her hand touched her heart and pointed at Henry. He simply smiled and nodded, turning back to the gate.

Angry Home
(1942)

Henry sank into his seat and spoke very little on the long bus ride home. He truly felt bad, imagining the concern he had caused. But he'd had to go. And he'd deal with the consequences. There was a strange, abiding comfort in knowing he could no longer let his father down. Not anymore. What more could there be to disappoint him? What more could he withhold from Henry as a punishment?

His mother, though. He worried about her. He'd left an additional note on his pillow for her to find later. Just a little something to keep her from worrying—too much anyway. The note told her that he was going to visit Keiko, that a friend would be coming along to keep him company, and that if all went well, he'd be home by late Sunday night. The money jar on his dresser was empty, so she'd assume that he had plenty of money for the trip. But in his entire life, he'd never been gone overnight. This would worry her immensely, especially with his father ailing.

When Henry had left Seattle, he'd imagined that he felt the same way his own father must have felt leaving home at age thirteen. Scared, excited, and confused. For his father, leaving at age thirteen was a matter of pride, even though, deep down, Henry sensed a lot of emptiness and sadness along with it. Now, on the bus heading home, he knew what his father had felt. Hurt and loneliness—but also a need to do what was right. To his father, that meant helping causes back in China. To Henry, it meant helping Keiko.

When he and Sheldon finally said their good-byes at the Seattle bus station, Henry was exhausted, despite having slept on the bus all day.

"Everything going to be okay for you back home?" Sheldon asked.

Henry yawned and nodded.

Sheldon looked at him, his eyebrows raised in concern.

"I'll be fine," Henry reassured him.

Sheldon stretched and said, "Thank you, sir, you have a fine day now," and headed for his home, walking in the direction of South Jackson, suitcase in hand.

Henry had assured him it would all be okay. But now, walking up the steps to his apartment, he realized it barely felt like home anymore. Somehow it all felt smaller. More confining. But he knew it was the same place he'd left.

The door was unlocked. A good sign.

Inside everything was dark and quiet. Their small home had a humid smell of rice cooking and the burnt, raw tobacco smell of the Camel cigarettes his father favored. His mother smoked them too, but not as frequently as his father had. That was the one thing that had changed when his father fell ill. His ability to smoke had disappeared, along with his desire. What will he had left seemed aimed at denying Henry's existence and focusing on the maps of the war in China.

The only light was a small ceramic lamp in the kitchen that his mother had made at the Yook Fun artisan shop years ago, before he was born. She'd had such a different life before Henry came along. He wondered whether she'd return to that life if he ever left. Next to the lamp was a small plate of food, cold rice and wind-dried sausages made from duck. Henry's favorite.

Looking over, he saw his parents' door was all but closed. Henry wasn't sure what surprised him more. That his mother had left such a nice dinner for him, or that she wasn't sitting here waiting for him, ready to pounce on his every excuse.

The silence was numbing.

He grabbed a pair of chopsticks and took the plate of food to his room, setting his small suitcase down just inside. He was stunned and confused as he looked at his bed and saw a large black suit laying there. On the floor were a pair of brown leather dress shoes that looked two sizes too big. The suit jacket was Western in cut but had an embroidered spiral design on the pocket, his mother's doing—modern, but giving it a touch of the Orient. A sense of place in a modern world.

Then it hit him. *My father's dead.*

Henry had never worn such a fine suit in his entire life. The nicest clothes he had were the ones he wore again and again to Rainier Elementary. He wore them several days in a row, doing his best to keep them clean, then his mother would hand-wash and dry them and he'd wear them again. His appearance was more important to her than the fact that he was teased mercilessly for being too poor to have any other school clothes.

But as Henry touched the fine fabric of the suit, he remembered that it wasn't white. If Henry were to wear such a suit to his father's traditional funeral, surely his mother would have insisted that he, as the birthright son, wear the color of his father's traditions. White was a funeral color, not black. This suit would never do.

Henry opened his door and stepped across the hall to his parents' room. Peeking in, he could see his mother sleeping, and the outline of his father. Henry could hear his father's jangled breathing, no better, but no worse than when he'd left three days ago. His father hadn't died. Henry sighed and felt his guilt make room for quiet relief.

Back in his room, Henry sat on the bed, looking at the suit, eating his cold dinner. The sausage was sweet and chewy. Fresh too. His mother must have made it while he was away. Chewing the last bite, he noticed the corner of a small envelope that must have been tucked in the inside breast pocket of the suit jacket.

Reaching in, he opened the jacket, which now looked too big for him. It was his mother's way. Everything had to have room to grow. Everything had to last.

Pulling out the envelope, he touched the label, which read "China Mutual Steam Navigation Co."—it was a cruise line. Henry didn't have to open it to know what was inside. It would be tickets—passage to China.

"It's for you. From your father and me." His mother was standing in his doorway, wrapping herself in a flowered robe, speaking to Henry in his familial Cantonese, a language he hadn't spoken all weekend. "Japan is losing," she said. "The Kuomintang has forced the Japanese Imperial Army north once and for all. Your father has decided you can go to Canton now. To finish your Chinese schooling."

Henry stood by the bed, facing his mother. On the bus ride home, he had heard the latest reports on the fighting on Guadalcanal. But to his parents, the war with Japan was always seen from the Chinese side. They fought a different war. Still, Henry was thirteen now, a man's age in his father's eyes. Those same eyes that no longer regarded Henry as his son. Yet here he was, being given the one thing his father had always wanted most for Henry—a chance for him to return to China, a place he'd never known, never been, to live with relatives he'd never met. To his father, this was the most precious thing he could give Henry. And as much as Henry had feared this day would come, part of him wanted to go, at least to be able to come back with an understanding of what made his father who he was.

But Henry knew better. "He's just doing this to keep me from her," he said. He studied his mother's face, searching for a confirmation in her expression, in her reaction.

"This is his dream. He's worked and saved for years to give this to you. To do this *for* you. So you can know where you came from. Haven't you dishonored him enough?"

The words stung. But Henry had been stung before. "Why now?"

"The army . . . the Japanese . . . it's finally safe . . ."

"Why now? Why today? It's not any safer getting there. The Japanese submarines have been sinking half the ships in and out of southern China. Why do I know all this? Because that's all he's talked about for my entire life!"

"This is his house. You are his son!" his mother snapped back, not loud enough to wake Henry's father but in a forceful way he'd never seen before. His mother had always walked the fence of conflict between him and his father. Striding with one foot firmly planted on each side of the neutral zone that Henry and his father never crossed. Now she was exerting her own will. She loved Henry as a son, he had no doubt, but she had no choice but to honor her husband's wishes. Henry's father was bedridden and could barely speak or move, but he still was head of the home.

"I don't want to go. This is his dream. Not mine! I was born *here,* I don't even speak the same dialect as the village he came from. I won't fit in *there* any more than I fit in at the all-white school he sent me to. Haven't I done enough?"

"Done enough? You have done plenty! You have taken sides with the enemy. The enemy of China—*and* America. We are *allies*. They are the enemy. You have become his enemy. And still he does this for you. For you!"

"It's not for me," Henry said softly. "And I didn't do this to him." As the words came out, he almost believed them. Almost. But looking at his mother—tears streaming down her face, the anger and frustration so measured she was shaking—he knew he'd always be haunted by this, by the effect his actions had had on his father.

Henry looked down at the suit. It was hand-tailored, and expensive. The tickets were expensive too. He had no idea where he'd be going, where he'd be staying, or for how long. And, looking at his crying mother, who now spent her days caring for her dying husband, for her dying father, Henry felt his resolve crumble. Maybe thirteen wasn't old enough to escape the pain and pressures of his family. Maybe he'd never escape.

"When do I leave?" The words fell out of his mouth, rising like a white flag of surrender. He thought about Keiko, feeling farther and farther away from her as each moment passed, as if his heart were already onboard the ocean liner and being pulled far away, to the sweltering hot South China Sea.

"Next week," his mother whispered.

"For how long?" Henry asked.

He watched her pause. This was obviously hard on her as well. She was sending him away, fulfilling the wishes of her husband, letting go of her only son. Henry looked up at her, not wanting to go.

"Three, maybe four years."

Silence.

Henry mulled it over. Realistically, he had no idea when Keiko would be coming home, if she ever came home. After all, what home did she have to come back to? Maybe the war would go on forever. Maybe she'd be sent to Japan. It was all unknown. *But four years?* It was unthinkable. Henry had never been away from his parents for *four days*. "I . . . can't do that."

"You must. You have no choice. This is decided."

"I will decide. I'm the same age Father was when he left, when he made his own choices. If I go, it will be my choice, not his," Henry said. He sensed the conflict in his mother—wanting to obey her husband's wishes but not wanting to lose her son. "My choice, not his. Not yours."

"What will I tell him? What would you have me say?"

"Tell him I'll go, but not now. Not until the war's over. Not until she comes back. I told her I'd wait. I made a promise."

"But you won't even see her—for years maybe."

"Then I'll write to her every week."

"I cannot tell him—"

"Then do as I've done these past years. Say nothing."

She put her head in her hands, rubbing her temples. Rocking back and forth. "You are stubborn. Just like your father."

"He made me what I am." Henry hated saying it, but it was true, wasn't it?

Letters
(1943)

Henry wrote to Keiko, telling her about his father's ill-timed intention to send him away. Back to China, a small village where his father grew up, just outside of Canton. Henry still had distant relatives there. People he'd never met. Some not even blood relatives, but they were *calabash,* as Henry's father put it, using some strange slang of quasi-English. They were together. They were of one mind. Everyone in the village was considered family. And they looked forward to visitors from America—Henry knew from his father's stories that his visit would include a warm *homecoming,* and a lot of work as well. Part of him wanted to go. But part of him wanted nothing to do with what his father had manipulatively planned for him.

And he couldn't go now. Keiko or her family might need him, and they knew so few people outside the camps. He was all they had.

Much to Henry's surprise, Keiko thought he should go. *Why not?* she'd asked in her most recent letter from Camp Minidoka. She was a prisoner, they were apart anyway, *might as well use this time,* she'd said—for Henry to complete the schooling so many parents of American-born children wished for their sons.

Stubbornly Henry refused to give in to his father's wishes. His father wanted nothing to do with Keiko. And had disowned him. Henry couldn't set that aside. So he stayed, and continued *scholarshipping.*

He also wrote to Keiko, every week.

Henry spent his days at school, helping Mrs. Beatty, and his free evenings wandering up and down South Jackson listening to the brightest jazz musicians the city had to offer. He caught Oscar Holden and

Sheldon when he could, but other nights he just stayed home and wrote to Keiko.

In return she sent Henry notes, with sketches from inside the camp and even outside, when she was allowed beyond the fences. The stringent rules had been eased a bit after the camp had been completely settled—Keiko's Girl Scout troop was even allowed beyond the barbed wire to have an overnight campout. *Amazing,* Henry thought. Prisoners being allowed outside, only to return freely. But that was where their families were, and besides, where else could they go?

At least she kept busy. Henry did too, walking down to the old post office on South King, near the Yong Kick noodle factory. As the months rolled by, his weekly journey had become more of a habit—one still filled with anticipation.

"One letter—overland carriage, please," Henry requested, handing over the small envelope with the letter to Keiko he'd written the night before.

The skinny girl who normally worked the counter looked to Henry to be about his age—maybe fourteen, with dark hair and rich olive skin. He assumed she was the daughter of the postmaster assigned to Chinatown, helping out her parents in Chinese fashion. "Another letter? This one carriage mail, you say? That's going to get expensive—twelve cents this time."

Henry counted out the change from his pocket as she stamped it. He didn't know what else to say, he'd done this routine dozens of times now. Long enough to know what was coming next, already seeing the disappointment in the young clerk's eyes.

"I'm sorry, Henry. No mail for you today. Maybe tomorrow?"

It'd been three weeks now, and no letter from Keiko. He knew that military mail had priority over all domestic shipments, especially letters going to someone with a Japanese surname—not to mention that mail in and out of the prison camps was notoriously slow. But this was troubling, on the verge of heartbreaking. So much that Henry began mailing all his letters by overland carriage—special bus service that cost ten times the normal postage but got there quicker. Or so he was always told.

Still, no word from Camp Minidoka. No word from Keiko.

. . .

On the walk home, Henry caught Sheldon wrapping up an afternoon gig on the corner of South Jackson.

"I thought you were playing at the Black Elks Club these days?" Henry asked, pausing on the street where he used to give Sheldon his lunch each day.

"Still do. Still do, that's for certain. More sold-out shows than ever. Oscar's packing them in every night, even more now that there's so many white folks moving their business into these parts."

Henry offered a solemn nod of agreement, looking down toward what was left of Japantown. Most businesses had been sold for pennies on the dollar, or the local banks had seized the frozen businesses and resold the real estate for a profit. Those that were funded by local Japanese-owned banks were the last to fold, but fold they did as the banks themselves became insolvent since their owners had been sent to places like Minidoka, Manzanar, and Tule Lake.

"I guess I just like to come down and reminisce with my horn once in a while. Think about the good ol' days, you know?" Sheldon winked at Henry, who didn't feel like smiling. Those times were gone. Things were different. *I'm different,* Henry thought.

"Looks like you're heading home empty-handed?" Sheldon half-asked, half-stated—as if Henry's sad walk home from the post office would be made any better that way.

"I guess I don't understand. I thought we'd write more. Is it wrong to think that? I know she's busy. Her last letter said she's in school now, playing sports—even on the yearbook staff." Henry shrugged. "I just didn't think she'd forget about me so quickly."

"Henry, there's no way she's forgotten about you. *I guarantee that.* Maybe there's just more to do, more to be busy with, what with ten thousand Japanese folks all crammed into one area. Beats what she was used to up at that white-bread, blue-blood elementary school y'all used to hang out at."

"At least we were together."

"At *most* you were together—and that's a beautiful thing," Sheldon said. "Don't worry, she'll be back someday. Keep the faith. Keep writing. Time and space is a hard one to deal with, let me tell you. Moving all the way up here from the South, I can testify to that one. People relations is hard business. Hard to keep that going. But don't give up, something good will come of it all—things have a way of working out just fine, you'll see."

"I wish I was as hopeful as you are," Henry said.

"Hope is all I got. Hope gets you through the night. Now you run along now, go home and take care of that mama of yours—and you have a fine day, sir!"

Henry waved good-bye, wondering if he should try to see her again. Then he thought of what Keiko's life must be like right now. How wonderful it must be for her finally to go to school with nothing but Japanese kids, all just like her. A whole community growing in the desert. Maybe there was more for her there than here with me? Maybe she was better off. Maybe.

"Good news, Henry." The young Chinese clerk brushed the hair from her eyes and held out the tattered envelope with both hands. "Looks like she does care after all."

Henry looked up and took the letter, detecting a wisp of a sigh. "Thanks" was all he could muster. It had been three weeks since the last correspondence. He had grown nervous and sometimes even anticipated a Dear John letter—the kind of dreaded brush-off normally reserved for enlisted men.

He held the envelope in his hand, unsure of whether to open it or not, then walked outside and around the corner, finding a bench at the nearest bus stop.

Opening it, Henry drew in a deep breath and exhaled slowly as he unfolded the letter. He noticed the date immediately; it was from last week. Seemed like the mail was still occasionally running on time.

"Dear Henry . . ."

It wasn't a Dear John letter. Just one of Keiko's normal heartfelt missives—catching Henry up on the crazy day-to-day life in the camp. About how all the men were required to sign loyalty oaths, which would then make them eligible for the draft and military service fighting the Germans. Some, like Keiko's dad, had signed up immediately, so eager to prove their loyalty. Others became resisters, refusing to sign; the worst of them were taken away and imprisoned somewhere else.

The note made little mention of Henry's own letters, saying only that she missed him dearly, and hoped he was doing okay.

Henry wrote her again that night and mailed the letter the next day.

This time he waited months for a reply, and when it came, Keiko seemed more confused and busy than ever. He'd written her two more times while waiting and couldn't tell which letter she was responding to. Or had a letter been lost?

Henry was learning that time apart has a way of creating distance—more than the mountains and time zone separating them. Real distance, the kind that makes you ache and stop wondering. Longing so bad that it begins to hurt to care so much.

Years
(1945)

Henry rounded the corner of South King and ran into Chaz heading home from the post office. Henry had grown a foot since he last saw Chaz and now realized he wasn't just looking directly into the eyes of his former tormentor. He was actually looking down an inch or two. Chaz looked small and weak, even though he outweighed Henry by twenty or thirty pounds.

Face-to-face, all Chaz could muster was a grudging *hello*. He didn't even smile. Henry just stared back, doing his best to look cold and intimidating. Chaz, by contrast, looked soft and doughy, cracking first, stepping around Henry and passing him by.

"My father's still going to own your girlfriend, Henry," Chaz muttered as he walked past, just loud enough for Henry to hear.

"What did you say?" Henry grabbed Chaz by the arm and spun him around, a move that surprised both of them.

"My father's still buying up what's left of Nip-ville, and when your girlfriend gets back from that concentration camp she's holed up in, she's not going to have anything to come home to." He shrugged Henry off and backed away, more pathetic and annoying than menacing. "Then what are you going to do?"

Stung, Henry let him go, watching him waddle off, up the hill and around the corner out of sight. Henry looked down the street to what was left of Nihonmachi. Not much. The only fixtures that remained were the larger buildings, too expensive to buy, like the Panama Hotel, which stood as the sole remaining evidence of a living, breathing community. Little else remained that wasn't completely gutted, torn down, or taken over by Chinese or white business interests.

Henry could hardly believe that two years had passed. For his father it had been two years of air raids and war updates—from Indochina to Iwo Jima. For Henry it had been twenty-four months of writing to Keiko, occasionally getting a reply, maybe every few months. Just catching up, her concern for him waning.

Each time he visited the post office, the same young clerk looked at him with what Henry regarded as a sad combination of pity and admiration. "She must be very special to you, Henry. You've never given up on her, have you?" The clerk didn't know much about Henry, just his writing habits and his dedication. And maybe she sensed his pang of emptiness, a hint of loneliness as Henry left the post office empty-handed each week.

Henry thought about taking another bus trip. Back in the *belly of the big dog,* as Sheldon liked to put it, that long Greyhound bus ride through Walla Walla all the way to Minidoka. But he let those thoughts go. He was busy here helping his mother keep up with things, and Keiko seemed okay from the few letters that he received.

In her early letters, Keiko had wanted continuous updates on life in Seattle. At school, and in the old neighborhood. Henry had slowly broken it to her that little remained of what she'd once called home. She never seemed to believe that it could disappear like that, in such a short amount of time. She loved this area so much—a place with so many memories. How could it be gone? How could he tell her?

When she asked, "What's become of the old neighborhood—is it still deserted?" He could say only, "It's changed. New businesses have moved in. New people." She seemed to know what that meant. No one seemed to care what happened to what was left of Nihonmachi. Chaz had gotten off on his vandalism charges years earlier—the judge wouldn't even hear of it. Henry kept that news to himself, and in the meantime, he'd updated Keiko on the jazz scene on South Jackson. How Oscar Holden was once again holding court at the Black Elks Club. How Sheldon was a regular in the band and even played a few of his own numbers. Life was moving forward. The United States was winning the war. There was talk of the war in Europe being over by Christmas. The Pacific would be next. Then, just maybe, Keiko would be coming home. Back to what? Henry wasn't sure, but he knew he'd still be here, waiting.

. . .

At home, Henry spoke politely to his mother, who seemed to regard him as the man of the house now that he was fifteen and helping with the bills. He'd taken a part-time job at Min's BBQ, though he didn't feel particularly helpful. Not when other kids his age were lying about their birthdays and enlisting, fighting on the front lines. But it was the least he could do. Despite his mother's best intentions and his father's wishes, Henry remained at home—his schooling in China would wait. It would have to. He had promised to wait for Keiko, and that vow was one he intended to keep, no matter how long it took.

His father still had not spoken to him. Then again, since the stroke, he spoke very little to anyone. He'd had another mild one, and his voice was little more than a whisper. Still, Henry's mother turned the radio off and on near his bed when there was a report on the fighting in the Philippines, or Iwo Jima—each battle in the Pacific drawing a breath closer to the expected invasion of Japan itself, a daunting task since Premier Suzuki had announced that Japan would fight to the very end. When the news was over, she'd read the newspaper to him and report on fund-raising activities at the benevolent associations that dotted Chinatown. She told him about how the Kuomintang had expanded their office into an outpost where expressions of nationalist pride could be printed and distributed, along with various fund-raising efforts to arm and equip the factions that were fighting back on the mainland.

Henry would sit occasionally and have one-way conversations with his father. It was all he could do. His father wouldn't even look at him, but Henry was certain the man couldn't turn his ears away. He had to listen; he was too weak to move on his own power. So Henry spoke gently, and his father, as always, stared out the window, pretending not to care.

"I ran into Chaz Preston today. Do you remember him?"

Henry's father sat motionless.

"He and his father came by a few years ago. His father was looking for your help in buying some of the vacant buildings—the ones left behind after the Japanese left?"

Henry continued despite his father's lack of response. "He tells me they're buying up the last of Nihonmachi—maybe even the Northern

Pacific Hotel. Maybe even the Panama." Despite his father's silence and frailty, he was still a highly regarded member of the Bing Kung Benevolent Association and the Chinese Chamber of Commerce. His age and health only made him more revered in certain circles, where honor and respect must be paid to those who had given so much. After he had raised so much money for the war effort, Henry's father's opinion still mattered. Henry had often seen members of the business community come by to get his father's blessing on business arrangements in the neighborhood.

"You don't think they'd let Chaz's family—the Prestons—buy the Panama, do you?" Henry had hoped the hotel would remain unsold until Keiko returned, or at least that it might be bought by Chinese interests. But few had the money to make a worthy offer.

Henry looked at his father, who turned back and, for the first time in months, intentionally made eye contact with him. It was all he needed to know. Even before his father mustered the energy for a crooked smile, Henry knew. Something was in the works. The Panama Hotel would be sold.

Henry didn't know what to make of it. He had waited for Keiko for nearly three years. He loved her. He would wait longer if he had to. But at the same time, he wished that, when she came home, it would be to more than just him; that part of her old life, part of her childhood would still be there. That there might be a few of the places she had drawn in her sketchbook, those memories that meant so much to her.

Meeting at the Panama
(1945)

After breakfast, Henry helped his mother carry the laundry upstairs from where she'd hung it to dry in Canton Alley and then sat next to their old Emerson radio, listening to *Texaco Star Theater,* a variety show—not the usual news program his father listened to. Henry looked up as his mother wheeled his father into the living room and next to his old reading chair. Behind her ear was a fresh starfire lily that Henry had picked up at the market earlier.

"Put it on your *father's* show," she implored in Cantonese.

Henry just turned the radio down, then off completely with a hard click.

"I need to talk to him about something. Something important, do you mind?" Henry asked as politely as possible. His mother just threw up her hands and walked away. He knew she didn't see the use in his having these one-way conversations.

Henry's father looked at him for a moment, then cast his frustrated eyes on the radio, as though Henry were a bill collector or a houseguest who had long overstayed his welcome.

"I'll get to that," Henry said, eyeing the radio. He left it off to make sure his father was listening, undistracted. "I just want to talk about something first." In his hands was the travel scrip from the China Mutual Steam Navigation Co.—his passage to China.

Henry let a moment of silence exist between the two of them. A period on the end of the sentence of their whole fractured father-son relationship.

"I'll go." As the words punched the air, Henry wasn't sure if his father heard him. He held the travel envelope up for his father to see. "I said, I'll go."

Henry's father looked up at his son, waiting.

Henry had considered his father's offer to go back to China to finish his schooling. Now that he was older, his time there would only be a year or two. Traveling overseas by steamship and starting life again, far away from everything that reminded him of Keiko, seemed like a reasonable alternative to moping up and down the crowded streets of South King.

Still, part of him hated to give in to his father. His father was so stubborn, so bigoted. Yet the more Henry thought about it, the more he realized maybe there was something good to be had from the whole sad affair.

"I'll go, but only on this condition," Henry said.

Now he really had his father's attention, weak and frail as it was.

"I know the Panama Hotel is for sale. I know who wants to buy it. And since you're an elder member of the downtown associations, I know you have some say in the matter." Henry took a deep breath. "If you can prevent the sale, I will do as you wish, I will go and finish my schooling in China. I'll finish the rest of the year here in Seattle, then take the August steamer to Canton." Henry examined his father's paralyzed expression; the stroke had taken so much of who he was already. "I'll go."

Henry's father's hand began to tremble in his lap; his cocked head straightened on the frail stem of his weakened neck. His lips quivered as they formed to make sounds, to speak words Henry hadn't heard in years. *"Do jeh"*—thank you. Then he asked, *"Why?"*

"Don't thank me," Henry said in Chinese. "I'm not doing this for *you*, I'm doing it for me, for the girl, the one you hated so much. You got your wish. Now *I* wish something. I want that hotel left as is. Unsold." Henry didn't quite know why. Or did he? The hotel was a living, breathing memory for him. And it was a place his father wanted gone, so having it spared somehow suited him. Somehow balanced the scales in his mind. Henry would go to China. He'd start over. And maybe, if that old hotel were still around, Nihonmachi could start over too. Not for him. Not for Keiko. But because it needed a place to start from. Sometime in the future. After the war. After the bittersweet memories of him and Keiko were long since paved over, he'd have one reminder left. A placeholder that would be there for him sometime in the future.

The next day, Henry mailed his last letter to Keiko. She hadn't written in six months. And then she'd only talked about how much she loved school there, going to sock hops and formal dances. Life for her was full and abundant. She didn't seem to need him.

Still, he wanted to see her. In fact, his hopes were high that it might actually happen. And who knew, maybe he would have a moment with her again. Word was that many families had been released as early as January. And since Minidoka was known as a camp for "loyal internees," Keiko might be out right now. If not, she'd be coming home soon. Germany was losing. The war on both fronts would be ending sooner rather than later.

Henry hadn't written in several weeks, but this letter was different.

This letter wasn't just a good-bye—it was a farewell. He was wishing her a happy life, and letting her know that he'd be leaving for China in a few months, that if she might be returning soon, he'd meet her, one last time. In front of the Panama Hotel. Henry chose a date in March—a month away. If she were coming home soon, she'd get the invitation in time. And if she were still in the camp and needed to write back, there was time for that as well. It was the least he could do. After all, he still loved her. He'd waited over two years for her; he could wait one more month, couldn't he?

The clerk took the letter and attached the twelve-cent overland carriage postage. "I hope she knows how much you care about her. I hope you tell her." She held up the envelope and then reverently set it on a pile of outgoing letters. "I hope she's worth the wait, Henry. I've seen you come and go for all these months. She's a lucky girl, even if she doesn't write back as often as you'd like."

Or ever, Henry thought, smiling to hide his sadness. "This is probably the last time you'll see me, 'cause this is my last letter to that address."

The clerk looked crestfallen, like she'd been following a soap opera that had taken a turn for the worse. "Oh . . . why? I hear the camps are sending people home left and right. She might be coming home soon, to Seattle, right?"

Henry looked out the window at the crowded streets of Chinatown. If people *were* leaving the camps, few were returning to their original homes. Because they weren't there any longer. And besides, no one would rent to them. Stores still refused to sell them goods. The Japanese were no longer welcome in Japantown.

"I don't think she's coming back," Henry said and turned to the postal clerk and smiled. "And I don't think I can wait any longer. I'm going to Canton to finish my schooling in a few months. Time to look forward. Not back."

"Finishing your Chinese schooling?"

Henry nodded, but it felt almost like an apology. For giving in, and for giving up.

"Your parents must be so proud then—"

Henry cut her off. "I'm not doing it for them. Anyway, nice knowing you." He forced a polite smile and turned to the door, looking back, detecting more than a hint of sadness in the young clerk's face. Some things aren't meant to last, Henry thought.

One month later, just as Henry had said he would, he waited on the steps of the Panama Hotel. From his vantage point, the view had completely changed. Gone were the paper lanterns, and the neon signs for the Uji-Toko Barber and the Ochi Photography Studio. In their place stood Plymouth Tailors and the Cascade Diner. But the Panama remained as a bulwark against the rising tide of opportunistic development.

Henry brushed the pants of his suit and straightened his tie. It was too warm for the jacket, so he kept it in his lap, occasionally brushing the hair that hung across his face to the side as the wind blew it back again. The suit, the one his father had bought and his mother had tailored, fit him well—he'd finally grown into it. Soon he'd be wearing it on his voyage to

China. To live with relatives and attend a new school. A place where he'd be *special* all over again.

Sitting there, watching handsome couples stroll by arm in arm, Henry allowed himself to miss Keiko. He'd pushed those feelings aside months ago, when her letters stopped, knowing that time and space don't always make the heart remember—sometimes just the opposite. At the thought of Keiko not coming back, or the more dreaded yet all-too-real alternative—that she'd forgotten or moved on—Henry grew less worried and simply began to despair. After school, sometimes alone, sometimes with Sheldon, he'd walk down Maynard Avenue, looking at what was left of the once vibrant Nihonmachi. The time he'd spent there, walking Keiko home, sitting and watching her paint or draw in her sketchbook—it all seemed like a lifetime ago, someone else's lifetime. He didn't really think she'd show up. But he had to try, to make one last noble gesture, so when he boarded that ship, he could leave knowing he'd given it his all. One last hope. Hope was all he had, and like Mr. Okabe had said as he and his family had left on that train almost three years earlier, hope can get you through anything.

In his suit pocket was his father's silver pocket watch. Henry drew it out and opened it, listening to the sweeping, ticking sound to make sure it was working. It was. It was almost noon, the time he'd said he'd be here—waiting. He looked at his reflection in the polished crystal of the pocket watch. He looked older. More grown-up. He looked like his father when his father had been in his prime, and it surprised him. The seconds ticked by, and in the distance he could hear the noon whistle blow at Boeing Field and then an echo on the wind as Todd Shipyards signaled their lunchtime hour.

Time had come and gone. He was done waiting.

Then he heard footsteps. The unmistakable *clip-clop* of a woman's heels against the pavement. A long, slender shadow bled across the steps and blanketed his reflection in the watch, revealing the second hand and the hour hand, straight up, twelve o'clock.

She was standing there. A young woman, in fine black leather heels, bare legs, a long blue pleated skirt that rocked back and forth from her hips in the cool springtime air. Henry couldn't bear to look up. He'd waited so long. He held his breath and closed his eyes, listening—

listening to the sounds on the busy street, the cars cruising by, the chatter of the street vendors, the wailing of a saxophone on some nearby street corner. He could smell her jasmine perfume.

He opened his eyes, looking up to see a short-sleeved blouse, white, with tiny blue speckles and pearl buttons.

Looking into her face, he saw her. For a brief moment, he saw Keiko's face. Older, her long black hair parted to one side, wearing a touch of makeup, just enough to define her supple cheeks, something he'd never seen before. She stepped to the side, and Henry blinked, staring into the sun for a moment before she blocked out the glare and he could see her again.

It wasn't Keiko.

He could see her clearly. She was young and beautiful, but she was *Chinese*. Not Japanese. And she held a letter in her hands, offering it to him. "I'm so sorry, Henry."

It was the clerk, the young woman from the post office. The one Henry had said hello to for over two years, coming and going, mailing letters to Minidoka. Henry had never seen her dressed up before. She looked so different.

"This came back, unopened, last week. It's marked 'Return to Sender.' I'm afraid she's no longer there . . . or . . ."

Henry took the letter and studied the ugly black return stamp, which had stepped on the address he'd so lovingly written in his best penmanship. The ink had bled across the face of the envelope, streaking like tears. When he turned it over, he noticed the letter had been opened.

"I'm sorry. I know I shouldn't have, but I just felt so bad. And then I hated the thought of you sitting here, waiting for someone who was never going to come."

Henry felt numb with disappointment, and a little confused. "So you came to bring me this?"

He settled into the sidewalk and looked into her eyes, seeing them in a way he'd never seen them before, noticing how pained she looked. "Actually, I came to bring you *this*." She handed Henry a bundle of starfire lilies, tied with a piece of blue ribbon. "I see you buying them in the market once in a while. I guess I figured they were your favorite, and maybe someone should give *you* some for a change."

Stunned, Henry took the flowers, looking at each one, inhaling the sweet fragrance, feeling the weight of them in his hands. He couldn't help but notice her earnest, hopeful, fragile smile.

"Thank you." Henry was touched. His disappointment melted away. "I . . . I don't even know your name."

Her smile brightened. "I'm Ethel . . . Ethel Chen."

V-J Day
(1945)

Five months. That was how long Henry had been dating Ethel.

She was a sophomore at Garfield High School and lived up the hill on Eighth Avenue with her family, of whom Henry's parents immediately approved. In many ways, Henry felt like Ethel was a second chance. He'd hoped, even prayed for Keiko to come back, or at least to write and explain where she'd gone and why. Not knowing hurt almost as much as losing her—because he never really knew what had happened. Life got complicated, he supposed. Yet in some strange, loving way, he hoped she was happy wherever she was and with whoever she might be with.

Henry on the other hand was with Ethel now. And Sheldon from time to time, of course—as always. Still, Henry could never forget about Keiko; in fact, each morning he'd wake up, think of her, and ache for what he'd lost. Then he would remind himself of Ethel and imagine a time, years from now, when he might actually forget about Keiko for a day, a week, a month, maybe longer.

On a park bench at the corner of South King and Maynard, he and Sheldon sat and soaked up the warm August afternoon. His friend didn't play the streets much anymore. His regular gig at the Black Elks Club paid the bills, and the streets just weren't the same, Sheldon complained. He'd even headed north along the waterfront, looking for new corners to play, new tourists to play for, but his heart wasn't in it. The club was where he belonged now.

"I'm gonna miss seeing you around these parts, Henry," Sheldon said, cracking a roasted peanut, tossing the shells into the street, offering the bag to his friend.

Henry took a handful. "I'll be back. This is home. Right here. I'm going to China to learn all I can, see some long-lost relatives, but that's not who I am. This place is who I am. This is home for me. Still, it's hard to believe that in one more week I'll set sail for southern China and a village filled with relatives I've never seen with names I couldn't even pronounce."

"You do sense the irony now, don't you?" Sheldon asked, spitting a piece of peanut shell out the side of his mouth.

"That I waited for her—for Keiko—and now I'm asking Ethel to wait for me? I know, it doesn't exactly make sense, but she said she'd wait, and I believe her. She will. My parents love her. And as much as I hate to see my father so happy under the circumstances, he is. But he did his part. I told him I'd go if he'd do me a favor in return, and he kept his word. He wants to talk all the time now, but I just don't know . . ."

"About your old man?"

"We lived under the same roof, but didn't speak for two, almost three years; at least he didn't speak to me, didn't acknowledge my presence. And now he wants his proud son back, and I don't know *how* to feel. So I just let Ethel talk to him, and that seems to work."

Sheldon cracked open another peanut, shaking his head, sucking the salt off the shell before tossing it. "Speaking of . . ."

Henry looked up to see Ethel running across the street, crossing into traffic.

They had begun dating the day Henry waited at the Panama Hotel. She'd bought him lunch, and he'd bought her dinner. Although they went to different schools they saw each other as much as they could. They spent all day together on Saturdays—walking arm in arm along the waterfront, or catching the No. 6 bus to Woodland Park, splashing in the wading pools, and chasing each other through the zoological gardens. They even shared their first kiss atop the Smith Tower, thirty-five stories up, watching the sun set over the city, lighting the harbor, shadowy mountains in the distance. Henry kept the admission ticket, a worn stub for fifty cents that reminded him of that perfect evening, in his wallet.

One place Henry never took Ethel, though, was the Black Elks Club. He never even mentioned the smoking joint where Oscar Holden held court and Sheldon played backup. That memory was special to Henry, something he couldn't easily share. Sheldon never asked about it. He seemed to understand without needing an explanation.

As Henry stood up, she threw her arms around him, squeezing him, shaking him, looking frantic and ecstatic at the same time.

"Hey . . . hey, what's the hurry? Did I miss something? What's the matter, are you okay?" Henry said as she tried to get the words out.

"Shhhh . . ." was all she could muster, holding Henry's hand. She was almost hysterical, blissful in her abandon. "Listen! Listen! Can you hear it?" She reached out and took Sheldon's hand as well.

Henry looked down the street in stunned amazement. All the cars on South King had stopped, frozen. Some right in the middle of the intersection with Seventh Avenue. People were running into the streets, pouring out of shops and office buildings.

In the distance, everywhere, Henry heard bells ringing, then cars honking. The commuter ferries that sat in their terminal moorings sounded their foghorns. The sounds roared from open windows and storefronts. Not the wailing siren of an air-raid drill. Not that piercing, menacing horn blaring from the rooftops, but cheering—that roared like a wave, crashing into all parts of Chinatown, the International District, and the whole city of Seattle.

The news spread from person to person, house to house, block to block—the Japanese had surrendered. Everywhere Henry looked, people flooded into the streets, dancing on the hoods of parked cars. Grown men were screaming like little boys, grown women, even stoic Chinese women, openly crying tears of joy.

Sheldon broke out his horn, slipped in the reeded mouthpiece, and began to wail, strutting around in the middle of South King between a milk truck and a police car, whose sirens flashed in slow, lazy circles.

Ethel wrapped her arms around Henry. He looked down and kissed her. Everyone else was doing it; even total strangers embraced and cried. Others brought out glasses of wine, glasses of anything.

Deep down, Henry had known the war's end was imminent. Everyone knew. Everyone felt it. He'd wondered what he would feel. Joy? Relief? He'd wondered what his father would do to occupy his time now that the Japanese had surrendered. Then again, he knew the war would go on in his father's mind. This time it would be the Kuomintang, the nationalists versus the communists. China's struggle would continue, and so would his father's.

Despite the years of *scholarshipping* at Rainier, and the hordes of Chinese kids who had shouted "White devil" as he walked to school each morning, Henry had never felt more American than right then, celebrating the greatest victory in the history of history. It was a joy that was simple, unexpected, and carried with it a quiet peace. It was a happy ending that brought the promise of a new beginning. So when Ethel finally let go, her lips still wet and soft from Henry's kiss, the words came out like a secret confession. And somehow it made sense. Somehow it fit. If Henry had had doubts before, they were obfuscated by the ringing church bells and yelling, crying crowds.

"Ethel . . ."

She straightened her hair and pulled the seams of her dress, trying to look composed in the frenzy of the moment.

"Will you marry me?" No sooner had Henry said it than alarms went off in his head. The realization that words aren't toys to be played with, and hearts were at stake. He didn't regret asking, he was just a little surprised that he had. After all, they were young. But no younger than many of the picture brides who had come over from Japan. Besides, he was leaving in a week for China. He'd be gone two years at least, and she had said she'd wait. Now she'd have something worth waiting for.

"Henry, I could have sworn you just asked me to marry you."

Jazz musicians began pouring into the streets from the clubs on South Jackson, some cheering, other riffing spontaneously.

"I did. I'm asking you now. Will you marry me?"

She didn't say a thing. The tears in her eyes from the happiest day in the history of Seattle flowed again for a whole new reason.

"Is that a yes, or a no?" Henry asked, suddenly feeling naked and vulnerable.

Ethel, on the other hand, looked inspired. Henry watched her climb on the hood of a police car even before the officer could get out to stop her. She turned to the crowd in the street and yelled, "I'm getting married!" The crowd roared its approval, and men and woman tilted their glasses back and toasted her.

As the officer helped her down, she found Henry's eyes and nodded. "Yes," she said. "Yes, I'll wait . . . And yes, I'll marry you. So hurry back, I might not wait forever."

It was during that moment, that exchange, when all fell silent in Henry's mind. The crowds and the horns and the sirens lowered their volumes. And he noticed for the first time a few Japanese families in the crowd. Trying their best to go about their business unnoticed. Saddled with the poor luck of somehow being related to the losing team, or coming from the wrong side of town due to unfortunate circumstances beyond their control. Some Japanese families, scores in fact, had trickled back in the previous months. But they found little left of their belongings and even less in the way of opportunity to start again. Even with the assistance of the American Friends Service Committee, a group that offered to help Japanese families find homes and rent apartments, few stayed.

It was during this stolen moment, this spot of quiet melancholy, that Henry saw what he most wanted, and most feared. Standing across the street, staring directly at him, were a pair of beautiful chestnut brown eyes. What did he see in them? He couldn't tell. Sadness and joy? Or was he projecting what was in his own heart? She stood motionless. Taller now—her hair much longer as it drifted away from her shoulders in the direction of the cool summer breeze.

Henry rubbed his eyes and she was gone, lost in the celebrating crowds that still flooded the streets.

But it couldn't have been Keiko. *She'd have written.*

Walking home along the littered, ticker-tape-covered sidewalk, Henry wondered how his father was taking the news. He knew his mother would probably prepare a feast, something to celebrate was so rare during times of rationing. But his father, who knew?

Inside, in Henry's quiet thoughts, he couldn't escape the memory of Keiko. The what-ifs. *What if* he had said something differently? *What if* he'd asked her to stay?

But he couldn't forget the love, the sincere feelings Ethel had as she delighted in her engagement, holding Henry close, giving all of her heart so unselfishly.

Around the corner, Henry looked up at the window of his Canton Alley apartment—he'd be leaving it next week for China. As he was thinking of how his mother would hold up during his farewell, he heard her shouting his name. Yelling, in fact. Not the vocal celebration of the others on the street—this was something else.

"Henry! It's your father . . ." Henry saw her waving frantically through the open window, the same one she hated for him to leave open.

He ran.

Up the street, and up the steps to his apartment. Ethel tried to keep up, then shouted at him to go on. She knew, even before Henry knew. She'd spent far more time with Henry's father than anyone but his mother.

In the apartment he shared with his parents, Henry saw Dr. Luke once again. Closing his black bag, looking broken and defeated. "I'm sorry, Henry."

"What's happening?"

Henry burst into his parents' room. His father was in bed, looking pale. His feet curled in at impossible angles, rigid and lifeless from the knees down. His breathing rattled in his chest. The only other noise was that of Henry's mother crying. He put his arms around her, and she held him close, patting the side of his face.

"He doesn't have long, Henry," the doctor explained sadly. "He wanted to see you one last time. He's been holding on for you."

Ethel arrived in the doorway, out of breath and looking pained as she saw the condition of her future father-in-law. She patted the arm of Henry's mother, who began to have that vacant look of quiet acceptance.

Henry sat next to the frail shell that was left of his once domineering father.

"I'm here," he said in Chinese. "You can go now, your ancestors are waiting. . . . You don't need to wait for me anymore. The Japanese

surrendered—I'm going to China next week. And I'm marrying Ethel."
If the words were a surprise to anyone, no one had cause to show it at the
moment.

His father opened his eyes and found Henry. *"Wo wei ni zuo."* The
words rattled out between haggard breaths. *I did it for you.*

That was when Henry knew. His father wasn't speaking about sending him to China, or about his planning to marry Ethel. His father was
superstitious and wanted to die with a clear conscience so he wouldn't be
haunted in the next world. His father was confessing.

"You fixed it, didn't you?" Henry spoke with quiet resignation, unable
to feel anger toward his dying father. He wanted to feel it, but unlike his
father, he wouldn't allow himself to be defined by hatred. "You used
your position with the benevolent associations and fixed it so that my letters never made it to Keiko. So that hers never got delivered. That was
your doing somehow, wasn't it?"

Henry looked at his father, fully expecting him to die at any moment,
leaving him with that question unanswered. Instead, his father inhaled
one last time, one long draw, and confirmed what Henry had already
guessed. With his dying breath he nodded, and said it again. *"Wo wei ni
zuo,"* I did it for *you.*

Henry watched his father's eyes widen as he stared at the ceiling, his
mouth releasing one long, slow breath that rattled in his chest. To Henry,
he almost looked surprised as his eyes closed one last time.

His mother clung to Ethel, both crying.

Henry couldn't look at either of them. Instead he left his father's side
and looked out the window. The excitement of the Japanese surrender
was still palpable in the air, and people wandered about the streets looking for a place to continue their celebrations.

Henry didn't feel like cheering, he felt like screaming. He did neither.

Bolting from his parents' room and out the front door past a saddened Dr. Luke, Henry ran down the stairs and headlong down King
Street—south, in the direction of Maynard Avenue, in the direction of
what used to be Nihonmachi.

If that really had been Keiko he'd seen in the street, she'd go there to
retrieve her things.

He ran first to her old apartment, the one she'd vacated over three years ago. The apartments in the neighborhood were now being rented to Italian and Jewish families. There was no sign of her. Amid the celebration and revelry, no one noticed Henry running down the street. Everywhere he looked, everyone seemed so happy. So satisfied. The opposite of how he felt inside.

He kept looking, but the only other place he could think of to go was the Panama Hotel. If her family *had* stored some of their belongings there, they'd have to go retrieve their things, *wouldn't they?*

Running down South Washington all the way past the old Nichibei Publishing building, which was now occupied by the Roosevelt Federal Savings & Loan, Henry saw the steps of the Panama—and in front, a lone worker. The hotel was being boarded up again.

It was empty, Henry thought.

All he could do was hold his breath, and the anger toward his father, as he scanned the streets for Japanese faces. He looked for Mr. Okabe, imagining him in an army uniform. Keiko's last letter had said he was finally allowed to enlist. He must have been one of the thousand Henry had read about from Minidoka who'd joined the 442nd and fought in Germany. *A lawyer.* They sent a Japanese lawyer to France to fight the Germans.

Henry wanted to shout Keiko's name. To tell her that it was his father, that it wasn't her fault or his. That this could all be undone, that she didn't have to leave. But he couldn't bring himself to speak; like causing ripples on a placid lake, some things are better left undisturbed.

Henry stepped forward, just to the edge of the street. If he took another step toward the hotel, he knew he'd break Ethel's heart, and he knew she didn't deserve that.

As he turned around, remembering to breathe again, he saw Ethel standing there, maybe ten feet away, parting her way through the crowded sidewalk. She must be worried about me, Henry thought. He pictured her running after him, so upset about Henry's father, about Henry himself. She approached him, but kept her distance a bit, as if not knowing what Henry needed. Henry knew. He held her hand, and she relaxed, her eyes wet with tears from the up and down emotions of the day. If she suspected, or wondered, she never said a word. And if she had had an inadvertent hand in the loss of Henry's letters, she never spoke of it. But Henry knew her heart—too innocent to get caught up in his father's drama. She simply let Henry feel everything and never questioned. She just was there when he needed her.

Walking home with Ethel, Henry knew he had much to do. He had to help his mother prepare a funeral. He had to pack for his trip to China. And he had to find a suitable engagement ring. Something he would do with a certain sadness.

He'd do what he always did, find the sweet among the bitter.

Broken Records
(1986)

Henry hadn't heard from his son in a week. Marty didn't call asking to borrow a few bucks. He didn't even pop by to do his laundry or wax his Honda. Henry thought about his Chinese son, engaged to his Caucasian girlfriend, driving around in a Japanese car. Henry's own father must have been spinning in his grave. The thought made him smile. A little.

Marty didn't have a phone in his dorm, and the community phone in the hallway just rang and rang each time Henry tried to reach him.

So after his visit to Kobe Park, Henry walked over to the south end of Capitol Hill and past the security desk at Seattle University's Bellarmine Hall. The front desk watchman was busy studying as Henry strolled to the elevator and pressed six—the top floor. Henry was grateful that his son had moved up from the fourth floor before his senior year; four was an unlucky number. In Chinese, the word for four rhymed with the word for death. Marty didn't share his father's built-in superstitions, but Henry was happy nonetheless.

Henry smiled politely as he stepped off the elevator, nearly running into a pair of coeds in bathrobes returning from the showers.

"Pops!" Marty yelled down the hall. "What are you doing here?"

Henry ambled to his son's room, around two young men wheeling in a keg of beer in a shopping cart and past another girl with an armload of laundry.

"Are you okay? You never come here," Marty said, his eyes questioning Henry as he stood in the doorway, feeling out of place and beyond his years. "I mean, I'm graduating in a week, and *now* you show up—when everyone is kicking back. You're gonna think all that hard-earned tuition went to waste up here."

"I just came by to bring you this." Henry handed a small thank-you card to his son. "It's for Sam. For making us dinner."

"Ah, Pops—you didn't have to . . ."

"Please," Henry said. It was the first time since Ethel had died that he'd made any attempt to visit Marty. During his freshman year, Ethel had made it a point to hand-deliver care packages when her health allowed her to get out once in a while. Henry, by contrast, had never come alone.

Looking around Marty's room, he saw Keiko's sketchbooks spread out on the desk. Henry didn't say much. He didn't like talking about Keiko's things in front of Marty—as if his excitement and joy at finding them somehow tarnished the image of Ethel. *Too soon.* It was far too soon.

"I'm sorry 'bout what Samantha said, Pops, about finding Keiko. She's just a little caught up in the moment—you know what I mean?"

Henry did. It was understandable. The belongings at the Panama Hotel were drawing the attention of a few local historians. A certain fascination was to be expected.

"She's fine," Henry said.

"But she does have a point?"

"About returning the sketchbooks to their rightful owner—"

"No, about finding out if she's alive, where she might be."

Henry looked at Marty's shelves. On them sat a Chinese tea service and a set of porcelain rice bowls that had been given to him and Ethel for their wedding. They were worn, chipped, and cracks were everywhere just beneath the hardened finish.

"I had my chance."

"What, back during the war? She was taken from you. She didn't want to leave and you didn't want her to go. And the things Yay Yay did and said, the way he interfered—how can you just accept all that?"

Marty had an old rice cooker simmering on a table near the window. Henry pulled the steamer away from the wall and unplugged it out of precautionary habit, letting it cool. He looked at his son, unsure of how to answer.

"You could have been together—"

Henry interrupted, drying his hands on a towel as he spoke. "I had my chance. *I let her go.* She left. But I *also* let her go." He hung the towel from the closet door handle, his hands clean. He'd thought about Keiko so many times over the years. Even during those empty, lonely nights while Ethel was taking that long, slow journey toward her final destination. He'd been barely able to hold her because she was in so much pain, and when he did, she was so heavily medicated she didn't know he was there. It had been a hard, bitter road he had walked alone, as he'd had to walk to and from Rainier Elementary as a boy. Keiko—how he'd wished she were there in those moments. But I made my decision, Henry thought. I could have found her after the war. I could have hurt Ethel, and had what I wanted, but it didn't seem right. Not then. And not these past few years.

"I had my chance." He said it, retiring from a lifetime of wanting. "I had my chance, and sometimes in life, there are no second chances. You look at what you have, not what you miss, and you move forward."

Henry watched his son listen; for the first time in many years, Marty seemed content to listen. Not to argue.

"Like that broken record we found," Henry said. "Some things just can't be fixed."

Hearthstone
(1986)

Henry couldn't quite bring himself to run through the sleepy, well-appointed halls of the Hearthstone Inn. Running just seemed to fly in the face of the quiet dignity the quaint and elegant nursing home maintained. Besides, he might run over some old lady and her walker.

Old—what a relative term. He felt old whenever he thought about Marty getting married. He'd felt old when Ethel passed, yet here he was, feeling like a little kid who might be scolded for running in the halls.

When Henry had got the call that Sheldon's health had taken a turn for the worse, he didn't grab his coat, wallet, or anything. Just his keys and out the door he flew. He'd let little slow him down on the drive over, rolling through two red lights. He'd received *the call* before and was used to a variety of false alarms, but he knew better this time. He recognized death when it was sitting right there waiting. After having listened to Ethel's breathing change, that shift in her state of mind, he understood. And now, visiting his friend, he knew the end was close.

Sheldon had taken ill on several occasions, usually because of a lifetime of untreated diabetes. By the time he began to take care of himself, and by the time he fell into the hands of the right doctors, the damage had already been done.

"How is he?" Henry asked, stopping at the nearest nurses' station and pointing to Sheldon's room, where a nurse was wheeling out a dialysis machine. No use anymore, Henry thought. They're taking him off everything.

The nurse, a plump, red-haired woman who looked about Marty's age, read her computer screen and then looked back to Henry. "It's close.

His wife was just here—she left to go get more family. It's funny. After all those little strokes, you fight off the visitors, just as part of the process of letting someone rest, hoping they'll recover soon. But when it's this time, this close, it's nothing but family and friends. It's that time, I'm afraid."

Henry saw the genuine concern in her eyes.

Knocking on the half-open door, he slipped inside. He padded quietly across the tiled floor, looking at the array of equipment usually assigned to Sheldon—most of it had been unplugged and wheeled to a cluttered corner.

Henry sat down on a wheeled chair next to his friend, who was propped up so he could breath more easily, his head slumped to one side, nestled against a pillow facing Henry, and a thin, clear tube draped around his nose. The whistling sound from the oxygen was the only sound in the room.

There was a CD player near Sheldon's bed. Henry adjusted the volume to low and pressed play. The smooth bebop rhythm of Floyd Standifer filled the quiet of the empty room like a steady flow of sand filling the bottom of an hourglass. Less time each second.

Henry patted his friend's arm, mindful of the IV protruding from the back of Sheldon's hand, noting scabbed-over dots marking the landscape of his medical condition and recent removal of other tubes and monitors.

Sheldon's eyes opened, eyelids flicking, his chin falling from side to side, his eyes finding Henry. He felt saddened for his friend—a sadness that was mollified when Henry spied the broken record next to Sheldon's bed.

I've been here too many times, Henry thought to himself. So many years with my wife, now with my old friend. Too soon. It's been a lifetime, but it's still too soon for everyone. Henry had clung to his grief and sadness with Ethel's passing, and now this.

He saw the confusion in Sheldon's eyes. He recognized the vacant stare of not knowing where you are or why you're here.

"Home . . . time to go home" was all Sheldon kept saying over and over again quietly, in a way that sounded almost pleading.

"This is home for now. Then I think Minnie will be coming back with the rest of your family."

Henry had known Sheldon's second wife, Minnie, for years but hadn't got around to visiting them as often as he'd have liked.

"Henry . . . fix it."

"Fix what?" Henry asked, feeling oddly grateful for those hard final weeks with Ethel. That experience made this difficult exchange seem normal. Then Henry saw what Sheldon was looking at—the old vinyl 78, split in two. "The record. You want me to fix the Oscar Holden record, don't you?"

Sheldon closed his eyes and drifted off into deep sleep, the kind of in and out that only someone in his condition can accomplish. Such heavy, labored breathing. Then back. Eyes open. Lucid again, like waking up to a new day.

"Henry . . ."

"I'm here . . ."

"What are you doing here? Is it Sunday?"

"No." Henry looked at his old friend, smiling, trying to be cheery despite the circumstances. "No, it's not Sunday."

"That's too bad. All these midweek visits. Must be time for my final performance, huh, Henry?" Sheldon coughed a little and struggled to make his aching lungs work the way they should.

Watching his old friend, still so tall and dignified, even lying here dying, Henry looked at the old broken record that sat on the wheeled nightstand next to the bed. "Earlier you were asking me to fix it. I'm guessing you meant fix this old broken record, maybe find someplace to restore it . . ."

Looking at Sheldon, Henry wasn't sure if, in his state, he remembered the conversation they'd started just minutes before.

"I think it's time you fixed it, Henry. But I wasn't talking about that old record. If you can put those broken pieces together, make some music again, then that's what you should do. But I wasn't talking 'bout the record, Henry."

Henry looked at the Oscar Holden recording—the one he'd hoped would still be there in the dusty basement of that old hotel.

Sheldon reached over and held Henry's hand. His old, dried up, brown-bag fingers still felt strong to Henry. "We both"—Sheldon paused, then caught his breath again—"know why you were always looking for that old record. Always known.".His breathing slowed. "Fix it," Sheldon managed to say one last time, before drifting off to sleep, his words disappearing into the soft hissing of the oxygen.

Tickets

(1986)

Stepping inside Bud's Jazz Records, Henry could smell the vanilla tobacco that Bud favored. The proprietor was smoking and chewing on an old pipe, looking at a coffee-stained copy of the *Seattle Weekly*. He lowered his paper just enough to give Henry a nod and a dip of the pipe, which hung precariously from the side of his hang-dog mouth; as always, he looked about three days late for a good shave. In the background a woman sang some sweet old-school number. Helen Humes? From the thirties? Henry couldn't be sure.

Tucked under Henry's arm was a brown paper sack. And inside was the broken Oscar Holden record. Henry had haunted Bud's place for years in search of it. Sure, he had felt a little bad taking it from Sheldon's room, but his old friend had been sleeping, and when he was awake, he was more and more disoriented. The silent lucidity gave way to moments of confusion and bewilderment. Like his old friend's ramblings about fixing what was broken. The record? Henry himself? That was unknown.

Still, after all these years, Henry wanted to hear the song embedded in these two broken slabs of vinyl—and maybe it would be good for Sheldon to hear it one last time as well. Henry didn't know the first thing about restoring antique records, but Bud had been here forever. If anyone could point Henry in the right direction, it would be Bud.

Henry walked up to the counter and set the bag on the cracked glass display case that held old sheet music and vinyl and wax disks too brittle to be handled.

Bud set down his paper. "You returning something, Henry?"

Henry just smiled, enjoying the last strains of the woman singing in the background. He always favored the gravelly tenors, but on occasion a bluesy, brandy-soaked voice like the one playing could keep him awake all night.

"Henry, you okay?"

"I have something I need to show you."

Bud tamped out his pipe. "Why do I get the feeling this has something to do with that old, busted-up hotel on Main Street?"

Henry reached into the bag and slid out the record, still in its original paper sleeve. It felt heavy in his hand. The label through the cutaway in the sleeve was clearly visible, a yellow, faded printing that read, "Oscar Holden & the Midnight Blue."

Henry watched Bud's heavy eyes widen, and the bitter grooves in the old man's forehead smoothed out like a sail caught up in a full breeze as he smiled in bewilderment. He looked up at Henry, then back down at the record, as if to say, "Can I touch it?"

Henry nodded. "Go ahead, it's real."

"You found this down there, didn't you? Never gave up looking for it, did you?"

Never gave up. Knew I'd find it eventually. "It was there all these years, waiting."

Bud slid the record out as Henry watched it give in his hand. The two broken halves sagged in opposite directions, held together by the pressed label. "Oh no—no, no, no. You're not gonna tease me like this, are ya, Henry? It's broke, ain't it?"

Henry just nodded, and shrugged his apology. "I was thinking maybe that was something you could help me with. I'm looking for someone who can do some kind of restoration."

Bud looked like he'd found out he'd won the lottery, only to be paid off in a lifetime's supply of Monopoly money. Exciting, but useless. "If it wasn't *completely* in two, you could send it someplace and they'd use a laser to record off every note. Wouldn't even touch it with a traditional needle, not even a diamond. Couldn't risk more scratches and pops. They could suck off every nuance ever recorded here and save it for you digitally." Bud rubbed his forehead. The wrinkles all came back. "Ain't nothing you can do with a busted record, Henry. Once she's gone, she's gone for good."

"They couldn't just glue it or something . . ."

"Henry, she's gone. It'd never play, never sound the same. I mean, I love holding it and all, and this does belong in a museum or something. A little piece of history, for sure. Especially since those in *the know* never knew for sure if it was actually recorded."

Bud knew it. Inside, Henry knew it too. Some things just can't be put back together. Some things can never be fixed. Two broken pieces can't make a lot of anything anymore. But at least he had the broken pieces.

Henry walked home. It was probably more than two miles, up South King and around toward Beacon Hill, overlooking the International District. It would have been much easier to drive, even with the traffic, but he just felt like walking. He'd spent his childhood canvassing this neighborhood, and with each step he tried to recall what used to be. As he walked, he crossed over to South Jackson, looking at the buildings that used to be home to the Ubangi Club, the Rocking Chair, even the Black Elks Club. Holding that broken record at his side, now looking at generic storefronts for Seafirst Bank and All West Travel, he tried to remember the song he'd once played over and over in his head.

It was all but gone. He could remember a bit of the chorus, but its melody had escaped. Yet he couldn't forget her, couldn't forget Keiko. And how he'd once told her he'd wait a lifetime. Every summer he'd thought of her but never spoke of her to anyone, not even Ethel. And of course, telling Marty had been out of the question. So when his impetuous son had wanted so badly to go to the Puyallup Fair each year, and Henry had said no, there was a reason. A painful reason. One that Henry shared with almost no one but Sheldon, on the rare occasion when his old friend would bring it up. And now Sheldon would be gone soon too. Another former resident of a small community in Seattle that no one remembered anymore. Like ghosts haunting a vacant lot because the building had long since vanished.

At home, exhausted from the long walk along the dirty, littered streets, Henry hung up his jacket, went to the kitchen for a glass of iced tea, and drifted to the bedroom he'd once shared with Ethel.

To his surprise, on his bed was his best suit. Set out like it had been all those years ago. His old black leather dress shoes had been polished and placed on the floor next to an old suitcase of his. For a moment, Henry felt fifteen again, in that old Canton Alley apartment he'd shared with his parents. Looking at the tools of a traveler bound for ports unknown. A future far away.

Mystified, Henry felt the hair on the back of his neck prick up as he turned back the lapel of his suitcoat and saw, like a mirage, a ticket jacket in his breast pocket. Sitting on the edge of the bed, he pulled it out and opened it up. Inside was a round-trip ticket to New York City. It wasn't to Canton but to another faraway land. A place he'd never been.

"I guess you found my little present." Marty stood in the doorway, holding his father's hat, the one with the threadbare brim.

"Most children just send their aged parents to a nursing home, you're sending me to the other side of the country," Henry said.

"More than that, Pops, I'm sending you back in time."

Henry looked at the suit, thinking about his own father. He knew only one person who had ever talked about New York, and she'd never come back. She'd left a long time ago. Back in another lifetime.

"You sending me back to the war years?" Henry asked.

"I'm sending you back to find what's missing. Sending you back to find what you let go. I'm proud of you, Pops, and I'm grateful for everything, especially for the way you cared for Mom. You've done everything for me, and now it's my turn to do something for you."

Henry looked at the ticket.

"*I found her, Pops.* I know you were always loyal to Mom, and that you'd never do this for yourself. So I did it for you. Pack your suitcase. I'm taking you to the airport; you're leaving for New York City . . ."

"When?" Henry asked.

"Tonight. Tomorrow. Whenever. You got someplace else you gotta be?"

Henry drew out a tarnished silver pocket watch. It kept poor time and required frequent winding. He flipped it open, sighed heavily, then snapped it shut.

The last time someone had laid out a suit and a pair of dress shoes with a ticket purchased for a faraway place, Henry had refused to go.

This time, Henry refused to stay.

Sheldon's Song
(1986)

Sheldon didn't have much time left, Henry knew for certain. With his friend's failing health, the desire to go to New York to find Keiko would have to be put on hold. It had been forty years, he could wait awhile longer—he would have to wait.

At the Hearthstone Inn, Sheldon had enjoyed a steady stream of visitors—family, friends, and former co-workers. Even a few loyal music fans who recognized his place in the paved-over history of Seattle's once-vibrant jazz scene.

But now most of his well-wishers had come and gone. They'd paid their last respects to a man they loved. Just his family remained, along with the minister from Sheldon's church, trying his best to comfort the family.

"How is he?" Henry asked Minnie, a silver-haired woman ten years the junior of the old sax man.

She hugged Henry in the doorway and let go, but still held on to his elbows. Her wrinkled eyes puffy, showing the redness from so much crying, her cheeks still damp. "It won't be long now, Henry. We know that. I know that. We're just so ready for him to have his peace, to not be in any pain," she said.

Henry felt a quiver in his lip, something that surprised even him. He bit his tongue and stood up taller, not wanting his tears to add to Minnie's grief.

"Is this your doing? The music, I mean? The record?"

Henry felt horrible. He'd taken the record, and now everyone knew it was missing. He held it tight under his arm, beneath his coat to keep it out of the misty rain that filled the Seattle air. "I . . . I can explain . . ."

"No need to explain, Henry, I mean"—she was searching for the right words—"it's amazing, like a miracle, really. Listen. Can you hear it? It sounds like a miracle to me."

And for the first time in forty years, Henry heard it. Playing in Sheldon's room was the long forgotten song he'd first heard in the Black Elks Club. The Oscar Holden song he and Keiko had shared. Their song—but Sheldon's too. And it was playing, loud and clear.

Walking into the room, Henry saw a woman standing there. In his mind's eye, he thought it might be Keiko, her caring smile was almost as bright. But it was Samantha, sitting next to an old portable record player, the boxed kind you could check out of the public library years ago. On it spun a complete vinyl recording of Oscar Holden's lost classic "The Alley Cat Strut," the song he'd dedicated to Henry and Keiko.

Sheldon lay unconscious, drifting in and out of that gray, empty space between life and whatever fate had in store for him next. Beside him were an assorted collection of kids and grandchildren, many of whom Henry recognized from earlier meetings or from the photos Sheldon had proudly shared when he and Henry would get together over the years.

"I like Grampa's record," a little girl confided. Henry estimated her to be about six, a great-granddaughter perhaps.

"It's wonderful, Henry," Samantha said, smiling with bright eyes wet but hopeful. "You should have seen him smile when we put it on and played it the first time. Like he'd been wanting to hear this, needing to hear this, all these years."

"But . . ." Henry took out the broken record he held in his coat. "Where?"

"*She* sent it." Samantha said it with a glowing reverence, like a bit player in awe of a featured performer about to set foot on the main stage. "Marty found her living on the East Coast, and she asked about you, asked about everyone, Sheldon too. And when she found out, she sent the record immediately. Can you believe that? She kept it all those years, the Holy Grail you knew existed." She handed Henry a note. "This came for you."

Henry hesitated, not quite believing what he was hearing. He gently tore open the envelope. He felt as though he were sleepwalking as he read Keiko's words.

Dear Henry,

I pray that this note finds you in good health, good spirits, and among good friends. Especially Sheldon, whom I hope is comforted by this record. Our record really—it belonged to all of us, didn't it? But more important, it belonged to you and me. I'll never forget seeing your face in the train station or how I felt standing in the rain on the inside of that barbed-wire fence. What a pair we were!

As you play this record, I hope you'll think of the good, not the bad. Of what was, not what wasn't meant to be. Of the time we spent together, not the time we've spent apart. Most of all, I hope you'll think of me . . .

Henry folded the letter with trembling hands, unable to continue. He had had a hard time revealing the true nature of what was found in the dusty basement of the Panama Hotel that day. He'd felt as if it might tarnish the way his son looked at him, or the way he might look at his mother. But in the end, as in so many of Henry's father-and-son moments, he'd had it wrong. Marty wanted him to be happy. To Henry, Keiko was lost in time, but to Marty, a few hours on his computer, a few phone calls, and there she was, alive and well, living in New York City, even after all these years.

Henry smiled, reached out, and grabbed hold of Samantha's hand. "You're amazing." He struggled to find the words. "Marty has done well. Amazingly well."

Looking at Sheldon, Henry sat on the edge of the bed, his hand on his friend's arm, watching his rattled breathing. His body shutting down, laboring for each breath. Sheldon looked hot and feverish; his body was losing the ability to regulate his own temperature. He was burning himself up.

As Henry watched his dying friend, he listened to the record, waiting for a saxophone solo he hadn't heard in four decades. As the band slowed and the brittle recorded melody kicked in, Sheldon opened his eyes. He looked up, as if regarding Henry.

Sheldon's mouth moved, straining to get the words out. Henry moved in, placing his ear close, to hear Sheldon's whispered words. "You fixed it."

Henry nodded. "I fixed it." *And soon, I'm going to fix everything.*

. . .

Three hours later, with Minnie at his side, surrounded by a lifetime supply of family and grandchildren, Sheldon opened his eyes again. Henry
was there, Marty and Samantha too. In the background the strains of
Oscar Holden and the Midnight Blue echoed in the shadowed corners
of the room. The lungs that had once powered the sounds of South Jackson, playing to the delight of a generation, breathed slowly one last time
and whispered the final notes of his song.

Henry watched Sheldon's eyes close and his body lighten, as if his entire frame were waving a slow good-bye.

Beneath the simple bars of the tune playing, Henry whispered to no
one but the spirit of his friend, "Thank you, sir, and you have a fine day."

New York
(1986)

Henry had never been to New York City. Oh, sure, maybe once or twice in a dream. But in full, waking reality, it was a place he'd thought of often over the years but never allowed himself to visit. It seemed a world away. Not just across the country or on another coast, but someplace beyond the horizon, lost in another time.

In the forty-dollar cab ride from La Guardia Airport, Henry held the complete Oscar Holden record on his lap. It had been played at Sheldon's funeral. The same one he had hand-carried on the plane from Seattle—his one piece of carry-on luggage, a conversation piece everywhere he went.

When he explained where the record came from, its unique history, and the circumstances of life at the time, people always gushed their amazement. Even the young blond woman sitting next to him on the plane, who was flying to New York on business, couldn't believe he was hand-carrying the only remaining playable copy. She'd forgotten how horribly cruel the Japanese internment was. She was in awe of the Panama Hotel's survival. A place of personal belongings, cherished memories, forgotten treasures.

"First time to the city?" the cabdriver asked. He'd been eyeing Henry in the rearview mirror, but his passenger was lost in thought, staring out the window at the brick-and-mortar landscape that rolled by. A nonstop ebb and flow of yellow taxis, sleek limousines, and pedestrians who swarmed the sidewalks.

"First time" was all Henry could manage to say. Marty and Samantha had wanted him to call first. To call ahead. But he couldn't bring himself to pick up the phone. He was too nervous. Like now.

"This is it, twelve hundred block of Waverly Place," the driver called out; his arm, which hung out the open window, pointed to a small apartment building.

"This is Greenwich Village?"

"You're looking at it, pal."

Henry paid the driver an additional thirty dollars to take his bags one mile over to the Marriott, where he'd drop them off with the bellman. A strange thought, trusting someone in the big city, Henry noted to himself. But that was what this trip was really all about, wasn't it? Blind faith. And besides, he had nothing to lose. What were some luggage and a change of clothes compared with finding and fixing a broken heart?

The apartment building looked old and modest, but a flat there still probably cost a fortune compared with the simple home Henry had occupied in Seattle for the past forty years.

Looking at the address Marty had given to him, Henry went inside and found himself on the eighth floor, a Chinese lucky number. Standing in the hallway, he stared at the door of Kay Hatsune, a widow of three years. Henry didn't know what had happened to her husband. If Marty knew, he hadn't said.

Just that Kay was indeed . . . *Keiko*.

Henry looked at the record in his hand. When he took it partway out of the sleeve, the vinyl looked impossibly new. She must have taken impeccable care of it over the years.

Putting the record away, Henry straightened the line of the old two-piece suit his son had set out for him, checked his hair and the shine of his shoes.

He touched his face where he'd shaved on the plane.

Then he knocked.

Twice, before he heard the shuffled steps of someone inside. A shadow fell across the eyepiece in the door, then he heard the tumble of the locks.

As the door opened, Henry felt the warmth from the inside windows shining through, illuminating the darkened hallway. Standing in front of him was a woman in her fifties, her hair shorter than he remembered, with an occasional streak of gray. She was slender, and held the door with trim fingers and manicured nails. Her chestnut brown eyes, despite the lifetime she wore in the lovely lines of her face, shone as clear and fluid as ever.

The same eyes that had looked inside him all those years ago. Hopeful eyes.

She paused momentarily, not completely recognizing him; then her hands cupped her mouth—then touched her cheeks in surprise. Keiko sighed, a confession in her smile. "I'd . . . almost given up on you . . ." She opened the door wide for Henry to come in.

Inside her tiny apartment hung an assortment of watercolors and oils. Of cherry blossoms and ume trees. Of lonesome prairie and barbed wire. Henry knew the paintings were all Keiko's. They had the same touch, only a grown-up version of the way she'd expressed herself as a girl. The way she remembered things.

"Can I get you something, some iced tea?"

"That'd be nice, thank you," Henry answered. Amazed that he was having this conversation, and that it sounded so normal, like a natural extension—a follow-up to where they'd left off forty years earlier, as if they hadn't each lived a lifetime apart.

While she disappeared into the kitchen, Henry was drawn to the photos on her mantel, of her and her husband, her family. He touched a framed photo of her father, in an army uniform, a member of the famed 442nd. He and a group of Japanese American soldiers were standing in the snow, smiling, proudly holding a captured German flag—written on it were the words "Go for Broke!" Henry found a tiny silver frame nearby. He picked it up and wiped a thin coat of dust from the glass. It was a black-and-white sketch of him and Keiko from Camp Minidoka. He had a peaceful, contented grin. She was sticking her tongue out.

Minidoka was gone now. Long gone. But she had kept the drawing.

Near a window, an old stereo caught his eye. Next to it sat a small collection of Seattle jazz recordings—vinyl 78s of Palmer Johnson, Wanda Brown, and Leon Vaughn. Henry carefully removed the record he'd been carrying and gently placed it on the turntable. He turned the old dial, watching the label begin to spin as he delicately set the needle in the outside groove. In his heart music began to play—Sheldon's record. His and Keiko's song. Complete with bumps and scratches.

It was old, and hollow sounding, imperfect.

But it was enough.

When he turned around, Keiko was standing there. The grown-up woman Keiko had become—a mother, a widow, an artist—handing him a glass of iced green tea, with ginger and honey from the taste of it.

They stood there, smiling at each other, like they had done all those years ago, standing on either side of that fence.

"*Oai deki te . . .*" She paused.

"*Ureshii desu,*" Henry said, softly.

Author's Note

Though this is a work of fiction, many of the events, particularly those dealing with the internment of Japanese Americans, did occur as described. As an author, I did my best to re-create this historic landscape, without judging the good or bad intentions of those involved at the time. My intent was not to create a morality play, with my voice being the loudest on the stage, but rather to defer to the reader's sense of justice, of right and wrong, and let the facts speak plainly. And while I strove mightily to be true to those facts, the blame for any historical or geographical errors lay firmly at my feet.

Because many people have asked, let me say, yes, the Panama Hotel is a very real place. And yes, the belongings of thirty-seven Japanese families do indeed reside there, most of them in the dusty, dimly lit basement. If you happen to visit, be sure to stop in at the tearoom, where many of these artifacts are on display. I highly recommend the lychee blend—it never disappoints.

Bud's Jazz Records is there too. Just down the street, in the heart of Seattle's Pioneer Square. It's easy to miss but hard to forget. I popped in once to take some publicity photos. The owner simply asked, "Is this for good or for evil?"

I said, *"Good,"* of course.

"Good enough for me" was his smooth reply.

However, if you're stopping at either place looking for a long-lost Oscar Holden recording, you might be out of luck. Though Oscar was certainly one of the great fathers of the Northwest jazz scene, to my knowledge, a vinyl recording does not exist.

But, you never know . . .

Acknowledgments

As the saying goes, writing is a lonely business. Fortunately, I've had my wife, Leesha, and our children—Haley, Karissa, Taylor, Madi, Kassie, and Lucas—to keep me company. Feel free to hum the *Brady Bunch* theme song—we do all the time. Thank you for allowing me to write these strange things called books, even though we have a perfectly good TV.

And beyond the crayon-covered walls of my own home, I am indebted to the following people for their contributions to this book:

To the faculty and alumni of that last bastion of bohemianism—the Squaw Valley Community of Writers—a group that I am humbled to be a part of. Special thanks go to Louis B. Jones, Andrew Tonkovich, and Leslie Daniels. And of course a big *doh je* to fellow alumnus Yunshi Wang for double-checking my Chinese.

To Orson Scott Card and my fellow Bootcampers: Scott Andrews, Aliette de Bodard, Kennedy Brandt, Pat Esden, Danielle Friedman, Mariko Gjorvig, Adam Holwerda, Gary Mailhiot, Brian McClellan, Alex Meehan, Jose Mojica, Paula "Rowdy" Raudenbush, and Jim Workman. Thanks for all the tough love.

To readers Anne Frasier, Jim Tomlinson, Gin Petty, and Oregon's poet laureate (as well as former internee), Lawson Inada, for their valuable time and generous praise of an early manuscript.

To Mark Pettus and Lisa Diane Kastner of the fledgling *Picolata Review,* for accepting a sliver of a story that would later become this book.

To historian and activist Doug Chin, for his charismatic and inspirational insights.

To Jan Johnson, owner of the Panama Hotel, for a three-hour tour of the basement and her relentless dedication to preserving the spirit of

Nihonmachi. Without her, the Panama would have been bulldozed into oblivion by now.

To the staff and volunteers of Seattle's Wing Luke Asian Museum, for remembering what others might choose to forget.

To Grace Holden, for allowing me to channel the spirit of her father.

To my über-agent, Kristin Nelson, for her relentless optimism. (And Sara Megibow, because where would Batman be without Robin? Where would peanut butter be without jelly? Where would KISS be without makeup?)

And finally to the saintly Jane von Mehren, Libby McGuire, Brian McLendon, Kim Hovey, Allyson Pearl, Porscha Burke, and the amazing team at Ballantine—for welcoming Henry and Keiko with open arms.

HOTEL ON
THE CORNER OF
BITTER AND SWEET

Jamie Ford

A Reader's Guide

A Conversation with Jamie Ford

Random House Reader's Circle: Where did the idea for *Hotel on the Corner of Bitter and Sweet* come from?

Jamie Ford: It really started with the "I am Chinese" button, which my father mentioned wearing as a kid. There was a bit of an identity crisis in the International District in the wake of Pearl Harbor. Many Chinese families feared for their safety, especially as the FBI was rounding up prominent members of the Japanese community. It piqued my curiosity and really led me to research the whole period.

From there I wrote a sliver of a short story, really nothing more than a vignette, and I submitted it to the now-defunct *Picolata Review,* where it was ultimately accepted. A few weeks later I was accepted to an intensive, immersive, week-long literary boot camp run by science fiction and fantasy writer Orson Scott Card, where we literally read and wrote fifteen to seventeen hours a day. It was while attending that camp in Virginia that Scott inspired me to write what he termed "a noble romantic tragedy." That story was called "The Button," about a Chinese boy (Henry) that tried to prevent his best friend (Keiko) from being taken away. I workshopped the story, changed the title to "I Am Chinese" and sent it off to *Glimmer Train,* where it became a finalist in their 2006 Short-Story Award for New Writers. That story became a chapter in the book.

RHRC: You're part Chinese. Tell us about your Chinese family. And the name Ford, where does it come from?

JF: Actually, I didn't even know the whole story until last year. I finally tracked it all down. It turns out my great-grandfather, a man named Min Chung, immigrated to America and later adopted the name William Ford—supposedly from the famous outdoorsman, not the father of Henry Ford. My grandfather, oddly enough, switched back to Chung as a screen name, going by George Chung and appearing as an extra in movies during the '50s. He went on to be a consultant for the '70s TV series *Kung Fu.* His son, my father, was 100 percent Chinese and fluent. Unfortunately, I don't speak Chinese—I had four years of German and that doesn't get me very far at family reunions.

In general, I had a very American childhood, though when you're half Chinese, you never fully fit in. You don't feel white and you don't feel Chinese—you're half, or *hapa,* as they say in Hawaii. Census forms don't have a box to check for half.

RHRC: How did you come to learn about the Panama Hotel?

JF: That came about as I was researching a different story—one dealing with the Wa Mei Massacre, which was a mass shooting in the mid-'80s at a backroom casino in Chinatown, where my grandfather once worked. I was paging through some old news articles and there was an unrelated mention of the Panama Hotel about the owner finding the belongings of all these Japanese families. When I wrote *Hotel on the Corner of Bitter and Sweet,* I dug further into that story and eventually contacted the hotel owner and flew out to Seattle. It was amazing and humbling to see what still remains to this day in that dank, dusty basement.

RHRC: Do you personally know anyone who was affected by the Japanese Internment?

JF: I do, but I didn't know it at the time. I lived in Ashland, Oregon, until I was twelve, and one of my best friend's fathers had been uprooted as a child and sent to a camp in Arkansas. I never knew that until I was doing my research and saw that he'd written a book of poetry about his camp experiences (five actually). His name is Lawson Inada—he's now Oregon's Poet Laureate, by the way. We were able to reconnect and he was kind enough to read an early version of my manuscript.

RHRC: Do you see any parallels between the Japanese Internment and, say, the desire by some to lock our borders, or round up Muslims because they might be a threat?

JF: Only vague similarities. The empire of Japan had been cornered, and lashed out by attacking Pearl Harbor, Singapore, the Philippines, etcetera—it was an unexpected, vicious attack, but it was an all-out declaration of war between nations with very obvious borders. It's very different than having cells of foreign-sponsored terrorists within our country or operating overseas. And now, for the most part, we're a much more integrated society. Rounding up 120,000 Japanese Americans didn't slow down the ambitions of the empire of Japan, and I don't think rounding up Muslim Americans will stop the machinations of evil-minded people along the Afghan/Pakistani border. Let's hope that we learned our lesson sixty-five years ago.

RHRC: What about people like conservative columnist Michelle Malkin who have spoken out in favor of the Japanese Internment, even writing a book about it—saying it was a just endeavor?

JF: First of all, I really set out to write a people story—a love story and a family story. It ended up as a bit more than that, but any kind of oblique political thing was not my intention. However, after I'd written *Hotel on the Corner of Bitter and Sweet,* someone pointed out the Malkin book and I guess my answer to that is this: Ronald Reagan, the most beloved conservative in recent memory, was the one who signed legislation apologizing for the Internment and authorizing $1.6 billion in reparations to be paid to those who lost their homes and livelihoods in the camps. Case closed.

RHRC: You delve a little into the Seattle jazz scene of the '40s. How did that come about?

JF: I've always had a fascination with the paved-over history of China-town and Nihonmachi. My grandparents were always having these anniversary dinners at the China Gate restaurant—this funky old place that was originally a Chinese theater and after that a jazz club where greats like Cab Calloway and Duke Ellington played. As a kid, I was always fascinated by that. It's sad because now the International District is ripe with decay, but in its heyday—from Prohibition until the Internment— it was the place to go for a wild time on a Saturday night. You could find booze, gambling, and jazz. I find it sad that these great places, like the Black Elks Club where Ray Charles had his first paid gig, have basically vanished.

Also, growing up in Seattle my grandfather would always take me to his favorite seafood restaurant, which was in Rainier Beach between a soul-food restaurant and a Hispanic grocer. I was always fascinated with how Seattle's ethnic communities ended up right on top of one another. Turns out it was because of the zoning laws in the '30s and '40s. It was illegal (though how well enforced, I don't know) to sell land to certain minorities outside of certain zones.

RHRC: The novel is told in a split-narrative: past and present. What made you decide to go that route?

JF: I wanted to give the book a more redemptive ending. That's a literary way of saying, "And everyone lived happily ever after."

The short story wrapped up on a fairly tragic note. And even if I continued the story in the '40s, there really wasn't a way to give it an ending that felt satisfying. I mean, after the war was over, it didn't suddenly get better for Japanese American families. Their lives had been completely turned upside down—sort of like people who survive a hurricane. Sure the wind stops blowing and the floodwaters recede, but what do you have left except rubble, and does that provide happiness, or just relief? It took decades for most of these families to recover. It just seemed natural to have that redemptive ending come years later as well.

Also, I think that most people can relate to seeing their first love again, at a class reunion or just by chance, and there's this wave of nostalgia and melancholy—it's very poignant and universal, I think. Plus, as a writer, it was interesting to explore Henry's character as an adult. As the saying goes, everyone has two chances at a parent/child relationship, once as a child and once as a parent. To me, that was a rich dynamic worth exploring.

RHRC: You've written a compelling and touching novel, which also sheds light on an important time in American history. Which of those elements came most naturally to you?

JF: I'd have to say that the "love story/family drama" came most naturally. If I were to list my all-time favorite movies, they tend to be complicated people stories, a bit sentimental, and devoid of car chases and epic gun battles—it's just what I relate to and what I like writing about.

The historical aspects are a close second, though. I love cultural history and am always pleasantly surprised at how much I enjoy the research process. I feel like an archaeologist, dusting off the past and presenting it to the reader. And of course, it adds context to my characters, giving them a rich world to splash around in. I find the whole process incredibly motivating as a writer.

Plus, deep down, I think most of us like entertainment that is somewhat enlightening. My grandmother used to watch *Jeopardy!* because it was "educational." Do game shows really boost your IQ? Probably not, but they can be strangely satisfying to a lot of people.

RHRC: What is your writing process?

JF: It seems as though some authors meticulously outline everything, while others just write extemporaneously—working without a net. I tend to do a little bit of both. I do start with a few notes that are probably the least amount of words on a page that could possibly be mistaken for an outline—really nothing more than a beginning and an ending, with maybe a few scene ideas in the middle. But that ending is all-important for me. And by ending, I mean a real, unambiguous, nonmetaphorical ending. I look at storytelling as either banking or spending emotional currency with the reader. Good or bad, happy or sad, the ending is where those emotional debts are paid—if that makes sense? Plus, if I have a clear ending in mind, then the more nails I lay in the path of my characters, the more motivated I am as a writer to help them overcome them. And of course along the way I'll take a lot of spontaneous twists, turns, and unexpected detours.

Process-wise, I try to get the entire story nailed in one draft—one chapter or one scene at a time. I'll start my day by cleaning up what I wrote the previous day and just keep going from there, occasionally backing up a chapter and starting over. I try not to slather words on the page with the intent to clean the whole thing up later. If I do, my stories tend to suffer a "death of a thousand cuts."

RHRC: Is Henry you?

JF: I think readers sometimes feel that there is some sort of linkage between protagonists and their creators. The truth is, there's a little bit of me in Henry—a small bit. Growing up in Oregon, I was the only Chinese kid in my grade school and my best friend was the only Japanese kid. That's probably where the Henry/Keiko dynamic came from. But we weren't outcasts—I think one year we were the class president and vice president. See what a difference thirty years can make!

RHRC: Do you have a favorite character in the book?

JF: Honestly, I tend to fall in love with the characters that I'm writing at the moment. I'm working on a new book so I'm sort of emotionally vested in these other characters right now. But in the world of *Hotel on the Corner of Bitter and Sweet,* I really love Sheldon—Mrs. Beatty, too. I love them so much that I've written short stories starring each of them. I just wasn't ready to say goodbye, I guess.

Reading Group Questions and Topics for Discussion

1. Father-son relationships are a crucial theme in the novel. Talk about some of these relationships and how they are shaped by culture and time. For example, how is the relationship between Henry and his father different from that between Henry and Marty? What accounts for the differences?

2. Why doesn't Henry's father want him to speak Cantonese at home? How does this square with his desire to send Henry back to China for school? Isn't he sending his son a mixed message?

3. If you were Henry, would you be able to forgive your father? Does Henry's father deserve forgiveness?

4. From the beginning of the novel, Henry wears the "I am Chinese" button given to him by his father. What is the significance of this button and its message, and how does Henry's understanding of that message change by the end of the novel?

5. Why does Henry provide an inaccurate translation when he serves as the go-between in the business negotiations between his father and Mr. Preston? Is he wrong to betray his father's trust in this way?

6. The United States has been called a nation of immigrants. In what ways do the families of Keiko and Henry illustrate different aspects of the American immigrant experience?

7. What is the bond between Henry and Sheldon, and how is it strengthened by jazz music?

8. If a novel could have a soundtrack, this one would be jazz. What is it about this indigenous form of American music that makes it an especially appropriate choice?

9. Henry's mother comes from a culture in which wives are subservient to their husbands. Given this background, do you think she could have done more to help Henry in his struggles against his father? Is her loyalty to her husband a betrayal of her son?

10. Compare Marty's relationship with Samantha to Henry's relationship with Keiko. What other examples can you find in the novel of love that is forbidden or that crosses boundaries of one kind or another?

11. What struggles did your own ancestors have as immigrants to America, and to what extent did they incorporate aspects of their cultural heritage into their new identities as Americans?

12. Does Henry give up on Keiko too easily? What else could he have done to find her?

13. What about Keiko? Why didn't she make more of an effort to see Henry once she was released from the camp?

14. Do you think Ethel might have known what was happening with Henry's letters?

15. The novel ends with Henry and Keiko meeting again after more than forty years. Jump ahead a year and imagine what has happened to them in that time. Is there any evidence in the novel for this outcome?

16. What sacrifices do the characters make in pursuit of their dreams for themselves and for others? Do you think any characters sacrifice too much, or for the wrong reasons? Consider the sacrifices Mr. Okabe

makes, for example, and those of Mr. Lee. Both fathers are acting for the sake of their children, yet the results are quite different. Why?

17. Was the U.S. government right or wrong to "relocate" Japanese Americans and other citizens and residents who had emigrated from countries the U.S. was fighting in WWII? Was some kind of action necessary following Pearl Harbor? Could the government have done more to safeguard civil rights while protecting national security?

18. Should the men and women of Japanese ancestry who were rounded up by the U.S. government during the war have protested more actively against the loss of their property and liberty? Remember that most were eager to demonstrate their loyalty to the United States. What would you have done in their place? What's to prevent something like this from ever happening again?

If you enjoyed *Hotel on the Corner of Bitter and Sweet,* you won't want to miss *Songs of Willow Frost,* the next enchanting novel from *New York Times* bestselling author Jamie Ford, coming in hardcover and eBook in September 2013.

Read on for a preview . . .

Sacred Hearts

(1934)

Mother Angelini was all smiles as William walked in and sat down, but the stained-glass window behind her oaken desk was open and the room felt cold and drafty. The only warmth that William felt came from the seat of the padded leather chair that had moments before been occupied, weighed down by the expectations of another boy.

"Happy birthday," she said as her spidery, wrinkled fingers paged through a thick ledger as though searching for his name. "How are you today . . . William?" She looked up, over her dusty spectacles. "This is your fifth birthday with us, isn't it? Which makes you how old in the canon?"

Mother Angelini always asked the boys' ages in relation to books from the *Septuagint*. William quickly rattled off, "*Genesis, Exodus, Leviticus . . .*" on up to Second Kings. He'd memorized his way only to the Book of Judith, when he'd turn eighteen and take his leave from the orphanage. Because the *Book of Judith* represented his own personal exodus, he'd read it over and over, until he imagined Judith as his forebear—a heroic, tragic widow, courted by many, who remained unmarried for the rest of her life. But he also read it because that particular book was semiofficial, semi-canonical—more parable than truth, like the stories he'd heard about his own, long-lost parent.

"Well done, Master William," Mother Angelini said. "Well done. Twelve is a marvelous age—the precipice of adult responsibility.

Don't think of yourself as a teenager. Think of yourself as a young man. That's more fitting, don't you think?"

He nodded, inhaling the smell of rain-soaked wool and Mentholatum, trying not to hope for a letter or even a lousy postcard. He failed miserably in the attempt.

"Well, I know that most of you are anxious for word from the outside—that God's mysteries have blessed your parents with work, and a roof, and bread, and a warm fire, and that someone might come back for you," the old nun said with a delicate voice, shaking her head as the skin beneath her chin shook like a turkey's wattle. "But . . ." She glanced at her ledger. "We know that's not possible in your situation, don't we, dear?"

It seems that's all I know. "Yes, Mother Angelini." William swallowed hard, nodding. "I suppose, since this is my birthday, I'd just like to know more. I have so many memories from when I was little, but no one's ever told me what happened to her."

The last time he saw her he'd been seven years old. His mother had half-whispered, half-slurred, "I'll be right back," as she had been carried out the door, though he might have imagined this. But he didn't imagine the police officer, an enormous mountain of a man who showed up the next day. William remembered him eating a handful of his mother's butter-almond cookies and being very patient while he packed. Then William had climbed into the sidecar of the policeman's motorcycle and they drove to a receiving home. William had waved to his old friends, like he was riding a float in Seattle's Golden Potlatch Parade, not realizing that he was waving goodbye. A week later the sisters came and took him in. *If I had known I'd never see my apartment again, I'd have taken some of my toys, or at least a photo.*

William tried not to stare as Mother Angelini's tongue darted at the corner of her mouth. She read the ledger and a note card with an official-looking seal that had been glued to the page. "William, because you are old enough, I will tell you what I can, even though it pains me to do so."

That my mother is dead, William thought, absently. He'd accepted that as a likely outcome years ago, when they told him her condition had worsened and that she was never coming back. Just as he accepted that his father would always be unknown. In fact, William had been forbidden to ever speak of him.

"From what we know, your mother was a dancer at the Wah Mee Club—and quite popular. But one day she made herself sick with bitter melon and carrot-seed soup. When that didn't work, she retired to the bath and tried performing . . ."

Performing? His mother had been a singer and a dancer. "I don't understand," he whispered, unsure if he wanted to know more.

"William, your dear mother was rushed to the hospital, but she had to wait for hours and, when they did get around to her, the admitting physician wasn't entirely comfortable treating an Oriental woman, especially one with her reputation. So he had her remanded to the old Perry Hotel."

William blinked and vaguely understood. He knew the location. In fact he used to play kick the can on the corner of Boren and Madison. He remembered being frightened by the ominous-looking building, even before bars were added to the windows and the place was renamed the Cabrini Sanitarium.

Mother Angelini closed her ledger. "I'm afraid she never left."

When William finally arrived at the Moore Theatre on Second Avenue, the younger boys had forgotten about their mothers and fathers in the rush to spend their nickels on Clark bars or handfuls of Mary Janes. Within minutes their lips were smeared and they were licking melted chocolate off their fingertips, one by one.

Meanwhile, William struggled to shake the thought of his mother spending her final years locked away in a nut-house—a laughing academy, a funny farm. Sister Briganti had once said that if he day-dreamed too much he'd end up in a place like that. *Maybe that's what happened to her.* He missed his mother as he wandered the lobby, looking at the movie posters, remembering her taking him to old photoplays and silent films in tiny second-run theaters. He recalled her arm around him, as she'd whisper in his ear, regaling him with tales of his grandparents, who were stars in Chinese operas.

As he lingered near the marble columns in the lobby, he tried to enjoy the moment, greedily palming the silver coin he'd been given. He'd learned from previous years to save it and follow the smell of melting butter and the sound of popcorn popping. He found Sunny, and they put their money together, splitting a large tub and an Orange Crush. As William waited to be seated, he noticed hundreds of other boys from various mission homes, institutions, and reformatories. In their dingy, graying uniforms they looked shrunken and sallow, frozen in line, a fresco of ragpickers. The prison-like uniforms the other boys wore made William feel awkward and overdressed, even in his ill-fitting jacket and hand-me-down knickerbockers that hung eight inches past his knees. And as he sipped his drink his gullet pressed against the knot of black silk that barely passed for a bow tie. But despite their differences, they all had the same expectant look in their eyes as they crowded the entrance, buzzing with excitement. Like most of the boys at Sacred Heart, William had been hoping to see *Animal Crackers* or a scary movie like *White Zombie*—especially after he heard that the Broadway Theatre had offered ten dollars to any woman who could sit through a midnight showing without screaming. Unfortunately, the sisters had decided that *Cimarron* was better fodder for their impressionable young minds.

Gee whiskers, William thought. *I'm just happy to get away, happy to see anything, even a silent two-reeler.* But Sunny was less enthusiastic.

When the bright red doors finally swept open, Sister Briganti put her hand on his shoulder and rushed Sunny and him to their seats.

"Be good boys and whatever you do be quiet, keep to yourselves, and don't make eye contact with the ushers," she whispered.

William nodded but didn't understand until he glanced up and saw that the balcony was filled with colored boys and a few Indian kids like Sunny. There must have been a separate entrance in the alley. *Am I colored?* William wondered. *And if so, what color am I?* They shared the popcorn and he sat lower, sinking into the purple velvet.

As the footlights dimmed and the plush curtains were drawn, a player piano came to life, accompanying black-and-white cartoons with Betty Boop and Barnacle Bill. William knew that, for the little boys, this was the best part. Some would barely make it through the previews, or the Movietone Follies. They'd end up sleeping through most of the feature film, dreaming in Technicolor.

When the Follies reel finally began, William managed to sing along with the rest, to musical numbers by Jackie Cooper and the Lane Sisters, and he laughed at the antics of Stepin Fetchit, who had everyone in stitches. He laughed even harder than the kids in the balcony. But silence swept the audience as a new performer crooned "Dream a Little Dream of Me"—staring wistfully into the camera. At first William thought, *She looks like Myrna Loy in* The Black Watch. But she wasn't just wearing makeup, she was Chinese like Anna May Wong, the only Oriental star he'd ever seen. Her distinctive looks and honeyed voice drew wolf whistles from the older boys, which drew reprimands from Sister Briganti, who cursed in Latin and Italian. But as William stared at the flickering screen, he was stunned silent, mouth agape, popcorn spilling. The singer was introduced as Willow Frost—*a stage name,* William almost said out loud, it had to be. And best of all, Willow and Stepin and a host of Movietone performers would be appearing LIVE AT A THEATRE NEAR YOU, in VANCOUVER, PORTLAND, SPOKANE, and SEATTLE. Tickets available NOW! GET 'EM BEFORE THEY'RE ALL SOLD OUT!

Sunny elbowed William and said, "Boy, I'd do anything to see that show."

"I . . . have to go" was all William could manage to say, still staring at the afterimage on the dark screen while listening to the opening score of *Cimarron,* which sounded farther and farther away, like *Oklahoma.*

"Keep on wishing, Willie."

Maybe it was his imagination. Or perhaps he was day-dreaming once again. But William knew he had to meet her in person, because he had once known her by another name—he was sure of it. With his next-door neighbors in Chinatown, she went by Liu Song, but he'd simply called her *Ah-ma.* He had to say those words again. He had to know if she'd hear his voice—if she'd recognize him from five long years away.

Because Willow Frost is a lot of things, William thought, *a singer, a dancer, a movie star, but most of all, Willow Frost is my mother.*

PHOTO: © LAURENCE KIM

Jamie Ford is the great-grandson of Nevada mining pioneer Min Chung, who emigrated in 1865 from
Kaiping, China, to San Francisco, where he adopted the
Western name "Ford," thus confusing countless generations. Ford is an award-winning short-story writer, an
alumnus of the Squaw Valley Community of Writers,
and a survivor of Orson Scott Card's Literary Boot
Camp. Having grown up near Seattle's Chinatown, he
now lives in Montana with his wife and children.

www.jamieford.com

Jamie Ford is available for select readings and lec-
tures. To inquire about a possible appearance, please
contact the Random House Speakers Bureau at
212-572-2013 or rhspeakers@randomhouse.com.